Resist

USA TODAY BESTSELLING AUTHOR

AVA HARRISON

Resist
Cover Design: Hang Le
Editor: Readers Together, Robin Covington
Proofreader: Editing4Indies, The Ryder's Proof

Dedication

For those who love a sexy grump . . .

"We must laugh in the face of our helplessness against the forces of nature—or go insane."
—Charlie Chaplin

Prologue

Paxton

COMING HERE PROBABLY ISN'T ONE OF MY FINEST DECISIONS. Despite this being part of the job, I have way too much shit to do. Standing around at a party, throwing a Hail Mary for a project that's not even guaranteed to pan out should not be on top of my list of priorities.

It's a long shot that the man who can make it happen will even be here.

Reaching into my pocket, I grab my cell and check the screen. Fuck.

I'm waiting for a call that could help this night, and my decisions, make sense. So far, there have been absolutely nothing to give me that validation.

Go fucking figure.

I'm trying to make something huge happen for two of my clients—and me. If the stars align, this could be the big one.

The screenplay is in my hands, and the lead actor is already on board. All I need is a director attached to the project to sell this as a package deal to a studio.

We'll still need a leading lady, but with Brad Wright at the helm, we can have the pick of the best of Hollywood to play opposite him.

My thoughts are a jumbled mess of options and ideas when my phone finally pings. When I see my assistant's name light up on the screen, I just about fucking embarrass myself by fist-pumping the air.

Kevin: Stefan Linburg is a no-show. Didn't RSVP. But since you're already there, have fun. Maybe get laid…

All the air deflates from my chest, and my hand balls into a fist at my side.

I should've known. The man is a recluse who refuses to take traditional meetings, but I had hope. Fickle. Fucking. Hope.

This needs to be pitched in person, and tonight was my best shot. Now I'm back to square one, wondering *what's the next step*?

I reread the text, and a laugh rips through my chest at Kevin's suggestion. *Get laid.* At least he has ideas. Kevin is ingenious like that and always down for forcing me to optimize bad situations.

A good lay would do wonders for my ego at the moment.

Looking around the room, I scan the options. Most of the women here are actresses, which won't bode well for a one-night stand, seeing as I'm a talent agent.

I have no interest in shitting where I eat.

Been there. Done that. Lesson learned.

In the early days of my career, I thought I was a king on my throne. I learned quickly that I was simply a page, needing to understand my role and play the part. After being burned, I left Hollywood, relocated to New York, set up shop, and have since become one of the leading talent agents in the city.

My clients are on top of the world, and I simply oversee their climb. Making kings and queens behind the scenes. I'm fine with it. I'll ride that train all the way to the top of my station and rake in the money that comes along with it.

I decide to cut my losses and head home to lick my wounds instead of a random pussy.

That's when I see her.

Who the hell is that?

She's breathtaking.

With long, blonde hair and the face of a goddess, I can't pull my gaze away.

She flashes an infectious smile at anyone in her vicinity, and I'm fascinated. It's hard to make out the color of her eyes, but I strain to see. Searching her face, I try to determine who the beauty is but come up short, which is a great thing.

She would be the perfect distraction for the night. No strings. No expectations. No complications.

I almost groan when she turns her back on me to talk to some asshole who's grinning down at her like a lunatic.

I should probably save her from the Jeffery Dahmer-wannabe, who's looking at her like his next meal.

I'm altruistic like that.

Her hair spills down her back, and her off-the-shoulder dress gives me a peek at her creamy skin.

I can't take my eyes off her.

This has potential.

It's not often that these sorts of events lead to options that won't impact my job. Add to that the fact I was immediately intrigued when I saw her. Typically, I'm forced to endure painful conversations with women who are so full of themselves that it takes one—or ten—drinks for me to tolerate them.

I haven't said two words to this woman, and somehow, I know it would be a fun distraction. Something to pass the time.

The question is, would she be up to the challenge?

I smirk because I know that this is a game I'm sure I can win.

No time to waste, Pax. Get your ass a-movin'.

It only takes a few long strides before I place myself in front of the idiot monopolizing her time and boring her to tears if her yawn is any indication. She needs to crane her neck to look up at me. Even with the heels she's wearing, I still tower over her.

And I love that.

"Pax." I extend my hand, and she doesn't waste time taking mine in hers.

"I'm Mal." She smiles broadly.

I rack my brain for any Mal that would make this off-limits and come up short. No Mal on the do-not-fuck list, and I'm relieved. Up close, the woman is even more breathtaking. Her large icy-blue eyes practically sparkle in the light.

For fuck's sake, the woman is already making me an idiot.

I incline my head toward the table I've been sitting at. "Care to join me for a drink?"

Her lip tips up. "I was in the middle of a conversation." She looks around my body at the douche I'd forgotten about.

I internally roll my eyes but recognize that this is a game we're playing, and she seems like the type of woman who would disapprove of a rude man.

"Sorry, partner. Didn't see you there."

The guy glowers at me, but I tower over him, too, so he quickly shoves down any hint of animosity, lifting his hands, palms out.

"No problem. I was just going to get another drink."

He looks around me as he says it. I haven't moved to block his path from Mal, but I'm still not convinced he doesn't plan to throw her in the back of his white van and whisk her off to his mom's basement somewhere in the hills.

Who is this guy, and how did he get an invite?

"Mal, it was a pleasure to meet you."

She offers a kind smile. "You, too, Paul. Have a nice night."

He scurries off, and I watch him the whole way. When I look back at Mal, she's smirking up at me. "Care to tell me what all that was about?"

I shrug. "That guy looked like a serial killer. I was doing my civil duty to ensure your safety."

She laughs. "Paul? He's harmless."

Mal looks down at her almost-empty glass of champagne and then over to the full bottle in the center of the table. I can practically hear her thinking, weighing out the options, but then she bites her bottom lip, hitting me with a sexy smile that damn near brings me to my knees. "About that drink . . ."

She steps forward, and I place my hand on the small of her back to guide her to the banquette. There's something about the way she moves that has me hard as a rock. Her ass sways effortlessly, almost like she's gliding on air. She's graceful and sexy all at the same time, and she's not even trying.

This night is turning around quickly.

The music is loud, but it won't be so bad where we're headed. We'll be able to hold a conversation unlike in other parts of the place. I picked this area specifically to pitch Stefan on coming aboard to be the director of the adaptation of *Twisted Lily*.

Turns out, the seats won't be wasted after all.

"So what do you do, Pax—"

I cut her off, shaking my head. "Let's not do that."

She chuckles. "Do what?"

"Play the Hollywood game. We're obviously here for our own reasons. Wouldn't it be refreshing to leave the Hollywood bit out and just pretend for a minute?"

She purses her lips, searching my face, and for a moment, I wonder if she'll get up and walk away.

"A drink?" she says, motioning toward the bottle.

I don't waste time filling her glass, and then I pour myself one, too.

Taking a swig, the bubbles in the champagne fizz on my tongue. I glance up at Mal and find her staring at me. I can't help but grin because that simple look says it all.

She wants to fuck me as much as I want to fuck her.

I take another drink, giving her the floor. This is one of those moments when remaining silent is in my best interest. I'll let her take control.

She sips her drink and continues to stare directly into my eyes. It's unnerving but hot as hell. The one thing she doesn't do… talk. We're in some sort of foreplay stare down, and neither one of us is giving in. I'm a patient man who prides myself on standing firm.

This fucking woman has me caving within minutes.

"Tell me something not Hollywood related?" The words fall off my tongue, and I internally kick my own ass.

Real smooth, Ramsey.

Mal laughs and shakes her head. "This should be interesting. We're at an after-party for one of the biggest awards shows of the year, and you want me not to mention Hollywood?"

"That's what makes it fun."

She places her glass down, then folds her hands on top of the table.

"It makes it difficult. It could take me a long time to come up with something." Her voice is light and airy as she continues to beam at me.

"I've got all night, sweetheart," I reply, winking. Her cheeks stain pink. It's dark in here. I could be imagining it, but I don't think so.

She's fucking gorgeous, regardless, and the dim lighting of the room makes her eyes sparkle even more.

Her fingers drum on the table as she mentally runs through her options. "Maybe you should go first."

I really want to convince her we should leave this place. Every second in her presence has my pants tightening to uncomfortable levels and my patience slipping.

There's no rush, except for the fact that I might combust if she flashes that hot-as-hell grin my way one more time.

If she needs to take this slow so we get to know each other, I'll play along. She'll still end up in my hotel bed tonight either way, and this foreplay isn't hurting anything.

Reaching across the table, I place my hand on hers, stopping the drumming.

Her eyes widen, and as I follow her gaze, I see it's resting on where our hands touch.

What the hell?

Does she not like to be touched?

"Sorry about that—"

I go to move my hand, and she shakes her head. "No." She smiles, bright enough to light up the whole damn room. "It's fine."

The way she lowers her lashes in invitation settles my concern, and I eliminate the distance between us, moving closer to her.

My lips move to the shell of her ear, and she trembles. "I know we said no work talk, but I have to ask… you're not an actress, right?"

"No." Her reply comes out breathy and sensual, the proximity and my mouth to her ear affecting her in all the right ways.

"Thank fuck."

I pull away just in time to see her eyes widen.

"You don't like actresses?"

"I didn't say that, but with the thoughts running through my head, I won't lie and say I wouldn't be disappointed."

Her eyes narrow in on me. "And what exactly are those thoughts?" She licks her lips and I watch the movement.

I grin. "Do you really want to know?"

She offers me a nod.

"For starters… I want to kiss you."

She clears her throat. "If I were an actress, that would be a problem? Why?"

"I don't kiss actresses."

She picks up her glass, pressing it to her lips. She tips it back, draining the glass of half its contents, before placing it back down. It rattles on the table, and I don't miss how her hand tremors slightly.

"Well, then it's a good thing I'm not an actress."

She's no master of seduction at the moment, but she doesn't need to be; her meaning is coming in loud and clear. I'll be taking her home tonight.

I place my fingers under her chin and turn her face so we look right at each other. "Is this okay?"

She bites into her lower lip as she nods.

It's her eyes that give away the lust inside her. They glitter with need; her pupils dilate as she leans into my touch.

"Words, Mal," I growl, losing control.

I need to touch this woman in other ways.

"Yes. Please kiss—"

I don't let her finish the sentence before my mouth crashes against her, shutting her up.

She grows soft in my arms. The taste of champagne explodes on my tongue as she parts her lips.

I cup the back of her neck, deepening the kiss.

She tastes delicious. Like the finest delicacy, and I can't wait to leave here. I want her away from prying eyes. All to myself. I want to lay her down on my bed and see if her pussy tastes just as sweet.

A whimper escapes her as my tongue swipes against hers.

Devouring.

As my tongue fucks her mouth, I lose the sense of time and space. My free hand drops down to the hem of her skirt.

We need to leave. Too many important people are around, and I need to be alone with this siren.

Her hand encases mine, and I think she'll push me away, but instead, she guides me to where she needs me.

I stroke her pussy over the cotton that covers her. Circling until she dampens beneath my touch. Her hips lift, but I don't stop; I just continue to drive her mad with need, my mouth still plundering hers. I dip my finger beneath the cotton, then swipe it against her slit.

Mal's so damn wet and ready for me.

She squirms as I play with her. "More."

"Not here." I pull my hand away, and she groans in protest. "Do you want to get out of here?" I ask between kisses.

"Yes," she pants.

"Let's go." I move out of the banquette and extend my hand.

The hand whose fingers were just inside her. She looks adorable as her eyes widen, a deer caught in headlights. Not quite the dirty girl I hoped, but we can change that.

I lift the hand to my mouth and lick her essence off, which is like nothing else I've ever tasted before.

My new favorite taste.

I extend my dry hand this time. Her mouth is open, but her lips slam together every time she attempts to talk.

I smirk.

Her arm reaches out, but just before our hands entwine, I hear the voice of the very person I came to see tonight.

"Paxton."

Shit.

"Stefan," I greet him, unable to hide the irritation from my voice.

I need him, but I can't help but resent his horrific timing.

"I know I said I wasn't coming, but I moved stuff around." He hurries toward a seat, motioning for me to sit.

Has he not noticed the incredible blonde in our company? Surely, he can't be *that* blind.

"I want in. I want *Twisted Lily*." The words come out in a rush, as though he's been holding that in for far too long. "This will be the project of the century. The script. I see it now."

He's talking so fast that I'm having trouble keeping up. My brain is too foggy from the allure of Mal and the raging hard-on I'm attempting to hide.

Fantastic timing.

"All we need is a young, innocent actress. Combine the purity with Brad's seasoned masculinity, and we will change the world—"

"Stefan." I look over at the girl in my arms. "Can you just give us a few minutes?" I ask her.

Her eyes ping-pong back and forth between Stefan and me before she stutters out, "I'm—I'm just . . . I'll be leaving." Her voice pitches as she steps away from me, and I instantly feel like the world's biggest asshole for pushing her aside.

Why?

She was only meant to be a distraction from this man's absence. He's here now, and my entire career rests in his brilliant hands.

Still...

"Mal—"

"Another time." It's all she says before she turns her back on me. Blonde hair swishes as she practically glides away.

She's gone, and I'm left standing here hard as a fucking rock and desperate for her.

Nonetheless, this is a dog-eat-dog world, and business comes first.

Always.

Chapter One

Mallory

@Stargossip: Word around town is the project of the century has imploded before it even got off the ground. If our sources are correct—and they are—Teagan Steward has left negotiations. Guess the teeny-bopper princess is too good for Hollywood legends. Thoughts?

> **@Ihatehollywood:** She couldn't act if her life depended on it.
>
> **@Fairytalelover:** I love Teagan. It's Brad who's got to go!
>
> **@Deathtothesystem:** Burn it all to the ground!

I CAN DO THIS.

Or at least that's what I tell myself as I stare out at the view of the city from the conference room where I'm sitting . . . patiently.

The floor-to-ceiling window overlooks the large buildings like a massive frame, stretching from one end of the room to the other. It's a view I'll never tire of. It's absolutely breathtaking, but what really captivates me is that every time I look, there's something new to see.

Luckily, the view of New York City keeps me company because my appointment is making me wait.

My knee bounces up for the four millionth time in the last minute, calling me out on my lie.

I'm not patient.

Nope.

It's not in my nature.

I'm a take charge and make things happen kind of girl. Which is why I'm currently in this conference room, a place I shouldn't be, and drumming my nails on the armrest of the chair.

My meeting was supposed to start thirty-five minutes ago, and my anxiety is firing up. The monotonous tapping of my fingers echoes throughout the space and calls me out. It's a nervous habit.

I should stop, but alas, it's like trying to stop breathing for me.

In the distance, I can hear the chatter around the office. The sound of voices makes my pulse beat frantically.

Each footstep has me looking around, ready for someone to appear.

Still, I'm left waiting.

My heart hammers in my chest as I sit here, fighting off the anxiety crawling up my stomach to sit firmly in my chest. Is that a bit of fear, too?

You got this. You know why you're here. You're a fucking legend.

Oh, the things we tell ourselves to tamp down the self-doubt. I'm here to get my client more money, and that's always nerve-wracking.

What I'm asking for is a lot.

I'm pretty sure my client would kill me if she knew.

I take a deep breath, willing strength to fill my lungs.

She deserves this, and it's my job to ensure she gets what she deserves.

The sound of footsteps approaching pierces through the air. I take a deep breath, composing myself. I'm about to be thrust full force into the biggest moment of my career.

My heart skips a beat as I look up.

The air is knocked out of my lungs.

It's him.

The man from the party. The one who played my pussy like a goddamn guitar right in the middle of Hollywood's elite. And I would've let him take it all the way without one thought of who witnessed my fall.

I thought I would never see him again . . . Pax.

Holy hell.

My memories don't do him justice. He's so incredibly tall.

Staring back at me are still the bluest eyes I have ever seen. They rival mine, and I've been told a time or two that mine radiates. Cringey, but it's been said.

Pax's gaze is like the sun, gently warming my skin and making me feel alive. He's beautiful.

Probably not the right word.

He's more than beautiful.

With a strong jawline that brings out his chiseled features, I feel like I'm gawking.

His eyes twinkle devilishly at my perusal. Mesmerizing yet unattainable.

I can't stop staring.

I've never forgotten how he tasted when we kissed—cherry with a hint of vanilla. Nor what his fingers felt like inside me.

The most delicious sin.

His lips are still full and inviting, like the sweetest of ripe fruits ready to be tasted. I wonder if his voice will still be like honey cascading down a waterfall, smooth and tantalizing.

My cheeks start to warm to uncomfortable levels.

Despite having already met Paxton Ramsey and kissed him, I am not at all prepared to see him again. He was supposed to be a slight reprieve from a shitty night.

Right before I arrived at the party, I had gotten into World War III with my father. All I wanted to do was get drunk and forget . . . enter Paxton.

Of course, the one time I decided to throw caution to the wind and make a reckless decision with a stranger, he'd end up being the agent for the actor opposite my client.

I continue to stare at him, and the moments drag as I wait for him to acknowledge me, but he doesn't. He doesn't say a single word, only furthering my awkwardness.

He continues to peer at me blankly, and my belly drops.

He doesn't remember me.

His jaw clenches, and I realize he *does* remember . . . but he's not happy I'm here.

"I'm too busy to see you now."

"Mr. Ramsey—"

"Oh, it's *Mr. Ramsey* now?" His voice is hard and taunting.

"If I could just have a moment of your time."

"As I said before, I understand that my assistant made this appointment, but unfortunately, something has come up."

"Pax, if we could—"

He holds his hand up. "No. I don't have time for this—"

"But."

"You know what? *Fuck it.* I tried to be nice, but you have a lot of nerve coming here."

My head jerks back at the animosity directed at me. He's livid, and I'm shell-shocked.

"I can't say that I'm surprised." He huffs, slamming a folder on the table and leaning toward me. "Your father strung me along, gathered information about my connections . . . but I never did get that job." He laughs, but it lacks all humor. This is pure, unadulterated hate, and I don't know what to do with that.

So, like a mute idiot, I don't say a word. I simply sit here and play the part of a verbal punching bag.

"Instead, he poached my clients right out from under me. It

was a rookie mistake, but I'm not the same man I was then." He points a finger at me, and I swallow in response. "Got to hand it to you, I didn't see it coming—not over the innocent vibes you were throwing. I guess the project was too good not to try the seduction route." He claps, nice and slow. A pure indication he's mocking me. "Good job, Mal."

His words cut through me like shattered glass being sunk into my skin.

Seduction route?

Does he think . . . ? Oh, my God.

He thinks I approached him at the party to—what? Get Teagan the role? My stomach churns, bile rising up my throat at the implications.

Speak, Mallory. Say something. Defend yourself.

"Let's get on with this." His deep voice cuts through the silence of the room, and although it is exactly as I remember it, the undertones are not. They reverberate through my chest, making my heart lurch.

This man hates me, and I search for something to say to explain that he has it all wrong. His narrowed eyes and hard-set jaw indicate my words would go unheard. My attempts would be futile.

I sit up taller in its wake, needing to fortify my walls. My mouth suddenly feels as dry as parchment paper. I swallow, desperately trying to wet my tongue to get my words out. His chin drops down, and his brow lifts.

"I'm ready when you are."

I feel like a complete fool in front of him, but I don't let that stop me as I stand. I take one step forward, and he strides to meet me.

Good.

Give me the ammunition I need to be strong and go head-to-head with him.

The ground itself shifts beneath his feet, and I know I can't fuck this up.

This is it. My defining moment.

It's my chance to prove myself, to show what I'm capable of.

It's now or never, Mal.

Fear builds in my chest, but I push it down. With one last deep breath, I take that final step forward, standing taller and readying myself for what I need to say.

"Thank you for meeting with me." I extend my hand, prepared to be professional despite all that's been said.

Unsurprisingly, he doesn't take it.

Typical egotistical ass.

His condescending stare makes me shiver, and I hate it. I don't like feeling beneath anyone, especially men in this industry. I've worked my ass off just as hard as the rest of them to get where I'm at, and I deserve some respect.

"I think we're past handshakes, don't you?"

My breath hitches, and for one second, I'm afraid he will drop all decorum and speak out loud about what I allowed him to do that night.

He sidesteps me. "Plus, I wouldn't thank me yet."

Oh, thank you, God.

I pivot my body to follow his movements, and my eyes widen at what I see. Paxton Ramsey looks at me as if I am a bug on the floor he wants to flatten.

Despite him thinking he has a reason to hate me, I'm still surprised by his behavior.

From everything I've heard about this man, he's not an asshole. The look of disdain on his face says otherwise.

"So, please inform me what is so urgent that we had to meet. It's highly unorthodox."

My hand falls to my side, and I tap my fingers along the side of my thigh.

"I'll be frank."

He cocks his head. "This should be good."

I draw in a breath and then exhale, trying to push our past aside. This is business.

"I don't think my client is being offered her fair share."

His hands shoot into the air. "This contract has been on the table too long. And to be frank," he mocks, "I don't understand why you think it's appropriate to meet with me."

"Well, I—"

He cuts me off. "If your client doesn't want to sign, that's not my problem. And it's certainly not my problem that the studio doesn't want to pay her more."

"If you'd let me speak," I half yell, yet it doesn't even get a reaction from him.

He's a stone wall of pissed-off man, and it's chilling.

"They are offering her five hundred thousand for her role in the film. Your client is making closer to ten million for his role. How is it even debatable she's getting railroaded?"

"Are you really here to compare your client's pay stub to mine? Brad has a track record of box office smashes . . ." He levels me with a hard stare. "You think she deserves what he gets?"

"I'm not saying she deserves the same amount, but I think she deserves at least a million. She will bring a unique energy and talent to the project. She might not have the same mileage to her career that Mr. Wright has, but she's fresh, crisp, and sought-after. You and I both know she's received high praises for her role in *Sunset High*," I reply fervently, my voice rising with every word.

Paxton lets out a dry laugh. "It's her first role. We have no idea what she'll bring."

I place my right hand on my hip. "This isn't her first role."

"I hardly think her previous appearances are relevant here. This will be her first feature film, and that's the only thing that matters. The stuff before was child's play."

My heart hammers in my chest, but I refuse to back down. "And who are you to say that?" I argue matter-of-factly.

"The man you saw fit to ask a favor. Because that's what you're about to do, right?"

I glance away. "I think both parties will have to make some concessions."

"You think my client has to make concessions?"

My eyes snap back to him, eyelashes blinking rapidly. "I didn't mean it like that."

"Don't backpedal now," he says with a smirk. "You're greedy. Always wanting what isn't yours. Guess the apple doesn't fall far at all."

I pause and consider my options. It's clear he's in no mood to speak rationally with me. We've argued long enough, and I can see no end in sight for this dispute. I search his face for any hint of leniency, but it's just a blank slate.

"Okay, let's meet somewhere in the middle," I say finally. His expression shifts to stone-cold.

"My client is arguably the biggest actor in Hollywood."

"And imagine how good his reputation will be once the media finds out that he offered a piece of his salary because he believes the gap between the leading man and woman shouldn't be the Grand Canyon."

He smacks his lips together. "Practicing your speech?"

"Just imagine the headlines, Mr. Ramsey."

His eyes roll, and he huffs a laugh. "And what exactly are those headlines, princess?"

"Princess?" I arch an eyebrow. "The sexism doesn't sto—"

"Seeing as your dad's a Hollywood king."

His words stop me cold, and I turn my head, not letting him see how his comment affects me. If he only knew how cutting they were.

He'd probably rejoice.

I blow out air, pushing my shoulders back. I need to stay strong in front of this man. If I give him an inch, he'll take a whole mile.

I need this more than he does.

The truth is, if my only client walks, I won't have any other choice but to grovel where I don't want to.

This is my last shot, and if I lose, he's right. This job will be temporary.

Scouring my brain, I try to think of a rebuttal, and then it hits me.

"Your client has had some serious complaints spewed about him in the past. His behavior toward leading actresses . . . It's one reason the producers wanted a 'no name', as you said, to play his counterpart."

His gaze narrows.

"Wouldn't this be the perfect spin? A great way to bridge the gap on the allegations that he treats his costars like they are his subordinates."

Paxton's jaw locks. "Comes as no surprise that you play dirty." His lips smash into a thin line. "Very well. I'll pitch the idea to my client. No promises."

Paxton doesn't wait for me to respond. He turns on his heel and strides out of the room, just as pissed off as when he arrived. Maybe even more so. I can't help but feel a little satisfied that this dispute is finally over. The contract hasn't been signed, but I know it will be. My job here is done.

Despite the complete torture I had to endure to get to this point.

Chapter Two

Paxton
Three months later . . .

@Stargossip: I have it on good authority that the set of *Twisted Lily* is bananas. Diva actors and a flighty director lead to tension and tears. What do you make of this?

> **@twistedtealover:** Sounds typical for Hollywood!
>
> **@loveandmovies:** How are we surprised by this?
>
> **@teagonstewardfanclub:** Teagan is no diva!!
>
> **@Deathtothesystem:** The whole thing needs to be canceled . . .

S OMETHING IS TO BE SAID ABOUT MONDAY MORNINGS.
Most hate them. It's often a dreaded word that is synonymous with a funny GIF of a man crying at his desk.

But I am not like most men. To me, it's the beginning of a new week. The potential is endless, leaving all the shit from last week behind.

A distant memory.

Usually hidden under new scandals thrust upon the public over the weekend when most of the debauchery happens.

Where most see a crisis, I see opportunity.

There's no such thing as bad publicity, after all, and with a short call to a publicist, I can leverage any scandal to get my clients more work.

So, yeah, to me . . . Mondays are fucking amazing.

Looking around the space, I take a deep breath. My favorite time of the day is now, when the office is quiet, and no one is around to disturb me.

I'm here before anyone else. Story of my life. I play hard. Work harder.

As if summoned by my thoughts, the phone rings on my desk, breaking the peaceful moment. Leaning forward in my chair, I reach for it and hit the speaker button.

"Paxton Ramsey."

"Thank fuck." Brad Wright's all too-familiar whine grates on my nerves.

It's way too early to speak to this man, but he makes me enough money that I have no choice but to humor him. Much to my displeasure.

"Brad. My man. Everything okay?" I don't care, but I can't let him on to that fact. Again, time is money, so he gets my time.

"No, everything isn't okay." My shoulders stiffen at his sharp tone. "I have been trying to call you for an hour. Yet despite how much money I make you . . ." His implication isn't lost on me.

But his accusation makes no sense. I didn't get a call from him.

"Hold one second." I place the call on hold and reach into my pocket to grab my phone.

Fuck.

He did try to call, and not just one time. He called five times.

"Brad, I'm back. What's going on?"

"You need to get your ass here right this fucking second."

"Here? As in, fly to an island for something other than a vacation?"

"Yes. Here. Filming. I need you."

I take him off speaker and bring the phone to my ear. I must be hearing him wrong. In all the years I've worked for this man, he's never demanded I be on set. That's not how our relationship works. Sure, he's a needy bastard, but this is next level. I'm not a babysitter.

"The shoot is going to shit. You set this disaster up, and if you know what's good for your career, you'll get here."

"Brad, take a deep breath. You know I'm here to help, but threatening me isn't going to have the outcome either of us wants. I've got you."

"That's not a threat, Paxton. That's a promise. It's your fault this unprofessional teen is my costar. You made the mess, so you clean the mess up."

Fuck. I knew giving in to Mallory would bite me in the ass.

The day she demanded a meeting, my anger clouded my judgment. Despite my feelings about her, I felt like an ass and subsequently made a stupid-as-fuck decision.

My jaw ticks. "What did the teen twit do?"

"Why don't you check Twitter or Exposé? They both have the whole scoop somehow. Then get your ass on a plane and get here."

I packaged this deal, so Brad is right. I need to be there and make sure this ship doesn't sink, but I won't allow him or anyone else to think they can railroad me like this.

"Tell me what you need me to do, and I'll make some calls. Surely, I don't need to pack a suit and head to the heat."

"That's exactly what you need to do, Paxton. What I say goes, and I say you get on a plane and fix this."

My eyes shut, and I have to work to control my temper. It takes a lot to send me over the edge, but Brad has mastered it.

"With all due respect, I have other clients. None of which will be fine with me whisking off to some remote location to play favorites."

"With all due respect, I'm your number one client. If I walk—and trust me, this is not an idle threat—I *will* take all your clients with me. We actors talk, you know."

I know, much to my chagrin. But I'm not about to let some privileged shit with a freakishly chiseled jaw hold me by the balls because he's good at reciting lines.

"I have no skeletons in my closet, buddy. I'm solid."

"A story here, a story there. It'll be easy to ruin your reputation."

"Are you fucking blackmailing me?" My voice rises, but I refuse to scream. I won't allow this little prick to get the better of me.

"Yes, and you'll fold within the year. And the kicker? I'll go straight to Thomas Reynolds just to piss you off."

I knew getting drunk with Brad back in the day was a bad idea. One too many fingers of scotch, and I was telling him all about my hatred of Thomas Reynolds.

At the time, Thomas wasn't Brad's favorite either. We bonded over our mutual hatred, and Brad signed. Thomas Reynolds, the father of Mallory Reynolds—the little nepo princess who convinced me to go to bat for her client, Teagan Steward.

The woman who let me finger her at a Hollywood event.

Focus, Paxton.

Now Brad's using that tidbit to grate on my last nerve and prompt me into action because he knows damn well that I'll go to the ends of the earth to ensure Reynolds doesn't get another fucking client.

I run my hands down my face, feeling the fight bleed out of me. "This is not how I do business."

"I need you on a plane. I need you dealing with this shit. I need this. I need the Oscar. You're my agent. Get here."

Despite what I want, the truth is, he has me by my balls. I knew what I was getting into when I signed him all those years ago from his previous agent, and I say previous because he's no longer an agent.

He was ruined by rumors. Rumors I can now deduce were

obviously spread by Brad himself. At the time, I didn't see the connection. But now, years later, and schooled by experience, I see the writing on the wall.

Back then, I was desperate to make a name for myself.

My teeth gnash together. I've put everything I have into my company, and this piece of shit could ruin everything, all because I had to make a deal with the devil.

Everything about this movie is fucked, but I'll be damn sure it gets made and that he wins an Oscar.

I refuse to put my reputation on the line, so that is exactly what I'm going to do. I'm going to fly to God knows where and deal with this shit. I lean back in my chair.

"I'll see you tomorrow. The studio will send a jet," Brad says. Before I can object, he's gone.

My fist clenches and then hits the desk with a thud.

Motherfucker.

Chapter Three

Mallory

TODAY IS NOT GOING AS PLANNED.

First, there was the frantic phone call from Teagan. *Now, this.*

"What are you doing here?" Paxton hisses as his footsteps halt in the aisle of the private jet.

My heart hammers in my chest. Of course, he's here, Mal. You didn't really think the studio sent a plane just for you. "I could be asking you the same question."

He looks down at me, his jaw tight. His disdain for me is written all over his handsome features. "Well, seeing as your client and her mother are making filming nearly impossible, I'm flying out to do damage control."

"I'm only here to ensure that my client is all right and is getting what she needs."

He huffs a laugh. "Your client will never be satisfied. She's a brat."

I gasp. "Pax—"

"Go home, princess. Leave this to the adults."

My arms cross over my chest. "Because you certainly act like one," I mutter under my breath.

His right eyebrow rises. "What did you say?"

"What was that?" I play confused.

From where he's standing, he assesses me like I'm an annoying fly. Hopefully, one he doesn't want to swat and kill.

To everyone who sang this man's praises, I don't know what Kool-Aid they drank, but it's obviously been spiked. He's the world's leading asshole.

He shakes his head. "You don't even have your training wheels off in this industry. If you're going to survive in this business, you will have to learn how to have a backbone."

I'm not sure what to make of this. Patronizing? Yes. Solid advice from a seasoned agent? Possibly.

"I said"—I cough, clearing my throat—"you certainly don't act like one." I smile broadly. "If you must know."

He rolls his eyes before taking the seat directly across the aisle from me.

Great.

This plane has seven other seats. Couldn't he pick one a little farther away?

All I need is this man breathing down my neck for lord knows how long. I'm not even sure how *long* this flight is. In my hurry to prepare, that was the one thing I didn't bother to check.

Once the doors close and we start to taxi down the runway, I position myself toward him. His upper body angles to face out the window, so I can only see his side profile.

It's clear he's not happy to be here. Like me, I assume he doesn't like being summoned on set due to movie drama. But it's more than just a disruption of his day.

He has to share this disruption with me.

Serves the idiot right. His reasons for treating me like dirt are misplaced, but I won't bother telling him that. I'm not stupid enough to believe anything I say will change his mind. He thinks I buttered up to him to get information on this project, a belief that couldn't be farther from the truth, but there is no dealing with this man.

Despite my research on Paxton Ramsey, and yes, I did plenty of it at that . . .

Everyone loves and respects him.

I have yet to find one person who has ever uttered a bad word about this grumpy man.

They've called him charming.

Witty.

Irresistible.

While all true, they left out arrogant jerk.

I shake my head, knowing I shouldn't engage with him, but despite myself, I find my mouth opening and words spewing out. "So, are you just going to sit there and ignore me the whole trip?"

He doesn't so much as look in my direction when he says, "That was my plan."

"Seems a bit ridiculous. As you so elegantly pointed out, you're an adult . . . and adults don't throw tantrums."

He turns toward me, lifting one brow. "I don't recall saying anything like that."

"Even if you didn't, you're still acting like a damn child." My harsh voice is much louder than necessary, considering our proximity.

His head tilts to the side. "Am I now?"

"Hmm," I drawl, tapping a finger on my chin. "Ignoring me on a small airplane. Let me think about it . . ." I place my right hand on my forehead and tap. "Yep."

"Somehow, you manage to pull off the childish behavior far better than I ever could. Bravo, Mallory. You should quit your day job and become an actress."

I let out a long-drawn-out groan at his words.

"Are you scoffing? And now she's rolling her eyes . . ."

"No, asshole." This time I *do* huff.

"And the colorful language. Such a lady."

My head lolls back on yet another groan. "Please, go back to ignoring me. Anything is better than listening to you having a mental breakdown every time I dare to breathe."

I spin my body away from him.

Unfortunately for me, this plane, although beautiful, isn't as large as a commercial aircraft, making it impossible for me to block him out entirely. I can hear him, and I swear he's chuckling to himself.

If I didn't think the window would break, I'd throw something at him, but my fear is great enough to have me clenching my jaw instead.

As the plane prepares to take off, I shift back to my original position, determined not to allow him to give me a pained neck later from sitting awkwardly. The copilot enters the cabin and proceeds to go over the safety protocol for this aircraft. If you've heard it once, you've heard it a million times, but it's protocol, so I do my best not to be offensive and put my headphones on.

"Relax and enjoy your flight," the copilot says, offering a small smile. "We'll be taking off momentarily."

My fingers start to nervously drum on the armrest.

Tap.

Tap.

Tap.

"Great. Bad flyer?"

I turn toward Paxton. "Oh, now you want to speak with me?"

He adjusts in his seat to face me. "Want to?" His head shakes. "No."

"Then why bother?" I fix my attention out the window beside Paxton, watching the building pass as the plane drives toward the main runway.

"Because you're liable to break something with the way you're fidgeting. The last thing I need right now is explaining to the studio why their plane is damaged and the lead actress's agent is bleeding when we land."

"Exaggerate much?" Despite my words, the rhythm of my fingers picks up as the plane takes off.

Tap. Tap. Tap.

"Hardly," he mutters, and I pull my gaze away from the window and find that he's staring at my hand.

I let out a long-drawn-out sigh. "It's not that I'm afraid of flying. I'm just afraid of flying in a plane this small." I motion around.

"It's just like flying in any other plane."

"Hardly. The wind could blow this thing down if it's too forceful."

My fingers frantically tap on the armrest as we lift into the air. If anything is going to happen, it will happen now. Most plane crashes occur at takeoff. Or is it landing? I have no clue.

"Have you ever flown private before?"

I shake my head, and the plane chooses that exact moment to wobble around the sky.

Tap. Tap. "It's just a cloud," Paxton says. "So Daddy dearest never took you on the company plane?"

Inhale. Exhale. Everything is okay. "Not that it's any of your business, but no."

Tap.

"Any particular reason?"

Tap.

"No. Again, that's not any of your business."

"You're a child."

Tap.

"Sure am."

Tap.

"I promise you . . . you're safe." His tone is gentler than ever, and his brows are pinched when I look at him.

Is he worried about me?

"And I should believe you, why?" I level him with a hard stare.

"Don't. Doesn't make a damn bit of difference to me what you do, princess."

Arrogant jerk.

Chapter Four

Paxton

@**Stargossip:** We might focus on the stars, but can we all agree that Paxton Ramsey, agent to the stars, is smokin' hot??

    @**spankmedaddy:** I'd let him paddle me . . .

    @**hotboysofsummer:** Hells yeah! The man is FIRE!

    @**sophisticateddreamer:** This is gross. Just stop!

    @**Deathtothesystem:** He's a douche from what I hear.

S HE'S DRIVING ME CRAZY.

    Despite me telling her that she has nothing to fear, her fingers still relentlessly drum on the surface of the armrest.

Usually, I consider myself a rather patient person.

I'm also empathic.

But with this woman, all bets are off.

I don't know how much longer I can put up with her.

Unfortunately, I have no choice. It's just my luck that I'd be forced to share air with Apate, the goddess of fraud, deceit, and trickery.

The worst part: I can't even drown out her sounds.

Like a world-class idiot, I forgot my noise-canceling headphones, which would've been the perfect solution to this annoying part of what's sure to be an awful trip.

This is new territory for me. I'm the fun guy. The life of the party, who doesn't take myself too seriously. She brings out something in me that puts the D in dick. I can't help but push her buttons and make her squirm.

Not like she doesn't deserve it.

Taking a deep breath, I pretend she's not here . . . because that's mature.

I pull out my laptop and queue up some documents I need to review. It's not an easy feat as the plane sways, but I manage to get through one and begin the next.

I'm unsure how much time passes, but the ride gets progressively bumpier. The plane dips with turbulence, and the drumming of Mallory's fingers intensifies.

Princess needs to relax.

Her words still amaze me. Knowing who her father is, I find it strange that this is her first time on a private plane.

I'm well-versed in his company. They have a corporate jet, and he and his agents constantly fly to meet his clients. It's one of the perks new agents who get hired boast about.

Since everyone knows she'll eventually take over for him, I would've assumed she'd traveled by that jet numerous times. Has she not gone along with him to meetings in the past? Apparently, not by his plane. There's no way she can fake her fear.

She's sucking in big gasps of oxygen, sounding on the verge of hyperventilating. One hand continues to tap while the other clenches with white knuckles. I really . . . *really* don't want to make small talk with the woman, but it's against my nature to allow someone so scared to practically collapse with fear.

"Do you always get this worked up when you fly?"

"No. I mean . . . maybe?"

This girl will be the death of me. "It's either a yes or a no."

"Not everything is black and white, Paxton," she bites back, voice cracking on a screech as the plane tilts a bit.

"You're either afraid of flying, or you aren't."

She exhales deeply. "I'm afraid of flying. On all planes. Large or small." I don't miss the grimace as she says those words.

Instead, I focus on her. Her jaw is tight, and her skin looks a shade paler than when we first got on the plane.

Yep, she's in the middle of a panic attack.

"You know they make drugs for that," I respond. "Your life would probably be easier if you took one."

"Thanks, ass." She huffs. "I'm aware that they make pills. But the thing about pills is it's never as simple as just taking one." There's a bite to her voice. It sounds like there's a story there, but to be honest, I don't want to know.

"Classy, princess. Name-calling suits your whole immature persona." I smirk.

"Stop calling me princess. If you knew anything about me, you'd know I'm the furthest thing from that."

"Whatever you say." I turn to look back at my computer, but it's not worth attempting. I'm distracted by the turbulence and that incessant freaking tapping. I close the laptop and stuff it into my bag. The sound of her damn fingers drumming doesn't stop. It intensifies tenfold.

Before I can think better of it, I'm reaching across the small aisle of the plane, and my hand lands on hers, squeezing gently.

She yelps at the contact as though I've somehow managed to frighten her more.

The sound makes me lift my gaze to meet hers. The shock of my actions is clearly written all over her face.

Her mouth is open, her pink lips forming an O, and her eyes are wide.

There's no question she wasn't expecting me to touch her. Hell, *I* wasn't expecting to touch her.

For a second, we just stare at each other. Gently, I squeeze her hand again. "There's nothing to be afraid of," I tell her, offering a small smile of reassurance. Now it looks like her eyes might pop out of her head.

I guess the only thing more shocking than my touching her is my being nice to her.

The irony isn't lost on me.

Most people only know the fun, carefree Paxton. This gesture wouldn't be out of the norm for them. I'm a hugger. A lover.

But to her, I'm anything but.

She sees me as a villain.

A tyrant.

Probably an egomaniac trying to ruin her life.

To be fair, I'm all of those things to her, and she deserves it.

Regardless of my feelings, I refuse to let her drum her nails to the bone out of fear. In turn, it would only manage to drive me crazy.

It's a survival tactic. That's all.

I lift my hand off hers, but she's still looking at me. Our gazes are still locked.

"When I was a kid, I was afraid of flying," I admit, shrugging like it's no big deal.

My voice knocks her back to reality, and she blinks. "Is there a story to go with this statement?" she fires back, still off-kilter from my gesture.

Me too, princess, me too.

"Obviously, there's a point to my comment. I don't talk just to talk." She purses her lips and lifts a brow. "Okay, sometimes I do. But not with you." The bite is not something I can control. When she's around, my inner dick waves his red flag at the bull, preparing for the showdown.

"Don't keep me in suspense."

"The point is, I was flying alone, and a flight attendant must have noticed I looked scared. She came over to where I was sitting, kneeled beside me, and told me something that changed my whole outlook."

With narrowed eyes of skepticism, she asks, "What, pray tell, is that?"

"Hey, listen, if you don't want my help, it's no skin off my nose," I say, raising one shoulder in a devil-may-care expression.

"Sorry," she says, clearing her throat and licking her bottom lip. "Go on."

I shake my head but continue because I've already come this far. I might as well finish the goal. Paxton Ramsey does not leave a story untold.

No way.

"Okay, where was I?"

"She was kneeling beside you," she prompts, showing she's listening.

"Yeah, okay, so she was kneeling beside me, and she said the one thing that made sense. The one thing that made flying a little less scary."

"And that was . . .?" She flips her hand in the air, signaling for me to get on with it.

"Think of the air as a road. The plane is your car. When you drive, you hit potholes, but that doesn't stop you. It's annoying, sure, but they aren't going to kill you."

"Well . . ."

"No. A simple pothole won't kill you, Mallory. The point is, you aren't afraid of a pothole, and turbulence is the pothole. Turbulence will never bring a plane down."

"You don't know that—"

"Historically speaking, yes, I do. Sure, it might feel scary, but it's just like driving."

"Except on a tiny plane," she deadpans.

"Did you know that jets are just as safe as big commercial

aircrafts? Actually, due to their size, they can maneuver better around turbulence. They can actually fly to a higher altitude to go above the clouds, and if need be, they can change flight plans easier, too."

"Wow, aren't you a wealth of knowledge?" Her sarcasm is not lost on me, but I don't allow that to deter me.

"I am."

She smirks. "And modest, too."

"That I'm not." I shake my head back and forth.

"Well, on that note . . ." She removes her hand from the arm-rest, reaches into her bag, and places her earphones in her ears, clearly dismissing me.

Guess my interference did its job. She's on to the next thing.

Even better? She hasn't drummed her fingers since I told her my story.

I call that a win, even if I still want to shake the woman.

Chapter Five

Mallory

@Stargossip: The hot news on the set of *Twisted Lily* is that reinforcements have been called in to wrangle in the circus. The reps are en route, and this little birdie has heard that trouble is brewing on multiple ends in paradise.

> **@Deathtothesystem:** Finally! This movie is gonna suck anyway . . .

> **@Iloveme:** F that! Get to work!

> **@PetrafiedDivaDog:** Boo . . . I heard that we'd get a peek at Brad's a$$!

> **@Deathtothesystem:** @PetrafiedDivaDog: Eww . . . who wants to see that?

A SMALL, BROKEN DINGHY WAS NOT ON MY BINGO CARD.
After getting off the plane and heading here, I didn't think it was possible to have one crazier thing happen . . .

Welp.

Here I am, standing on the dock, hand on my hip, mouth hanging open, staring at the tiniest boat I have ever seen. One that has seen better days. I'm shocked, and I shouldn't be.

"This isn't a boat. I'm aware I sound like a Karen . . . but with all due respect, this isn't a boat." I turn to look at Paxton, begging this all to be a joke. Hoping he'll start laughing at any minute.

If looks could kill, I'd be dead by the way he's staring at me. "I applaud you for recognizing that you are, in fact, a Karen. The moniker fits your personality to a T."

"You can't be serious." My voice pitches, and I stamp my foot like a child.

Wonderful. I'm feeding right into Paxton's hands.

"I hate to break it to you, but this is, in fact, a boat—*our* boat, to be exact," Paxton quips.

I blink, incredulity rising by the minute.

"Not one you would take across the open ocean, right?"

Please laugh.

Please tell me you're fucking with me.

From where he's standing, the bright sunlight streaks across his face, making him squint. "It is, and we are, princess."

"You can't be serious?"

"You literally just said those same words, and my stance hasn't changed." He lifts his hands to run his fingers through his hair, tugging on the root, clearly annoyed by my behavior.

Hell, *I'm* annoyed by my behavior, but that thing can't be safe.

"Just get on the boat."

My head shakes violently. "Hell no."

Paxton's jaw works back and forth, and I swear I can hear his teeth grinding. Maybe they'll crack, and his image can match closer to *his* personality.

Ugly. Inside and out.

"Listen, princess, we can stand around all day, having you stare like a dog waiting to be walked, but basically, it comes down to this. You have two choices." He lifts his pointer finger. "One. You get on the boat, you do your job, and we fix whatever problem is going down on the ridiculous set." He lifts his middle finger. "Or two, you go home to Daddy and all the others who've contributed to turning you into the spoiled brat you are."

I feel like I've been punched in the gut.

He thinks I'd run home to my father, but that is the last thing I'd ever do. It's the very thing I'll avoid at all costs.

"Nothing to say? No snarky remark?" He's baiting me, and I know it.

The truth is, I'd rather fail than ask my dad for help.

"You think you've got it all figured out, Paxton. Why should I attempt to convince you otherwise?"

He huffs. "Save your breath, princess."

Paxton thinks he has it all figured out, but he couldn't be more wrong. A princess? It's laughable, and the farthest thing from the truth. Yes, in name, I might be considered Hollywood royalty for some, but if he saw the way I lived and how I acted with everyone but him, he'd know how wrong he is.

My bank statement can attest to that fact.

Anger boils deep inside the pit of my stomach. It fills me to the point of rage. I won't let him see the fire inside me, though. Instead, I tamp it down and take a deep breath.

"Let's go," I say through gritted teeth.

There's nothing more to say. I don't have a choice; I have to go with him on this death trap. Doesn't mean I'm happy about it. Nor does it mean I'm not scared. It's practically rotting out in front of us.

He takes a step forward.

I follow suit.

My moves are tentative as I make my approach. The boat is ancient, at least fifty years old, if not more . . .

Probably seventy.

It's covered in rust and grime. Once upon a time, it was probably white, but now it's murky like the ocean below it.

I move closer, but there are no steps. Only a small landing before you enter the boat.

There's barely enough room in the thing for the captain, let alone Paxton and me.

"Well, are you getting in or not?"

Pulling my gaze away from the water, I peer up at Paxton. "Stop rushing me," I mutter under my breath.

"What did you say?"

I shake my head. "Nothing." There's no point in repeating myself. It would make no difference, regardless. The man's going to be pushy, and if I say something about it, he'll likely turn it up. Anything to get a rise out of me.

If I don't get in, my career will be over before it's really started.

Sure, I've been in the business for two years already, but this is my big break. I'm barely getting by as it is.

That's what Paxton doesn't realize. I don't intend to clue him into the fact, but at some point, I'll have to take up a new career if this doesn't pan out.

He thinks of me as this nepo baby, one where everything comes easy to me, but that's the last thing I am.

Hell, even my one client didn't know who I was when she first came to work with me.

When I approached her, I didn't tell her who my father was. I wanted to represent her because she believed in *me*. Not my capability due to my birth.

Lucky for me, she was young and didn't do her research. Her mother, on the other hand, had dug for all the details.

It's the reason she didn't fight with her daughter, who decided to sign with me. She thought I was bringing the big guns and probably still does.

Which is one of the reasons I need this movie to be a success. I have managed to keep my one client even though I never used my father's success for my own benefit, but if this crashes and burns to the ground, her mom will only let me get away with so much.

I cannot afford, literally and figuratively, to lose my only client.

If I thought telling all of this to Paxton would convince him to get off my back, I'd happily do that, but I know men like him, stubborn guys who think they know everything.

Men like my father.

"Is this thing stable?" I practically squeak.

"Yes, miss," the captain responds, but I don't miss his eye roll as he turns his back on me.

I look toward Paxton, an eyebrow lifted in question, and boy, are there a lot of questions.

Will this make it to the island? Will we get stuck? Is there a radio on board just in case we do?

And most importantly—will we die?

"Get on the boat. If we don't leave now, the waters will get too rough for us to leave, and we will have to stay here overnight." He gestures behind us to the run-down dock. There was nothing on the way here from the airport, so there will most likely be no place for us to sleep.

The idea has me shivering at the thought of being stranded on the beach in the middle of nowhere with this man.

With careful steps, I make my way onto the boat. Beneath my weight, the back end rocks forward.

Then Paxton gets in after me.

The captain grabs our two bags and throws them in the back of the boat. He doesn't lock them up or anything.

An uneasy feeling weaves its way through me.

What if we hit a bump?

Will all my stuff get ruined?

Paxton moves up to sit near the captain, but I hang back, instead choosing to sit in the very back next to my bag. I place my foot on the suitcase as if my leg will act as a restraint.

Probably a dumb idea.

Paxton pivots his body and looks at me. "You plan to sit there?"

"Yeah. You have a problem with that?"

His lip tips up, but he keeps his mouth shut as he shakes his head. Just as I get my legs locked in the correct position, the small boat takes off.

It's going much faster than I anticipated, and although I know the back is better than the front for rocking, I can still feel every single bump. *And don't get me started on the water spraying my face.*

Now his question makes sense. I should be in the middle of the boat.

Despite knowing I should move, I don't dare. I'm holding on for dear life, sending up prayers to all the saints and whoever else is listening to deliver me safely to the island.

My pride is already pretty banged up by all the terribly awful things Paxton has said to me since we boarded the plane.

Laughter pulls my head in the direction of the captain and Paxton, who are getting along very well for having just met. Go figure. He gets on with everyone but me.

I didn't ask my father what he knew about Paxton Ramsey because that would require me to discuss business with him, and that's out of the question. Not that it matters. Sounds to me like there's bad blood between my father and Paxton.

Plus, calling my dad isn't on my to-do list.

Every time I talk to him, it's the same bullshit. "When are you going to abandon this pipe dream and come work with me?"

Um, never.

My body jerks, and I'm shaken out of my thoughts.

Holy crap.

From where I'm sitting, I have a clear view of the ocean. It's vast and never-ending. The water is choppier than anything I have ever seen. Large waves are forming in the distance, and my heartbeat quickens.

Can this boat make it?

I squint my eyes to see if I can make out the island from here, but I have no visibility. Between my hair whipping in my eyes and the saltwater burning my eyeballs, I'd prefer to simply keep my head down.

I'm thankful I'm seated and don't have to walk anywhere because I can't imagine that I could for any reason.

The salty air lingers in my nostrils, and I'm practically choking on it.

I hate this.

"You okay back there?" Paxton asks me. Although his question is one of concern, his facial expression says otherwise.

He's smirking.

His eyes are alight with mirth, and I wonder what he's up to.

I don't have to wait long for my answer.

It comes in the way of a giant wave, and the boat crashes right into it. The ginormous splashback drenches me all the way through.

I might as well have just jumped into the ocean.

I have to look like a drowned rat, and as much as I don't give a damn what Paxton Ramsey thinks of me, I do care what others think. Showing up on the set looking like this isn't professional, even if it wasn't my fault.

I purse my lips together, watching as the two idiot men cluck like hens, laughing about me, if their stares in my direction are any indication.

Great. Just great.

The first thing I do is lift my hand and scrub at the salty water clinging to my skin. My eyes burn even more now, and it takes a few minutes to regain my sight. When I do, I realize that being wet isn't my only problem.

This is not my finest moment.

My travel outfit was not planned for a soaking, compliments of a half-crazed captain and a scallywag skipper.

Sopping wet, dressed in a white tank and white shorts.

My pert nipples are on full display.

My shorts cling tightly to my bottom, leaving little to the imagination.

"Need a jacket?" Paxton calls out, grinning widely. "Oops. Left that back home."

Jackass.

As if my life couldn't get any worse, the engine sputters as we near the coast.

"Give me a fucking break," I yell up to a sky that has become dark and mocking.

Great, just great.

I keep looking at the angry clouds above. "It's going to rain, isn't it?"

"Sure looks that way," Paxton says, eyes tipped toward the sky.

The boat continues its sputtering, jerking back and forth.

"Are we . . . are we running out of gas?" My voice pitches.

"Seems likely." Paxton uses that moment to look at me. "Look on the bright side, princess. You can't get any wetter."

FML.

Chapter Six

Paxton

@**Stargossip:** Is it just me, or is the silence from the *Twisted Lily* reps telling?

    @**Nobodycares:** Just you.

    @**Stopinthenameoflove:** Paxton Ramsey and Mallory Reynolds boarded a private jet.

    @**Dontdogthedog:** Production is shut down. The movie is toast!

    @**Deathtothesystem:** I find it hysterical!

S HE TRULY IS A SIGHT.
    Drenched from head to toe, I can't stop staring at her.

I want to for so many reasons, but I'm finding it nearly impossible to turn away.

She's dressed in all white, and her clothes have gone see-through.

I might not like her. Hell, I might hate everything she stands for, but even I can admit she's fucking gorgeous.

This might very well mean I'm a pig, but what's a man to do? Between her smart mouth and her killer body, it's a lethal combination. If she were anyone else, I wouldn't hesitate to make my move.

She looks like a sea goddess.

A siren trying to lure me to my death.

Mallory has me under a spell at this moment, and I can't pull away.

She might truly be a witch because my control is damn near gone.

Starting at her feet, I lift my head slowly, taking in her long, lean legs. Not that I haven't noticed them before. They're hard to miss. This morning when we got on the plane, I had to turn toward the window so I didn't stare at them.

But now, with the glistening saltwater making them stand out even more, they are something else entirely. The type of legs I want wrapped around me as I—

Nope. Not going there.

She's an entitled princess with a last name that ruins any chance of that. Ever.

But even while I tell myself this, I still let my eyes travel up her body. Moving up over her flat stomach encased in the tight white shirt clinging to her skin, landing on her ample breasts, and that's when a lump forms in my throat and my heart pounds in my chest. Her pebbled nipples stand out like beacons under her shirt. I am simply a mortal unable to control my body's reactions to a pair of tits. Perfect or otherwise.

It's not like I want to rip her shirt off and see them.

Okay, I do. I *so* do. Instead, I force myself to keep moving upward until I'm peering at her face.

That's when I realize my error. Her eyes are hard, and her face is a mask.

"Take a picture. It will last longer," she chides.

"Great. Say cheese and give me two thumbs-up." I pretend to pull up my phone, and she groans in frustration. Her lips are pursed, and a small line forms between her pinched brows.

"This is my first encounter with a sea hag." I shrug one shoulder. "A guy's gotta remember such a monumental event."

Her bottom lip trembles, her eyes blink way too fast, and my stomach bottoms out.

Ah, hell. Is she going to cry?

That's the one thing I can't take. A crying girl is tough to watch. It's even worse when I'm the cause of it. It's not something I ever set out to do. I'm not that guy. I don't like to hurt people.

This girl has me wound tight. I'm seconds from snapping. She rubs me the wrong way, and that's not a feeling I'm used to. A woman like Mallory is hard to have empathy for.

But as the boat sputters again and the engine stops, I can't help but feel bad for her.

It's not her fault that this boat is a piece of shit and now has us stranded. It's also not her fault that we represent infants who can't act professionally.

Despite the way I acted, her assessment of this half-ass motor craft wasn't wrong.

I grew up on boats, and the second I saw this one, I knew we'd be lucky to make it to the godforsaken island. I'd have offered an alternative if I had thought there was one.

It was pretty clear from the moment I stepped off the plane that we wouldn't get luxury.

Unfortunately, the director is quite peculiar with his choices of location—along with just about everything else the man decides—but it works for him.

One movie. Every ten years. It will be a shoo-in for an Oscar, which is the only reason I'm on this damn boat right now. For any other client, on any other picture, I'd have put my foot down, but I know full well Brad would go through with his threat.

This project is too big for him to lose—for *me* to lose.

If this goes as planned, I'll have plenty of "Brads" on my doorstep begging for representation, and Brad's departure will no longer pose an actual threat to my career. Let him try to spread rumors, but people in this industry know my character, and they're learning his.

I'm on this boat to secure my station.

I'm also staring at a girl I truly despise and contemplating the issues with admitting I'm attracted to her.

What does it matter?

I blame evolution. My reactions to a beautiful woman—brat or not—are normal.

A sound from beside me has me pulling my focus away from Mallory and looking over at the captain.

He's mumbling curses under his breath and stomping around like an angry buffoon. He doesn't pay any attention to us as he's hitting his hands on the steering wheel, giving the impression that he's seconds away from well and truly losing his shit.

I'm about to intervene when he turns toward Mallory and stops.

He goes quiet, his mumbling fading into the distance as he inspects her.

Good lord.

The last thing we need is another weak man aboard when it comes to her.

He sees what I see. A gorgeous woman who might look even hotter drenched head to toe and covered in sea salt. Next to women wrestling in a vat of Jell-O, I wouldn't be surprised to learn that the average adolescent male fantasizes about this very image. A soaked woman wearing white under a halo of sunlight raining down on her.

Except we're missing the sun.

The sky's about to open up and drench her even more. Me, too. And I will not look as good soaked through.

The more the man stares, the more uncomfortable the small area becomes.

Despite my feelings toward her, I can't help the way my fists clench by my sides as I stand abruptly. I take the few steps to where she is and stand in the way of the captain's view.

I was wrong to stare and so is he. She's a person and deserves respect. Right?

Right.

I don't explain, and I don't look at her when I pull off my T-shirt.

"Here," I say, passing her the shirt. "Take this and use it as a cover. Assuming you want a dry shirt to change into?"

Her mouth hangs open, and her eyes are practically bugging out of their sockets. She looks like a fish out of water. Her lips slam together and then open. She wants to say something but seems unable to find the words.

I don't give her a chance, turning my back to her.

That doesn't stop my thoughts from running wild.

The rustling of clothes, the sound of a heavy wet shirt hitting the floor . . .

My pulse picks up as I imagine her naked body behind me.

I shake my head. Nope. Please stop.

Another sound pierces my eardrums, but I still don't turn around and look. I refuse. I'm not that pervy guy trying to get a peek. I don't need to. I'm Paxton Ramsey, and as egotistical as it might sound, I have no problem getting laid. I don't need to obsess over a woman I hate everything about, other than her appearance.

"The coast is clear. You can turn around." Her voice is sugary sweet, notwithstanding the situation, and that gives me pause.

Why on earth is she being nice after everything I've said to her?

I turn around, and I'm met with something far worse than seeing her in a wet T-shirt. She's in a dry shirt—*my* shirt. It falls to her upper thighs, leaving nothing to the imagination. It's a dress on her. A dress that should be illegal.

"How long do you think it will take?" She lifts her hand to scrub at her face, and the fabric rises, giving me an even better view of her toned thighs.

"What?" I ask, clearly too distracted to understand what she's asking.

"The boat. How long until it's running?"

I shake my head and try to clear my foggy brain of stupid, idiotic thoughts.

Our eyes lock, and it's clear she knew very well that I was gawking.

Her cheeks stain red at my perusal, and her eyes drop to her toes.

I clear my throat, not at all obvious that the situation is awkward . . . so awkward.

"I don't know, but now that you're situated, I'll go check it out."

Turning away from her, I breathe out a sigh. I shouldn't want this woman. I *don't* want this woman.

I'll keep repeating that in hopes my brain and my dick get on the same page ASAP.

She's fucking hot. That's fact. It's also fact that I put her on the off-limits list a long time ago.

"Do you know anything about boats?" she asks from behind me.

"You can say that. I've been driving them since I was a kid," I say over my shoulder.

"Driving is not the same as fixing."

I blow out a breath, and I swear my eyes cross in utter annoyance.

"I know what I'm doing, Mallory."

"Really?"

I turn over my shoulder to look at her, trying hard not to glare. "Why would I lie about that? I grew up on Long Island. Cold Spring Harbor. I used to work on boats all the time."

The sound of metal hitting metal has me pulling my gaze away from Mallory.

The goddamn captain is now hitting the steering console with a screwdriver.

For fuck's sake. He'll have us well and truly stranded, and that won't work for me. I need the hell off this boat before I go and do something monumentally stupid.

I don't finish my thought, nor do I say another word to Mallory. Instead, I dart off to where the captain is because we are too far from the coast to have him breaking this thing.

I'm sure I can fix it. I just need him not to do anything stupid in the meantime.

Seems like an easy ask.

When I get to where he is, he's cursing to himself yet again.

This isn't gonna be good.

I wave him off, telling him I'll look at it.

"I'm more than capable of fixing my own damn boat."

Great.

"I don't doubt that at all."

I totally doubt that.

"It just seems like you might be frustrated, and I'd like to help so you can take a minute to calm down," I say, meeting his eyes and hoping he buys the lie.

Begrudgingly, he nods before taking the few steps away from his captain's chair. He finally does the first helpful thing by picking up the radio and calling someone for assistance.

Who knows if anyone is close enough, but at least he isn't breaking anything any further than he already tried to.

I tinker around, looking at all the typical issues, and it isn't long before I identify the problem. I turn around and find that Mallory has taken a few steps closer, practically looking over my shoulder. No doubt inspecting every move I'm making, as though she has a clue what any part of this boat is called or its function.

"Is there anything I can do to help?"

My lips form a thin line, and the temptation to say something biting is intense. But like the adult I am, I tamp it down. "Nope, I got this."

"If you say so."

Those words grate on my damn nerves. So typical of a Reynolds to think they know everything.

She sits back down, and I go to work, silently cursing her proximity and the fact I can't stop thinking about her wet.

Chapter Seven

Mallory

@Stargossip: An insider has shared that the location is remote and lacks proper accommodations. The talent is sleeping under the stars . . . literally!

> **@suckstocry:** And this is news?

> **@SavageTurtle:** I'd sleep anywhere with Teagan Steward!

> **@Deathtothesystem:** The whole industry should burn.

THIS TRIP MIGHT VERY WELL BE THE DEATH OF ME.

The heat in my cheeks has not abated since realizing that all my goods were on full display to the two surly men on the boat.

Paxton was practically staring daggers at me while the captain was accosting our only transportation with a screwdriver.

You can't make this stuff up.

Finally, after an hour, we're back en route to the island, and I couldn't be happier.

Paxton gave me his shirt, and I'm no longer cold and wet, but other problems have arisen.

His shirt barely falls to my upper thighs, leaving my legs on full display. The captain has not stopped staring, which is a hazard, considering he's supposed to be driving. I feel as exposed as I did before. The only upside is that I'm warmer.

The bigger problem manifests itself as Paxton. Since we're on the water in the middle of nowhere, in a boat that doesn't seem to be working properly, replacing his missing shirt doesn't appear to be high on his priority list.

And why is that a problem, you may ask yourself.

I'll explain. Gladly.

I've spent the last hour trying desperately not to stare at him. On top of not having access to my clothes, I apparently forgot my damn sunglasses, as well, leaving me open to being caught.

This mission to ignore Paxton . . . yeah, I'm failing horribly.

Even though he's probably the biggest prick I've ever met, I can't stop the way my heart beats a little faster when he's nearby. Nor can I silence the voice inside my head, wondering what it would be like to kiss him again. To have him trail his fingers along the same path his eyes wandered earlier.

His face was stone. No emotion while he perused my body unabashedly, and that left me vulnerable beyond measure. He saw nothing of interest. Meanwhile, I'm practically panting at his bare chest.

My body and mind are damn traitors.

Let's just say a shirtless Paxton Ramsey should be illegal.

Every time he moves, his muscles flex, and now that he's standing in front of me, I can really appreciate the view. Luckily for me, he hasn't noticed my thorough inspection. He's too busy making sure the boat will be okay.

What a fun option that could've been. Something to keep me entertained on this work trip. A fun island romp to break up the shit I'm about to deal with.

If only he weren't a complete asshole.

Made only worse by the fact that I shouldn't want him, yet I do.

Not that anyone could blame me. He is the most gorgeous man I've ever seen, and that was my opinion of him before he removed his shirt.

As the boat takes off, cutting through the water, I change locations so that this time I don't get the splashback from the wave. It also means I'm sitting much closer to him.

I can't avoid it.

"Changed seats." It isn't a question. More like an observation he's making out loud.

My face scrunches up as I watch him war with himself.

For goodness' sake . . . is it that much of a hardship to simply *sit* by me?

Finally, he nods as though he's telling himself everything will be fine, and I want to throw something at him. He takes the seat across from me, which might've been the worst decision. At least beside me, we wouldn't have to look at each other.

We both do our best to look anywhere but at each other. My gaze focuses on the horizon. Neither of us says a word, and that's fine by me. I'll enjoy this last bit of peace before the chaos ensues.

I don't know how long I'm staring out at the scenery when I feel his eyes on me. Tingles start at my toes and work their way up to the top of my head. The reaction doesn't sit well with me because I know I can't have what my body is screaming for.

I'm about to combust.

If he keeps staring, I might lose my mind and do something stupid.

Thankfully, it isn't long before I see the shadow of land. I lift my hand to block out the sun's glare that trying to emerge from the clouds and sigh in relief.

The island is approaching swiftly.

"We should be there soon," Paxton says.

"Great. Should we make a game—"

"No."

"You didn't even know what I was going to say," I snap back, irritated for so many reasons.

"I don't want to talk business yet. It's been a day from hell."

He isn't wrong.

"Understood." My fingers twist together in my lap, the awkward silence getting to me. "I just figured that we could discuss a strategy—"

"Again . . . no. There is no strategy. There's no brainstorming. I'm traveling to meet with my client, who has already briefed me on all the issues. Your only job is to get your girl in line." He rubs at his temples. "Her mother, too. Because if this falls apart—" He shakes his head. "Doesn't matter."

His head falls, and the mask of stone disappears for a minute. The vulnerability catches me off guard.

"No, please. Why don't you finish your sentence?"

He sighs. "Because if this falls apart, unlike you, this can affect my career. I don't have a daddy who is just waiting for me to take over, princess."

I open my mouth and then shut it. I'm grasping for words and trying to find a rebuttal. I shouldn't want to convince this man, who is practically a stranger, that I'm not what he thinks I am.

That his own prejudice has clouded his judgment.

He doesn't know me.

He doesn't want to know you.

Nothing comes out of my parched mouth, and I stop fighting the need to explain. Words are just words. Nothing I say will make someone like him believe me. A man like him will never admit he's wrong.

Actions speak louder.

It shouldn't matter to me at all what he thinks. However, that's always been a problem of mine. I do care what people think. I care what *he* thinks.

Deep-rooted daddy issues.

Wanting approval.

Needing it.

The crushing realization that I would never get it from the person I wanted it from most.

That's one of the reasons I need to make it on my own and be successful. And why, despite everything, I strive to do this without help.

Paxton's not wrong. If this doesn't work out, I could go to my father, and he would give me a job, but I'd never do that because I'm going to earn my place in this business. On my own. I don't want my father's handouts.

Maybe that makes me stubborn.

Or stupid, depending on who you ask.

What people don't realize is that life under the shadow of my father has always been cold, and I don't wanna spend the rest of my life shivering.

"Nothing to say?" he goads.

"What's the use, Paxton? It doesn't matter what my truth is. You don't want to hear it, and I'm well aware. All I wanted was your respect—"

He huffs a dark and humorless laugh. "That you will never get, Mallory. Ship's sailed on that front. What you can do is fix your client's mistakes. Make her see reason, and then you won't have my disdain," he seethes.

I bite my tongue because it will do no good to lash out at him. His battle is against my father, and yet again, I am the casualty. We knew each other for two seconds, and somehow that demanded my loyalty to him?

Bullshit.

Either way, I did nothing wrong. It's his loss for thinking the worst.

With me not responding, he goes back to ignoring me, his head turning to face the direction in which we're going.

The land grows as we make our approach. It's no longer a faint shadow in the distance. I can't wait to get off this boat, but the closer we get, the more my back tightens.

Once on land, I need to start figuring out what the heck is going on.

I don't take much stock in the gossip channels, but from what I've gathered from Exposé, it's a disaster, and my client is the cause.

The filming of this movie is apparently not only filled with unnecessary drama, but it's also unsafe. The speculation is that the two leading actors are driving each other crazy. The director is driving everyone crazy. Most annoying is that Teagan's mom can't stop meddling. Not at all a surprise. For the years that I have known her, she has always been a lot to handle. Having her on set was sure to be an absolute nightmare for everyone. But Teagan insisted. It was part of her contract.

The worst part is that if what is being written is true, it's unlikely that this movie will ever be finished, which means my career is sunk before it's even begun.

All that aside, the reason I got on that plane and rushed out here is because Teagan is hurt, which leads to many questions about the safety of the set.

The boat slows down, and it isn't long before we are pulling up to a rickety old wooden dock.

This thing is about as safe as the boat I'm sitting in.

The wood is splintered and broken. Even the metal is cracked where the boat is supposed to be tied. This dock is on its last leg. Yet another casualty in the making.

Hell, it's barely tethered to the land, but even if it was, something tells me with a big enough storm, the dock would be gone.

How is this okay?

Don't they have another dock that we can use?

Mallory, put your big girl panties on and stop bitching.

You've already been labeled a princess. Give this man more ammunition, and he'll blow up the entire place.

It's time to take care of business.

That's why I'm here.

Not to complain.

Not to fight.

But I'd sure like to wipe the smug-ass smirk off Paxton Ramsey's face.

That would be a bonus.

I practically jump off the boat and dash across the dock until I'm back on flat ground.

"Don't worry, princess, I got your bag," Paxton yells.

Shit. In my mad dash to get off, I forgot about my stuff. Now I really do look like the princess he's pegged me as.

I cannot win at this point.

There's no way I'm not going back. I quickly truck it across the warped dock until I'm standing right across the little exposed bit of water. I don't step back onto the boat, but I lift my hands up and signal for him to pass me my bag.

He shakes his head and shoots me a look that clearly tells me he's not going to do that.

Instead, he has my bag in one hand, and in the other, he has his.

"Go back on land," he says. "I have it handled."

I don't want to obey him, but the truth is, looking down at the wobbly wood and the sound it makes under my feet, I'm not sure it can maintain my weight. Let alone Paxton and mine simultaneously. What should be a rich, dark wood is weathered from years of abuse.

Rather than argue, I heed his suggestion and backtrack to safe ground.

He steps out of the boat, crossing the space in two large steps, not bothering to look at me as he passes.

"Come on. They expected us hours ago." Paxton is halfway down the path, leaving me to practically sprint to catch up.

I'm not sure how much time has passed. We've walked in complete silence. I focused on trying to keep up with his long strides, practically panting next to him.

Note to self: The gym is calling.

We make it to a clearing, and that's when I see a group of peo-ple sitting around a fire.

What I don't see is equipment, lodging, or any of the modern luxuries that most of these people are accustomed to.

This is so much worse than I thought.

Chapter Eight

Paxton

@Stargossip: Our sources say sparks are flying, and they aren't the butterfly-inducing type. Things are heated on the set of *Twisted Lily*. Who do you think will bail first?

> **@starstruck:** Teagan . . . obvs!

> **@Deathtothesystem:** They're all divas. Who cares?

WHAT THE FUCK.

What the actual fuck?

This place isn't suitable for farm animals, let alone people.

I'm beginning to see that Brad's phone call was justified. For once in his miserable life, his concerns are valid.

I think he downplayed the severity of the island on purpose because had I realized what I was walking into, I might've told him to go fuck himself. I'm young enough, at only thirty-three, to find another career.

This place is a disaster.

From the boat to the dock, to the freaking path here, the place is a shithole.

Hell, even this makeshift setup in the middle of the grass where everyone is gathered is likely to go up in flames. The grass is dead and ripe for catching fire. There's no question that this place is unsafe.

One of the things about Stefan, the director, is that he's a nutcase. He prefers primitive locations that he feels bring out the best in the actors. I call bullshit.

The fact that he's even doing this project is a miracle, but that doesn't excuse this mess.

"Come on. Let's go find Stefan," I call over my shoulder to Mallory.

Surprisingly, she doesn't argue with me. She follows with no question as I lug around our bags in search of the reclusive director.

We walk through the crowd sitting around the campfire, and they don't so much as notice us. They're a lively bunch, probably all drunk.

There's not much else to do in these parts, so it would seem.

Dusk is settling over the island, and I realize how lucky we were to fix the boat in such a short amount of time. If night had fallen, we would've been stuck out there.

This place is very secluded.

Who even knows what provisions they have? I even question if help would've arrived. I'm not sure Mallory wouldn't have lost her mind if she had been told she had to sleep on the boat. She almost didn't get on the thing to begin with.

The shit I do for Brad is ridiculous.

He wanted an Oscar, and this is his shot. His success is mine.

I'll just keep repeating that so I don't knock his ass out for bringing me here.

Princess over there can fix Teagan's issues, which, in turn, should fix Brad's.

Unlikely.

I'm not sure I can do anything about the state of this set.

Not that I'm surprised. They're filming a movie about a plane wreck and a deserted island. The story centers around a girl and her guardian. It's a story about forbidden love and survival.

The book was not only critically acclaimed, but it also won a Pulitzer.

This film is projected to be the film of the decade. Or it will be if we can get it back on track.

If he sets the location to get the best out of the actors, it's no surprise he'd choose this spot. It's sure to bring out the desperation in everyone to get off this island.

After a few more minutes, I see the director's assistant, Michael. He fidgets, looking frazzled. It's the same way he's always looked whenever I've seen him. Stefan must drive him crazy.

"You're here." Michael's face lights up like a kid on Christmas morning. Things must be really bad for him to get so excited at my appearance.

"I said I'd come," I say in a deadpan, not sharing his feelings on my presence being needed here.

"And you're here, too." He looks at Mallory. "Good. We'll need all the help we can get with those two."

He's obviously referring to the actors.

My gaze leaves his and darts around the field. "And what about Stefan? Where's he?"

He shrugs. "He's being Stefan. He films and then disappears."

My head swivels around. "To where?"

"Beats me. I don't question his brilliance. There's a method to his madness, and he'll make gold out of this…."

I arch a brow. "A bronze statue, I hope."

"That's the plan. Which is why we need both of you here." He huffs. "Let me show you where you'll be staying."

Mallory and I share a glance. If I'm reading her right, she's thinking the same thing as me. *This oughtta be good.*

"Please," I say, sweeping my hand out in front of me. "Lead the way."

Michael walks us down a different path. One that goes deeper within the island.

I pride myself on my bravery and chivalry, but this place gives me the creeps. It has horror movie vibes, and with every rustle of the trees, the hairs on the back of my neck rise a little higher.

Pull yourself together, Ramsey.

Michael points a finger in the opposite direction from where he's taking us. "Everyone else is staying on that side in the main group of huts."

Mallory stops walking. "Did you just say huts?"

Michael turns to her, and even in the waning light, his face pales. "Yes, umm. Why?" He nervously shifts his weight from one foot to the other.

"Thank you for giving us better accommodations. After the day we've had, we could use some good news." She chuckles. "I'd have died if you walked us up to a hut."

I don't have to be a genius to know she's read it all wrong.

We won't be getting anything luxurious. He's simply giving us more private huts.

He swallows. "Well… actually… you see—"

"Dear God, Michael. Stop stalling." I turn to her. "You'll be sleeping in a hut, too."

"What?" she screeches. Her head snaps from his to mine.

"That's accurate." Michael looks down toward the ground and then back up. He's clearly uncomfortable having to be the bearer of this unfortunate news.

It's my turn to step forward because that's one thing Brad did not mention. "Where are the actors' suites?"

He rocks back on his heels, blinking uncontrollably. "Everyone is staying in huts." His voice squeaks, sounding like a dog's chew toy being attacked by a mastiff.

Mallory paces as she worries her lip in thought. "Do they have electricity?"

"Some."

She stops pacing, sliding right up in front of him.

"Explain . . . some."

"Stefan wants everyone to rough it, but not that much. He knows that we need some technology to function. Just don't expect fast Wi-Fi." He chuckles awkwardly, trying and failing to make a joke.

There is no joking about this. It's the truth of the situation.

We'll be lucky if we have cell service out here.

"Wait—are you serious?"

"Unfortunately, yes. But this is the way he wants it." Michael turns, done answering questions.

"How am I supposed to work while I'm here?" Mallory asks, and I laugh.

"You have one client, princess. How much work do you need to do other than getting your actress on board to, you know, act?"

"I—"

"You nothing. If anyone should be worried, it's me, but you don't see me complaining. The faster you get your girl—"

"It's not just my girl." She scoffs.

"Maybe not, but she and her irritating mother are certainly not helping with all the other problems."

"Let's not pass judgment until we know all the facts." Mallory's voice is sharp with an edge I haven't heard from her before.

She's protective of Teagan.

Good to know.

"What do you say, Michael? What's really going on? The only information we have is from the tabloids. Are the rumors true? Is the set a ticking time bomb?" I ask him.

He grimaces. Shit. "There have been a few accidents."

Fantastic.

I level him with a stare. "How many?"

Michael lifts his hands in the air in defense. "I haven't been counting."

"Wonderful. So you're telling us we're walking into mayhem?"

Worse than even the tabloids have said.

"I'd say mayhem is a tad understated."

My eyes close, and my lips smash together. I don't lose my temper. I pride myself on also being patient and understanding.

"Brilliant." It's all I say, because what more is there?

This is a nightmare.

What shit did you get me into, Brad?

"The environment isn't ideal. You'll soon see." And just like that, his words become reality. The wooded terrain opens in front of us, giving a clear view of the huts.

And they are much worse than I imagined.

Based on Mallory's yelp, she's feeling the same way.

"Saddle up, princess. It's gonna be a long night."

For both of us.

Chapter Nine

Mallory

@Stargossip: Breaking news . . . the stars of *Twisted Lily* are roughing it in huts! Can you imagine? HUTS!

> **@TeaganStewardFans:** OMG! Nooooo!

> **@Losethetude:** First world problems. *Rolls eyes*

> **@Deathtothesystem:** How barbaric. Teeheehee

THIS HAS GOT TO BE A JOKE.

I blink my eyes, certain that when I open them, I'll be back in New York City, lying in my comfy bed, snuggling into my warm down comforter, dressed in my coziest pajama set, freshly bathed and slathered in lavender lotion.

Instead, I'm standing in front of what I don't even think qualifies as a hut, as Michael so poignantly called it.

It's a hovel, missing half of its roof.

My mouth is glued shut. I'm keeping all my thoughts to myself.

There is no need to give Paxton any more reason to kick me down further. I'm at rock bottom.

For this nightmare to be over, we need to get along. We have to join forces to get things rolling and get this movie wrapped up.

That obviously does not mean that we need to be best friends. We only need to be cordial to each other.

"Not quite the Ritz. Is it, princess?"

I turn my head in his direction. Even though I don't want to admit it, he is most definitely the most beautiful man I have ever seen.

His brown hair looks almost blond in this light, and the wind has ruffled the soft locks, pushing it forward so it sweeps across his forehead.

As if he can hear my thoughts, he lifts a hand and runs his fingers through his hair.

He still has no shirt on, and his muscles flex at the movement. He shouldn't be this good-looking, making it hard for me to remember what he just asked me, but then, like a sledgehammer bashing against concrete, he speaks and ruins the moment.

"What? Not up to your standards?"

My face contorts before I force it back to neutral.

"I highly doubt this is up to your standards, either."

"That's something we can both agree on."

I turn toward him, brow raised. "No cutting remark? That's new."

"What's the point? It's obviously not the luxuries you're accustomed to."

A humorless laugh escapes me. "You'd be surprised what I'm accustomed to," I fire back.

He doesn't know about the struggles I've had or what I've done to get to this place in my life. He assumes by looking at me and knowing my last name, that I just take money from my father.

The list of everything he's got all wrong is growing by the minute.

I bite my lower lip and stop myself from saying anything rude.

That's not who I am, and I won't allow him to make me something else.

Typically, I'm happy. This man just brings out the worst in me, and apparently, I bring out the worst in him.

I don't need to impress him, so I won't say more. I have one goal, and that's to get the hell off this island and away from him as soon as humanly possible.

Without anything more to say to him, I take a step up. The wood creaks beneath my weight. Never a good sign.

"Be careful where you step."

As the words leave his mouth, I understand what he's saying.

I yelp as I lurch forward.

I'm vaguely aware of my surroundings, and my head swims as a set of firm arms wraps around me.

It takes me a few seconds to understand what just happened and who I'm pressed against.

My foot went through the rotted wood, and I was about to fall forward, flat on my face. Somehow, as if he were a superhero with lightning-fast speed, Paxton was able to drop the suitcases and grab me.

Which means, right now, the warmth surrounding me . . . Yep. That's all him.

My heart hammers in my chest, and if I'm being completely honest, my cheeks start to warm at his proximity.

I would think after the day we had, he would be sweaty and probably smell bad, but instead, it's the complete opposite.

Paxton Ramsey smells divine.

Leather and sandalwood mixed with salt and sea. An intoxicating aroma that has my knees weakening further.

Despite my better judgment, I inhale, leading my body to relax against his embrace.

"Careful, princess, get any more comfortable, and I'll think you still want me."

That comment knocks me back to reality with a proverbial slap to the face.

I struggle to get out of his embrace, but he just chuckles behind me.

"You do that, and you'll most definitely fall flat on your face," he warns. "Let me help you."

I look over my shoulder, and our gazes lock. He wears an interesting expression on his face, but I can't read it from the way he has me positioned. His shirt, a.k.a. my makeshift dress, has risen up my thighs, nearly exposing my panties that have finally managed to dry.

"While I'm holding you, I'm going to need you to bend down and move your foot."

"Won't I fall?" I breathe out.

"You're going to have to trust me."

A huff escapes my mouth. "Well, that is unlikely, seeing as—"

"Stop that line of thought. The only thing you need to know right now is that I am going to help you out of this."

"You are?"

Dear lord, I sound like some idiot damsel in the arms of her knight.

This man is no knight. A *night*mare, maybe.

"Yes. So be careful, because you don't want to cut yourself. Nor do you want to get any splinters out here in the wild. You'll likely lose a foot." He lifts a brow, indicating that too many things could go wrong, and he's right.

I nod in agreement.

"Now, with me holding you, wiggle your foot gently."

I attempt to dislodge myself, but I'm having absolutely no luck.

He shuffles behind me, then his hands lower. I stiffen at the touch of his hands on my exposed thighs. This is not the time for butterflies and tingles, but they're there anyway.

It can't be helped. His hands on my skin bring too many memories.

Our time together may have been a blip, but I can still remember the feel of his fingers working me over. The way my body ached for him.

OMG. Stop it right now.

His other hand leaves my skin, and my body cries out in protest. He pushes out the wood and manages to dislodge my foot.

When it's free, he helps me back up, all while still holding me.

I need to breathe, but all the oxygen has left me.

His hands haven't moved, and they are warm against my skin. The feeling of his touch has the butterflies fluttering in my stomach even worse than before.

Breathe, Mallory.

I place my hand on his and push his fingers off, desperately needing the distance.

"Thanks," I mutter, and then look down and take another step.

I fling the door open, and the moment I do, the smell of stagnant air hits my nostrils.

Gagging, my hand flies to my nose.

"Oh, God," I moan.

I'm going to have to air this place out.

Wait. Bugs.

Maybe that's not a good idea.

"Let me show you where everything is," Michael says from behind me.

"Not sure that's necessary," Paxton deadpans.

I step into the hut, knowing I don't have a choice. I move aside, making way for Paxton and Michael to follow me in.

Paxton drops my suitcase on the floor. He peers around as Michael steps forward and points out various things.

"There is electricity. The island does have internet, but I must warn you, both are temperamental."

"Good enough for me," I say with a forced smile.

It might not be ideal, but I've gone camping before. *At least this has internet*, I tell myself.

"Over there is a bathroom, and you can unlatch the windows if you need air. You can also drop a bug net from the ceiling. That way, nothing gets in. I know it seems a bit much, but when you've worked with Stefan for as long as I have, you know he is a genius."

"Everything will be fine. This is perfect."

Lies. Lies. Lies.

"Okay, Pax, let me show you to your hut," Michael says.

"You're leaving me?" The words are out before I can think better of it. "I mean . . . yeah. Okay."

Paxton's eyebrows are both lifted to his hairline, but he doesn't say anything. I'm sure he can see the unbridled panic all over my face, and thankfully, he takes pity on me.

"I'll be nearby if you need anything."

I'm not sure why those words comfort me coming from him, but they do.

I offer a tight-lipped smile and nod, watching as the two of them leave.

It'll be dark soon, and I'm exhausted. I had every intention of going back down to the fire, but I think I'll cash out for the night and get an early start the next day. Something tells me I'm not ready for what tomorrow brings.

Let the chaos begin.

Chapter Ten

Paxton

@Stargossip: Do you think there are killer snakes on the remote island where *Twisted Lily* is being filmed? That's a hard pass for me!

> **@twistedtealover:** Probably. Would serve Brad right to get bitten.

> **@Lostintranslation:** Brad will save Teagan . . . or place the snake in her bed . . .

> **@Deathtothesystem:** One can only hope. Maybe that will finally stop this horrific movie.

B Y THE TIME I SITUATE MYSELF IN MY ROOM, IT'S PITCH-BLACK outside. This place is fucking awful.

Hell, I can see why Brad is freaking out.

I'm barely containing my ire.

While I have no idea if his accommodations are better than

mine, I can still see how, even if they are marginally better, this isn't what he signed up for.

Nowhere did the director indicate that the actors would be roughing it.

Listen, I grew up outside. Camping. Sailing. Hell, I was a fucking Boy Scout. I can appreciate the ambiance, but that's me. And most people aren't like me.

Take princess, for example.

She was shocked. While she tried to play it cool, I saw the way her footsteps stumbled when the huts came into view. The stress was evident by the way her damn fingers tapped her leg continuously. Now, sitting here, I debate what to do—go to bed or go meet up with everyone.

I'm a little hungry, and seeing as food options are limited, I'll need to head back to civilization to find something to eat.

Craft services are most likely still set up.

I open the door and look around. There is absolutely no visibility. My gaze darts toward Mallory's hut, and I realize that if she's hungry, she may not be able to find her way at this time of night.

Mallory is not your problem. She can fend for herself.

But . . . if something happened, I wouldn't forgive myself. No matter my opinions of her, I'm not that guy.

In the end, the gentlemanly part of me wins out, and I walk over to her hut, sidestep the hole and knock on her door.

At first, nothing happens. I don't hear anything and wonder if maybe I'm wrong. Maybe she already left. She may be down by the open field with everybody else.

Then I hear a rustling sound, a series of groans followed by footsteps.

The door swings open, and a small light streaks out across the distance. It's coming from her bathroom, but it does nothing to illuminate the space.

Instead, it casts a soft glow over Mallory.

I take her in. She looks as if she was sleeping. Her hair is disheveled, and her eyes are swollen.

After staring for far too long, I track my eyes down, and that's when I realize her mistake. She is barely dressed. She's wearing a skimpy white tank top that does nothing to cover her.

What's with this girl and her poor clothing choices?

Her nipples are pebbled through the thin material. I let my gaze drop, and she has little shorts on, too.

They're not tight, but what they are is short, and her toned legs are not hidden from my view. Her hand lifts, making me look back up until our gazes lock.

She scrubs at her eyes, clearly confused.

"I was coming to see if you wanted to walk back with me, but seeing as you fell asleep, I'm assuming no."

Hopefully, she says no, because as much as I don't want to admit it, the idea of her wearing this in public makes my blood boil.

I'm not sure where that thought came from, but I don't like it.

The group at the fire mainly consisted of men, and out here, that's dangerous.

She opens her mouth and then closes it. It's as if she's thinking about what she wants to do, but ultimately, she shrugs.

"I'm just gonna go back to bed."

"Works for me," I say, turning around to get the hell out of here.

I head toward the field where I assume everybody is. The more time that passes, the more worried I am for Mallory.

There were no other huts on our side, leaving her completely alone out here.

Not your problem, Pax.

She'll be fine.

As I get closer, the noise of people talking confirms that I walked in the right direction, and all thoughts of Mallory disappear with my growling stomach.

It doesn't take much longer before the path opens to the clearing.

There seem to be different groups set up, but one thing I do notice is that there aren't a lot of people. Far smaller crew than usual for this type of movie.

Then again, in the meetings, Stefan had said a lot of the filming would be done with a handheld camera to feel more natural in scenes.

When Brad's character lusts over his young ward, the scenes will be shot from an angle to make it feel like you're looking at the world from the hero's point of view.

It should be interesting to watch. That is, if all goes as planned.

Within a few seconds, I spot Michael. He sees me, too, and his arm reaches up into the air as he waves me over.

"How did you get situated?"

"Everything is good. I'm actually looking for Brad."

"I think he's over there. I believe he's drinking." Michael points in the opposite direction.

Great. Just what I need. A drunk, pissed-off client, who's already demanding.

Hopefully, that's not the case, but if it is, I'll let him know I arrived and then head back to my hut on the other side of the island.

I take the path Michael pointed at and see where Brad is. He's sitting on a chair, sharing a bottle of—what is he drinking?

I squint my eyes. It's rum.

Fantastic.

He lifts the bottle, and from the way his hand sways, it's clear he's three sheets to the wind. I consider turning around, but before I can, he sees me. "You're here!" he hollers. "Get your ass over here. It's about fucking time."

I make my way over to him. "You called me yesterday," I deadpan.

"Exactly, it took you long enough."

"Glad to see you, too." I take a deep breath and assess him. "How much worse is it?"

He places the bottle down and tilts his chin up to meet my stare. "It's worse than the tabloids think it is."

"How the fuck are the tabloids getting so much intel? There's hardly anyone here."

"No clue. No one knows who's leaking the information. It's 100 percent an inside leak because the gossip columns aren't that far off."

This whole thing is beyond peculiar. This set is supposed to be a closed one. How are the stories getting out?

"Stefan fired half the crew." Brad's sharp voice cuts through my thoughts.

"Are you serious?" I step closer.

Brad reaches for the bottle and takes a swig. "Yes, and it's causing a host of issues. Production being slow is one of the biggest." He lifts his hand and offers me the bottle. I lift my hand to decline. "I didn't sign up for this, Pax."

I nod. It's not something I can argue. He made a fortune, but that doesn't have anything to do with contracts.

"Are the safety issues true or false?"

"Well, seeing as we're missing half the crew now, that is a major safety issue. But even before Stefan fired everybody, there were accidents. At first, it was only Teagan getting hurt." He lifts his hands like it's no big deal. "I figured she was clumsy."

That's concerning. What's going on that she is getting hurt? No wonder her mom is flipping her lid.

"After Stefan went rogue and fired people, more accidents have been happening. Which isn't a surprise."

I shake my head, taking in a deep breath.

"How is Teagan?"

His lips tip up into a lecherous smirk. "Hot."

"Be serious. I meant physically."

His eyebrows waggle, and I regret my words immediately.

"I am serious. What I would do to have those lips wrapped around my cock. Fuck, she's so young. I bet her pussy is tight, too—"

"Brad." I level him with my stare. "Please stop. And don't even think about laying a hand on her. She's off-limits. Got it?"

That's the thing about Brad. Fame has gone to his head, but despite his inappropriate comments, he has yet to step over the line fully.

People have complained that he's difficult, but nothing about those complaints has actually come to fruition . . . yet.

One day, it could, but in the meantime, men like him simply think they are gods.

"I do what I want, Paxton. You just make the deals and collect on the money *I* earn."

Arrogant fucking prick.

The moment he gets his Oscar, I'm cutting him loose.

This relationship has run its course. One more comment I don't like and I'm liable to strangle him.

On that note, I decide it's best I leave. My appetite is now gone, thanks to this man. "I'm calling it a night. I need to be on my A game tomorrow. Don't do anything stupid."

"You sure you don't want a drink?"

"Positive."

Another thing about Brad, one minute, he'll threaten your career and your whole livelihood, and the next, he'll ask if you want to party with him.

He's a big enough narcissist not to understand that I hate his ass.

He probably shouldn't be left unattended in this state, but enough people are around to ensure he doesn't step out of line. I'm not a babysitter.

Turning my back on him, I make my way down the dark path. I need to get my head in the game, and I can't do that around him.

Something tells me tomorrow will give today a run for its money.

I'm not looking forward to it.

Now, to get a good night's sleep, without dreams of long-legged women wearing my shirt and looking like my wet fucking dream.

Chapter Eleven

Mallory

@Stargossip: What are the chances that Teagan falls twice? Stick around . . . we'll keep you posted.

> **@TeaganTrain:** I'll play the net! No need for her to worry!
>
> **@LosttoLust:** @TeaganTrain F*$& the net . . . I'll play the tree!
>
> **@BeamMeUpTeagan:** Hopefully, she gets back up there . . .
>
> **@Deathtothesystem:** She's a drama queen!

EARLY MORNING SUNLIGHT STREAMS THROUGH THE SMALL cracks in the straw . . . or whatever this place is made of.

I left the makeshift windows open last night, opting to use the mosquito net. The entire place needed airing out, or there was no chance of me getting any shut-eye.

It's not overly warm, thankfully, but I'm used to the air conditioner in my apartment, so sleep didn't come very easily for a host of reasons, including the fear of being murdered out here.

Too many nights were spent watching true crime

documentaries, and now I have an overactive imagination. Every sound had me clutching the threadbare sheets and pulling them up to my chin. At this rate, I might never sleep.

As I stretch my hands over my head, I realize just how much I tossed and turned in the little sleep I did manage, because my neck is stiff and my back aches. A typical casualty of traveling. Stifling a yawn, I move to get out of bed.

My bare feet hit the warm and sticky wood floors as I force myself to get moving. I need to search for coffee, stat.

The hut isn't as bad as I thought it would be. It has running water, a bathroom that flushes, and electricity. It works. The greatest flaw? No coffee machine.

I hope the huts the actors are staying in have more amenities. Otherwise, the list of grievances I'm sure to hear about today might bury me. It won't even be Teagan doing the complaining. Her mother, Theresa, is the worst kind of momager. She's horrible to deal with on a normal basis. This experience is sure to bring out the worst in her.

Walking to the bathroom, I turn on the faucet. It sputters alive. Well, I guess not the best plumbing, but again, it works.

I'll take it.

Slashing water on my face, I make quick work of ridding myself of the remaining dregs of sleep and the grime I accumulated overnight.

My morning routine is simple. I get by with the basics: teeth brushed, bladder emptied, and dressed to attack the day.

Once I throw on a pair of black leggings and a T-shirt, I make my way outside and follow the path to where everyone gathered yesterday.

I'm not exactly sure that's where I'm supposed to be going, but seeing as I've been given little to no information and have yet to connect with Teagan, I'll stick to what I do know.

I follow the small empty passageway through the trees. It winds around almost like a maze, and I'm officially lost. I didn't see that as a possibility, considering the island looked small from the water. With no other option, I keep walking and eventually stumble upon another clearing.

This is much larger than the one from last night.

It's large enough to build a decent-sized hotel in this spot, and it makes me wonder about the island. Who owns it, and why haven't they considered building it up? It's a beautiful space.

In the center of the clearing, craft services have set up a food buffet, and my stomach rumbles in response.

I let out a long-drawn-out exhale, grateful for small indulgences.

The smell of coffee permeates the air, and my body shivers with delight. I'm practically running to the table when I hear my name called out.

Dammit.

I turn to look over my shoulder, and from the edge of a different path than the one I traversed, Teagan is waving her hands frantically at me.

"You're really here." She's practically screaming, and several heads turn to see what the ruckus is about.

Despite my desperation for coffee, I make my way toward her.

"I told you I'd come."

She pulls me into a hug, squeezing harder than I'd think possible from a girl so tiny.

Pulling back, she stares into my eyes, smiling wide. "And I told you it wasn't necessary."

"Well, your mother disagreed."

She practically growls at the mention of her mom, which wouldn't be the first time she's shown her lack of interest in having the woman around.

"You should have let me handle Theresa."

I place a hand on her shoulder, squeezing in reassurance. I don't want her to think that I'm inconvenienced. I am, but that's not something she needs to worry about. I'm here now, and I came to help.

"It's okay, Teagan. I understand why she was so frantic." I glance around the area, realizing, not for the first time, how unconventional of a set this is.

"She's dramatic. I'm fine."

My head tilts as I take her in. She looks tired and pale. Not the picture of health and vitality someone so young and on top of the world should appear.

"She's concerned you're going to throw in the towel."

"No . . . she's concerned about losing money."

The anger and hatred radiating from Teagan is concerning. Does she not realize what this film could do for her?

"This picture has the potential to be huge, Teagan. It will set you up to take over Hollywood."

Her chin dips, and her eyes fall to her shoes. "Don't remind me."

Are those nerves? This girl is a star. Can't she see that?

"You have nothing to worry about. Just show up and do your thing, and you'll be gold." I try to reassure her, but it's obvious she's nervous.

How could she not be? This could make or break her career. She's worked so hard to get to this point, and one wrong move could end it all.

I hope she realizes I'll do anything to help her flourish, including fly to a deserted island with a man who hates me, and even play nice with the ass.

"If you say so." Despite the way her voice rises an octave, she's not fooling me. Nothing I'm saying will make her feel at ease.

Until the film wraps, she will be a bundle of nerves, and I can't blame her.

"Come on, show me where the coffee is."

Teagan lets out a laugh. "Struggling?"

"You know it."

"Can't have that." Her hand reaches out, tugging my arm, leading me toward the tables. A lot of people are already halfway done with their meals, but that's no concern to me. I don't make eye contact with a single person, heading straight to the coffee.

I don't know anyone, which suits me perfectly. I'm not here to hobnob. I'm here to ensure Teagan has everything she needs to get this movie done.

Grabbing the largest mug I can find, I serve myself.

The robust fragrance filters in through my nose, and my eyes close as I breathe it in further. This is what I need. This will make things better. Lifting it to my mouth, I take a swig before finding a place to sit.

Teagan has ditched me for food, and I don't mind. I'm by myself, able to take in my surroundings. As expected, I know no one. This is a closed set with very few crew members.

I wonder where Paxton is and what he's been up to this morning. I didn't even check to see if he was still in his hut. My mind was too preoccupied with finding caffeine. A man approaches the table, staring at me. He looks vaguely familiar, but I can't place him.

"Mallory Reynolds," he says, smiling wide. "It's been forever."

I smile back, trying and failing to place the man.

"I'm not sure if you remember me. We met years ago through your father."

I try my hardest to refrain from grimacing at the mention of my father. Just what I need, a reference to him, of all people.

Here I am, trying to break out on my own, and my Achilles' heel, aka my dad, is still hovering over me.

I'm hoping he puts me out of my misery and introduces himself, and luckily for me, he does.

"Jeffrey Trainer."

He extends his hand for me to shake, and I do. Immediately after, I use both hands to lift the coffee mug to my mouth, to buy some time to figure out what to say next. I'm not usually this awkward, but I usually don't encounter people who know my dad before I've even had my coffee.

"How is your father?" he asks, and I internally groan that this is how my morning has started.

Not a good sign for today.

I shrug. "Good, I guess. I haven't spoken to him recently." I hope my answer keeps him from pressing the issue because I'd rather discuss fungus growing on trees than anything to do with my father.

"Well, I imagine so, since the service here is so spotty." He laughs. "As a producer, I don't have much of a choice. Stefan sure can be difficult sometimes." His shoulders shake with continued laughter. "My next project will *not* be on a deserted island."

I offer a tight-lipped smile but continue to drink my coffee.

"It's great to get to spend some time with you," he says, and for a moment, I think he's going to sit across from me.

"It will be nice. Rain check? I need to find my client."

He nods. "Of course. I'll see you around. Not many places for you to hide."

Creepy way to put it, but accurate.

With that, Jeffrey walks off, and I'm thankful. My eyes scan the area, looking for Teagan because I don't want that man to find me still sitting here and come back.

She's sitting by herself at a table closer to the edge of the clearing.

Coffee in hand, I make my way to her, sitting across the table. "Everything okay?"

She scrunches her nose. "I guess I'm just nervous for today."

I lift a brow. "What's happening today that has you nervous?"

"We're filming a scene that we tried to do last week." She blows a stray hair out of her eyes. "It was a total disaster."

She has to be referring to the scene that hit the tabloids.

"When I'm up in the tree . . . well, all my lines . . . they just evaporate from my brain. I'm not a fan of heights to begin with. I'm afraid that after last week, with how dangerous it was, I won't be able to—"

"Do you want help running your lines?"

The key to getting rid of her nerves rests in diverting her train of thought. If we can get her focusing on the lines, she won't be thinking about the height. We can't have her working herself up before she's even in the tree.

"You wouldn't mind?"

"Of course not, Teagan. That's what I'm here for." I smile wide, hoping to ease her discomfort. "I'm here to make your life easier. I'll do whatever is in my power to ensure you're comfortable and able to fulfill your commitment."

I stress that last word, hoping it hits home. She signed a contract, and a breach wouldn't be good for any of us.

Her forehead crinkles, and two lines form between her eyebrows, then she nods.

"I appreciate you. You really are one of a kind."

At least someone thinks so.

Chapter Twelve

Paxton

@**Stargossip:** What would you do to have one night with Brad Wright on a remote island with nothing but the stars as witnesses?

> @**GunsandPoses:** I'd give up my cat . . . and my Pokémon collection!

> @**Lacklusterlover:** No thanks. I need a challenge . . .

> @**SunshineDaisy:** Can I trade him for Teagan? I'd switch teams for that!

> @**Deathtothesystem:** Brad's a pig. Pass!

B Y THE TIME I FIND MY WAY TO CRAFT SERVICES, A CROWD HAS already formed to get food.

With a tilt of my head, I search the area, my gaze landing on Brad. He's across the clearing, talking to Stefan.

I have no desire to speak to him this early in the morning. I don't deal with idiots before coffee. Before I'm seen, I make a beeline in the opposite direction, my eyes landing on Mallory.

She's got her coffee cup in hand, but she doesn't get far. Within a few steps, Jeffrey, the executive producer of the film, steps up to her.

I'm too far away to hear what they're saying, but I can only imagine. As a part of the elite, surely, Jeffrey knows exactly who she is. Despite not working for her father, she is still Hollywood royalty, and this little world of glitz and glamour is rather small. I have the perfect view of him, and I don't miss how quickly he juts out his hand to introduce himself.

I pivot away, not wanting to watch that any more than I want to talk to Brad. It's yet another reminder of nepotism in Hollywood and how birth elevates the lucky few.

I'll work my ass off to rise to the top on my own. Thank you very much.

I'm not interested enough in their budding relationship to stand here gawking at them. They'll shake hands. She'll bat her long eyelashes. The next thing you know, she'll be booking Teagan left and right because of all the connections the last name Reynolds makes.

The truth is, for the next few days, I'm gonna have to deal with a lot of shit, and starting my morning off being reminded that she's the daughter of a man I hate, isn't helping my surly attitude.

I head over to where the food is set up, grab a piece of bread, and take a bite before making my way to get some coffee. I'll need it before speaking with Michael.

He's standing next to an attractive blonde who's overdressed for this neck of the woods. I vaguely remember her as a publicist, which makes sense, but who does she represent?

She certainly doesn't represent Brad. Although it would be good for his reputation, Brad does not employ women, not for the publicist role, at least. I've often wondered why, but for the sake of my working relationship with the asshole, it's best I don't understand his inner workings.

My job is to negotiate the deals, keep him busy, and ensure that he follows through with his contractual obligations without causing too much shit in the process.

I know Teagan has a very modest staff, which leads me to believe this woman is the publicist for the movie.

Good idea to bring her here, considering the lousy PR the film is already getting in the tabloids.

I'm sure they are hopeful whoever was leaking information on set is gone with the round of firings, but having a publicist in place, just in case, could give the film enough time to spin it for the greater good. Or at least one would hope. By the time I'm standing in front of them, Michael is about to leave.

"Morning. Got to run. But I'll see you on set," he calls over his shoulder, rushing off to be at Stefan's beck and call.

"I'll be there."

The blonde slides in front of me, offering a coy smile as she extends her hand. "Hello, Paxton. We've never officially met," she coos at me. "I'm Natasha. I'm the publicist—"

I reach out, taking her hand in mine because that's what a gentleman does.

Her full, injected lips part, and she inhales, exhaling a choppy breath.

Is she flirting with me?

My eyebrow lifts, waiting for her to say something more, and when she doesn't, I decide it's best to run along. The last thing I need is a complication while I'm stuck here.

Now on my list of no-go flings—publicists on movie sets.

"Hi, Natasha. It's nice to finally meet you."

Lies. I had no idea who she was. My best guess was the publicist by deduction only. I have a reputation for being the nice guy, and I'll maintain that no matter how awkward the situation.

She pushes her chest out, showcasing her ample breasts, and I have to bite down on my tongue not to laugh.

"If you'll excuse me, I have someone I need to speak to."

Not really, but I'll say whatever I have to in order to evade more passes.

"See ya around?" I say, brandishing my signature smile.

Her eyelashes flutter, and she bites her lower lip.

Dear God. This woman is thirsty.

I quickly turn and spot Mallory again. My eyes narrow as I take in the scene.

Teagan is animatedly talking, her arms flailing around. From here, she looks like a deranged chicken trying to fly.

What is happening? Brad better not have caused this.

That's when I notice the script on the table in front of Mallory. Her mouth moves, and I realize she's running lines with Teagan.

Thank God.

For a second, I thought I was witnessing one of Teagan's notorious meltdowns. That would not have been a good start to the morning.

"Mallory Reynolds?" Natasha says, and I turn to look over my shoulder.

"So it would appear."

I try really hard to keep the animosity from my voice but fail miserably. Nobody needs to know my feelings toward Mallory. This is business, and when it comes to this set, I will be professional in front of every person on this island, save for my nemesis.

"Don't bother talking to her. I hear she's a bitch."

I stare at the woman for a moment too long, and based on her crooked smile, it appears she might've misconstrued that as me being interested. Which I'm not.

"That's funny. I've never heard that about her."

Which is true. Nobody has ever said a negative thing about Mallory. In fact, until recently, she flew under the radar in a way most people of her status wouldn't.

"Well, when Daddy owns the most successful talent agency in Hollywood, I guess it's no surprise that you can land your nobody client a major movie picture."

Her words are no different from my thoughts, but for some reason, as they leave her fake lips, my blood boils.

My reaction is puzzling, but I push away the thought and keep my face neutral.

"She doesn't work for him. Mallory's a solo act."

She scoffs. "For now, but everybody knows that's temporary." Her hatred for Mallory is evident by her sour tone.

I lift my brow, wondering how this woman knows so much about the Reynolds family. She's a publicist. Sure, we all work in Hollywood, but she has a completely different role to play, and it would suit her well to butter up to the rising agent.

"Is that so?"

She rolls her eyes, and for a publicist, I'm not at all impressed with her behavior. "Yep, Daddy Dearest told me himself."

Well, I guess my first opinion of Mallory was correct. What's their endgame? Send her out to underhandedly steal clients to funnel to dear old dad before she joins forces? It wouldn't be a new strategy for Reynolds.

I thought maybe I was wrong about Mallory for a second, but I should've known to always trust my gut. It rarely leads me astray. The confirmation is all I need to steer clear and keep Brad far away.

"Nice talking to you, but I need to get to my client."

She offers a wide, toothy smile. "I'll be here all day . . . and night."

Subtly isn't her forte.

I nod before turning in the opposite direction of both Mallory and Natasha, moving toward Brad like my feet are on fire. The women on this island are batshit crazy. They both likely want to fuck me in one way or another. I typically prefer Natasha's method, but in this case? Pass.

By the time I reach Brad, he's already standing, hands on his hips, glaring at me as if I'm late.

"You coming to the meeting?" he asks, cocking his head in the direction of where we're supposed to be discussing the issues on set. "Or were you planning to get your dick sucked by blondie over there?"

I rub at my temples, not ready to deal with him today.

"There will be no dick-sucking for you or me on this island. Understood?"

"Who pays who?"

Fucking arrogant prick.

"Seems like you're confused about how this works," I say, tapping my chin. "I find you opportunities. You agree to a project, and I make a deal. Then *they* pay us." I smash my lips together, widening my eyes. "Isn't that a novel concept?"

"Are you going to do your job or what?" he says, completely ignoring my reminder that he does not, in fact, pay me dick.

"I am." A yawn escapes me, and he narrows his eyes in on me. "I'm going to get some more coffee first."

"You better, because I need you on your toes. The bullshit around here needs to be fixed and fast. When we shoot later today, everyone needs to act like professionals."

I choke but quickly mask it with a fake cough. Brad, of all people, talking about being professional is a wholly ridiculous contradiction. He doesn't seem to notice my slight because he keeps blabbering on.

"Doubt it. But one can hope. The last time we tried to film this scene, Teagan fell."

My eyes widen. "That's the scene they're filming today?"

Now Teagan's arm flapping and overall crazy-toon actions make sense.

"Yep."

Brad doesn't need to clarify whether I know what scene he's talking about. It's the scene that made all the gossip influencers' feeds only two days ago. It's why we're all here on this isolated island, sleeping in run-down huts.

The set isn't safe, and the branch Teagan stepped on was not secure. It can't happen again.

The influencers insist someone had broken the branch. Why would someone sabotage the set and put Teagan, or anyone else here, in harm's way?

I think it's bullshit. Someone was sleeping on the job and didn't bother to do a safety check. I chalk it up to an overzealous influencer trying to go viral by concocting a conspiracy.

Not that it matters. Nobody should've known what was going on here. It's a closed set, so the news was leaked from within. One of many leaks that started the moment filming began. The question is, did Stefan fire whoever had loose lips? Or are they still standing in the wings, waiting to share the next glitch?

The appearance of Natasha leads me to believe Stefan's not so sure the culprit's gone.

Fantastic.

If someone is trying to ruin the film, the larger question is why? What do they have to gain?

Only time will tell.

For now, my focus is on getting this film rolling and keeping Brad's dick in his pants.

Fuck my life.

Chapter Thirteen

Mallory

@Stargossip: Brad was the Wright guy for the role, but we've been told that Teagan continues to look like a deer in headlights. Sounds to us like her spot should've gone to a seasoned actress. Someone who deserves to be next to the likes of Brad. What do you think?

    @BitchPleaseMe: He sure is fiiinnneee!

    @ShakeItOn: Give the girl a break. She's poppin' her cherry!

    @FreshLinenLicker: @Stargossip Stop feeding into rumors!

    @Deathtothesystem: Replace them both! They're the worst . . .

HAVEN'T BEEN HERE FOR A DAY, BUT FROM THE MOMENT I stepped off that junker boat, it was clear the set had problems. I don't need a TMZ article to figure that out. The writing is all over the walls or, in this case, the trees.

I'm as nervous as Teagan is about today, but I can't let her see that. She needs all the confidence she can muster going into today.

So do I.

I'm about to go head-to-head with whomever I need to in order to ensure my client's safety.

I follow the path that Michael instructed me to take to find Stefan and Jeffery. Just up ahead, there's a hut, not unlike mine, but a little bigger.

The door is open, and I wonder if I'm the last to arrive.

Unlike last night, I look down as I take the steps up. The last thing I need is to embarrass myself in front of everyone by getting my foot stuck again.

It had been humiliating enough in front of Paxton.

But he helped you.

Doesn't matter. There will be no incidents happening in that regard again.

When I step inside, Teagan, Brad, Paxton, Stefan, and Jeffery are already here, as I feared.

Shit.

The person who I'm surprised not to see is Theresa. She's typically stuck to her daughter's side, causing all sorts of headaches for everyone. I quickly wipe that from my mind, not wanting to inadvertently manifest the Wicked Witch of the West into existence. For whatever reason, she isn't here, and I'm grateful.

"So nice of you to join us." Paxton drawls as he lifts his wrist and checks the time. Making it clear to everyone watching that I'm late.

I narrow my eyes at him, doing my best to communicate that I will cut him. Into paper-thin turkey pieces. I'm talking real thin here. It has no effect. Instead of shutting up, he smirks. *Asshole.*

"Some of us have a company to run and want to settle this," he adds.

Piss off.

"How about instead of continuing to harp on my timing, we get to work?" I turn to the director and producer. "I apologize for keeping you waiting. I'm ready." I look back at Paxton. "Let's discuss why we're here."

"I'm not working with her," Brad blurts out, garnering everyone in the room's attention.

"Brad—" Paxton chides, but it does no good.

"No, Paxton. She's unprofessional, and I don't have time for this."

"*I'm* unprofessional?" It's Teagan's turn to chime in. "You're a drunk!"

Paxton rubs at his temples, and I swallow a lump forming in my throat. We've just gotten started, and it's already a shit show.

"Do I need to remind you both that you signed contracts?" Jeffery says, leveling them both with a hard stare.

"Which is why *we* are here," Paxton interrupts, motioning between himself and me. "No one is walking." He practically glares at Brad when he says this. "Let's discuss the grievances like mature adults."

Brad throws his hands up in the air. "She's basically a kid." He bares his teeth like an animal. "A bratty one at that."

She glowers in his direction but doesn't say a word. Good girl, Teagan. Show the group that the issue is Brad.

"Her age is irrelevant." I address the group when I point this out. "I'd like to hear from Teagan about what's going on."

I dip my chin, signaling that she has the floor.

"The set is unsafe." She shrugs. "I refuse to work until it is."

"Bullshit. It's an excuse." Once again, Brad shows his ass, speaking out of turn and seemingly unwilling to act like an adult.

Based on the way Paxton's jaw works back and forth, he recognizes it, too.

"Brad, is your only issue with my client that she's not showing up to the set?"

He purses his lips, crossing his arms over his chest like an entitled jackass. "That, and she's not prepared."

I look over at Teagan, giving her an opportunity to rebut.

She chews on her cheeks, indicating there might be some truth in what Brad's saying.

Great.

I'm about to speak when she finally talks. "I know my part."

Teagan and I used to run lines together. Seeing as she's my only client, I've had the time to cater to her every whim. I think something more is going on here.

Confidence maybe?

I need to talk further with her about this, but not in a room full of men who've been at this for far longer than her. I won't embarrass her.

"Listen, let's not do this." I sit up taller. "We all want this picture to be made. The best way for that to happen is for us to shoot here and now. Don't you agree, Jeffery, Stefan . . .?"

"There's no question that if I tell the studio that production has halted or if we have to recast"—he looks at Brad as he continues—"the chance the film will be made is next to zero."

"I'm sure you know what's at stake if that happens." My eyes remain locked on Brad, who appears to be mulling over what he's heard.

It's no mystery that Brad is hoping for the Oscar. This is his chance. Is he willing to throw it away because of ego? I decide to ride that train of thought and see where it takes me.

"Although you have a long career ahead of you, you won't have many opportunities like this."

Brad's forehead scrunches at my words.

"Knock it off," Paxton snaps at me, likely catching on to my antics. "If we want to replace Teagan, that's exactly what will happen." His sharp voice cuts me deep. "But that doesn't mean we want to go down that route." He says this last part to Teagan, much kinder in tone, but the threat is already there.

I know it. He knows it. Now Teagan knows it. Her part in this movie is precarious. Despite what I said, he brought this package to the studio. Her role isn't guaranteed.

She's easily replaceable.

With Brad at the helm, the perfect screenplay, and a well-respected, seasoned director, Teagan is the movable piece.

"I agree. No one wants that to be the outcome," Jeffery says, offering a tight-lipped smile in Teagan's direction.

This wouldn't just be a massive loss for Teagan, but for me, too. I'm not typically emotional, but my future rides on her keeping this part. I tamp down the emotion building in my chest because I need to present a strong front for both Teagan and me.

"What can we do in the meantime?" I inguire, proactively. "How do we fix this?"

Jeffery shares a look with Stefan, who's been oddly quiet this entire meeting. "In corporate America, when problems arise within the work force we do team building," Jeffery states. "Seeing as Brad and Teagan can't seem to work together maybe we should try this method, too."

"Team building?" Brad guffaws as though Jeffery just suggested the most ridiculous idea.

It isn't a bad idea. If this is a confidence issue for Teagan, team building could go a long way in bridging the gap and making this work.

"I think it's a fantastic idea," I offer.

I don't miss the way Paxton's eyes half roll before he catches himself.

"It works," Stefan interjects. "I've been on sets where we've used this method before, and the outcome was a wrap and several academy nominations."

He's speaking Brad's language now, and it's evident his words hit their desired mark by the way Brad is now smiling.

"We're already set up to shoot the scenes. It couldn't hurt." He shrugs as if he's still not sold on the idea, but he's the team player.

Gag me.

"Wonderful. Before we shoot, Brad and Teagan will work together on each scene. That way, by the time they shoot, they're comfortable with each other," Jeffery explains to the group. "Moving forward, we'll continue team-building activities for them. Would that work for you, Stefan?"

"Only if I can shoot the activities."

I lift a brow, not understanding why he'd want to film team building.

"If an organic moment happens, I don't want to miss it," he says, picking at his fingers.

If that's what Stefan wants, it will have to work for the collective. Everyone knows that Stefan loves full immersion into a role. Seeing as we're staying on a barely habitable island, I can understand his need to capture all moments. Not to mention, editors can do wonders with all types of footage.

"I can live with that," Paxton says, turning to Brad. "How do you feel?"

"Let me get this straight . . . we are basically filming a reality TV show. That must make you so happy." He glares at Teagan.

My teeth bite down to refrain from unleashing my anger on Brad over his treatment of Teagan, but based on everything that's happening, it would be best to play nice . . . for the time being.

"Next on the agenda: the leak," Paxton says, keeping the conversation rolling.

"I fired everyone." Stefan doesn't bother looking up from his fingers when he says it.

"Yes, and that opened up the set to accidents," I remind him. "How are we going to remedy that?"

"I've arranged for new staff to be flown in. They should be here in the next few days."

Jeffery's eyes widen, indicating this is news to him.

"In the meantime, I'll delegate two remaining crew members to inspect all the equipment. Everything will be checked before we shoot. Is that okay with you guys?" Jeffery looks back and forth between Paxton and me.

"That works," Brad responds, despite the question not being addressed to him.

Paxton takes a deep breath. "That is a good idea."

Teagan remains quiet, but since Brad had his say, she gets hers, too.

"Teagan? Will that make you feel safer?"

She nods but doesn't say a word.

"Teagan," I press. "Do you have something more to say?"

She shakes her head. "No. That all sounds better."

"Okay, that's settled, so team building, safety . . . What else?" Jeffrey looks around, giving us the opportunity to steer the conversation toward our greatest issues.

"Natasha is here," Paxton states. "Will she be working on damage control?"

Jeffrey nods. "She will."

"Excellent." Paxton turns his gaze to Teagan. "Are you willing to do what she says to get this done?"

"Excuse me? It's not just my client—"

His hand shoots up, stopping my tirade. "My client knows the drill. He's a seasoned vet." He inclines his head. "I'm simply ensuring that your team is prepared."

Yep. Got that message loud and clear.

Teagan and I are the newbies. We are nobody—basically idiots. I hate this man.

"Yes," Teagan mutters, clearly not happy to be called out, and I don't blame her. I want to rip this man a new one.

"Lovely chat." Paxton stands. "Jeffrey. Stefan. Thank you for your time and swiftness to ensure our clients are taken care of." He offers them a dazzling smile that I'm sure he's spent numerous hours in front of a mirror perfecting. "I'm sure we all have things to do. Like shoot the next scene." He claps his hands together and then strolls out the door with Brad.

I wish he would get lost in the woods and never come back.

Now that would be a story for the press.

I've never been on a real film set. Sure, I've seen television shows being filmed, Teagan's, to be exact, but a movie—nope.

This is a first, and I'm trying to remain professional and not act like the kid in the candy store because this is exciting. It was always a dream of mine to be part of the movies. Growing up with Thomas Reynolds as my father, one would think movie sets were my playground, but he never let me accompany him.

After the meeting, I follow Teagan to hair, where we continue to run lines. When they switch to makeup, I decide to head toward where the scene will be filmed today to verify that people are checking over everything.

As small as the island appeared from the water, I'm surprised by how immense it feels once you're on it.

Maybe it's the towering trees or the labyrinth of paths, but I feel small here, surrounded by nature.

Despite the size and various clearings, Stefan has ensured it's bare bones where accommodations are concerned. The luxuries are nonexistent.

I catch a glimpse of Michael, surrounded by a few other people I don't know.

Small talk is not in the cards for me right now, so when I see Jeffrey lift his hand and try to wave me down, pointing at the seat next to him, I politely smile and shake my head to decline.

When he doesn't take no for an answer, I lift a finger to signal him to give me a minute. At that, he finally nods, turning back to speak to Michael.

How the hell am I going to avoid that?

This is such a different experience from Teagan's television show. That was shot in the studio with a limited set and green screen most of the time. The entire premise of the show was a group of kids hanging in the lead's basement, talking about life and the hiccups of being a teen.

It wasn't a hit.

A man climbs up on the tree, likely to inspect it, as discussed at the meeting. It's holding him all right, so hopefully, that means it's sturdy enough to hold a small girl like Teagan just fine.

I would *not* want that job.

From what I gathered from reading lines with Teagan this morning, in this scene, a wild boar has tried to attack her character, and she must climb up the tree to stay safe. Brad's character finds her and tries to coax her down, but she's frantic and scared. It's a powerful scene, and I know she'll nail it.

For the next few minutes, I likely look like a micromanager as I watch everyone preparing, but so be it. Whatever keeps Teagan safe is worth it.

One by one, everybody does what they're supposed to do, and the actors are called on set.

I get tired of standing. Knowing full well that this could be a very long day, I find an empty chair in the back and attempt to disappear into the background. It's far away from Jeffrey, which was my main objective.

The hairs on my arm rise because I feel eyes on me. I search the vicinity to see if I'm going crazy or if somebody really is staring at me. A man I've never seen before is peering right at me. When our eyes lock, he quickly turns away.

Who is he?

I turn in the other direction to find Paxton striding toward me. *Ugh. Why?*

He takes the seat right next to mine, and I prepare for whatever issue he's about to lie at my feet. When he doesn't say anything, my eyes narrow in on him.

What the hell?

I would sit next to Jeffrey before him, and I can't imagine he feels any differently. I pull my gaze from the side of his head and realize that no other chairs are available. Every one, aside from the seat he's in now, is occupied.

That makes more sense.

He doesn't acknowledge me, nor do I acknowledge him. I'm purposely avoiding eye contact, staring in the opposite direction.

It does no good. Sitting this close to him makes it hard to ignore his presence.

I can feel his warmth.

I can hear the rustling of his clothes with every shift of his body.

I'm hyperaware of the proximity. Our chairs are so close that it's almost as if I'm sitting on his lap.

His cologne wafts over me, and my eyes close as I inhale the intoxicating fragrance. Damn, he smells good.

A loud voice booms through the space, and my eyes fly open.

Teagan walks across the grass, and Stefan fires off directions as he talks to her. The crew moves into position, and the surrounding area goes silent.

A man comes up behind Teagan and lifts her into the air, helping her scale the tree. This time, unlike the last, a brown foam pillow sits around the trunk in case of a fall.

It's not viewable, but at least Teagan knows that if she falls, she won't land on hard ground. Hopefully, that's enough to keep her calm.

"Quiet on set!" Stefan yells out.

The air around us is still. Every person waits with bated breath for what's coming, not uttering a sound.

It's almost creepy how quiet it is.

Please, universe, make this scene work.

If a pin dropped, you might actually be able to hear it, and so would Stefan. From what I've heard, that would be enough to witness him blowing a gasket. Something tells me it wouldn't be a pretty sight, either.

The man is a nutcase when it comes to his art.

I'm watching intently as the camera rolls, and Teagan opens

her mouth. She's shaking like a leaf, part of the role, but I know Teagan, and her fear is real, even from where I'm sitting in the back.

I can see the tears forming in her eyes. I'm so engrossed in what's happening that I am taken aback when a hand rests on my hand.

A shriek bubbles up in my mouth, but I don't dare allow it to escape.

I follow the hand up until I meet Paxton's gaze.

I'm not sure why he's touching me, and I narrow my brows and shake my head in confusion.

His eyes go wide, and he looks down to where my other hand rests on the wooden arm of the chair, indicating something.

Then it hits me.

My hand was drumming.

My nerves won out again. They have a mind of their own, and I almost disrupted the shoot.

My sole purpose in being here is to keep things running smoothly, to make sure that everything goes off without a hitch, and that the movie is made, and I almost ruined it for everyone, including my client.

I would have if it weren't for Paxton.

Time stands still as I feel the heat of his skin on mine.

I expect him to remove his hand. As I'm now aware of what I'm doing, he has no reason to keep touching me, but he doesn't let go.

Inclining my chin, I motion for him to let go, but he shakes his head.

Then he mouths, "You can't be trusted."

My mouth drops open, and I want to argue, but instead, I bite down on my lower lip. I force myself to stay quiet and not argue with this insufferable man.

But I don't because I know this isn't about me. This is about his client, and the longer the scene takes, the longer we're here. Which, in turn, means the longer we have to work together.

So yes, I bite my tongue, inhale deeply, and let the scene play on.

All the while feeling the burn from his touch.

Chapter Fourteen

Paxton

@Stargossip: They say not to work with family . . . guess Teagan Steward missed the memo. Our sources say that her mother is a tyrant and half the reason *Twisted Lily* is about to sink.

    @PumpedUpKids: That woman is psycho! Get her off the set!

    @Deathtothesystem: Some people shouldn't reproduce.

I'T'S NOT EVEN A SECOND AFTER THE DIRECTOR CALLS CUT AND gives the cast and crew a five-minute break that all hell breaks loose.

When it happens, I'm not surprised Teagan's mom is striding across the grass and getting in her daughter's face.

Of course, she is.

"Aw, hell . . . here we go," I say, rubbing my hands together.

Theresa Steward is the most overbearing woman I have ever met. She gives the moms on all those reality dance shows a run for their money. She's certifiable.

"What's she saying? Tell her to turn it up," I practically whisper for Mallory's ears only.

Theresa's yelling, but I have no idea what she's going on about.

"Will you shut up? It's not funny," she hisses.

"Au contraire. If all our careers are about to go up in flames, we might as well sit back with popcorn and watch the blaze light."

"Asshole."

Mallory quickly stands and dashes over to intervene, but it might be too late. The whole scene has drawn a crowd.

"What's happening?" Natasha asks from behind me, placing her dainty hands on my shoulders.

"The Wicked Witch of the West is on set. I'm just waiting for the house to drop on her so I can steal the red shoes."

"Ruby slippers," she corrects, and I shrug.

"This isn't good. Look at Stefan. Something like this is going to be the end of *Twisted Lily* and all our earnings."

She says the words, and I'm sure my face pales. She's right.

Before I know what I'm doing, I spring up out of my seat and take off straight into the fire.

Lord knows she'll likely need reinforcements to get Theresa under control, and if I have to play backup to Mallory to save our asses, so be it.

This fight might have nothing to do with Brad, but if Theresa messes up today's filming, it will.

One foot in front of the other, I pick up my pace and arrive just as Mallory steps forward, essentially blocking mom from daughter.

"Is this how you repay me?" Theresa shouts, her voice sounding brittle.

"Mom. Please."

Theresa points a finger in Teagan's face, and the poor girl allows it.

"No, Teagan. One job. You have one job—"

"Mrs—" Mallory attempts to stop the tirade but is cut off at the knees.

"This is none of your concern, Mallory—"

Her features harden, and her shoulders roll. She looks like she's preparing for war.

This I've got to see.

"That's where you're wrong. This is exactly my concern. My job, in fact."

"Your job is to get my daughter movie contracts." Theresa places her hands on her hips, leveling Mallory with a glare that singes. "Seeing as we're here, your job is complete. I'll speak with my daughter alone." She practically growls when she turns back to her daughter. "Remind her what's at stake."

"What's at stake is you being the reason your daughter is removed from the film permanently," I say, unable to allow this woman to speak to Teagan or anyone like she is for another second.

She doesn't belong here, and I intend to make it clear.

"And who the hell do you think you are?"

"Nobody important. Just the person behind the existence of this project." I shrug.

"Mallory." Teagan's voice cuts through the thick air. "I'm okay. The director's going to want to get on with filming. We've already— just . . ." She shakes her head, appearing defeated. "You can leave." She looks at me. "You can *both* leave."

Mallory's head tips to the side. "If you're sure."

"I am." Teagan reaches her hand out. "Thank you."

There's not a shadow of a doubt that Teagan genuinely likes and cares for Mallory, and as I look over and see the scowl on Brad's face, I can't help but be furious.

Furious for how Theresa Stewart talks to her daughter and Mallory, who's only trying to help.

Furious about the impact this moment might have on the future of *Twisted Lily*.

More than anything . . . I'm furious that I'm furious.

What the actual hell is going on?

I don't stand around. Instead, I find myself striding back toward my chair and fuming the entire way.

From a few feet behind me, I can hear the soft sound of Mallory's faint footsteps. My back muscles tighten as I halt my steps and pivot to face her.

Her eyes go wide, and I'm not surprised. I'm pissed, and she can tell.

My jaw is locked tight, and my posture is rigid.

"What's wrong?" she asks.

"This." I motion around.

"The shoot?"

"No, *you*." My hand lifts, motioning toward Teagan. "Her."

"What are you talking about?"

"Your client is out of her depth. You can't even handle her mother, who has no business being on a closed set, to begin with."

Her head shakes with confusion. I watch her mouth open and close, trying to find words, but she must come up with nothing because she stares at me.

"Why do you hate me so much?" she asks, catching me off guard. That was the last thing I expected her to ask.

"I don't hate you," I snap. "But I do blame you."

I'm not even entirely sure what I blame her for. The respect she gets from her client? The fact that she's unable to handle an unruly mother?

All of it?

She places her hands on her hips. "How is this *my* fault?"

"You are out of your element. Not schooled enough for this kind of shoot. You shouldn't be here."

"And you should?"

I take a step forward, and Mallory doesn't even budge.

"I have years of experience. I own my company. I'm damn good at my job."

She tosses both hands up in the air, throwing her head back. "And I'm not?"

I lift my right brow in answer.

"That's bullshit. You know nothing about me. *Nothing.*"

"I can say it because it's the truth. You barely have your training wheels on in this profession. You should be working your way up from the mailroom, just like everyone else."

"You have no idea what you're talking about."

"I know that you had an unfair advantage. I know you are in no way prepared for this shit show. I know that your client is too new and too naïve to survive this picture. And I know the damage it will cause my client when this fails."

"And what would you have me do? Walk away. Not try to help? Leave her to flail on her own?"

I shrug.

"If you think I'd ever walk away from someone who needs me, you don't know anything about me."

She walks past me, and after a few steps, she stops.

"You're the one who brought my proposal to your client. Teagan is here because of you, just as much as me. You didn't have to say yes." She places her hands on her hips and cocks her head.

She has a point. If I were smarter, I would have told her to fuck off. The truth is, if I were smarter, I'd never have had a meeting with her in the first place. We'd had that one interaction that went too far and almost cost me my career before it got off the ground.

The meeting followed a phone call regarding Brad. His reputation was hanging in the balance, and we needed some good publicity. Stat.

It bought some time to come up with a plan to push the narrative that he's not a tyrant to work with. That he treats his costars fairly. That he's a mentor looking to help new talent succeed.

Good publicity.

Looking back, I see none of this was worth it.

I'd have been better off letting Brad sink. Instead, despite my better judgment, I let this woman throw my client and me a lifesaver.

And here we are, in the middle of the ocean, adrift anyway.

"I wasn't about to run the risk that you'd play unfairly like your daddy."

"What are you insinuating?" she grits through her teeth, which only makes me grin in return.

"You would've twisted things around and spun something useful to benefit your client. Poor Teagan, shot down by the bully." I shake my head and huff. "Nope. Working with you seemed like the lesser of two evils."

"I'll ask you again. Why do you hate me so much?"

"Hate you? That implies I give a fuck about you, princess."

"From where I'm standing—"

I lift my hand and stop her words. "I don't. You are a means to an end. I need this project to happen. I can either have your help or not. I don't give a shit."

Her light blue eyes lock on me, her teeth biting her lower lip. She's out of her element.

Despite growing up with a shark of a dad, she's flailing.

I turn, giving her my back.

"Where are you going?"

"Back to the set. We're already behind on filming because of your client and her mother."

"I'll speak to them," she shouts at my back, but I ignore her.

I don't have to look to know that Mallory is trying to keep up. I make my way back to the chair I had vacated only minutes before and plop down onto the seat.

When Mallory doesn't follow suit and find a seat, I glance around to find her.

She's across the grass talking to someone.

Jeffrey.

What's she up to?

You know what? I don't give a fuck.

Chapter Fifteen

Mallory

@Stargossip: The rumor mill has been a bit silent. Should we be worried about the state of *Twisted Lily*?

> **@PenTen:** I'm more concerned about world issues!

> **@Deathtothesystem:** No . . .

THE LAST THING TEAGAN NEEDS TO DEAL WITH TODAY IS HER overbearing mother.

However, I'll honor my client's wishes and back down.

If it were up to me, I'd tell her she's not welcome on the set. Teagan is eighteen, so she doesn't need her mother here.

I'm not sure what it is or why she has this hold on her, but unfortunately, she does.

It's hard for me to understand that type of relationship since I never wanted my parents around.

My mother ignores me. Often too busy getting her Botox and

fillers. When she's not injecting some poison into her face, she's going shopping with her friends and lunching.

She's the quintessential trophy wife. My father, on the other hand, is a condescending prick who truly doesn't believe in me at all. He thinks that I should just get married and pop out children.

Not that there's anything wrong with that, but since he finally understands that's not my life goal, he wants me to work for him. And it isn't because he wants me beside him, building an empire, but because he has no faith in me not to sully his name and reputation.

He wants me under his wing to control me and the narrative. So, I guess in that regard, I do understand Teagan's relationship with her mother.

My father is controlling and overbearing, but unlike Teagan, I don't let him.

I'll make something of myself and flip him the finger when I manage without him.

I take a deep inhale, realizing she's still young. I'm ten years older than her. Maybe by the time she's my age, she'll understand, and she'll stand up for herself, too.

Then there's Paxton.

Yet another man who thinks he knows it all and has the world under his control.

I can't be anywhere near him right now.

My teeth grind together. I clench so hard I'm afraid a tooth will crack.

Instead, I move toward where a group of people are gathered far enough away that they don't interrupt the shoot but close enough that they can still observe. I'm already too close when I realize my mistake. Jeffrey waves me toward him.

It's not that he's done anything to bother me, and truly, I should be cozying up to him, seeing as Teagan is having so many problems on the set. He's the producer, after all. But every time I look at him, I think of my father, which is ridiculous, but it doesn't stop it from happening.

Instead of trusting my gut, I head toward him. A lump forms in my throat the closer I get. I'm not looking forward to this conversation.

"Mallory."

"Hi, Jeffrey. It's a pleasure to see you again." I give him a small, tight smile, hoping it's enough for him to think I'm busy and can't sit and chat.

However, he doesn't seem to get the drift as he motions to the empty chair.

"Come. Take a seat."

"I can't. I need to—"

"Oh, nonsense. Your client is working. What else do you have to do?"

I open my mouth to respond when, suddenly, he's waving his hand again. "I won't take no for an answer. Sit."

Seeing no polite way out of this, I do just that. I plop down in the seat and move until I'm comfortable.

I cross my arms in front of my chest and let out a breath. *Let's get this over with.*

"Heard anything from your father?"

Great. Just fucking great. He doesn't even pretend to wine and dine me. He just goes right in for the kill.

No finesse.

No bells and whistles.

Just straight to the point.

I'm not interested in you and what you bring to the table. I simply want to get to your father through you.

"Not since you last asked." As soon as the words leave my mouth, I realize how rude I sound, and I can't make an enemy out of Jeffrey.

Plus, as much as I don't always get along with my father, I also don't want people to think we're estranged or have familial problems. It's nobody's business.

"I'm sure he's good. I've been busy. So has he, obviously." A small, nervous giggle escapes my mouth.

"Oh, that's good to know."

I shake my head in confusion. "What's good to know?"

He licks his lips. "That your father's been busy."

My head tilts to the side as I stare at his profile. "I'm not following you."

"I've reached out to talk to him about a project I'm working on."

And there it is. Just as I suspected.

Jeffrey doesn't want to shoot the shit with me. He wants to interrogate me about my father. Story of my life and the reason I have one client.

Despite years of practice trying not to give a crap, his statement still flies through the air like an arrow, hitting me in the heart. Even knowing the drill, it still hurts.

For years, the shadow of my father has cast his larger-than-life ego over me. This is the reason I don't work with him. I'll never shine under his shade.

In high school, I learned very fast not to talk about him because even school-aged kids were tasked by their parents to get intel on him from me. People played at being my friend for that sole purpose. It was devastating for me as a child.

But even that wasn't enough. Everyone who wanted to be an actor who has ever crossed paths with me has tried to use me for him. To get an in to be represented by him.

Boyfriends.

Teachers.

Coaches.

You name it. I've never known who is real and who isn't.

Teagan was the only one who didn't know.

Eventually, she found out, but by then, the ink was dry on our contract, and I could feel pride at having landed a genuine client.

Which was a good thing because she knew off the bat that I wouldn't ever use my father's connections to help her.

This man, however, doesn't know that.

Seeing as I'm on his set and everything is already going to shit, I can't say it outright.

I'll have to play this the right way.

But how?

"Yeah. He's been crazy busy. I'm sure he'll get back to you soon." I uncross my arms and lift my right hand to my head, closing my eyes as if I'm thinking. "He actually might be out of the country."

That might buy me some time.

"Oh, yeah? That's good to know. I really do want to talk to him. I think one of his actors would be perfect for a movie I'm producing."

I nod at him. From the outside, I look cool and collected, but what he doesn't see is that I'm biting my cheek. The coppery taste of blood fills my mouth as I listen to him tell me about his project.

I'm sure he hopes I find it exciting enough to call my father and sing his praises, but he doesn't know me at all.

"That sounds wonderful." I move to stand. "I do have to go."

"If you speak to him—"

"Yes, of course."

"Thank you, Mallory. And if there is anything you need while you're here. Anything—"

I smile, but it's forced. "Thank you."

Before he can say another word, I scurry off, and as I make my way to the path out of here, my body moving faster than it should on the rugged terrain, I smack right into a wall.

Nope. Not a wall. A person.

Shit.

My hands lift, and I steady myself. When I'm no longer dizzy, I look up and find Paxton grinning down at me.

Double shit.

Chapter Sixteen

Paxton

@**Stargossip:** Seems some people have friends in high places or, in this case, family. How did I miss that Mallory Reynolds is *that* Mallory Reynolds*?* Daughter of Thomas . . . Heir to the largest talent agency in the world? Maybe that's why Teagan hasn't gotten the flip-flop. The movie takes place on an island, so a flip-flop is more fitting than a boot. *Shrugs*

> @**Iloveme:** Must be nice. F*cking hate nepo babies.
>
> @**SavageTurtle:** Who cares? She's hot.
>
> @**Deathtothesystem:** The bigger problem is the movie, not the staff.

MALLORY DOESN'T KNOW WHAT SHE'S DOING, SLIDING UP next to me. I'm in a mood I can't seem to shake, and I can't help but blame her. It might not be fair, but shit, so is life.

"You looked rather cozy with the producer. Why am I not surprised?" The words flow from me, oozing with disdain.

Mallory's cheeks color fiercely at my words. If she were any other person, I might mistake the warm red glow for a blush, but that's not at all what this is. She sucks in her cheeks like she's biting the inside of them, and her eyes are hard and steely.

I narrow my eyes and take in her rigid posture. Her hands are clenched tight at her side, and instead of her hand tapping, it's her foot this time.

She's good and pissed.

Not that I care. I made a simple observation. If she can't handle the criticism, she's not cut out for this industry, no matter who her daddy is.

I decide to poke the bear, because why the hell not?

"It must be such a comfort to have friends in such lofty places. I'm sure you'll be swimming in clients before long." I grunt. "Putting some other well-deserving, hardworking agent out of business just because you can hobnob with the best of them. You're probably already on a first-name basis with half of Hollywood."

She glares at me as she steps forward. "What's your problem, Paxton? Scared I'll come for yours?"

I guffaw, impressed by her gall, but the more I think about it, the angrier I grow. It's just the sort of thing her father would do. He's notorious for poaching other agents' clients.

"You can try, but everyone knows you're just a second-rate agent, whose one and only client can't seem to fulfill her obligations without a damn fuss."

Okay, I probably went too far, but I'm on a roll now. Might as well dig that hole a little further.

Her chest puffs out in anger. "You son of a—"

"Watch it, Mallory. You'll pop a blood vessel."

She's trying her best to look unaffected and strong. Unfortunately for her, she isn't fooling anyone.

I tower over her petite frame, likely a foot taller than the five-foot-two I have her pegged at. My hope is to intimidate her enough that she backs down and gets out of my hair.

She straightens her back, craning her neck. "I hate you," she seethes. "You are such an arrogant ass."

"Calm down, princess. All that is pretty obvious." I take another step toward her so we're toe-to-toe. "For the record, you're the only person on this earth that brings that out in me."

Not entirely true. There are a few others on that list. But she's quickly climbing to the top with her hoity-toity, holier-than-thou attitude.

"I get it. You don't like me. You don't like my advantage. But I don't even work with him. I own my own company."

I bark out a laugh. "That's all you think this is?"

Her eyebrow lifts, and a smirk spreads across her face. Despite the heated moment and topic, the way she's grinning at me has my dick hardening in my pants.

Not cool.

"Wow, Paxton, I didn't think you were so hard up for a hookup that you're still thinking about a kiss we shared months ago."

"Kiss? Is that all that was?" I wipe under my lips and grin back, leaning down so we're now eye to eye. "I still remember how your pussy tastes, Mal."

She gasps, eyes darting around.

I move my mouth to her ear and bite down just hard enough that she yelps. I'm not sure why I do it; it's too intimate. I'm too turned on for my own good.

This woman is a nightmare—a conniving devil woman. But when I'm this close, breathing in the same air, inhaling her scent of lavender, I can't help myself. The way she unravels me with a look. She must be casting spells because she has me riding a very fine line between hate and some other foreign emotion.

And it makes absolutely no damn sense.

My lips linger at the shell of her ear before I whisper, "It wasn't the best I've ever had."

She squeaks, pushing at my chest. I stumble back, caught off guard, just in time to watch her cross her arms over her chest and glare at me as though she's attempting to light me on fire with a look alone.

I watch her for a second, and that's when I notice the rhythmic tapping of her index finger on her upper arm.

Aw . . . did I hurt your feelings?

Impossible because a woman like her has none. She uses people to get ahead, and that's the one type of person I can't be kind to.

"Or could it possibly be that I figured you out? You're not much different from *him*, after all."

"You don't know anything," she bites out, turning to walk away.

"Touch a nerve, sweetheart?" I yell to her back, and she spins around, taking two long strides toward me, poking me in the chest with her finger.

"No, Paxton. It doesn't bother me. Wanna know why?"

I purse my lips and shrug a shoulder. "Not particularly."

Mallory's face looks hard, and bitterness spills over her words. "You're pathetic. You run around with your quick wit and faux charm like you're some kind of god around town."

"Thank you," I cut in, smiling widely at the backhanded compliment.

"Don't thank me because I know you're nothing special. You're just like every other playboy, using his looks to climb the ladder." She huffs a laugh. "So, tell me, Paxton . . . how does that make you superior?"

"You think you have me pegged?" I chuckle darkly. "You don't have one fucking clue."

"And I don't want to. You've shown your true colors, and I'm fine never to speak to you again. If you can't see that I'm nothing like my father, that's your loss. Either way, I don't give a rat's ass."

I step back, assessing as I peer down at her. She's got a fire in her that I have to admit is impressive.

From the corner of my eye, I see movement and turn to watch as Teagan runs off the set.

"Great," I snap. "Where's your client going?"

Her eyes narrow. "What?"

"Teagan. She just ran off. From what I gathered this morning from Michael, she's filming all day." I move closer, smirking down at her. "You need to do your job better. There are some things not even Daddy can make better."

Mallory lets out an audible gasp. "You are such a—"

"Careful . . . word around town is there's still a leak on set. I'd hate for your reputation to be tarnished."

"Ass."

That makes me smile.

Moving back up to my full height, I shake my head. "You better go see where the hell she's off to. We can't afford more Teagan theatrics."

An instant later, she's doing just that, rushing off in the direction Teagan went.

With her out of sight, I take in a calming breath, trying to get my anger and hard-on under control. I shift, trying to readjust, so it's not noticeable when someone steps up beside me.

"What has her running off?"

I clear my throat, and turning, I find Brad staring off toward the tree line where Mallory just disappeared.

I shrug. It's not like I have any of the details.

"Following her client, I assume," I say, hoping it'll prompt him to share what he knows. When he doesn't offer, I press. "What happened back there? Teagan ran off like someone was chasing her."

"Who knows?" He smirks.

My eyebrows tilt inward as I take him in. "I think you do know." When he remains silent on the subject, I level him with my stare. "Brad—"

"What?" He lifts his hands in the air. "I had nothing to do with that."

I incline my head, two seconds from snapping. "How come I don't believe you?"

"Ugh. Fine." He shuffles his feet, looking up at the sky. "I might have said something about Theresa."

My hands lift to my temples and rub. "What, pray tell, did you say?"

"It doesn't matter."

"Brad," I snap, tone hardening to something that says *I'm not backing down*. Not until he tells me.

He rolls his eyes, and the impulse to strangle him is so intense that I have to take a page out of Mallory's book and tap my hand to my thigh. "I might have implied that I could help her."

"Help her how?" When he looks away from me, I know he couldn't help himself. "Goddammit, Brad. We've spoken about this. There's no coming on to your costars."

"It was a harmless joke."

"Harmless joke that had her taking off." I motion toward the trees.

He bites his cheek, moving his shoulders. "Well, maybe not that harmless."

Fuck. The last thing I need is more bad press for Brad. Making a pass at a costar, especially one so young and new to the scene, would not bode well if the tabloids got a hold of it.

"What exactly did you say?"

His eyes lower to his shoes. "I might have implied that one way to shut her mother up and have her back down would be if we were friends . . ."

"And by friends, you meant . . .?"

"Fucking. If we were friendly fucking."

"Goddammit." I lift my hand and run it through my hair, pulling at the roots. A headache has formed, a headache named Brad. "You need to cut this shit out."

"And you need to back down, Pax. We already established this," he deadpans. "You have a lot to lose if you piss me off."

"And *you* don't if this leaks?"

"First off, I never said 'fucking' to her. I said 'friends'. I offered my help."

"At a price," I groan.

"Well, it wasn't clearly stated." He smiles. This man is way too confident in his skills of being discreet. There is nothing discreet about him.

Sometimes I wonder what the female population sees in the guy. He's a greasy, used-up salesman, conning young women into his bed with false promises of help.

Fucking gross.

I can feel my anger bubbling over. Truth of the matter is that I should just walk. Let him ruin me. I've lived through worse. Sure, it would suck, but many of my clients will stay loyal because they know him, and they know me. Very few people don't know what he's like. Unfortunately, his timing is not opportune. I've just taken out a massive loan to expand. I'm currently opening up a second office in Hollywood. If any of my clients walk, I'll be fucked. I'm leveraged too thin as it is. That's the only reason I'm here.

Get him the Oscar, then part ways.

"Just implied," I grit.

He nods. "Now you're getting it."

"Listen, as fun as this is, I have to speak with Michael. Stefan needs to get a new safety coordinator and hire more staff. This shoot is only supposed to take a month, but seeing as half the staff has been fired, I'm not sure how he's going to make that deadline, and your next project is quickly approaching."

I understand why Stefan was pissed, but firing so many people will do more damage than a few gossip articles. As much as I don't love Natasha, having her here is a good thing. She can convince him that any press, good or bad, is still good for the movie.

Anything can be spun to make it work.

The only thing that can't is no movie. And without staff, that's exactly where we'll be.

"Don't remind me," he says with a yawn.

I close my eyes and take a deep breath. "I'll speak to you later. In the meantime, stay away from Teagan unless you're shooting."

"Yeah, yeah. Go do your job."

I've only been here one day, and I've noted a million things that need to be fixed.

The only thing unfixable is Brad and his smug attitude.

Lord, give me strength.

Chapter Seventeen

Mallory

@Stargossip: Are the rumors true? Is Brad up to his old ways? Seems that there isn't a star in Hollywood he won't hit on.

> **@Bradforlife:** Cry me a river. Teagan would be lucky to have Brad.

> **@Ilovebrad:** B*tch doesn't deserve him.

> **@Betterthenfiction:** I hope Teagan is okay.

> **@Bradforlife:** @Betterthenfiction Why wouldn't she be? Again, she'd be lucky to have him.

> **@Deathtothesystem:** You're all ridiculous. Everything about this is toxic.

"TEAGAN!" I SHOUT AS I JOG TO CATCH UP TO HER. WHEN SHE shows no signs of slowing down, I pick up my pace.

I don't enjoy running, especially on rough terrain.

By the time I catch up, my chest pants in quick spurts, and puffs of oxygen escape my mouth.

I lean forward, bracing my hands on my thighs as I try to get my breath back.

"You okay over there?" Teagan jests, and my head snaps up to see her grinning down at me.

"Y… you ran off. I thought something happened."

I'm happy to see that I rushed here for nothing. I truly thought I would find her crying her eyes out, refusing to go back to the set. It appears whatever set her off isn't that bad.

"Nah. Nothing like that."

My head shakes, and I question whether I heard her right. The blood is pumping through my ears, and I can hardly hear. "Just give me a second," I say, lifting my hand with my pointer finger up.

"Take as long as you need." She inclines her head, and her brow lifts. "Maybe you need to start jogging."

"Har, har, har." I roll my eyes. "I'll have you know I'm in good shape. I just can't run for shit."

"Clearly." She taps her chin. "Sounds like you're a mouth breather, too. It's in through your nose, out through your mouth. Not in mouth, out mouth."

I level her with a look I hope conveys *shut up.*

Straightening my spine, I get my bearings before looking back at Teagan. "Okay, I'm good now. Care to tell me what happened back there?"

She starts to play with her fingers, looking everywhere but at me. "I needed a break."

"Teagan, you know that's not how this works." I press my lips together to stop from saying more. Although I'm her agent, I can't make her do anything she doesn't want to do.

Only the studio can. If she doesn't fulfill her obligations, she'll be wrapped up in lawsuits, having to pay more than she received, ruining her reputation to boot.

In the end, it's still her choice. If she wants to sink her career, that's on her.

She lets out a long sigh. "I know. I know. It's just—"

She kicks at the dirt, and all the while I wait for her to finish her sentence. Eventually, I grow impatient and snap.

"It's just what? Do you plan to keep me hanging?"

Teagan thrusts her hands into her pockets and begins to whistle.

"Very mature."

No reaction comes with the insult, and I'm growing more agitated by the minute. I came all this way to ensure she was all right, and she can't even be bothered to confide in me?

Good God, what is happening?

"Teagan . . . "

"It's nothing," she snips. "I'll be fine."

"It's not nothing." I lift my hand and place it on her shoulder. When I do, she takes a deep inhale, her body shaking beneath my touch. "You can talk to me."

Her eyes meet mine, and for several seconds, she's quiet.

"Fine," she finally says, exhaling a deep breath. "It was Brad."

My jaw tightens, and my fists clench at my sides. "What did he say to you?" I grit my teeth, waiting for her response. Brad is known to be a playboy who is inappropriate most of the time. I figured he'd make a pass at Teagan. She's young, naïve, and beautiful. His kryptonite.

The audacity of Paxton to tell me I need to do my job better. He has some nerve.

"It's—"

"Nope." My head shakes. "Don't do that. Don't make excuses for him."

She nods. "He was giving me shit about my mom. About being taken seriously in this field—giving me pointers."

I lift my brow. "And let me guess. The pointers would be done alone in his hut."

"Well, he didn't say that."

My eyes narrow. "But it was implied?"

Teagan raises her hand and scrubs at her face. "Not really." She groans. "I don't know."

It will do no good to interrogate the girl. Whether he did or didn't make a pass, one thing's for sure, he will.

"It's been a long day. Why don't you go back to your hut and rest?"

I know Paxton won't like it, but too damn bad. If she tries to shoot now, they'll only get shitty acting, which is just as bad as calling in sick. If not worse.

"You know I can't do that. I need to go back."

"You do, but not today. I'm sure they can film plenty of scenes of just Brad."

"Mal—"

"Don't Mal me. I got this. And you got a stomach bug." I wink. "I'll take care of everything."

Teagan gives me a small nod. "Okay. If you think . . ."

"I do."

She offers me a small smile before heading back toward camp.

I head in the opposite direction, taking my time so that I don't look like an idiot, huffing and puffing out of breath. Before I move into the clearing, I pat down my hair and my clothes. I'm sure I was looking disheveled, and I need people to take me seriously.

Once I'm happy with my appearance, granted I don't have a mirror to see the real damage, I head toward Brad. I don't care who he is. If he thinks he can proposition my client like that, he has another thing coming.

With my shoulders pulled back, I approach him, ready to say my piece and get this over with.

He's currently standing next to someone I don't know but recognize. It's the creepy guy who was staring at me. I think he's a cameraman, but I'm not sure. They're laughing boisterously, and I'm glad not to be in the know.

"Brad," I say once I'm standing in front of him.

He tilts his head up and meets my stare. A look in his eye tells me he's thoroughly amused, but I'm not sure if I'm the cause of his entertainment or if it's Teagan. Maybe it's something else entirely.

"We need to talk." I keep my voice level despite the fact that, for the first time in the past two days, I agree with Paxton. I am in over my head.

Despite knowing I have to say something to this man, I can't afford to piss him off, and by the cocky look on his face, he knows it, too.

"Do we now?"

"We do. Please." I tack on the last part out of professionalism.

"Very well." He turns to his little buddy and laughs. "We'll continue this conversation later."

"Have fun." The creep laughs as he stands to walk away, raking his pervy eyes over me as he does.

"Oh, I will." The innuendo in his voice makes my back muscles tighten.

I shiver in response, feeling dirty and appalled.

Nothing is comforting about knowing I'm stuck on an island with either of these guys.

Once no one is within hearing distance, I place my hands on my hips.

"What did you say to Teagan?" I practically bark out.

He raises his hands in mock surrender. "Whatever she told you is not true."

"She told me nothing, which is why I'm asking you. I'll repeat, what did you say to her?"

His eyes partially roll. "All I did was offer her some friendly advice."

"I'm sure it was extra friendly," I retort, shaking my head. "Just stay away from her when you're not on set." I go to walk away, but his words stop me short.

"I'll offer you some advice, too, sweetheart."

I spin back around, glaring. "Don't call me sweetheart."

"Very well, Ms. Reynolds. You are playing in a field that you don't understand. Hell, you don't even know the rules."

"I know enough to know hitting on your costar isn't what you need right now."

His lip tips up into a smirk, and then he laughs. "I like you—"

"Feeling isn't mutual."

"I really like you now. Maybe I'll have to get rid of Pax and try you out. I need someone who's got your spunk, and he's not very good at his job."

"If you aren't happy with your agent, that's your problem, but I'm certainly not interested."

"My agent is old news, but you . . ." His gaze lingers over me, making me feel even dirtier. "You're the future. When are you going to go work with your father?"

"You know what? This is pointless." I turn to leave, and he yells at my back.

"Let me know; I'm definitely interested."

I storm off, not in the mood for any more shit. I've only been here for less than a day, and I'm already dreading my decision to push this deal through.

Leaving here can't come soon enough.

I'm about to head in the direction of Michael and Stefan to tell them Teagan is sick for the day when a shadow steps in front of me.

I crane my head up and meet the familiar blue eyes that have driven me mad for the past few days.

"Paxton," I grit.

"Mallory, what a pleasure to see you. What has you stressed? Not a missing actress, by any chance?"

"You know what, Paxton? Why don't you worry about your own client? He needs to be placed on a tighter leash."

He narrows his eyes, and his jaw tightens. "What happened?" For the first time since I met Paxton, I hear something else in the way he speaks. There's no disdain in his voice. The only thing I hear is concern.

"Aside from his penchant for hitting on young girls?" His face pales at that, and for a moment, I consider fucking with him about how news has been leaked, but considering the real leak, it wouldn't be funny. "Seems he's not too happy with you. Wants to sign with me." I smirk. "Apparently, and I quote, 'You aren't very good at your job.'"

"He's all yours."

Chapter Eighteen

Mallory

@Stargossip: We hear our leading lady has a bug . . . the stomach bug, to be exact. Could it really be, or is she just sick of her costar? Signs point to the latter.

> **@Bitchpleaseme:** Someone should drop a house on Teagan.

> **@SpeakEasyToMe:** @Bitchpleaseme You're what's wrong with the world!

> **@Deathtothesystem:** If people are getting sick, it's time to shut this DOWN!

U NLIKE YESTERDAY, I'M IN NO RUSH TO LEAVE MY BED. MY BODY is bone-tired, and even this hard-as-hell bed feels like a cloud today.

Not even coffee can lure me from this cozy mass of sheets.

I know what's in store for me when I leave the safety of this hut, and it's all-out pandemonium. With Teagan taking the rest of the day yesterday to nurse her not-so-upset stomach, they'll have her make up for it with double the shots today.

Which will only serve to piss off Brad and make for a grumpy crew.

This whole production is a ticking time bomb. Eventually, it will blow, and I'm just hoping to be far from the island when it does. That or I will at least have a raft to keep me afloat.

Stretching my arms over my head, I admit defeat. Even if I don't want to go, I have to. Teagan needs me after yesterday, and I won't let her down.

Fifteen minutes later, I've showered, dressed, and am walking down the path. When I make it to craft services, I head right for the coffee and then walk to an unoccupied table, determined to get my bearings before being accosted by someone who needs something from me.

Around me is plenty of chatter, and from what I can gather from my eavesdropping, Stefan plans on shooting on the water today. Right next to the rickety dock.

That's a recipe for disaster.

In tomorrow's news, lead actress gets stabbed by rusted nail and contracts tetanus.

I lift my cup to my mouth and take a sip of my hot coffee. As always, the taste and smell help alleviate some of the stress lingering inside me. It's not a miracle worker. I'm still tense, but at least I'm waking up and ready to attack the day and all the shit it brings.

I hang back at the table until I see everyone start to get up, and that's when I finally push my chair back and stand, searching the area.

I haven't seen Teagan yet this morning. Hopefully, she's feeling better after yesterday.

Following the crowd of people, I head toward the dock and hang back as everyone gets to their places.

I'm standing in the corner, far enough away that I won't distract anyone, but close enough to have an unobscured view.

"Your client planning on coming to work today?" His gravelly voice makes my back go ramrod straight.

Goddammit.

It is too early for Paxton Ramsey to be this close to me.

And he is close. Like right up in my personal space, making it difficult to concentrate on anything but his masculine scent. Even out here in the open, it circles around me, and I sigh into it.

"Everything okay down there?" Paxton's humor-filled voice has me snapping back to the present.

Good Lord . . . did I just sniff him?

"Mm-hmm. All good."

I look over my shoulder, and the moment I do, I regret the move.

One thing is for sure, he's a handsome man in his white-collared shirt and navy shorts. Too bad he's such a douche.

"Good morning, Natasha. Bill." He nods to the pervy man, who is, in fact, a cameraman named Bill, apparently.

They all offer warm smiles and their own greetings.

Why can't he treat me like he treats everyone else?

Then I could have an ally.

A hot ally at that.

I like a little man candy every now and then, and he's just that.

"Something wrong?" His question has me shaking my head. I have no idea what he's talking about.

"Your cheeks." He smirks. "Are you getting sick? You're looking a little flushed."

Ugh. Of course, he'd notice that I'm blushing. I'm flushed because I couldn't resist ogling the enemy and got caught red-handed.

Great. Just great.

"I'm just warm."

"I'd imagine, wearing that getup. You're on an island. Nobody would fault you for wearing weather-appropriate clothes."

I look down at my black slacks and grimace.

Paxton turns his attention back to the set, ignoring me.

They have Teagan in the water, pretending to tread. In this scene, she almost drowns, and Brad runs to save her. Too bad the man's anything but a knight in shining armor. If anything, the woman should wear armor around him. He's the villain, not the savior.

When action is called, Teagan jumps into her role. For a second, as she floats in the ocean, I can see the fear in her eyes, even from a distance. They're enlarged, and her lips are pulled taut.

I *feel* the fear.

I'm transported to the water with her.

I'm drowning beside her.

It looks so damn real that I want to yell out for someone to save her.

As if summoned by my unspoken panic, Brad comes running in and pulls her to safety. Teagan's body begins to shake as she cries in his arms, and I have to wonder if that's contrived or real. I have never seen anything like this.

The way Stefan holds the small camera in his hand as he hovers right behind Brad, the viewer will watch Teagan through Brad's eyes.

It's truly profound.

For all the critics complaining about his tactics, it makes sense why he's considered the best. He goes to extremes, and in return, he gets extreme results.

"It's good, right?" Paxton says, and I turn to look over my shoulder. I had forgotten he was there.

I'd been so mesmerized by the events playing out in front of me that, for a moment, I forgot about all my issues.

"It is. Truly incredible."

"He's a genius. If they can pull it off . . ."

I nod. "It could be life-changing for everyone."

"For fuck's sake. What now?" Paxton groans, and I turn to see Teagan's mom stalking toward Stefan.

Somehow, she manages to rope him into an argument,

bickering loudly for all to hear. Stephan doesn't back down when the intimidating woman screams at him about how he has the angle all wrong.

"What the hell does she know about that?" Paxton mumbles, and I have to agree.

Theresa knows nothing. She was a cocktail server before her daughter landed her first gig.

Yet somehow, she thinks she has a say on the position Teagan should be in when she's retrieved from the ocean.

"Dammit," I say, rushing toward the argument, determined to get Theresa in check before she gets herself kicked off the set.

Paxton is right on my heels, and I'm not sure why, but knowing he's going to be there with me when I go toe-to-toe with the woman gives me more confidence.

Which makes absolutely zero sense, considering he's my biggest critic.

I'm almost to them when a piercing crack rings through the area. I stop in my tracks, swinging around to find the source of the noise.

"Holy fuck," Paxton says from beside me.

Before I can figure out what's happening, Paxton is taking off toward a wobbling dock.

Another crash and I stand in shock as Theresa and the director fall into the ocean.

The dock broke, and they were the casualties.

Oh. My. God.

I have to cover my mouth to smother the laughter as I watch Theresa splashing around in knee-high water, yelling curses. Stefan, however, is in the deeper part, and completely fine, albeit soaking wet with a likely ruined camera.

Paxton rushes in after Theresa, helping to calm her down and realize she can stand.

This is priceless . . . but also a nightmare.

Who knows what setback this will result in. A delay that none of us can afford. Time is money in this industry, and the longer we're on this set, the longer before Teagan's next role and my next paycheck.

My heart hammers in my chest, and I find my legs moving toward the commotion, ready to see what we're dealing with.

Paxton is pulling a surly Theresa out of the water, helping her to stand on dry land. He steps away, meeting a few crew members who are running up with towels.

I watch on as Paxton takes the reins, wrapping one around her and then Stefan, speaking to them both. Whatever he says to Theresa appears to calm her down, and I have to wonder what voodoo he's playing with to make that happen. He stands back, his chest rising and falling as he catches his breath. Dripping wet without a care.

I'm not sure what possesses me, maybe that magic Paxton's weaving, but I find myself grabbing a towel from a crew member and rushing toward him.

He helped everyone else. Someone needs to look after him.

Not you, Mallory.

When I'm a few feet from him, I stop short.

Paxton's hands are currently attached to the bottom of his wet shirt that clings to every muscle on his torso. He lifts it up and over his head, baring his sculpted abs and pecs, glistening with water under the bright sun.

I stand in front of him, towel in hand, mouth most likely hanging open.

He's a work of art.

All chiseled and tan. Wet and sexy as sin.

Look away.

But no matter how hard I try to stop staring, I can't.

I'm in a trance, unable to move.

"Mallory," his voice calls out, and I blink, trying to focus. "Is that for me?"

My gaze snaps to his face. His features are sharp and pensive, eyes trained on the towel in my hand.

"Umm, yes." I reach out my arm just as he does, and our hands touch. His wet fingers are cold against my skin, causing a shiver to run through me, but I feel warm at the same time.

"Still hot?" he asks.

My eyes narrow as I try to understand his question. "What? No."

His gaze drops from my eyes to my face, and I know my cheeks must be beet red.

Great.

"Okay, Mallory." His full lips tip up into the cockiest smirk I have ever seen, and I want to melt into the ground. Or smack his smug face.

Bastard.

Chapter Nineteen

Mallory

@**Stargossip:** What do you get when you put an overbearing mom and a seriously deranged director together? A splash. *You're welcome for the picture attached.*

    @**Movielover:** She's batshit insane.

    @**dramalover1234:** Someone make that picture a meme.

    @**Mario33:** That's asshole energy.

    @**Deathtothesystem:** How is this movie still filming?

A FTER THIS MORNING'S CHAOS, WE HAVE ALL BEEN BECKONED to a bonding session to try to fix the drama still erupting throughout the island.

Although this particular drama is all Theresa and Stefan. The added tension on the set has affected both Teagan's and Brad's ability to act, and that's a major problem. I wouldn't be surprised if Theresa is asked to leave.

She needs to, or else things won't get better.

"Are we really doing this?" I groan to myself, annoyed that instead of being out rubbing elbows and finding my next client, I'm stuck on an island, being forced to kumbaya with people I don't particularly care for.

Michael left a note on my hut's door requesting me to meet with the group by the small alcove near the beach.

This afternoon, the actors and agents are going to spend some time "breaking down the walls and getting to know each other." Stefan's words.

I don't care to break down walls around these people. When it was suggested, I thought only Teagan and Brad would be subjected to it. I felt like they needed to spend time together.

It turns out that's the last thing Teagan needs. Spending time with slimy Brad is a recipe for disaster.

I didn't realize my presence would be requested, too, but I guess it's best, considering I don't want my client alone with the predator.

"You seem thrilled." Hearing Paxton's smarmy voice from behind me has my back muscles tightening. This man drives me insane, and not in a good way.

To think, the first time I met him, I was prepared to make him a notch on my belt.

Nope.

Stop.

Not going there.

The proximity to this awful man is starting to warp my mind because even when I'm thinking about how awful he is, my brain short-circuits and reminds me how good a kisser he is and how skilled he is with his—

And there I go again.

No good will come from lusting after my archnemesis.

The closer his footsteps get, the more I can feel the tiny hairs on the back of my neck stand up. My legs wobble, and my palms begin to sweat. An intense ache forms in my core, and the need to rub it out is intense.

This isn't good.

My body isn't getting the memo, and it's a real issue.

I pick up my pace, determined not to feed my body any more ammo. I'm not in the mood to make small talk with him while we walk to the same place. It'll only lead to an argument.

"You can't escape me that easily." He chuckles. "We're headed to the same icebreaker, after all."

"Sounds like a horrible time. Can't wait," I call over my shoulder.

He's right behind me, which makes me pick up my pace even more. Before long, I'll be jogging.

Not obvious at all.

"The intention behind it is admirable."

"Welp, the road to hell is paved with good intentions and all that," I mutter, and it only makes him laugh harder.

As his smooth laughter washes over me, the tingles in my body start right back up.

Just what I don't need.

"Glad you find me so entertaining." I huff, turning my head to find him right next to me, grinning down like I'm some kind of clown here for his amusement.

"I find you something all right, but entertaining is certainly not it."

It takes everything inside me not to stop in my tracks and rip into him.

That wouldn't be a good idea at all.

He taps my shoulder with his as he strolls along beside me, and if I was an outsider looking at us, I'd think we were friends taking a leisurely walk.

But I know better.

"Do you have to stand so close to me?"

"Yep. Consider this the start of our bonding."

I let out a slow breath. I shouldn't allow this man to get to me.

"I'd prefer we don't," I grit through my teeth.

"Oh, come now, princess," his voice rasps, and my heart beats so fast it threatens to pound out of my chest. "That's what the producers want."

We can't always get what we want, as evidenced by how my body lights up around him, and he's strictly off-limits. He's damn sexy but, alas, an ass.

"Can't you just be quiet?" I snap.

Then, like an idiot, I find myself pivoting to look at him.

Dammit. It never gets old how handsome he is, and no matter how often I see him, I'm never prepared for the way my body responds. *Muscle memory from one encounter is pathetic.*

His face looks carved from stone, and his eyes appear sterner than normal. "What are you wearing?" he grits through clenched teeth.

"What?" I lift a brow, not understanding what he's saying.

His hand waves around, pointing at my outfit, and I follow the path and see that he's pointing at my low-cut tank. I changed after this morning's festivities for a couple of reasons. (1) his criticism of my dress pants (2) when I took the wet towel back from Paxton, my previous shirt got all wet when I held it against my chest.

Now it would appear that Paxton doesn't like this outfit either. Too damn bad.

"You can't wear this around the crew—"

I cut him off. "And why the hell not?" My voice pitches, the incredulity oozing from every word.

"Because anyone with a dick will want to fuck you."

My mouth drops open in shock at his crass words, and my body shakes with fury.

"You have some nerve, Paxton Ramsey." I purse my lips in disgust. "Kissing me once doesn't give you the right to put a chastity belt on me."

"This has nothing to do with me. Dressing like that can draw unwanted attention."

"You sound like a 1950's church pamphlet. Maybe that's what

I want." My chest heaves, and my hands ball into fists. "A quick romp in the middle of the island sounds pretty damn good right about now."

He scoffs. "Wanna put a bulletin out to the whole crew? I can start auditions for you."

"You're acting like you have a say in my life, as if you are anything to me," I say, trying to keep my voice level.

"Talking to you is pointless." He storms past me.

"No one asked you to," I shout at his back, picking up my pace to keep up.

A few feet away, the path opens into a clearing, and we're on the beach.

The waves crash against the shore as the salty air whips my hair around. I inhale deeply, taking in the calming essence that only the sea can provide. It does wonders at chasing away my fury brought on by Paxton.

"Mal!" Teagan waves from where she's standing closer to the water.

Kicking off my shoes, I make my way over to her. I allow the past few minutes to wash away with every ebb and flow of the tide. The coarse sand scratches at my now-bare feet, and I savor the feeling.

I might not love being on the open water, but I love the beach.

The farther out I walk, the more I realize how much I've missed this.

Growing up on the California coast, I'm used to spending time on the water. Now I'm in the city. I barely have time to relax, let alone find a beach to sit on.

Teagan moves toward a towel and takes a seat, motioning for me to do the same. I head in her direction, lowering myself next to her, and continue to stare out at the endless blue water.

"So, what are we doing here?" Teagan asks, seeming not to have gotten the same memo as me.

"Getting to know each other . . . I guess." I shrug.

"Maybe we're here to air our grievances," Brad mutters as he sits across from us.

Teagan doesn't flinch next to me, and I'm not sure how to take it. I'd figured after she rushed off the set and told me it was about him, that he bothered her. She doesn't seem too disturbed at all.

"Let's hope not," I say, not meeting Brad's eyes.

I don't need Brad or Teagan knowing I let Paxton touch me very intimately one drunken night, in the middle of a crowded party for everyone to see.

I look over my shoulder to see where everyone else is and find Michael heading our way. He smiles broadly at the three of us sitting together, likely misinterpreting our proximity as a good sign. Paxton must realize Michael is waiting for him, so he nods and heads over.

"Since Teagan and Brad are having a hard time connecting, we're hoping that a few opportunities to get to know each other with people they trust around might help."

"What can we do?" I ask, ready to get this shit show on the road.

"The thing is, Stefan wants each activity to tie into upcoming shots."

"And how do we go about that?" Paxton asks, sounding just as confused as me.

Thankfully.

"Instead of just running lines, Stefan wants them to understand the feelings associated with being stranded on an island. He wants you two to play along. Act as though you are also stranded here."

My eyes widen.

"What?" Paxton and I say in unison, both clearly mystified by the request.

"I'm not an actress," I say, looking back and forth between Michael and Paxton.

"Could've fooled me." Paxton mumbled the words under his breath, and I believe only I heard him.

I refuse to let him get to me in front of this group, so I ignore him.

"Mallory and Paxton, since you both have voiced concerns, as well, Stefan thought it would be best for you both to oversee the process by being players. Since your time on the island is short, this is the best way not to lose any time with filming and give you both peace of mind that issues are being resolved."

The panic I'm feeling is real.

Maybe the crazy-ass director is on to something, after all.

That or I might actually turn this into a murder mystery.

Paxton, be warned . . . keep your distance.

Chapter Twenty

Paxton

@Stargossip: Playing games is all well and good . . . until someone gets hurt in the middle of a half-deserted island with a crazy crew of nobodies.

> **@GeterDone:** Recipe for disaster . . .

> **@FMeRunning:** @GeterDone More like a lawsuit in the making!

> **@Deathtothesystem:** These people are deranged. Who's allowing this shit show to continue?

'M TYPICALLY A NICE GUY, BUT I BECOME UNHINGED WHENEVER I'm around Mallory.

Case in point, today.

What the fuck is she wearing? She might not have noticed because we were in the middle of a verbal sparring, but while we walked through the crew's hangout to get here, all eyes were on her. It wasn't a good thing. Some of these guys haven't been laid in . . . well, ever if their greasy appearance and creepy vibes are any indicators.

What the hell was Stefan thinking with this crew?

No one on this island should see her like that.

Only me.

No, fuck that. Not only me. No one.

If it weren't for the fact that I take my business seriously, I'd already be off this godforsaken island.

Unfortunately, I can't, and instead, I have to torture myself by being surrounded by a woman who, no matter how hard I try, I can't stop thinking about. What would it feel like to slip inside her? To feel her walls close in around my cock, milking my orgasm like a fucking pro.

Jesus, Pax.

If things were going well here, I'd be on the first plane back to get as far away from *her* as possible. But since I put this idea together, not only do I feel I owe Brad this movie, but I owe the author, the screenwriter I brought in, and also Stefan. Which is why I'm sitting on this damn towel about to partake in some bullshit team-building activity, pretending to be stranded on an island. Whatever the hell that entails.

News flash . . . I basically am.

Michael steps forward. "Obviously, you are here because Stefan believes we can get this movie to where it needs to be."

Fucking Michael and his incessant need to drag out shit that doesn't need to be.

"Just tell us what he wants us to do," Brad gripes, and for the first time in a very long time, I'm with Brad.

"He wants you to play a game called what makes you tick."

"What the hell is that?" Brad says, head bouncing from person to person for clarification.

"I think it's pretty obvious from the title," Teagan retorts, not looking at him when she says it.

"I'm not an idiot!"

"Could have fooled me," she mutters under her breath.

Of all of Mallory's shortcomings, her inability to stop this from escalating tops the list.

"I can see this is already starting perfectly." I look over at Brad and Teagan, who are both acting like five-year-olds.

If this project wasn't my brainchild, I wouldn't be here, which leads me to wonder why Mallory is. Sure, Teagan is her client, but it's not as if Teagan is keeping her company afloat. I'm sure Teagan is just a means to get her legs wet before she goes to work for her father, so why put herself through this?

"Stefan believes knowing what motivates each other will be a powerful asset to you both as we embark on filming, but he wants it to go a step further. He wants you to suspend disbelief, and instead of drawing examples from your own life, he wants you to be your characters."

"What's our part in this exercise?" I ask.

"Act as moderators but be in character, too."

"How does that help them? There isn't anyone else on the island in the movie."

He shrugs. "Stefan thought it would be a good idea. Perhaps he wants to portray their characters as losing their minds. Talking to people who aren't there. Who knows Stefan's motives?"

From beside me, I see her tense. "So we just make up lines? Act like part of the movie?"

"Precisely," Michael says.

Mallory exhales at Michael's words, but then Brad cocks his head in her direction.

"I think you should. If we have to do this, you might as well do it, too."

"It could be fun," Teagan chimes in. "I've run lines with you. You're good."

"Come on, Mal. It will be like role-playing." I wink. "You can pretend you're someone else and gather intel."

I know I'm a dick, constantly throwing what she did in her face, but it can't be helped. The girl brings out the worst in me.

Mallory's eyes grow wide, and there is no missing how hard her jaw locks. She wants to fire back at me but smiles boldly instead. "Sounds like a great plan. But wouldn't you think Stefan would want Brad to know more about Teagan's real personality? That way, if a problem does arise, he can refer to what he will have learned today and use that as a means to come to a resolution. Or, at the very least . . . refrain from being a dick?" She turns to Brad. "No offense. It's just hypothetical."

His brows lift. "None taken."

"She does have a point." Michael nods.

"Maybe we can do both?" Teagan adds.

"Yes, because we have nothing better to do than play games all day," I gripe, hating the way Mallory turns things around.

"At least I'm trying," Teagan mutters back.

"Children," Michael interrupts. "We need you all to get along—especially Brad and Teagan. Right now, the idea that you fall in love is so far-fetched that if the press got hold of your lack of chemistry, the studio could pull it. So do what you need to do." He turns to me. "Show them what real chemistry looks like." His head swivels to Mallory. "It's plain to see that you two have it."

My mouth drops open, and a squeak sounds from Mallory.

Michael doesn't notice the shift his words have caused, and he jumps right into the next ask. "Also, Stefan would like for you all to practice fishing."

"What the hell?" Brad balks. "I don't fish."

"You have to film a scene in the next few days where you build a net with the leaves of a palm tree, so you might as well practice this now while you get to know each other."

Michael doesn't wait for us to object before he points at the water. "Go. I have things to do."

"And us?" Mallory asks, voice so high she sounds like a Disney character.

"Observe. Help. Contribute."

It's all he says before he stalks off. Brad paces the moment we are left alone, but Mallory is already gathering leaves.

I have to hand it to her. Despite my feelings for her being handed everything on a gilded platter, she doesn't seem to mind getting her hands dirty.

Or maybe this is her way of distracting herself from the awkward shit Michael said about us. I'm not bothered. Shocked? Yes. Bothered? No. He isn't wrong. We do have chemistry. That has never been our problem.

As we all sit down on the towels to weave palm leaves, Mallory is the first to break the silence. "What makes everyone tick, or in our case, get ticked off? Let's each go around the circle and say something that ticks us off, and then we can problem-solve. Once we get the hang of it, Brad and Teagan can do it again in character? Sound good?"

"Yep. Not that I have a choice," Brad mutters, continuing to entwine the pieces together horrifically.

"Okay, then. Brad, why don't you go first," Mallory fires back.

Brad's eyes go wide, but he brushes it off just as fast. We all know what's at stake.

"No. I don't think I will—"

"Fine, I will," Teagan snaps. "Want to know what makes me pissed . . . off? Condescending behavior."

"You know what ticks me off?" Brad fires back.

"Nope, but I have a feeling it's me," Teagan taunts, throwing her palm leaves to the ground.

"As a matter of fact, it's not."

Teagan's lips form a straight line, and her nose scrunches. "Oh. Umm, then what does?"

"Crazy-ass directors who make me sit around building palm nets is what ticks me off." He lifts his haphazard net as evidence.

Teagan nods. "I have to agree."

"Come on, guys, let's be serious," Mallory says. "The sooner we get you two working in sync, the faster this whole thing can be done." She looks at Teagan. "On to the next project." Then she looks at Brad. "No more net building."

"You have something better to contribute? Why don't you go first?" I say, tired of Mallory's holier-than-thou act.

"Fine, I will. When people assume." She throws her own net. "When people think they know everything about you but are too stubborn to find out the truth."

My eyes narrow in on her petite frame before lifting to her eyes. "Well, what makes me ticked is when things come easily to someone when the rest of us have to work for it."

She throws her dainty hands up into the air. "Again, why do you assume? You don't know anything."

"Are we missing something here?" Brad asks.

We both turn toward him and shout, "No!" simultaneously.

"You have something to say? Something so profound that I don't know?" I continue, wanting to goad her into snapping.

I want her to show me her cards. All of them. Let her one and only client see how deranged she is.

"Umm, Brad . . ." Teagan's voice sounds like a dull whisper against my building rage. "Why don't we let them hash this out, and we can go over there and play this game as our characters?"

Mallory and I are in the middle of a showdown as they move away from where we are sitting on the beach.

"Let's do this once and for all," she practically spits.

I motion for her to begin. "Have at it."

"You have this expectation of what you think, and I hate to break it to you, but it's far from true."

"So . . . it's a coincidence that you were there the night I landed Stefan, and then you so happened to put your client up for the same movie?"

"Yes." She lasers me with a glare. "It was a role that was perfect for her."

"I find that hard to believe."

"Then don't believe it. It's no skin off my nose. I was invited to that party. I didn't come there to eavesdrop on someone I didn't even know."

"That's it? That's the big misunderstanding?"

I'm so sick and tired of the lies and half-truths. If she would just be honest. She was there to find Teagan a role, and my idea fell right into her lap at the moment my finger left her pussy.

"What's more for me to say? The fact that Teagan's mom brought *Twisted Lily* up to Teagan has nothing to do with me. If you must know, I didn't even know she was auditioning."

"How is that possible? You're her agent."

"Have you met her mother? She's a tyrant."

She's got me there. The woman's a lunatic.

"Teagan has the right to audition for whatever role she wants. You were the one who gave her the part!"

"Because your father made a call to the director. It was taken out of my hands."

She gasps, eyes wide before clouding over. My eyebrows tilt inward as I watch the range of emotion sweep across her face.

Shock.

Confusion.

Anger.

"He didn't," she whisper-yells.

"He did." I laugh darkly. "You get what you want, princess. Daddy makes a call and fucks us all over because he's the king."

A strangled sob gets smothered by her hands.

She isn't wrong; Teagan can audition, just like everyone else. I wouldn't have given a shit if she had shown up. It's the fact that Thomas Reynolds went around me and right to the director to ensure his daughter's one and only client got the role of a lifetime.

"I don't work with my dad. I've never worked with my dad. I will *never* work with him. I had no idea he did that, and if I had, I would've tried to talk Teagan out of it."

"Right," I snap, rolling my eyes. I shake my head and then nod. "No wonder you only have one client."

"What the hell is that supposed to mean?"

"Come on, princess, I figured even for you, that's obvious." I lift my hand to stop her tirade. "Your father plans to show the world just how up-and-coming you are by showcasing with one client how on top you are. He's pulling the strings so you can slink to his agency and dominate even more. Taking money out of my pocket and every other hardworking agent in the industry."

"Your beef with him is your beef with him, Pax. I have nothing to do with it. And let me repeat, I will *never* work for him." She takes a deep breath. "Listen, take it for what it's worth, believe me, or don't believe me. My client was actually supposed to take a break for a few months before I found her the next project. I was blindsided, too, when, during that break, her mother sent in her audition."

I narrow my eyes and watch her, looking for any signs of deceit, but I find none. She looks tired and defeated. She either needs to change career paths because she's the best actress in the world, or maybe she's telling the truth.

That doesn't solve all the problems I have with her, but—

"Paxton, I didn't do what you think I did. I didn't allow my father to call in favors for me. And if you just put aside your hatred for him for a minute, you might see that." She stands from the towel and then dusts off the sand on her leg. "I'm going to check on whether our clients are faring better than us."

For the first time, I begin to question if I'm wrong about her.

Fuck my life.

Another damn tweet.

My grip on my phone is so tight that I'm afraid the glass might crack. I guess Stefan was wrong about the people he fired. He only made the set unsafe. The problem still isn't resolved. Someone on this island is still leaking privileged information to the press.

But instead of the truth, a terrible accident that no one could have prevented was spun in a way to exaggerate the fight and how unsafe the island is.

The working conditions are being called into question.

Everything posted today was total bullshit; I'm pissed, and so is the studio.

The chatter is the higher-ups are considering pulling the plug on the whole project. Which means my main goal in life is to fix this shit.

Trekking across the path, I find Natasha. "We need to spin this."

"Good morning to you, too, Paxton." Her eyes sparkle with lust, and the last thing that should be on her mind right now is sex.

"I have no time for this bullshit, and I'm surprised you do. We need to get the truth out about what really happened."

"And that will help how, Paxton? The dock broke—the only dock on the island. Right now, it's pure speculation. Well, other than the picture of Teagan's mom and the director falling into the water. Yeah, that went viral."

But luckily, in that picture, all you can see is them falling. No dock.

She's not wrong, though. If the studio saw a picture of the broken dock going viral, they would pull the plug, and there is no way that can happen. Way too much rides on this.

"Can we at least counter the leak about the fight? Throw out a picture of them getting along."

"That we can do. We can feed them our own info. Not a bad plan, Pax . . . ." She moves closer to me, and I step back. "Good thing we have one professional on the scene." She scoffs. "Mallory Reynolds is worthless. Typical Hollywood nepotism at its finest."

It's no different from anything I've said or thought, but coming from Natasha, it doesn't sit well with me. She doesn't know a fucking thing about Mallory.

"That's bullshit, Natasha. She's working her ass off for Teagan. She's here just like me. Give her a goddamn break."

Natasha's eyes widen, and she stutters over her next words. "I-I-I didn't know."

"Just set up the meeting," I snap, turning my back on her.

"I will," she calls out, but I don't give her any more of my attention.

The only person here sleeping on their job is her. She should've already been spinning this shit, yet it was me who needed to feed her an idea.

Fucking worthless.

I head to today's location, fuming about what just went down. I don't have the energy to unravel why I'm so heated.

I come upon another clearing, this one smaller.

Logs are scattered all around, and Teagan is on the ground, Mallory behind her.

What are they up to?

I head toward them when I see Brad not far away, watching the girls intently.

"Pax," he calls out when he sees me, waving his arms.

Is it too late to walk away, career be damned.

"What's up, man? What are they doing?" I incline my chin toward the girls.

He crosses his arms at his chest. "Practicing."

My head tilts as I take in the scene again. "Practicing what?"

"For the next scene." He blows out a puff of air.

I shake my head. "I'm not following."

"It's the scene in the book where Teagan's character tries to start a fire. Most of the wood is wet, and she can't seem to get it going. My character sees her struggling and goes to help her."

I vaguely remember that scene.

It was a crossing point in their character arc. It was the moment he realized she wasn't what he thought she was, but something

153

more. He hadn't figured out what that was yet, but he was on the precipice of a breakthrough.

"What's Mallory doing?" I ask.

"Helping her client." He lifts a brow. "Something you're not very good at, but by all means, if you want me to get help from Mallory . . ."

I shrug and then let out a groan. "Move over."

Looking up, I find Mallory staring at me. She's watching me keenly. "How's it going over there?" I ask.

She smiles, but it's full of mirth. "Never been better."

I gather dry logs before collecting some twigs. "Do you normally build fires for your clients? Is this in the pitch?"

She smirks. "Why, are you jealous? Upset that at least I'm innovative on selling points?" she chides.

"What else do you have to offer?"

"I know what she has to offer," Brad mutters.

If murder was an option, I'd gladly rid the world of this idiot.

"Oh, shut up, Brad." Mallory rolls her eyes. "Never. Gonna. Happen."

I snort because that might be the first time I've heard a woman tell the guy no so brilliantly.

"Yeah, give the girl a break. Can't you see she's working hard on getting that thing lit?" I laugh.

"As if you're one to talk. I doubt you can do it either," he snaps, slinking down onto a log, pouting like a child.

"I'm a fast learner." I bend down, looking over the pile.

"I bet I get this lit before you." My eyes lift to find the challenge in Mallory's words.

I lift my brow. "Care to make this interesting?"

"A bet!" Teagan exclaims, clapping her hands together.

"Sure, but what are we playing for?" Mallory asks.

I tap my chin.

"I have a few suggestions." Again, fucking Brad can't hold his tongue.

"Not interested, Brad," Mallory fires back, and I can't help but grin at the continued rebuke.

"Traitor," Brad mutters behind my back.

"Since we've only been here a few days, what can we even wager?" Mallory looks around the circle, waiting for anyone to offer a wager worth making.

"Dry towels," Teagan says with a shudder.

Mallory stops moving and looks at Teagan with wide and scared eyes. "Wait, that's a thing? All your towels are wet?"

"No," Brad responds. "She's being dramatic."

Teagan shudders. "Speak for yourself. I haven't had a dry towel since I arrived on this godforsaken island."

"As fun as this is, Teagan, you need to practice, so let's get back to it," Mallory says, her voice serious.

I have to hand it to her; her work ethic is better than I expected.

"Don't be so serious," Brad says. "Teagan will be practicing, only to fail to make a fire."

"Fine," Mallory shoots back. "Winner has to jump into the water—"

"*Naked.*"

"Thank you, Brad, for your suggestion, but no," Mallory says, scrunching her nose.

"In underwear." He tries again.

"Again, no." Mallory shakes her head, growing as fed up with the idiot as I am.

"Then what's the point?" Brad looks like a petulant child who was just denied his favorite toy.

"How about a friendly wager? Bragging rights included," I answer.

Brad drops another pile of logs down beside me. "You're all lame."

"Teams?" Teagan asks.

"Well, it makes the most sense to have girls versus boys since

I'm helping Teagan practice. If we can do that." Mallory looks over at Teagan. "You can do both. Right, Teagan?"

"Sure. I'll run the lines while we try to build a fire. The added pressure of the competition will help the motivation of the desperation my character is supposed to feel."

"Great. Starting on three. One . . . two . . . three."

Everyone sets off. Brad mutters to himself as he collects more wood.

And I'm just observing.

Teagan is firing off lines as Mallory frantically works a stick back and forth on a log.

I still don't move.

It's complete chaos.

Lines are spoken. The scene rehearsed, and Mallory has sweat collecting on her brow.

"Aren't you going to help?" Brad stops rehearsing to ask.

"In a minute."

"She helps her client, and you're what? Too good for that?"

I really hate this man. I lift my finger. "I said, *in a minute.*"

I turn my attention back to Mallory, whose shirt has lifted as she's hard at work. Her chest rises and falls with her movements.

She stops for a minute, and our gazes lock.

My lips tip into a smile as she watches me.

I lift my hand, grab a log, then reach for a few smaller pieces, never breaking contact.

Muscle memory kicks in, and I'm working, all the while staring into the bluest eyes I've ever seen.

"You bastard! You did it!" Brad exclaims, but I never pull my gaze away from Mallory.

I shrug. "Boy Scout." Then allow my lips to tip up into a smirk.

Gotcha, babe.

Chapter Twenty-One

Mallory

@Stargossip: Sources say things are heating up on the set of *Twisted Lily.* Will fireworks be next? Our guess is the spark will burn out quickly.

> **@StruckbyStardom:** Vague posts suck.

> **@WhisperEyes14:** Brad and Teagan? That's HOT AF!

> **@Deathtothesystem:** Gross! The man's a wh*re, and she's too young.

H E SET ME UP.

Paxton knew exactly what he was doing. Playing it cool like he didn't have a giant advantage.

A Boy Scout? Seriously?

No doubt this whole idea was plotted to boost his ego and show us how much better he is.

I turn over my shoulder and shake my head, causing Teagan to laugh.

"Of course, he's perfect at making a fire, too."

"Too?" Her lips pucker. "What else is Paxton *perfect* at, Mal?"

I bite my bottom lip and pray to God that my cheeks are not as pink as they feel. Maybe the sun beating down on us is enough to cover my blush.

Doubtful. Teagan sees too much, apparently.

"Nothing. He's perfect at nothing."

"Sure." She winks, and I lift a finger in protest.

"No. No winking. I didn't mean it like that." I drop the log and sit with my legs crossed, trying to bring myself to center.

"I might not be a rocket scientist, but even *I* know that man isn't lacking in any department." Teagan's words catch me off guard.

Something twists in my gut. I don't like the fact that his charm is evident to everyone. It's dumb, but it's true. I hate the thought of women swooning over him.

"He lacks personal skills. He's an ass." I say it just to put that negative thought in her head, which is just plain wrong.

She has every right to form her own opinion of him. Just because he treats me like he does, doesn't mean he's like that to everyone else. In fact, that's half of my issue. He's a gem to anyone who isn't me.

"I don't know him, but from what I hear—"

"Yes, I know." I huff. "He's perfect at that, too."

Her eyes widen, and her lips tip up. "Well, I'm just repeating what I heard. If you say he's an ass—"

"I do."

At that, Teagan giggles again. "You're funny."

"Ladies . . ."

That voice. That damn sexy voice. Always washing over me at the wrong time. Doesn't he realize I'm over here trying to convince myself that he's Satan incarnate?

He will be the death of me.

"Let me show you," he says, bending down to my level.

"What?" I ask, dumbfounded.

He gestures to the pile of wood behind me.

"Let me show you how to start a fire. I'll teach both of you." He looks up at Teagan, whose smile is so large, you'd think he handed her the damn sun.

"Why bother with me? I'm not in the movie. Show her."

He smiles. "You never know when you will be stranded in the wilderness and need a fire."

"Never," I grunt.

"Stop being difficult, Mallory. He's just trying to help." I look over at Teagan as if she's a traitor.

"Fine." I throw my hands in the air. "Show us."

With a chuckle, a smirking Paxton sits down next to me, and Teagan joins.

The early afternoon sunlight peeks through the trees, cascading across his face.

In another world, in another place, I might have been able to carry out a torrid love affair with this man on this shoot.

Especially knowing how skilled his fingers are. It would be a nice way to spend my evenings.

Jeez, Mal, you've been reading too many romance novels.

I stifle a groan, wondering what the hell is wrong with me. I'm not that kind of girl. I don't fawn over a handsome man, and I sure as hell don't practically come undone when one is illuminated by the sun.

I'm losing my grip, and I blame this island.

His proximity has me hyperaware and practically panting.

"Teagan, gather some wood. You're next," he says. "Brad, watch me teach Mallory, then you will emulate it with Teagan. If you don't understand, I'll be here to guide you."

I'm about to suggest he work with Teagan so that when Brad joins the party, they'll be ready to run lines, but when he moves up so that his chest is touching my back, I forget all rational thought. The idea of pushing him toward Teagan is long gone.

His body's warmth makes me feel dizzy, but when he speaks

in that low and gruff tone, the vibrations work through me, and I almost pass out.

"Take the sticks and rub them together."

My hands shake as I try to follow his commands, and he must see it because he reaches out to help steady the wood. His hand brushes against mine, and all I feel is fire lightning from within—a burn I savor.

"No, Mallory." My name rolls off his tongue sinfully. "Like this." His hands wrap around mine, and I stop breathing. I turn to look over my shoulder, and our gazes lock. Neither of us blinks, but his fingers start to caress mine as he works to light the branch.

"Just like that." His voice is husky, and I shiver.

"Holy shit, you guys nailed it. Don't fucking think about kissing her!" Brad's voice acts as a bucket of water.

Pax's hands drop, and before I know what's happening, his heat is gone, and I'm left cold and shaky.

I hardly notice when Brad gets behind Teagan. I miss what prompts her to belly laugh. My attention is fixed on my hands, devoid of Paxton's.

Teagan fails miserably, and I can't focus enough to help.

Now that filming is over for the day, I can relax. It might have been tense in the beginning, but it all worked out, and I think they nailed the scene.

The friendly competition kept the energy levels high today and made all the difference. Teagan and Brad looked like different people out there. Connected and vulnerable.

No one fought.

They nailed it.

After yesterday, I call that a win.

Granted, yesterday was shit. The leaks just keep coming, and

I intend to get to the bottom of it. My bet's on the creepy camera-man, who always seems to be leering.

"Mallory." I look over my shoulder and see Natasha standing there.

"Hey. What's up?"

She better be here with some spin on the story. Something to change the rumors and make things turn around.

As Natasha approaches, I take her in. While the rest of us are dressed to get dirty on an island, this woman is perfectly put together, with hair perfectly coiffed and a full face of makeup. I wonder if she's the type of girl Paxton would go for and immediately hate myself for even caring.

She's exactly the type, and it's none of my business.

"I want to discuss yesterday and how we spin it."

"And you want to talk to me?" My eyes narrow in on the beautiful woman. "Should I get Teagan?"

She puckers her perfectly filled-in lips. "That's the thing. I'd like to pitch the idea to you first."

"Oh, okay." I move closer to her, watching as everyone heads toward craft services one by one.

After today, I'm starving, but I guess it will have to wait. This is more important than anything. Without a positive spin, this film is in great jeopardy. I didn't come all the way out here to live in a dilapidated hut for nothing.

Natasha moves closer and pulls out her phone. "I spoke to Paxton."

Of course, she did. Was she in his bed while talking?

Stop it, Mal.

"And he thought it would be a good idea for us to show the cast and crew getting along. I know you're all trying behind the scenes, but we need the public to see it, too."

My head bobs up and down. "Agree."

"I took some pictures."

It feels like I'm hit over the head with a sledgehammer as it finally dawns on me what today really was. It was a setup. The competition was all a ploy, concocted by a dashing Paxton and this woman.

They decided together that Paxton teaching Teagan and me how to light a fire would look good—his tenderness . . . all a damn show.

I'm such an idiot. I fell for his charm—hook, line, and sinker.

Later in the day, everyone joined us, and Paxton went about showing off his skills. Hell, even Teagan's mom participated. It was all for show.

For the camera.

The whole thing was manipulated.

Not that I'm surprised.

But I am something . . .

Disappointed?

Yeah, that's what the heavy feeling in my chest is. I'd felt like Paxton and I had a breakthrough. Like maybe we were turning a corner.

Wrong.

Paxton is a dick.

I lift my hand and run it through my hair. God, I'm an idiot. "And?" I ask, pissed I didn't know.

"I want to release them."

"I'm not seeing why you need my permission. You obviously have Paxton's. Are you planning to ask Teagan?"

"No, I don't have to. Per her contract, she signed off on promotional pictures."

My hands land on my hips. "Well, technically, that's not what she had in mind."

"Sure, it is. Rehearsing scenes to build hype is often released to the press." She picks at her red-painted nails.

"Then why do you need to talk to me?"

"You aren't an actress, Mallory." Her hand waves in the air like she's talking to a moron.

"You need my permission to release the photo." Now I understand, and the understanding has my hands clenching by my sides.

"Yes. I'll need you to sign off on using your picture. We're trying very hard to spin the narrative that everyone on set is friends. Not just Teagan and Brad. I'll also need Theresa's permission since she and Stefan's fight was the most recent incident. We need everyone on set to look happy."

I narrow my eyes. "Couldn't it lead back to the press that this is a setup?" My voice is sharp, my disdain evident.

"Oh, no one will see it. It's just for the files." She smiles broadly.

"Sure. You have my permission. I'll sign."

"Great." She walks to an empty table and rifles through her phone.

Her emails, most likely.

It's taking forever, though, and I'm starting to get annoyed. I haven't eaten since last night, and I swear I'm starting to get dizzy. My stomach keeps rumbling. Thankfully, it's loud enough outside that no one can hear its sounds.

I don't know how much more of this I can take. I swear, from where I'm standing, I see every person visit the table, pour food on their plate, and head off to eat.

I've been here so long that people are finishing dinner.

This is ridiculous.

My fingers start to tap, my annoyance growing by the second.

"Here it is," she calls out.

Thank God.

Natasha reaches over to me and swipes at her phone, showing me a document. I don't even bother to read it. Rookie mistake, but I'm near passing out.

"Is that all?" I ask.

She claps her hands together. "It is."

I give her the fakest smile I can muster. "Great." I turn on my heel and walk toward the food.

When I get to the table, I stop short.

Goddammit.

The table is almost all out of food. It's slim pickings. I have nothing to eat. As I'm about to admit defeat and sulk back to my hut, footsteps approach behind me.

"You missed the food."

My jaw clenches down.

In another place, in another world, I'd find his voice irresistible. The gravelly way he speaks, the way he looks at me, but today is an important reminder that nothing about Paxton Ramsey is genuine.

He has everyone fooled.

I turn to look at him. Only an hour ago, he was making my knees weak as he taught me how to start a fire. Now I feel dumb for allowing myself to feel that way.

"Yeah, apparently Natasha had to speak to me. Not that it needed to be done now . . . ." I roll my eyes.

"Were you okay with the pictures being leaked?"

"Do you mean was I okay being a pawn in your silly plotted charade?" I level him with my glower. "Yeah, sure, I'm fine with being used."

He shrugs, which manages to piss me off more. "It's for the greater good."

"I would have liked to be privy to the plan."

Instead of being blindsided when I thought you had changed. *That we were changing.*

I bite my inner cheek, a habit I picked up over the years not to tell my dad what I was really thinking.

"You're being a bit dramatic."

"I haven't eaten in over thirty-two hours. I'm tired and pissed. Just leave me alone."

"I didn't mean to upset you."

I cut him off. "Bullshit. You knew exactly what you were doing. You can't help but be a dick. Not telling me? Good plan, asshole. I let my guard down, and they likely got the pictures that'll work perfectly for their lies."

"You haven't eaten in how long?" he practically growls, missing the important part in all of this.

"That's all you heard?" My hands fly up into the air. I'm two seconds away from throwing a Teagan tantrum, and I can't do that.

I spin around and stalk toward my hut, desperate to get away.

"Where are you going?" he yells at my back.

"If there's no food, I'm going to bed."

My lack of food has the ground dipping below me, and I sway, almost face-planting. My sugar levels are seriously low.

"Hold up, Mallory."

I'm about to object, but then strong arms steady me, guiding me toward a table.

Once Paxton is sure I'm safely sitting, a plate of food is pushed in front of me.

"Eat," he commands.

I narrow my eyes at his plate. "Where did you get that?"

"Don't worry about that. Just eat before you pass out."

I look up at him. "Is this yours?"

"And if I told you it was?" he asks, and I push the plate away. "Exactly. Now eat. I can't have you passing out."

"Why do you care?" I retort.

"Because, believe it or not, I'm not a complete asshole."

"Two hours ago, I might have agreed."

A hand reaches out and touches my hand that is resting on the table. I raise my chin and meet his stare.

"Please." His voice sounds different, and I find I'm too weak to argue.

Picking up my fork, I look at the plate, contemplating eating it.

It was a nice gesture, sure.

But I don't for one moment allow myself to believe that this is anything more than another ploy. Something else for Natasha to snap a picture of.

Chapter Twenty-Two

Paxton

@Stargossip: Is anyone else thinking these latest photos from the *Twisted Lily* set are another ploy to convince us all that things are going swell?

> **@SuckMyToes:** Whatever the angle, I won't complain about shots of Paxton Ramsey . . . YUM!

> **@SpeakEasyToMe:** @SuckMyToes You're not wrong! The man's FIRE!

> **@Deathtothesystem:** They're all evil, and the photos are trash!

"I'LL BE BACK IN A FEW." STANDING FROM THE TABLE, I HEAD toward one of the few restrooms used by the whole staff. I make quick work, wanting out of here as soon as possible. It's fucking gross. On the walk back, I watch her from across the expanse as she pulls out her phone and attempts to find service.

Good luck.

She really is stubborn.

Or at least she is when it comes to me.

That's partially my own fault. I've been a dick to her since the beginning. I'm starting to think that maybe my anger was misplaced.

Since we've been here, she's done nothing but work her ass off for Teagan.

Running lines.

Practicing scenes.

Hell, she goes to bat for her every chance she gets.

When I'm only a few feet away, I hear Mallory on the phone, and she's not happy with whoever is on the other line. I don't intend to listen, but something catches my attention, and I decide to slink into the brush to avoid being seen.

Dick move, but whatever.

"Why? Why the hell would you do that?"

The person on the other line must be speaking because the only thing I hear is Mallory's deep breathing.

"I didn't ask you to make that call. I never would've. She's *my* client, and I'm capable of getting her roles," she practically yells. "I'll never work for you, Dad. I told you this. I want to make it on my own, and your interference prevents that. Stop, or this will be the last time I speak to you."

She ends the call and stalks back toward the table.

I stand here for several minutes, replaying what I just overheard. I can only assume it was her father on the other end. Could she have been talking about this role and his interference?

It's the only thing that makes sense.

Fuck.

I've been such an asshole.

I run my hands back through my hair, trying to figure out how to atone for my behavior.

Do I even care to?

Without any more thought to it, I head back toward her. The closer I get, I see how uncomfortable she looks, and I wonder why.

"I didn't touch the food, if that's what you're worried about."

Her head snaps up. "Wait, you haven't eaten either?"

I shrug.

"Have you eaten today at all?"

Again, my shoulders lift.

"Jeez, Paxton. I can't take this." She slides the plate toward me.

"Let's share." As soon as the words are out, I see the skepticism in her narrowed eyes and scrunched-up nose.

"Paxton."

"Mallory," I challenge back. "We're both starving. We can't work like this."

She looks down at the plate. There's plenty for both of us. Chicken, rice, and vegetables, but I only have one fork and knife.

I push up to stand. "But first, I need to get you something." Her eyebrow lifts. "A fork. Unless you want to share mine?" I wink.

Mallory shakes her head from side to side. "No. Another fork would be great. Can't be sharing—"

I smirk, and her cheeks turn a warm shade of red, which seems to be standard Mallory. The girl blushes at the drop of a hat.

She sure does get flushed around me a lot for someone who hates me. Across the grass, a small table is set up with utensils.

After today and all the work I see that the actors have to do to make the filming seem authentic, I'm surprised we even have craft services set up.

Knowing Stefan, I bet he would have been okay if we had to hunt and gather to eat.

Something tells me that's what Jeffrey is doing here.

When I reach the table, I grab what we need and turn toward where Mallory is sitting.

A man stands by her, engaging her in conversation.

From this angle, I can't see who it is. My eyes narrow at Mallory, whose posture has changed from relaxed to sitting upright.

She looks even more uncomfortable than before, and my hand

clenches around the fork and knife—the cold metal biting into my skin.

I stalk toward the table, and the man turns. It's one of the cameramen. Bill, I think that's his name. When he sees me heading their way, he rushes off, but not before I notice the look he gives her.

Fucking creep.

"Everything okay?"

She reaches her hand up and runs her fingers through her hair, a normal gesture, but it's the way her brows pinch in and the two lines that form between them that have me concerned.

"You don't look like everything's okay. What did he say to you?" I can't keep the steel from my tone.

If he said one inappropriate thing, I'll send his ass packing.

"Now you're an expert on the faces I make?"

"Mal—"

She inclines her chin down at the nickname.

"Stop, Paxton. We aren't friends. You don't need to protect me."

Placing the fork down in front of her, I lift my hand in surrender. "Let's just eat."

Sitting across from her, I look in the direction the camera guy came and then back at her.

I don't voice my comments or questions. Instead, I opt to stay quiet. She needs a minute to calm down from whatever bothers her because it's clearly not me.

I try my hardest to allow her the time she needs and the opportunity to open up to me, but when she continues to sit there, pushing her food around, I'm done giving her space.

"Did he say something to you? Anything inappropriate?"

She continues to push the food around the plate. "It's nothing."

"It's not nothing." This time, my words come out through clenched teeth.

"Typical comments."

"He hit on you?"

She peeks up at me through her lashes. "Yeah."

I nod, but I don't say anything. My hand fists on the table. Whatever he said is more than what she's letting on. "Has he made more passes since you arrived?"

"A few."

A moment of silence passes, and then she places her fork down. "You done?"

I nod because anything I say at this point would come out strained, and she'd misinterpret me as being short with her.

I grab the tray of food and the utensils. "Let's go."

She shakes her head in confusion before standing. "Where?"

"I'm walking you back to your hut."

She stands, crossing her arms over her chest. "Maybe I'm not ready for bed," she challenges.

"Princess, it's late. It's time for you to get your beauty sleep."

"I'm princess again, not Mal?"

"Well, you are being difficult." I shrug, as though that should be obvious.

I watch as the fight bleeds out of her, and a yawn escapes her lips. She's not just tired. She's exhausted.

She rolls her eyes. "Fine. You're right."

I smirk, steering us toward the path. I drop the plates in the appropriate bins and turn my head toward her. "Wow. How do those words feel coming out of your mouth?"

"Bitter. Like sucking on a lemon." She grins.

"After you." I reach my hand out in gesture, and when she steps up, it accidentally brushes her arm.

She darts off like I lit her on fire, and I follow quickly behind her.

I trail her, watching her carefully step over the fallen leaves and rocks.

Night has fallen on the island, and the farther we walk into the cover of trees, the darker it gets.

As we walk, I pull my phone from my pocket to shine a light ahead. It doesn't take us long to get there; it's only about a five-minute trip, but neither of us speaks. I'm thankful for the silence because I'm still trying to wrap my brain around the phone call I overheard and how it's changed my feelings toward this woman.

Only a few days ago, I wouldn't have cared who hit on her. Now I'm enraged not just that he did, but that she was made to feel uncomfortable.

Since when do I give a fuck?

You always did, to some extent.

When we get to her hut, she goes to walk inside, but I reach out my hand and stop her. My fingers lightly grip the exposed skin on her upper arm.

"Listen, Mallory." She looks at me over her shoulder, but what she must see in my eyes has her turning fully.

My hand slips from her skin. "I don't want you walking alone."

"Okay."

I'm taken aback by her quick agreement. That's unusual.

"No, I mean it. If you want to go somewhere, just don't go alone."

"How am I—"

"I'll go with you. Just tell me where and when, and I'll go with you."

She stares at me for several moments, eyes sweeping over my face and landing on my eyes. She must find whatever she was looking for because she nods.

With that settled, she turns around and goes inside without another word.

What the fuck, Pax?

Attaching myself to Mallory Reynolds will not end well for either of us.

Chapter Twenty-Three

Mallory

@Stargossip: Rain is in the forecast . . . oh, wait . . . that's just the tears of Stefan having to work with amateurs.

> **@TacosandHairclips:** That's just rude . . . .

> **@twistedtealover:** @TacosandHairclips What the hell does your handle even mean?

> **@TacosandHairclips:** @VadarDarthLife Wouldn't you like to know . . . stalker!

> **@Deathtothesystem:** I'd be crying, too. What terrible casting. Someone needs to be fired!

A KNOCK ON THE DOOR JARS ME, AND I ALMOST FALL OVER.
"Who is it?" I yell out, struggling to pull my leggings up. I bounce around, wrestling the black tights into submission.

Luckily, I win the battle. The last thing I need is to be caught on my hands and knees with my pants around my ankles. Especially if it's who I think it is.

As kinky as it sounds, Paxton, the ass, would never let me live it down. He'd torture me about it for as long as we're stuck on this island together, and Lord knows I don't need to feed him more fuel.

"Paxton. You ready?"

His voice alone has my heart beating a little faster. A vision begins to play in my mind. I was wrong. He doesn't make fun of me. Instead, he gets on his knees behind me, spreads my legs apart, and—

"Mallory?" The reminder that Paxton is just outside my door is like a bucket of cold water on my hot and dirty thoughts.

"One minute," I reply, needing to get myself in check.

Kittens. Sauerkraut. Popsicles . . .

Nope. That last one does not help.

My mind conjures all sorts of inappropriate things.

When he told me he wanted to escort me everywhere, I didn't truly believe he'd stick to that. It's easy to say at the moment, but I half expected him to ditch me and laugh about it with the crew he's likely friends with. The guy can get along with a tadpole if its name isn't Mallory Reynolds.

Here he is, keeping his word and knocking on my door bright and early. I guess he's capable of kindness where I'm concerned, after all.

Maybe this shouldn't be such a shock. The word around town is that Paxton Ramsey is one of the good ones.

Now, granted, he's been anything but nice to me. However, when I first met . . .

Well, maybe not then, either, but I have seen glimmers here and there of that good guy.

"Come on, princess. We don't have all day."

Yep. All lies. He's an ass.

Looking around my room, I find my hoody and grab it. I'm wearing a black tank, but the weather is a bit colder today compared to the last few days. The leggings are necessary with the wind that seems to be picking up. The cool air coming off the ocean is chilly on a warm day. Today, it'll just about do me in.

Dramatic? Obviously.

Once I'm situated, I throw open the door, and of course, he's standing there, looking larger than life.

The early morning sunlight streaks across his face, making his blue eyes take on the shade one can only find in the shallow waters of a tropical ocean.

Clear and almost translucent.

One could get lost in them, and as he shifts his weight to step back, I realize I just did.

This man is dangerous, especially now.

Now that I can see past the anger and walls he's built up.

"It's still a tropical island, Mal. What's with the parka?"

I pull a face, looking down at my clothes.

"It's weather appropriate." My voice pitches a bit, flaring with indignation.

"If you're in Alaska."

"Apparently, you've never been to Alaska if you think this is appropriate." I scoff. "Whatever. Let's do this."

I pull the sweatshirt off, feeling insecure from his criticism, which is stupid because I should be used to it.

I'm still thinking about it when I take a step down, and as I try to avoid the hole in the wood that still hasn't been fixed, Paxton's arm darts out, and his hand wraps around my upper arm. His touch is strong enough to steady but not one to wound.

Again, he's protecting me, and my traitorous heart melts.

It's becoming harder and harder to hate him when he keeps acting like this.

Being alone with Paxton when he's like this is dangerous because, apparently, I'm unable to think straight around this man.

It's not that I want him to be mean to me. Of course, I don't. But I don't know how to reconcile the two versions of Paxton.

A feeling blooms in my belly, warm and fuzzy. What if he's finally ready to move past his hate? What if we can get along?

"Why am I constantly having to rescue you?" His tone isn't exactly harsh, but it's not teasing, either.

Nope . . . definitely not ready to get along.

I'm not going to get my hopes up for that. The moment we're back around people, all this will evaporate into smoke, and the asshole will return.

When I'm back on firm ground, his hand on my arm lingers for a beat, then it drops to the small of my back as he lets me pass him.

Despite my best intentions, I can't help my shiver at the feel of his warmth.

By chance, my tank top has risen, and since the hoodie is in my hand, his skin touches the small, exposed area above my leggings.

It's only a finger, but it feels like my body is on fire.

It catapults me back in time to the way his fingers had their wicked way with me.

How I was begging, desperate, and ready to go home with him after only a brief conversation.

I let out a large breath. I need to rein myself in.

"Everything okay over there?"

"Just a lot on my mind."

You. Mostly you and your expert fingers.

"Care to talk about it? We have at least five minutes before we bump into anyone."

"Nope," I squeak, earning a raised brow from Paxton.

I'll take these five minutes before we bump into our high-maintenance clients and enjoy the island's peacefulness. Brad and Teagan have us both on edge, so I'll jump on any chance to relax.

The fact he wants to discuss anything with me is a complete one-eighty from only a few days ago, but I need time to pull myself out of the gutter.

"Mallory. Talk to me."

I stop walking and turn around. What I see makes my knees go weak.

His blue eyes look at me for the first time with zero hate. The stern glare is gone. They're soft and filled with compassion. "We can talk about our clients. Or whatever."

"Can we? Because right now, we are kind of at a cease-fire, and I'm afraid if we do—"

"All-out war will start again?" He chuckles, a sound that has my heart rate picking up.

Sure, I've heard him laugh, but with me, not in fun. The only time I've heard the sound was the first time I met him, and now, hearing it again makes my legs wobble.

"Basically."

"Believe it or not, I think we can. I'm a professional. You're a professional."

I lift my hand in mock shock. "Wait, I'm a professional now?"

His head dips, and I fear he's about to drop the niceties and chastise me. Instead, his lip tips up, and I realize he's playing with me.

And this is something that I'm not ready for because if I think moody Pax is hot, playful Pax is fire.

Chapter Twenty-Four

Paxton

@Stargossip: Is it just me, or do Brad and Teagan have zero chemistry?

> **@SpikesandCollars:** So true! I bet this is worse than that first vampire movie!

> **@twistedtealover:** We'll see. They might surprise us.

> **@Deathtothesystem:** @twistedtealover No chance. They both suck weeds.

'VE SHOCKED HER.

Well, good because I shocked myself. We both should be on equal footing in this.

It's hard to dislike her, knowing I didn't have all the facts. Based on the conversation I overheard, she wasn't involved in getting Teagan this role.

That was all her father. He's the one who I dislike. Not Mallory.

I was unfair to her, and while I might not say those words out loud, I'll do my best to steer the ship to water.

If I'm being honest, my opinion of her started to shift before that phone call. I have no idea when it happened, but somewhere between her going to bat for Teagan, reading lines with her at every free moment, and her unending determination to improve this situation, I realized she works hard and genuinely cares for her client.

I don't think it's all about the money, and it certainly isn't about the family legacy—two things I can admire in any agent.

In Hollywood, it's easy to lose sight of a passion to help. When money gets involved, the waters get murky.

I have no intention of telling her all this, but I'm tired of fighting. With no good reason to walk around this island going out of my way to be a dick to her, I'm waving my white flag.

An invisible one.

One in which Mallory can't look at me in the way she does, hands on her hips, and *I told you* so written all over her face.

We're halfway to the shoot location when it occurs to me that maybe Mallory doesn't realize the leak is still an issue. I stop and turn toward her, not wanting to have this conversation around everyone else. Not knowing who's responsible makes things difficult.

"Did you know that there has been a new post about the set every day, sometimes multiple times a day, since we've been here?"

"What?" she bites out. "Nobody told me! I thought that was handled."

"I've been checking every day."

Her hands fly up. "My phone hardly works here. I have barely been able to check any of my social media. When it does work for a brief second, I have business to handle. You're lucky enough to be established with employees."

She has a point.

She sighs heavily. "Stefan fired all those people for no reason."

I lift a shoulder. "Maybe. Maybe not. The person responsible for posting might be gone, but that means they have an accomplice feeding them information."

She nods. "So many possibilities."

"Exactly. Whoever is doing it needs to be stopped and fast." I run my hands back through my hair. "I didn't drop weeks of my life and desert my other clients to come to this isolated island for nothing."

"Same. Well . . . at least about the life part." She nibbles her bottom lip, and my eyes follow the movement. "This isn't good."

What's not good is that all thoughts of the leak have vanished because now I'm staring at her full, plump lips, imagining in great detail if they still taste the same. Going a step further and wishing to see them wrapped around my—

"When did Natasha arrive on set?"

"Huh?" My head shakes as I try to rid my mind of her lips wrapped around my cock. "No clue. Why?"

Her nose scrunches. "Just wondering if maybe she'd have some insight."

"No harm in asking." I watch Mallory closer, and I know something more is going on in her head. "But something tells me you have another theory."

She glances around the area, lowering her voice when she speaks. "You know that saying, there's no such thing as bad publicity?" Her fingers tap on her hip as she thinks.

I close the distance between us, reach out, and take her restless hand in mine.

Mallory is about as shocked as I am by my actions. While it's not the first time I've stopped her tapping, it is the first time I've held her hand in mine when I wasn't actively glaring at her.

It shouldn't be different, but it certainly feels different to me.

I lean into her. "You think Natasha is our leak?"

"I mean, while I have no proof, it makes sense to me," Mallory whispers. "She just gives me a bad vibe. That's all."

Reaching my free arm up, I run my hand through my hair again, wondering if she's right.

Natasha makes sense. She's shown a clear disdain for Mallory. Could that feeling extend to Teagan, as well?

I also realize that Natasha's main objective is to get eyes on the film. Anything to spike curiosity and get butts in the seats on opening week. She doesn't give a shit about Brad's or Teagan's reputation once this film's done.

"If she's a suspect, that means so is Stefan. Or Jeffrey, for that matter. If we're going under the assumption that they want publicity and don't care how or where they get it from, it could be all of them. We're the only idiots not in the know. All the while, they're sinking our clients' careers."

Mallory's face pales. For a moment, I fear she's about to get sick.

"Shit. How do we stop leaks if leaks are what they want?" Her voice shakes, and I have a ridiculous need to pull her into me. To wrap her up and protect her from the world.

I need off this island.

"We need to consider all the options." Dropping my hold on Mallory, I start to pace back and forth on our little path. "So, then, it's what? A disgruntled employee? Someone not happy to be here?"

"I'm not sure," Mallory says with a sigh. "The only person I fully trust is you."

I swallow. "Me? Why do you trust me after everything?"

"Neither one of our clients can afford the bad press, and they've both been painted in a terrible light. I would never, and I believe you wouldn't either." Her lip tips up. "Even if you do hate his guts."

I chuckle. "That obvious?"

She lifts her eyebrows. "You're not exactly subtle. Don't worry, I don't think he noticed. He's too much of an egomaniac to think anyone could ever not love him."

I roll my eyes. "You've got him pegged that fast?"

She nods, tapping her legs with her hand. "We just need the bad press to stop. You heard what Jeffrey and Stefan said. There's a real fear that filming could stop if the studio thinks there is a safety issue."

"Which should automatically rule those two out. Natasha, too. None of them benefit from production being shut down."

"Back to square one."

"Maybe. From what I remember of the latest tweets, they had nothing to do with safety. I'll have to revisit them to rule those three out."

She huffs. "We just need to make sure nothing insane happens to ensure nothing detrimental can get leaked."

"We can try." My eyes narrow as a thought occurs. "We can also plant our own story. Why not use the media to benefit us and our clients?"

"Do you have contacts?"

I grin. "Sure do."

She takes a deep breath, appearing to mull it over. "Let's revisit this later." She points down the path. "We should get going. With Stefan wanting character building before each scene, timing is an issue."

"Say no more." I swing my arm out, motioning for her to take the lead.

It's not long before we get to the location of today's shoot, and Mallory's whole demeanor shifts.

Fishing.

Apparently, they're shooting the scene where Brad tries to spearfish for food, as evidenced by the props lining the ground—everything from spears to nets made of leaves from the other day.

"Not a fan?" I say, grinning down at her.

She turns toward me. "No clue. Never done it."

"I'll teach you."

She offers a rare smile that reaches her eyes. "You've been doing a lot of that lately."

I shrug. "I can be a nice guy, Mallory."

We stare at each other for several long seconds before Mallory glances away, breaking the moment.

Thank God one of us has brains.

I might not hate her, but that doesn't mean I need to jump into the deep end.

Mallory walks off, heading toward Teagan, and I appreciate the distance. I need to get my head screwed on straight.

Teagan hugs her before she starts to talk animatedly. Her hands are moving faster than usual when she does, and I'm instantly on edge.

Now what? Another issue?

Teagan holds up a stick with a point at the end before pointing at her exposed midriff.

I make my way toward them, mostly to head off any additional issues. Mallory and I agree that we must do our part to keep the set free of problems. I'm at their side just before Teagan says, "I'm not wearing this."

"Teagan—" Mallory starts, but she's cut off.

"No, this is ridiculous. I'm practically naked."

For fuck's sake.

She can't be serious.

I want to interrupt and remind Teagan that she signed a contract, agreeing to not only wear this but also be partially nude for a sex scene.

I don't interrupt, though. Not my place.

The one thing I have learned since being on this island is that Mallory is the only person who truly knows how to handle Teagan.

"Listen." Mallory reaches her hand out and places it on her shoulder. "What's going on? You knew about all of this. You agreed. I asked you several times if you were sure before you signed."

Teagan's eyes dart around, and at first, I think she'll tell me to leave, but she doesn't. Her head continues to swivel around, and I realize she's looking for someone. I follow her eyes and land on her mom. Teagan shudders, and it's not hard to deduce this is an issue with Theresa.

Great.

Just fucking great. The woman is a continual pain in everybody's ass. To make matters worse, it's clear that her adult daughter doesn't want her here. So why the hell hasn't somebody sent her packing?

"I . . . I can't," Teagan stammers.

Mallory squeezes her shoulder. "Why?"

"I ate too much."

Mallory shakes her head, clearly confused. "What do you mean, you ate too much?"

"I shouldn't have eaten today. Mom said—"

"Stop right there, Teagan." Mallory's voice takes on a hard edge that tells me she'll go to war against Theresa for Teagan.

"Do not let your mom get into your head." She places her other hand on Teagan's opposite shoulder, bending to eye level. "You might not feel uncomfortable right now, but you are beautiful, Teagan. Don't let *her* issues become yours."

"I—"

"Nope. I will not have you entertain anything she says. You look great. You know the lines. You're going to nail this."

Teagan drops her gaze and doesn't look up.

"Take a deep breath, and now exhale that bullshit. I'm going to make sure she's not on set today."

Teagan inhales and then exhales, and she smiles. "You promise?"

Mallory places two fingers under Teagan's chin and lifts it. "Absolutely."

"What would I do without you?"

Mallory smiles warmly. "That's something you'll never have to find out."

Teagan throws her arms around Mallory, hugging her tightly before running off toward the water to practice with Brad.

I stand here, taking in what I just witnessed. It's something you only see in movies. Rarely does an agent have that kind of relationship with a star. Ego plays too much of a part in things.

"You're really good with her."

"She makes it easy." Mallory shrugs off the compliment, and I refuse to allow it.

"Nope."

She turns to me with narrowed eyes. "Nope?"

"It's you who makes it easy."

And dammit, I mean it wholeheartedly. Mallory Reynolds has me twisted up, and that's a real problem.

Chapter Twenty-Five

Mallory

@Stargossip: Some people fish for compliments, while high-paid actors just plain ole fish . . . or so we hear.

> **@Betterthanfiction:** Umm . . . pass!

> **@Bitchpleaseme:** I hate everyone. And I hate pants.

> **@Deathtothesystem:** More like overpaid actors! It's ridiculous!

It's been three days since I had Theresa removed from the set.

She didn't go without making a scene, but ultimately, Stefan agreed, and she was asked to leave.

They've been running the same scene since that day, and I'm hoping today will be a wrap and on to the next. The chemistry between Brad and Teagan is improving. It's just Stefan's wacky way of filming that has prolonged this particular scene.

He claims it hasn't hit peak performance.

Whatever the hell that means.

"Here," Paxton says, moving beside me and offering a piping hot mug of coffee.

I accept the offering with a small smile. "Thank you."

He nods, eyes never wavering from Brad and Teagan.

"How's it going so far?" he asks, taking a sip of his coffee.

"Not bad. Let's just hope Stefan gets what he's looking for and moves to the next scene." I huff. "At this rate, we'll be here another month."

Paxton groans. "If I don't return to the office soon, I'm afraid I won't have a team or clients outside of Brad."

I turn to him and make a face. "That sounds ominous."

He smirks. "I work with a bunch of petulant brats." He turns to look at me. "Did I mention the worst are the men?"

I grin up at him. "How shocking. You better take advantage of your downtime here. Sounds like things will be crazy when you get back."

He leans down, lips grazing the shell of my ear, and my entire body goes still, except for the tingles rushing over my skin. "Oh, I intend to."

If my heart could beat any faster, it might pop out of my chest.

I have no clue what's happening here, but when Paxton pulls away and our eyes lock, his eyes darken, and I swear something resembling lust crosses his gorgeous face.

I'm likely imagining things. Allowing his proximity to play mind games.

Snapping my head away, I clear my throat.

Stefan has called a break, and Brad and Teagan are just standing around.

"I'm going to go check on Teagan. Make sure she doesn't need anything."

"You care about her," he says, gesturing to where Teagan has taken it upon herself to begin rehearsing with Brad.

I'm so proud to see her coming out of her shell and taking

the initiative. The ways she flourishes when Theresa is absent is telling.

"I do care about her," I say, turning back toward Paxton.

His features shift, and I can only describe it as admiration, as if he's seeing me as someone entirely different. It's almost like the way a sculptor might look at his marble masterpiece after hours of chiseling away, marveling at how far it has come from what it was before.

I was always this person, Paxton.

"I was wrong before." His eyes glisten with an emotion that transcends words, and I can feel my heart melting. "About you." His voice is gentle yet strong, like a warm summer breeze ruffling the leaves of a tall tree.

I stand stock-still, shocked and overwhelmed. My cheeks flush with warmth, the air around us suddenly electric. I can feel myself being drawn in deeper by the intensity of his gaze.

"Thank you," I whisper, stepping closer to him without conscious thought.

There is something so powerful about the way he looks at me that my breath catches in my throat. I'm rendered speechless.

It's like he's finally seeing me for who I really am, like he finally sees past the shadow my father casts.

"No, thank you," he murmurs back, his voice like velvet as it wraps around me.

"For what?"

"For giving this your all. For not backing down when I gave you a hard time. For trying to fix this movie. Because I think we all need this movie to pan out."

"I certainly do." My lips slowly part into a smile, which he returns. A strange feeling settles over me, but not a bad one; nope, it's almost like clarity. An understanding that this moment is important. This is when everything changes.

He doesn't want to hate me anymore, and I don't hate him at all.

As Teagan and Brad rehearse, Paxton and I fall into a comfortable silence.

But unfortunately, it doesn't last for long because a screech rings out in the air, and if I'm not mistaken, the loud noise came from Teagan.

Before anyone confirms my suspicions, I take off, dashing across the space. *Please, no more drama. I've had enough of that for the next century.*

The closer I get, the more nervous I become.

She's no longer standing. Now she's on the ground, and her one hand is lifted, clutching her other arm.

As I rush to her side, my heart pounds in my chest so hard that it feels like it's ready to climb up and out of my throat.

People are shouting, but I don't stop to listen. I drop to my knees beside her, trying to assess what's wrong.

Her face is a mask of fear, her eyes wide and unblinking.

I reach across and take her arm in my hand. That's when I see blood. It's started seeping out of what looks like a deep scratch on her arm. It's an angry red line that is striking compared to her pale skin.

Gently, I touch her shoulder. "What happened?"

"I-I don't know." She looks over at the fake spear. "It stabbed me when I was rehearsing the scene."

"That shouldn't be possible," I say. "Isn't the one you're supposed to use during this scene rubber?"

"Yes," Teagan stammers.

"Shit. Are you okay?" I ask. "Can someone get me a first-aid kit?" I yell out, and people around me scramble.

As if waking from a trance, she nods slowly. "Y-Yes," she says in a small voice. "It was just a scare and a scrape. I'll be okay."

We look at each other, and we both let out a breath. A feeling of relief sweeps over me. It could have been worse.

I pick up the spear to find it's not the rubber one she's supposed to use. Didn't she realize that?

Probably not. When Teagan is in character, she's so focused on her lines that an error like this can easily occur if those responsible for the safety measures are sleeping on the job. There will be severe consequences when I find out who put this here. Right now, I'm focused on cleaning her up and making sure she doesn't get an infection.

I wrap my arm around Teagan's shoulders to comfort her. I know right now she needs me to give her strength. *My strength.*

A few minutes later, crew members come running up to us with towels, bandages, and antiseptic.

"It's nothing." She tries to brush them off.

"It's not nothing. Even if you're going to be okay, it's not nothing," I tell Teagan, squeezing her tighter against me. She looks up at me with a small smile of understanding and a sparkle of thankfulness in her eyes.

I've known her long enough to recognize when she needs me. Since she will never get compassion from Theresa, I will be that person in her life.

"I'm going to let them clean you up and get to the bottom of this," I say, lifting the spear.

She nods, releasing her grip on me.

"What's going on?" Paxton says, jogging up toward us. "Brad said the spearhead is supposed to retract, and it didn't."

I step closer to him so as not to be overheard. "Someone gave her the wrong prop." I lift the spear to show him. "This is what she was using."

"Fuck. That's not good."

"No . . . it's not," I agree, shaking my head. "If this gets out . . ."

"We won't let it."

I sigh, looking up at Paxton. "How are we going to manage that?"

"Teagan!" A scream pierces the air, and I don't need to turn around to recognize the voice.

Theresa is barreling toward us, and she's not worried. She's pissed.

"Who let her in here?" I say through my teeth.

"Want me to handle this?" Paxton offers, but I'm too focused on what's occurring in front of me.

"You stop being dramatic and get up."

Teagan shudders at her mom's words. Her mouth opens and shuts several times. It looks like she can't find her words, and to be honest, I understand because, right now, neither can I. "You need to get back up and finish this scene."

She moves in closer, leaning over until she's practically on top of Teagan. "We need this. You can't ruin this." Her words come out in a hissed, low whisper, but I hear them clear as day since I'm so close.

"Mom—"

I march toward them, looking down at Theresa. "Teagan will do no such thing. Everyone on this set will agree that she needs a moment."

"It isn't your place to say what she needs—"

"No, but it's mine," Stefan's voice rings through the air. "Everyone, that's a wrap for the day."

Before Theresa can object, Stefan strides away, not allowing her to say another word. She doesn't bother to ensure Teagan is being cared for before she storms off, too.

Turning back toward Teagan, I reach my hand out to help her up. The sun is setting now, its light reflecting on Teagan's face. She looks so fragile in the fading light, unshed tears filling her eyes.

"I know I'm not supposed to cry. I know better than to expect more from her . . ." she finally says, "but . . ."

I can hear the pain in her voice, and my heart breaks for her.

"It's all right," I say softly, squeezing her hand. "Let's get out of here and get drunk."

"I'm underage."

"On this island, the drinking age is eighteen." I wink.

Her face lights up with the first real smile I've seen from her today.

Chapter Twenty-Six

Paxton

@Stargossip: Name a song that comes to mind when you think of *Twisted Lily* . . . Go!

> **@TeaganTrain:** "Island Lover" by Shaggy.
>
> **@LosttoLust:** "Burn the Ships" by King & Country!
>
> **@Deathtothesystem:** "It's the End of the World as We Know It" by R.E.M.
>
> **@Stargossip:** @Deathtothesystem I couldn't have picked a better song! Bravo!

WHAT A DISASTER OF A DAY.

Even though Teagan wasn't badly injured, she was still hurt. Yet more potential fodder for the gossip columns. On top of that, filming was once again stopped.

I search for Mallory to check on Teagan and find them sitting on the grass, well on their way to tipsy.

Why not? Shooting is halted, might as well take the edge off.

Crossing the space, I swipe a bottle of rum from the table before heading in their direction.

Mallory's laughter breaks through the air, wrapping around me, resulting in my need to readjust.

Jesus.

Why does this woman make me feel like a horny teenager?

I sit beside her on the blanket, passing her the bottle of rum. She grabs it from my hand and takes a swig before passing it to Teagan.

She tips the bottle back, draining too much, too quickly.

"Thanks," she chokes out.

My eyebrow lifts into my hair, and Mallory smirks at me. Her eyes twinkle with amusement. I take back my earlier assessment. She's well past tipsy.

She lifts her empty bottle. "Ours ran out, so thank you for bringing us a new one." She hiccups on that last part.

I recline back on my elbows. "What can I say? I'm good for something, at least."

"You know what I hate about my mom?" Teagan says, clearly not in the mood to hold back. Her voice drips with sarcasm as she continues the conversation she must have been having before I sat down. "She thinks she can control me like some kind of puppet! No matter how hard I try to prove her wrong, she still won't let me be my own person."

Mallory shakes her head and chimes in with a smile. "I feel you."

I lift the bottle to my mouth, considering what Mallory is thinking. I don't know much about their family, but from the little she's said in the heat of the moment, her father is rather controlling.

The rum warms my stomach. It's like a small fire that spreads through my body, and I can feel it loosening the knots in my shoulders.

"It feels like everything that can go wrong is. Like there is a giant boulder we're all trying to push up a hill. No matter how hard we try, it just keeps rolling back down," Mallory says.

Teagan's voice is tight. "Yeah, that's exactly how it feels." Her hand reaches out toward me, and I give her a look.

"Sure that's a wise idea?"

She glowers, and I decide not to treat her like a child and hand over the bottle. She takes a swig and then sighs heavily.

"We'll get this movie done," Mallory says. "If it's the last thing I do, I'll make sure of it."

The bottle is passed back to me, and I grip it tightly and nod. I can see the fire in her eyes and know she means it.

"I'll make sure we do, too."

Teagan gives us both a tight smile. "Okay."

Time passes, and as it does, the sunlight fades and turns the sky black.

Laughter rings through the air as we continue to drink. Unlike the group to our left, we sit in companionable silence, taking turns sipping from the bottle.

I turn toward Mallory, and she has her head tilted toward the sky. The stars twinkle above us like tiny pinpricks of light against a backdrop.

A gust of wind blows across my face, and the air around us changes. There's no question a storm is brewing.

A drop of rain pelts me on the forehead, quickly followed by another.

I jump to my feet and turn to Mallory and Teagan. "It's going to pour any minute."

"I guess it's time to go." Mallory shrugs, sulking as she stands.

"I'm going to find my mom." Teagan gives us a tight smile. "I might be mad, but she's still my mom."

"Make sure you're indoors before this storm hits. It looks like it's going to be nasty," I warn, hoping she heads my words.

Storms on an island can get intense. The last thing we need is a tragedy.

She nods, rushing off toward her hut.

When it's just Mallory and me standing here, the rain picks up, and the storm soon becomes fast and furious. Wet strands of hair cling to her face as she throws her head back and laughs. Her eyes sparkle and shimmer brighter than the stars on a clear night.

She's a goddamn masterpiece.

Her beauty is beyond any words that I can think of. Stunning hardly cuts it.

What I wouldn't give to grab her, pull her toward me, and do all the wicked things I want to her.

That's the rum talking.

There's no time for that shit right now.

The wind continues to pick up speed, and I know we're running on borrowed time. "Stay right here."

Her eyebrows furrow. "Where are you going?"

I'm jogging backward when I call out, "To grab another bottle and some food before everything is ruined. I'll grab you some, too."

She nods, and I turn around and dash over to the table. There are large black totes under the food. I grab one, stuffing it with supplies, before hurrying back.

I grab Mallory's arm. "Let's go."

Together, we dash back to the path that leads to our huts.

When we get to hers, she sidesteps the hole in the step.

I follow her in, unloading half of the supplies I took before heading toward the door.

"If you need me—"

"I'll be fine."

I stand in the doorway, looking down into her blue eyes, which are a bit hazy at the moment. Neither one of us speaks or moves. We're staring into each other's eyes, both lost in the moment. I lean toward her, not sure what I'm thinking. When my lips are a hair's breadth away from hers, thunder booms, jolting us back to the present.

Mallory screeches, jumping back, eyes wide.

"You better go," she says, and I know the moment is ruined.

I nod, and she offers me a small smile before closing the door and shutting me out.

The sky opens up, and the winds are fierce.

I'm standing on her hut's porch while the rain soaks me through. Lightning streaks across the sky, and I know I have to move. No amount of standing here will bring back that moment. It's for the best.

I'll only think about it until morning.

It's going to be a long night.

Chapter Twenty-Seven

Mallory

@Stargossip: Just in . . . Teagan has been stabbed on set! We'll keep you posted on every detail we manage to uncover.

> **@LosttoLust:** Umm . . . why isn't the news picking this up?

> **@BeamMeUpTeagan:** WHAT?! Is she okay? Was it Brad?

> **@Deathtothesystem:** Somehow, it'll be covered up because it wasn't Brad . . . .

> **@Stargossip:** @LosttoLust They have PR on the scene . . . . I'm sure they're burying it.

IT DOESN'T TAKE ME LONG TO REALIZE I'M, IN FACT, WRONG.

I will not be fine.

A nervous laugh bubbles up through my mouth. Only me. This would only happen to me.

Right there, not a foot in front of me, is a huge puddle of water.

It's only a few feet from the bed, and I'm thanking the universe that I won't have to sleep in a pond tonight.

Plopping down onto the mattress, I place my hands on my head as I try to figure out what the hell I'm going to do.

It's only a matter of time before the whole place is wet. Rain pours through a gaping hole in the roof.

Of course, this is my life.

Why wouldn't this happen to me?

Everywhere I turn, something else goes wrong.

I can just imagine the cosmic joke being told up in the clouds right now. The gods, laughing and pointing down at me, shaking their heads in amusement as they marvel at how pathetic I must look.

Tears well in my eyes, but I push down the shattering feeling sitting heavy in my belly, and don't let them to fall.

I've lived through worse.

A mouse-infested apartment is probably not worse than a gaping hole with water pouring down in the middle of a tropical storm. Then again, my best friend Melissa would have burned the place to the ground. She'd sleep in a pond any day to avoid a single mouse.

Not me. I cannot be wet.

There is no way I can stay here. But where do I go? Is there even a dry hut to be found on this island?

Maybe the rain will let up soon and I can get someone out here to fix it?

No chance.

The hole was there when I arrived, but nobody rushed to patch it when the sun was out. I'm absolutely screwed.

I let out a long-drawn-out sigh before I head back outside and into the storm. The raindrops feel like tiny needles, piercing the skin on my face. I look up and see the broken part of the roof, and pieces of jagged wood are clearly visible.

Nope. That won't be fixed anytime soon.

Turning my head, I look over at the door to Paxton's hut, and then I look toward the path I could take back to the main camp.

The wind picks up, blowing my hair as I take a few steps in

that direction. I hesitate for a moment. Thoughts of Paxton and his smug smile fill my head.

He would love to see me like this—alone, wet, and desperate. No.

I shake the thought away. That's not how it is anymore. He was decent today. He even drank with Teagan and me. It's time to give the man the benefit of the doubt. I'll ask Paxton for help. I take a deep breath and make my way over to his hut. I pause just outside the door, wiping the rain off my face before giving three quick knocks on the door.

"Hold on," he calls from inside, his voice gruff.

"It's Mallory," I shout over the wind, my voice barely audible.

The door swings open, and Paxton stands there, looking at me with an expression of disbelief on his face. "You look like a drowned rat," he says, his tone shocked yet sympathetic.

I manage to give him a weak smile before pointing over at my hut.

"My roof . . . it's broken." I gesture to the spot on the thatched roof that's the reason I'm standing in front of this man like an idiot.

Paxton nods and steps outside into the rain. He looks up at my roof, his face turning grim.

"That sucks. No way is that getting fixed."

"That's what I figured," I say sadly, watching as Paxton watches me. "Can I—can I come in?" I ask hesitantly.

Paxton steps aside, allowing me to walk past him. My clothes are drenched with rainwater, and with every step I take, a puddle forms. Paxton quickly closes the door behind me. Then he dashes across the small space and returns a second later with a towel he must have grabbed from his bathroom.

I wrap it around my shoulders. "Thanks."

The room grows quiet around us, the only sounds coming from outside as the winds batter the wood.

"This is awful." I reach up and start to run my hands over my sopping hair. "I'm not drunk enough to deal with this."

He snorts. "We should remedy that. Not like there's anything else to do."

"Grabbing the rum was genius," I offer, meaning it.

"Sometimes I'm actually good for something." He winks before turning around and grabbing the bottle off the dresser.

Paxton doesn't bother with glasses before he takes a swig, and then he's handing the bottle over to me. My hands wrap around the cold glass of the bottle, and I don't mess with a sip. I gulp it down.

It's warm, yet the warmth is exactly what I need right now. After another large drink, I hand it back to Paxton, who takes a big gulp.

"What a fucking disaster." He shakes his head. "And I'm not just talking about the roof. Everything is a fucking shit show. The day. The movie. Everything."

"Sure is." I look at the floor before Paxton's hand touches mine.

He gives it a light squeeze, and that's when I realize what I'm doing. The feel of his hand on mine has me letting out a sigh.

"We'll figure something out." His calm voice is full of reassurance, and at that moment, I believe him. We will figure this out together.

"You can stay here." His voice cuts through my thoughts, and my heart stops beating for a second. Then, as if hit with a defibrillator, it jumps erratically in my chest, bashing against my breastbone.

He wants me to stay here.

With him.

"Y-You wouldn't mind?"

Shit. Do I even want to stay here with him?

I glance up and find him staring at me. His gaze unnerves me, especially in the confines of his personal space. The way he's looking at me makes my knees wobble.

I can't tell if he's back to hating me or if he wants to fuck me.

But regardless, he's my best option for the evening. Because if he says he's not serious, I'll have to trek down the path to find Teagan, and I might die if I have to do that.

He pulls his gaze away from me, and the moment is gone. I miss it. "It's fine. I'll crash on the floor."

I nod, feeling grateful, relieved, and, most of all, confused by my reaction.

"Sit." He motions to the bed, and I feel dumb, but I look down at my still-drenched outfit.

"I'm all wet—"

"Oh, shit. Yeah, hold on a second." Paxton walks over to the closet and grabs a shirt before returning and handing it to me. "Here."

"Thanks." I chuckle, looking it over. "This won't be the first time you've handed over your clothes to me."

His lips spread into that sexy smirk that makes my stomach feel like jelly.

Luckily, I don't need to tell him to turn around because he does it unprompted.

Once I know he's not looking, I remove the wet clothing and throw on his shirt.

It's huge on me, but I'm not surprised. When I borrowed his shirt on the boat, it also fit like a dress.

"All clear," I say once I'm covered. Paxton turns around and proceeds to look me up and down—a strange expression passing over his features. I feel like I should say something or maybe cover myself, but that's dumb. I am covered. My anxiety is peaking in his presence.

"This is becoming a habit." He speaks my prior thoughts.

"Sorry," I mutter, shrugging.

"I'm all right with it."

My eyes narrow slightly as I try to make out the meaning behind his words. The room sways a bit, and I need to sit.

Now that I'm no longer drenched, I do just that.

"Want more?" he asks, and I nod.

I reach for the bottle, and that's how it goes for several quiet minutes. We take turns passing the rum back and forth.

"Do you have any idea when this storm is supposed to stop?" I ask, breaking the silence.

"No clue. My service is gone. Can't even look up the weather."

"Surely by tomorrow."

He blows out a hard breath. "Let's fucking hope so."

A pang in my chest builds, and I question why. Is it because he wants me out of here?

Not that I can blame him. This hut should be his private space. A place to escape it all. Hard to do when you have a woman you hated only a few days ago stuck in your hut.

I go to stand, needing to use the restroom, and sway a bit more. I'm feeling the effects of the booze, and I can tell that Paxton is, too. His eyes are glazed over, and he has this lazy grin he's been sporting for several minutes. It's like he's stuck.

No matter. He's even more gorgeous when he's smiling.

The more we drink, the more the air between us shifts. I'm starting to relax and get comfortable when the smile drops.

His face grows stern, and I'm instantly on edge. He looks like he's struggling with something he wants to say, and one can only guess what.

"Something wrong?" I finally ask, hating the tension that's filled the space, desperately hoping that whatever he says won't ruin my buzz.

We're in a good place. He better not rock the boat. In my drunken state, I don't know if I'll be able to take it.

Paxton doesn't answer right away. He stares at the wall before he meets my gaze. "I was a fucking dick."

Not what I was expecting.

"You were." There's no point pretending he wasn't. He was, and I want him to own it. I won't say a word. I'll allow him to lead this conversation.

"Your father." He presses his lips together, and he continues to stare at me, but oddly enough, he doesn't say another word after that.

"I'm not him. We've established that. Can't you just move on?"

Paxton lets out a breath before nodding; his eyes look softer, a little dazed—maybe it's the booze. "You're right. I'm sorry, Mallory."

We sit there in silence for a few moments, both of us lost in our own thoughts.

"Let's not do this now," I say. "Things are stressful enough. Let's not talk about my dad."

Paxton takes a swig of his rum and nods. "Fuck, it's crazy out." He leans forward with a serious look, and as he says the words, a loud crash of thunder echoes through the air.

"It sounds like we pissed off someone up there." I point at the sky and then give a little laugh.

Paxton's face breaks into a smile. "Knowing you, you probably did." He smirks.

Another crash has my body jolting in place.

The storm rages outside, the rain pounding against the roof like giant fists. I can almost feel the air crackling with the electricity.

"It's like it has a life of its own," I say, gazing out the window as a flash of light illuminates the sky.

I turn to Paxton. "Think Teagan's doing okay, stuck with her mother?"

Paxton takes another swig of his rum before answering. "Nope."

"Great," I huff. "Sure to be a pleasant day tomorrow."

He looks out the window with a grim expression. "We'll be fine."

"Yeah, that was reassuring." I roll my eyes. "Also easy for you to say; you have a roof over your bed."

"And I already said you'll stay with me. We'll be safe here," he replies.

I nod, not sure if I believe him but grateful all the same.

Despite its ferocity, I am strangely comforted by the storm. The darkness, the thunder, and the lightning all offer a kind of wild beauty I haven't seen in a while.

"At least it's something to look at," I say as another streak of light flashes across the sky.

"Yeah," Paxton agrees. "There's that."

Paxton comes to sit beside me on the bed. Suddenly, the room is too small, and I feel like I can't breathe with him so close.

Paxton's larger-than-life presence eats up all the oxygen, making me light-headed. Or maybe that's the booze.

"Shit, I'm drunk." I giggle.

He grins. "Are you now?"

"Yeah." Another fit of laughs leaves my mouth.

"You know—" I start, and I cock my head. "If Stefan didn't come over that night . . ."

I'm about to continue, but then the whole hut shakes, followed by a crash.

My whole body shudders, and before I know what's happening, I'm being lifted into Paxton's arms.

"What the h-hell was that?" My jaw rattles from nerves. The wind batters against the walls, and the roof sounds like it's going to fall on top of us.

Tears stream down my face.

Usually, I don't cry in front of someone, but I blame it on the booze because, as Paxton holds me, my nerves win out.

Chapter Twenty-Eight

Paxton

@**Stargossip:** Welp, this is depressing.

> @**ZFleftBallSac:** @Stargossip Any word? It's been forever . . .
>
> @**Lexi_H:** @Stargossip You're going to leave us all hanging? We need info!
>
> @**IWannaMarryTeagan:** What gives? Give us the dirt!
>
> @**Brad4life:** @IwannaMarryTeagan I'm with you.

HOW THE HELL DID WE GET TO THIS POINT?
To this place where Mallory is encased in my arms, crying.

I feel helpless, which isn't a position I find myself in often. She's sobbing, and it's no wonder why. Between the weather, her damaged hut, and the stress of everything happening on the island, my own shitty contribution, who wouldn't?

Fuck, I've put her through hell and back. This whole damn

movie has basically chewed her up and spit her out, and I played a major role in a lot of her stress.

Mallory's sobs ring through the air, and the last remaining wall inside me crashes and burns.

This girl.

As her body shakes, the past few weeks flash before my eyes. All the bullshit sparring and barbs. The accusations and the condemnation about how she did her job. I'd pointed fingers and blamed her for Teagan's actions.

That would be like someone telling me it's my fault that Brad's an egomaniac sleazeball.

What the hell was I thinking?

Never in my life have I felt like a bigger prick than I do at this moment. I don't handle a woman crying well on a good day. This whole thing is nuts.

Despite her warranted reaction, I never expected her to come undone like this.

I guess between my antics and this shit show of an island, it seems the take-no-shit girl who showed up at my office fighting for the equal rights of her client is gone, replaced by a very drunk and sad girl.

And fuck is she drunk.

The smell of rum wafts off her.

Every time her small body jerks, it infiltrates my nostrils, making it feel like I've walked into a damn distillery.

There's no question Mallory will feel the aftereffects of the booze and likely curse herself when she wakes up tomorrow.

Maybe she won't remember this moment and will at least be spared her dignity.

It's not like she's embarrassing herself. It's a small blip of her letting her walls down and showing that she's human and can only handle so much.

If, by some miracle, she does forget this moment, I have no

intention of reminding her. Not when she's let herself be vulnerable in front of me. Something I know she would never do sober.

I can feel the wetness of her tears on my shirt as they drip off her chin onto my chest.

Neither of us speaks, but I hold her close.

Soon, her soft sobs fade away, and all that's left is the sound of her breathing.

For a moment, I wonder if she's fallen asleep, but then she lifts her head and looks at me through glassy eyes.

"Thank you . . ." She leans toward me, and the air between us grows thick as our gazes lock. It feels like time stands still as we watch each other. She tries to stand back up but stumbles back down before she can take a step.

Luckily, I'm there and reach my hand out to steady her.

"Easy there." I laugh. "You okay?"

She takes a deep breath. "Yeah, I'm fine," she slurs. "I'm not a f-fan of s-s-s-storms."

She leans against me for balance and wraps her arms around my neck. That's when she giggles.

"I'mholdingyou." Her words come out like one long word, then she hiccups.

"What?"

She shakes her head as if that will sober her up. "You're shaking. Are you scared, too?" She's adorable when she's drunk, grinning away and mumbling her words.

"I believe the shaking is all you," I say, trying and failing at smothering a laugh.

She looks up at me, her eyes sparkling with life and excitement, even in her drunkenness. I chuckle and shake my head at her antics. "You know . . . I'm not like him. I'm really not. If you got to know me, you'd know I'm nothing like my father."

Jesus . . . this again. We've been over this, and I'd prefer to move on with life. It's already been established that she isn't him.

Just one more indicator that Mallory is three sheets to the wind.

She looks away, embarrassed by her sudden vulnerability. I don't know what to do or say, so I just wrap my arms around her and hold her tight. She buries her face in my shoulder and takes a deep breath.

"Thanks," she mumbles again. This time her eyes flutter.

"You already thanked me." I chuckle.

Her lids pop open, and she looks around the room until she's staring at the rum bottle. "Why are we done drinking?"

"I don't think you need any more."

I eye the bottle with contempt, angry with myself for not having hidden it earlier. The last thing either of us needs tonight is another drop of rum.

She looks up at me, her vision blurry as she blinks a few more times. Then she narrows her eyes. "Why don't you like me?"

I sigh heavily and avert my gaze momentarily, annoyed this is still coming up. I understand she's drunk, but I'm doing my best to try to forget about how big a dick I was. Her constantly bringing it up only makes me feel worse.

"We've already established that I don't hate you, Mallory."

She shakes her head, disagreeing with my answer. "No, no, you do. I can tell. Everybody can tell." Her voice cracks, and she stares down at her hands in her lap.

"I don't," I say softly. "We've discussed this."

"But when I asked about the rum, you said I didn't need any more."

I smirk. "Tomorrow, you'll agree with my decision to cut us *both* off," I say, emphasizing the fact that I don't need more either.

"You did . . . hate me."

I nod, prepared to be truthful. "That's true."

"But not the first time you met me. You liked me then." Mallory giggles before slapping a hand over her mouth. "Oops."

For fuck's sake. The last thing I need with a drunk Mallory sitting in my lap is a reminder of that night.

"You're right. I did like you. A lot."

She inhales slowly and looks up at me with an intensity in her eyes that she doesn't usually have. "I like you now," she whispers as she closes the distance between us. Her body twists until her small hands land on my shoulder, and the next thing I know, her lips are on mine.

Through the haze of rum, I kiss her back.

I shouldn't. This is a bad idea on so many levels. But I can't help it. I want her. I think I always have—even when I was too busy hating her.

Pent-up emotions flood through me as I plunder her mouth with my tongue. Her fingers run through my hair, pulling at the strands and deepening the kiss.

But it isn't enough, and as my hands leave the side of my body and slide down hers, the haze of the booze and the moment start to fade.

Fuck.

I can't do this.

This kiss is wrong.

She's drunk.

Despite my dick being all in, I know I must stop this. Tomorrow, she might hate me if I allow this to go too far.

"Mal—" I say against her lips as I pull away. "We have to stop."

The look in her eyes practically undoes me. Her cheeks redden, but not from desire.

She quickly jumps off my lap, her eyes downcast. She won't look at me.

"Mal."

"Just . . ."

"You're drunk," I say, by way of explanation. When she says nothing, I add, "I think we should just crash for the night."

At that, she glares at me, and if looks could kill, I'd be dead. Then she pulls back the covers, and I watch her lie in bed. "You don't have to sleep on the floor. Just don't touch me." She turns to face the other wall, essentially shutting down any more talk.

Great. Just great.

I try to do the noble thing, and she's still pissed at me.

We're both silent. The storm raging outside is the only sound lingering in the room.

A wave of guilt washes over me for rejecting her and for fucking kissing her back in the first place.

Will we be back to square one tomorrow?

With one last look, I turn away from Mallory, hoping we won't.

Chapter Twenty-Nine

Mallory

@Stargossip: I got nothing. It's crickets from the island. Who wants to talk about another movie?

> **@Musty_rat:** What's this status? No, we don't want to talk about another movie! We want the TEA!
>
> **@Brad4life:** @Stargossip But is Brad okay????
>
> **@Cloudyqueen69:** Not a happy birthday to me, I guess.

SITTING ON THE EDGE OF PAXTON'S BED, I PLACE MY HEAD IN my hands and groan.

Kill me now.

Everything hurts.

My head.

My eyes.

My whole damn body hurts. It feels like my brain is being hit with a sledgehammer. Repeatedly. And slowly. By a *lot* of people.

I have the worst headache ever, and I only have myself to

blame. What the hell was I thinking? I'm here to work, not get bombed in front of my client and colleagues.

I don't even want to think about it, but Paxton's presence in the room isn't helping. He's looking down at me, rocking back and forth on his feet. Clearly, he has something to say, and I want to crawl into a ball and hide. I'd rather eat dirt than hear whatever he's thinking.

Some people get drunk and don't remember the next day...

I am not some people.

Every dumb thing I said and did yesterday has reared its ugly head in my mind.

I remember how I acted. How I threw myself at him.

How he rejected me.

Now, I'm giving him the cold shoulder. It isn't fair, but I'm not exactly in the right headspace to turn this train around. I see the tracks are broken up ahead, and I'm doubling down, rushing faster toward the derailment.

Not my finest hour.

But it's easier than saying *I'm sorry for being a drunk idiot.*

Plus, at this point, I'm sure all our progress is gone.

Paxton probably thinks I'm a lush, unable to be professional, and I can't blame him. I made such headway, only to drown it in one bottle of rum. Okay . . . maybe two . . . or three.

Who's counting at this point?

But inside my head is an unbearable cacophony of noise, reminding me that last night didn't just happen in some dream or alternate reality. It happened right here in this hut, and it was all my fault.

I take a deep breath and try to focus on the present moment, but all I can hear is the bitter echo of yesterday's mistakes playing on a loop.

A gust of cold air rushes through the room, and it's a welcome relief. It manages to cool my warm cheeks, hopefully hiding my embarrassment.

I look up, and Paxton remains standing there, watching me with those same concerned eyes.

Oh, just say it, for shit's sake.

I'm too embarrassed and upset to let him get close. So instead of engaging with him, I stand and head toward the door.

I'm not even sure if it's still raining, but I need to get out of here. I need space and time to process everything.

When the door opens, I find that it's still pouring rain. The sloped area by the path outside of our huts is flooded. I don't even want to know what condition my hut and possessions are in right now. Now's as good of a time as any to find out.

The moment I hit the first step, I slip, and I'm about to tumble down the stairs, so all I can do is brace for impact.

But the pain never does come because Paxton has once again caught me.

I hadn't even heard his approach. I'd been so fixated on my hut that I was oblivious to the fact he was following me.

"Think that's a good idea, princess?"

That name, and all the memories associated with it, washes the embarrassment away, and anger replaces it.

I tear my arm out of his grip. "Don't call me that," I snap, and his eyes widen.

With my mind on getting to my hut, I splash right through the muddy puddles, not giving a damn how dirty I am.

"Stop, Mallory," Paxton calls, but I keep going. "Dammit, stop being a brat."

That stops me short. How dare he call me that after everything? I bend down, filling my palm with a handful of mud. I stand and turn around to find Paxton up in my personal space. Without another thought, I smear the mud across his handsome face.

He blinks, and his mouth drops open.

"Did you really just do that?" His voice is low and raspy.

An ominous feeling takes over as I stare at his eyes and watch his features turn from surprise to something else. Something that screams, *this is war.*

"Paxton," I say, lifting my hands and giggling nervously. "I didn't mean to."

He leaps forward, throwing me over his shoulder. "That wasn't very nice," he growls, slapping my ass.

I yelp. Not because it hurt, but because it caught me so off guard. He doesn't sound mad, but playful.

What is happening?

He stomps toward his hut with me hanging down his back. I do the customary flailing, but it lacks conviction. "Paxton, let me down."

My words don't even sound believable. I might as well tell the caveman to take me to his lair and have his way with me, for all the ways my objections fall flat.

He stalks up his steps, lowering my feet to the ground. For the longest moment, we stay there, sharing a single breath of air, while the rain pours down around us.

His arms are still around me, pulling me close. I feel his heart beating against mine. As I look up into his eyes, I see something I haven't seen since getting to this godforsaken island . . . regret.

So, instead of pushing him away, I let him hold me. One good thing is that the adrenaline has seemed to help with my headache. It's still there, but it's a little less intense.

"Let's get inside. You're freezing," Paxton says, grabbing my hand and leading me into his hut.

He walks me right next to the edge of the bed, and my cheeks feel warm despite the chill from my rain-soaked clothes.

I was such an idiot last night. I haven't gotten that drunk since college. He might have called me princess, but I don't think he understands the effect that name has on me.

I associate it with all the bad times. Every insult. Every glare.

Standing in the middle of Paxton's hut, I wait for him to speak.

"What happened? What did I do?"

"Nothing," I mutter back.

I should be honest and tell him what's going on in my head, but I don't. I'm stubborn to a fault. Perhaps the one horrific trait I carry that is all my father.

He inclines his head, eyes narrowing. "Lose the attitude, princess."

My shoulders stiffen, and I glare at him. "Again, with the princess?" I grit through my teeth.

"That's your issue? The pet name?" he responds, looking truly confused.

"It's not exactly a term of endearment. It's a condescending nickname you gave me to put me in my place."

He shakes his head. "It's not. I never meant it as an insult. I see it as entirely different."

Had I read him that wrong this whole time?

"I only think of you, eyes closed and mouth open that night when my fingers were inside you. To me, it's a fond memory and a name that is entirely associated with that night."

The air is thick with tension, and I can feel my face getting hot.

No matter how hard I try to push away the feelings that have taken over me, I can't. Paxton's rejection still burns. Now I'm lashing out even though I know I shouldn't. He doesn't deserve it.

Paxton paces. I can feel the anger radiating off him, making my rage swell.

He disappears into the bathroom, leaving me to ponder what's coming. A few minutes later, he returns, face freshly washed free of the mud I'd plastered across his cheek, and a dry shirt to replace the soaked one.

Must be nice as I sit here soaking wet and freezing.

"You should really get out of those clothes. You're going to get sick." He motions toward my wet clothes.

His shirt, not my own. My belongings are next door, likely under a pond of water at this point.

"I don't have anything. It's all over there," I say, pointing toward my hut.

Opening a drawer, he pulls out another white T-shirt and throws it toward me.

"I don't want your shirt," I say, sounding petulant.

I know I need to pull myself together, but I'm too out of my element around this man.

He takes a deep breath. "Mallory, seriously, what's with the attitude today?" His words aren't said harshly.

I can feel the tears welling up in my eyes. I try to turn away from him, but he grabs my arm and pulls me back around.

"You've been angry since you woke up," he says. "What's going on?"

Staring into his deep blue eyes, I finally dare to tell him how I feel.

"I'm mad because you—" I huff, going over the words in my head and finding they sound ridiculous.

"No. Don't do that. Say what you're thinking. I'll stand here all day if I have to."

"You rejected me." The words fly out, and my hands lift into the air before dropping heavily to my side. My fingers start to tap on my leg. "I thought that you wanted me . . . forget it."

Paxton takes a step closer and pulls me toward him. His strong arms wrap around me, and I can feel the warmth of his body.

"Mallory." His voice is soft as his hands move up to cup my face, and he tilts my chin so I'm looking at him.

"Paxton, I—"

"Shut up." Then he slams his mouth against mine.

Chapter Thirty

Paxton

@Stargossip: Radio silence is never a good sign. Who thinks the island has turned into a game of Survivor?

> **@Twistedtealover:** My money is on Paxton.

> **@Moviesaremylife:** @Twistedtealover I think everyone's money is on Paxton.

> **@TeagansStewardFans:** Don't count Teagan out. My girl is scrappy.

> **@Holaypancakes:** All hail the coconut.

SLAM MY MOUTH AGAINST HERS. SWALLOWING HER WORDS OF protest. There won't be any more barbs or circumventing the issues. She's upset that I rejected her. I'll show her just how much I wanted her all along.

On a gasp, her mouth parts for me, and I take full advantage of the moment, slipping my tongue into her mouth and sweeping it against hers.

Our tongues tangle in a rhythm that is all ours.

And I can't get enough.

I've waited too long to kiss her again, and now that I am, I want more.

I'm mad with desire—the need to devour her whole coursing through my blood, zapping all my nerves to life.

It's chaos.

But it's the best kind.

Pulling my mouth away from hers, I look down at her. "You think I rejected you? You think I don't want you?" I rub my hard cock against her, and she groans at the friction. "Does this feel like rejection, Mallory?"

She shakes her head.

"Words."

"No," she whispers.

"Good girl. Tell me you want me, Mal."

She nods, and I shake my head. "I need words," I command again.

"I want you."

That's good enough for me.

I grab the bottom of her soaked shirt, pulling it up and over her head, discarding it to the floor.

"Fuck."

A goddamn siren.

My cock hardens even more at the sight of her pert nipples, begging to be tasted.

Her eyes heat, and I know she wants this just as much as I do.

Placing my hands on her shoulders, I gently lay her back on the bed and spread her legs.

"Pax," she whispers against my lips. "I need you."

This has been a long time coming.

Since the moment I met Mallory, and then when she came storming back into my life, we have been careening toward this moment, and I sure as fuck am not going to fuck this up now.

"Pax—"

"Shh. Before I fuck you, I need a taste."

Dropping to my knees, I place my mouth on her skin. Slowly, I trail a path up until I reach the tiny scrap of cotton covering her.

"These have got to go."

She lifts her hips as I slide the soaked panties down her toned legs. I throw them over my shoulder, eyes never leaving Mallory. I spread her thighs wide, giving me a perfect view of her pussy.

"Please," she pants, lifting her hips up again.

Mallory lying naked in front of me, legs spread, pussy on full display as she begs for my mouth, is my new favorite activity.

"Patience, princess," I say the name, hoping we've passed that hurdle.

Raw lust sparkles in her eyes, and I sigh with relief. I close the distance, moving closer and placing my mouth on her. My tongue swipes out, licking her before my mouth clamps down on her clit.

The sounds coming from her mouth should be illegal. No one should ever hear them but me. I want to drown in her, then feast on her again and again.

I do just that.

Licking. Sucking. Having my fill. The harder I lick, the heavier her panting becomes.

Despite her moans of desire, I take my time, drawing out her pleasure until she's a rubber band pulled so tight it's about to snap.

Mallory's body begins to shake, and I know what she needs. With one thrust of my finger inside her, she comes undone, pulsing around my digit.

Her hips thrust, meeting my finger stroke for stroke, riding out every last ounce of her orgasm.

I wait for her to come down from her high before I speak. "You taste amazing. Better than I could have ever imagined."

She sits up on her elbows. "What about me?" She grins, her face a warm shade of red from her orgasm. "Do I get to taste you?"

"Next time. I can't wait to fuck you."

Her eyes close as though she's already in ecstasy, and I'm losing control, needing to make her mine. The way her body reacts to my words alone is an aphrodisiac. I want more.

"This time, I want you to come on my cock. I want to feel every pulse. Every quiver as you ride my dick." I remove my pants, all the while telling her every dirty detail of what I intend to do to her. My shirt is off next. "Shit."

Her eyes fly open. "What?"

My eyes close with a groan. "Condom."

"You don't have one?" Her voice is thick with need.

I hadn't thought I'd be getting laid on the island, but one does not travel without being prepared. I just hope she doesn't think poorly of me when I admit I do.

I nod. "I never leave home without some. Precaution."

She smiles, showcasing her bright white teeth. She's relieved, which helps me relax. I don't waste time heading toward my bag and grabbing one.

While tearing the wrapper open, I watch Mallory, her pert breasts rising and falling with each breath. Her lips quiver as she watches me slide the rubber over my dick, her mouth parted with want.

With my cock in my hand, I stroke myself from root to tip. She observes my every move. A hunger lingers in her gaze, deep and intense.

My lips part into a smirk as I stroke my dick one more time before parting her and rubbing myself over her clit.

It's pure torture. Heat surges through me with each pass, but I don't rush it. No, instead, I drive us both past the point of insanity. Needing us both desperate before I give us what we both want.

Readjusting my hands under her ass, I slide through her folds.

I stare at her the whole time that I do. I watch as her lips part, her eyes glaze over, and her pants become heavier.

I need to be inside her—now.

My mouth finds hers, and as I run my tongue over the seam of her lips, I adjust her legs to wrap them around my hips and place my cock at her dripping-wet entrance.

With one sudden thrust, I plunge in.

Fuck.

Nothing, and I mean nothing, in the world has ever felt this good.

Pulling back, I watch my dick this time, enjoying the view as I retract and then push back in.

Fucking phenomenal.

Watching my cock as it sinks into her warm heat has my balls tightening and ready to explode.

But I don't. *Not yet.* I take a deep breath and push down the feeling.

She needs to come again.

Thrusting in and out, I watch my cock as it disappears inside her as I pump my hips roughly.

Sweat coats my skin.

No one has ever felt as good as Mallory.

We aren't even done, and I want to start all over again.

Her grip tightens around me, pulling me tighter to her body as her nails bite into my skin.

She's close.

I pick up my pace, and she claws at me, her inner walls fluttering.

"More," she begs. "Harder."

I answer her pleas, picking up my pace. Fucking her at a punishing clip.

My fingers tighten around her hips as her pussy contracts around me, sucking me in and strangling my cock. Mallory feels so good that if I could, I'd spend every minute of my day inside her.

Our skin slaps together. Her moans echo through the hut.

Then, like a flash of lightning, it happens. I come—hard.

It's official.

Fucking Mallory is the most sublime feeling in the world.

And I intend to enjoy that feeling all damn day.

Chapter Thirty-One

Mallory

@Stargossip: Where is everyone? It's been forever and no word from the set. It's official. The world is coming to an end.

> **@Betterthanfiction:** If it's the apocalypse, does that mean I can hang with zombies?
>
> **@Bitchpleaseme:** Zombies are our friends.
>
> **@Sparrowfan:** Something is wrong with you people.
>
> **@Bitchpleaseme:** @Sparrowfan Don't yuck my yum.
>
> **@Sparrowfan:** @Bitchpleaseme You need help.

M Y EYES BLINK OPEN, AND FOR A SECOND, I CAN'T remember where I am. Rain pitter-patters on the roof, and that's when it all comes back to me.

The storm. The rejection. The chase. The mud. *This is becoming a bit ridiculous.*

Then all the wicked things he did to my body take up residence in my head.

My cheeks flush, and my core tingles at the memories of his touch.

Where is he? Did I fall asleep?

Lifting my hands, I rub my eyes, and as soon as my vision returns, I see him.

Standing in the middle of the room is Paxton, getting dressed. His bright eyes seem to twinkle with mischief as he catches me staring. I can't help but smile back at him.

"Hello, sleepyhead." He crosses over to me, leans down, and kisses my mouth before moving back to an upright position beside the bed. "How was your nap? Sleep well?"

"I'm shocked I managed to fall asleep," I reply, the lingering fatigue in my muscles replaced with a surge of energy.

He grins. "I'm not. After that," he says, motioning toward the bed, "I'm surprised you didn't sleep longer."

My whole body warms at the gleaming look in his eyes, promising more where that came from.

Yes. Please.

"How long was I out?" I say, lowering my eyes and trying to get my head out of the gutter.

"A few hours. Long enough for me to catch up on some work."

He slides a black T-shirt over his head, and I want to beg him to take it back off. But I'll keep my dignity intact and not appear desperate for more of him.

"Without internet or power, how did you manage that?"

"I have my ways." His lip tips up into his signature smirk that makes butterflies swarm in my belly.

Heat courses through me as I stare at him. Desire bubbling through my veins.

"You have far too many clothes on," I say despite my earlier conviction not to. My eyes travel down his toned chest and notice the bulge in his gray sweatpants. I lick my lips.

"I was heading down to get us some supplies," he says, trying and failing to hide his amusement at my blatant gawking.

"Is it still raining?"

"Yeah, but we need food."

I push down the blanket and scoot to sit at the edge of the bed. "Do we, though . . .? You could just—" I lift my hand and run my fingers over the cotton sitting low on his hip. "Stay."

"Princess . . ."

My fingers wrap around the material, and I pull it down. His cock pops free of the confines of his pants, and I look up at him.

"What are you doing?" he growls.

"You told me I could have a taste." I bat my eyelashes at him.

He stares down at me for a second, his expression stoic, but then his lip tips up into his utterly lickable smirk. "Do you want my cock, princess?"

"Yes."

"Then what are you waiting for?"

Reaching out, I eagerly take his length into my hand and stroke him a few times before I lean down and place him in my mouth.

As my lips wrap around him, he threads his fingers through my hair, thrusting himself deeper into my throat.

I moan, loving the way he tastes, and each time I do, it must fuel something inside him because he slams himself into my mouth harder and faster.

Reaching around him, I wrap my hands to pull him tighter until he's fucking my throat.

Despite the position, I love having this power over him.

Being responsible for his pleasure, his desire.

His movements become more frenzied, and I think he might come, but then he's pulling out.

"Fuck, princess."

"Why—"

"Inside you." Then I'm being pushed back until my legs hang off the bed. "Need to fuck you."

Closing my eyes, I wait. In the background, I hear the telltale sounds of him rummaging next to the bed, the sound of the condom wrapper ripping, and then he steps between my parted thighs.

His cock is hard against me. I let out a desperate breath as I wait, and then he's doing just what he promised; he's thrusting inside me all the way to the hilt.

I feel so full with him inside me.

It's the best feeling in the world.

My entire being throbs with desire as he pins my hands above my head, my breasts shaking with his movements.

"You feel so fucking tight around my cock. Like a glove gripping me." Paxton slips a hand between us to rub my clit as he keeps pounding into me relentlessly. I whimper in response as wave after wave of my orgasm crashes over me.

His movements get faster, harder, more desperate, and then he shudders inside me, following me over the edge.

A few seconds later, Paxton is up and crossing the space, cleaning us up. The compassion he shows me as he gently cleans me off is so different from the man I argued with in his office—the man who taunted me here on the island.

I can't help but marvel at how far we've come, but at the same time, my pulse beats faster with the fear that if he leaves to go back to base camp, all of this will evaporate.

"Now, I *really* have to go," Paxton says, his words pulling me from my thoughts.

The sound of rain pattering against the thatched roof above us is terrifying; there's no way he should be outside. It's like a million tiny drums beating out an intricate pattern—each droplet angrier than the next.

"Seriously, you're leaving?" I gesture to the door. "In this."

He cocks his head, a full beautiful smile displayed. "Aw," he playfully coos. "Are you worried about me?"

"Umm. No." I roll my eyes, and he lets out a chuckle.

"I like it that you are, but there's nothing to fear. It's mainly just rain." A crack of thunder overhead has my eyebrows lifting into my hairline. "I got this. I'll be back in no time."

He leans down and kisses my forehead. "Very few people are going to be out in this. We should have our pick of food. I'm sure you're hungry."

That's when it occurs to me. He's doing this for me.

He's braving a tropical storm for *me.*

I'm overwhelmed by his care, and I can feel myself melting into the ground like a puddle of goo.

"I guess you better get going, then," I say, my voice thick with emotion.

He nods, heading toward the door. When he pushes the door open, it's easy to see it's well past a simple shower. He looks back at me one last time and winks before disappearing into the abyss of rain.

Being here alone in Paxton's hut is overwhelming. His things surround me, and I feel like an interloper.

The sound of rain on the thatched roof surrounds me as I wait for him to return, hands tapping on the sheets. The storm sounds intense, and my back muscles tighten as I wait. My heart is pounding. I can feel it reverberating through every cell in my body.

He shouldn't be out there. He shouldn't be risking himself like this. The thought of him in the storm has my hands balling into fists and sweat trickling down my forehead. I can barely keep still as I wait. And wait.

I jump up, needing to find a way to exert this pent-up energy. I'm pacing the floors, thinking about all that could've gone wrong out there. Did we need food? Well . . . yes. I'm starving, and I'm sure he is even more. This whole island hut thing was not well thought out. There should've been more provisions stocked. You can't tell me someone on the island didn't know a monsoon was coming.

I'm practically plastered to the window as I watch for him to return, fearing he won't.

That's when it hits me.

I'm falling for Paxton Ramsey.

This is bad.

Chapter Thirty-Two

Paxton

@Stargossip: Still no word from the island. I'm starting to get worried. Think they got washed away by the storm?

> **@Freshwaterlover:** Think they're dead?

> **@twistedtealover:** Seems likely.

> **@twistedtealover:** You know who's been quiet? @deathtothesystem

> **@twistedtealover:** Did we finally run you off? *Insert sad face*

IT'S BEEN POURING ALL DAY, AND ALTHOUGH THE PATH BENEATH my feet is slick with mud and fallen leaves, I venture on.

If it weren't essential for me to get food, I wouldn't be risking it, but we need to eat, and as if on cue, my stomach growls.

There better be supplies, or we're in trouble.

I wonder if Brad and Teagan are faring better than us. If they weren't, I have a feeling that, downpour or not, Brad would be pounding down my door. I'm sure he's livid to lose more days. His next project is looming; if we don't wrap this up quickly, we will be in a tough position.

The rain beats down on me like a thousand tiny hammers, and the trees around me shake from the wind battering the leaves. I'm not prepared for this weather, but I cross my arms in front of my chest the best I can, shielding myself from the storm. It does little to help.

All I can think about is Mallory waiting, and I need to get back to her. I take a deep breath, the smell of wet wood and moss filling my nose.

The thunder booms in the distance, and I pick up my pace, the urgency of getting back propelling me forward.

As far as I can tell, there's no shelter around here, just trees whose branches are caught in an awkward position.

I take a left at the fork in the road and then another right.

The rain's coming down harder now, so I pick up my pace.

Finally, the path opens up to the clearing.

The trailer looks abandoned, but I head over to it anyway, swinging open the door to see if anyone is inside.

No one. I breathe in relief. I really didn't want to bump into Brad or, worse, Theresa, but now that I know it's clear, I start digging around, looking for food.

"You're here!" I jump out of my body and spin around to see Michael standing there, surveying me with his eyes. "I wasn't sure if you guys were okay. Happy to see you are."

"Jesus, Michael. You scared the shit out of me."

He chuckles. "Sorry about that."

"All good. Just grabbing supplies to wait out the storm."

"Good idea. There are clean linens and towels over there." He points at a bin in the corner. "I know there are large sacks to carry stuff in around here somewhere."

He goes digging around, eventually lifting his arm into the air. A bag big enough to stuff a small child in is clenched in his fist.

"Here you go." He hands it over, and I get to work.

I make sure to grab two new sets of sheets and several towels. The bag fills up fast, and I know I can't fill it so full I won't be able to carry it back.

"Need help?" he asks. "There's another black bag if you think you can manage."

I can use the second bag for food. "I can do this."

You have to.

"Do you guys want to move down here? I'm sure Teagan would bunk up with Mallory."

"Trying to move all our stuff in this would be a nightmare. I think it's best we stay put."

It occurs to me that I should probably ask about my client, considering we're in a tropical storm and cut off from the world.

"Have you seen them? Are they okay?"

"Yes. I'm actually here grabbing food for both of their huts. They're fine."

I nod. "Good. I've been worried."

Lies. I haven't given two shits what that entitled prick is going through.

"You sure you don't wanna be closer to him?" His eyes are narrowed as if he knows exactly what we're getting up to on our private side of the island.

I smile even though I want to say *fuck no.* "Yep. But thanks, man." I turn away from him and start grabbing foods that won't go bad.

Water. Peanut butter. Bread.

By the time I have what I came for, Michael is long gone.

The rain has not slowed down in the slightest, but I'm used to it now.

Slinking the bags over my shoulders, I take off, running back down the path, the bags cracking my ass as if to say, *faster.*

I make it back to the hut in record time. I'm breathing a bit labored, and my arms ache.

They'll be sore tomorrow.

I see Mallory peering out the window, waiting for me. I can't help but laugh.

She opens the door and steps aside so I can enter. With a sigh, I step inside and join her in the warm, dry shelter. "You made it."

I wink at her and take off my wet clothes. "You miss me?"

Mallory smiles, her eyes twinkling as she walks over to me, towel in hand. "I did."

"How much?"

She wraps the towel around me and pulls me close, her lips brushing against mine.

"More than anything."

A clap of thunder rips through the sky, and we both jump apart, laughing.

"Thank God you weren't still outside," she whispers, and I can hear the note of fear in her voice.

I look at Mallory's face then, and my jaw tightens. Mallory must read my change of emotions because she squeezes my hand before pulling away. "Let's eat." I nod to the dresser, and I set the supplies down.

"What did you bring?"

"Peanut butter, bread, and a few surprises."

She sighs. "Thanks for doing this."

"Anything for you, Mallory." I take her hand in mine and bring it up to my lips.

Once we make sandwiches, we sit together on the floor and eat, all too aware of the storm outside. But here, in this hut, we're safe and content.

The rain and winds outside may rage on, but there's nowhere else I'd rather be.

Chapter Thirty-Three

Mallory

@Stargossip: Anything? Anyone out there? Earth to the island. We need news!

> **@Ilovebooks:** Maybe we should call in a search party?

> **@doglover626:** I think they died.

> **@Bradforlife:** Blasphemy. Brad is fine.

THREE DAYS HAVE PASSED, AND PAXTON HAS BRAVED THE weather to go back to camp for supplies, almost every one of them. It's allowed him to check on Brad and Teagan, as there is typically someone at camp who has information.

The rain has finally stopped, but the power still doesn't work. Something tells me that because this island is so remote, it might be a while before it's turned on. Production is halted for the time being, according to Michael.

All around our huts is a damn mess of mud and puddles that rise to mid-shin. Paxton has gotten us enough provisions to last a few more days without even having to venture out, but Paxton is obviously growing a little stir-crazy.

The farthest I've gone is across the short expanse to my hut. It's not in as bad of shape as I thought it would be. The bulk of the water is contained to the center of the room. My bed is soaked through, but because of the slits in the bottom of the hut, a lot of the water escaped, rolling down the incline and pooling at the bottom of the hill, making the path to camp a pond.

My suitcase had been stored in the bathroom, which, surprisingly, was the one area that didn't leak. Thankfully, most of my clothes were dry.

A small miracle, considering.

"Come on, let's go," Paxton says from across the room, and I narrow my eyes at him from where I'm lying in bed.

"Where are we going?" I'm still under the blanket, and I'm not in any rush to reenter civilization, and by civilization, I mean the cast and crew.

"We can't stay here all day," he says as he lifts his brow.

"Sure, we can." I drop the blanket and allow my breasts to show. I'm playing dirty, but I don't care.

If my boobs on display are enough to keep us right here in this hut, away from the world, I'll gladly pimp them out.

The idea of bumping into anyone right now and the bubble we've created bursting is too much for me to handle.

With my luck, I'll walk right into Jeffery, who will likely pitch me again. Pax will overhear, and this fun little romp between us will be over. I don't want that to happen because I'm insatiable with this man.

"You're dangerous." He laughs but still pads across the room and grabs my clean tank and shorts I salvaged last night from my hut. "Get dressed."

"No." I pucker my lips and shake my head. Yep, I'm acting like a petulant child.

"Princess . . ."

"I hate when you call me that."

I've repeated this several times, which only seems to encourage Paxton more. We might be on totally different terms than before, but it doesn't change the fact that he enjoys getting a rise out of me.

"Then stop acting like a brat." He winks before throwing the clothes at me.

I huff. "Fine."

Stepping out of bed, I push out my chest and put myself on full display. Paxton can't take his eyes off me, which is exactly what I wanted. I take advantage by seductively getting dressed, which is actually a thing. Not one I've attempted in the past, but based on his heated stare, I'm pretty good at it.

However, despite my goal of keeping him distracted, he doesn't waver.

"Not working, sweetheart." He grins.

"Sweetheart?"

"I like to switch it up."

When I'm only a foot away from him, he reaches out and pulls me into his chest before dropping a kiss on my forehead. "I have plans for us."

"Since when?" I pout, pressing my lips to his chest.

"Since now. I made them when you were taking your little nap."

"I don't want to see anyone but you." I groan, stepping out of his grasp and burying my face in my hands.

It's the truth. The storm gave me a much-needed break from all the drama on this island. I do not intend to return to the fray until the power comes back. Instead, I plan on taking this time as my little staycation from work.

"Oh, you won't."

That has my head snapping up to look at Paxton's face. "Promise?"

"Would I lie to you?"

I narrow my eyes. "Maybe."

He smiles, walks past me, and smacks my bare ass. "Shut it. Let's go."

I quickly throw on my clothes and follow him out of the hut. Instead of taking the usual path, he veers us down a different one. One I've never taken before.

I look around at the foreign trail that leads us in the opposite direction of the camp.

"Where are we going?"

"Nope." He laughs, shaking his head.

"Nope? What the heck does nope mean?"

He glances over his shoulder. "It means I'm not telling you. It's a surprise."

A surprise? What has he gotten up to while I slept?

I typically don't love surprises. In the past, they haven't served me well. But something about Paxton's boyish excitement has me excited.

"This oughta be good." I smile wide and continue to follow him into the unknown.

We walk for what feels like forever, but it's only ten minutes. The path clears and opens out to a small beach.

No, a lagoon.

A private one at that.

It's beautiful.

We're tucked back between rocks that reach up to the sky. It's like something out of a travel magazine. I'm in awe.

Paxton rifles through a bag that he must've brought here earlier. He pulls out a blanket and spreads it out on the remote part of the beach. He thought this through, and my heart swells at that.

What else does he have in his bag of tricks?

The lagoon itself is still, a peaceful mirror reflecting everything around me. I can hear nothing but silence, save for the occasional chirp of a bird somewhere up in the trees.

The clear and inviting water is a deep sapphire color. As we step closer, I can see the pebbles at the bottom. They're surprisingly colorful, ranging from dark blues to lighter grays.

I take off my shoes and step in to feel the water rush around my feet. It feels cool against my skin—refreshing after the long hike.

I take a deep breath and close my eyes, enjoying being surrounded by nature in its purest form.

At this moment, I can feel everything around me—the sun on my skin, the sand tickling my feet, the gentle breeze rustling through my hair, and Paxton's presence as he walks up from behind and wraps me up in his arms.

This is peace. Exactly what I need after the stress this trip has caused.

I wish I could stay here, like this, forever.

We stand together for several minutes, me wrapped in his warmth, looking out at the vast sea in front of us. The water is still, which is surprising considering the storm.

Paxton kisses the back of my neck and then drops his arms and walks off. I don't turn around, knowing he won't venture far.

I'm content, basking in this moment of quiet. I watch the waves crashing against the shore for a few more minutes before I turn from where I'm standing and find Paxton laying supplies on the blanket.

This day is just getting started, and it's already perfect.

Quiet and serene.

With zero power still on the island, it's slim pickings for entertainment, but being with Paxton is enough for me.

After taking a long breath, I head over to where he is and sit on the blanket. We sit like this for hours, talking about life. He's filled me in on his agency's beginning and how he grew his contacts.

He has a friend who owns a fancy club. He's rented out a VIP room every week to wine and dine current and future clients.

He's smart.

I get a glimpse of his humor that I've been unable to appreciate due to our rocky relationship. He's funny. Charming. Hot as hell.

Hours pass as we chat, cuddle, snack on the food he brought, and relax, far from the chaos that camp brings.

The sun is starting to set in the distance.

Streaks of pink dance across the sky.

Paxton sets off to gather some dry wood to build a fire. A task I'm sure is challenging after the storm. If anyone can find some, it's Paxton. He's determined to make this special.

He already has, and it's something I won't forget.

He returns with an armful of logs, no surprise there, carefully placing them in front of us. He pulls matches from his bag and my eyebrows lift.

"That's cheating," I chide, recalling he's more than capable of producing fire without matches. "Boy Scout, my ass."

He grins. "Don't tell Stefan."

I laugh, thinking about that day and how he'd tricked us all. It feels like a lifetime ago but isn't.

"Stefan? Fuck that. I'm telling Brad."

Paxton looks up at me with wide eyes. "He would mock me."

"Most likely," I agree.

"But it got the job done." He gestures to the wood.

The flames are now licking the sides of the logs. The fire's glow illuminates his face, and I can't help but feel mesmerized. He looks like a god. Barefoot and shirtless, manning the fire.

"You hungry?" he asks, and I shrug.

"In this place? Always."

"Good, because I brought plenty of food."

"Oh my God, if you tell me we have to fish, I will kill you."

He whips out whatever is in the bag. "And by fish, you meant s'mores?"

"S'mores? Oh, wow! You win."

"Yes, I do. I know the way to your heart is through chocolate. Sorry, I don't have wine."

I can feel my cheeks flush. He remembered our conversation the other day about my favorite things. Chocolate and Sauvignon

Blanc. He's done all of this for me, and I'm overwhelmed in the best way.

"Let's do this," I say, trying to stave off the tears welling in my eyes.

I'm emotional for many reasons and don't want to embarrass myself in front of Paxton.

The fire crackles and sparks, throwing orange light across the sand. "Do you have a stick?"

He gives me a look as if I've just asked the dumbest question in the world.

"I'm not an idiot. Of course, I have a stick." He rolls his eyes at me playfully.

I respond with a mature gesture. I stick out my tongue.

"Sorry, I forgot you're perfect at everything." My mocking voice only has him laughing.

"You think I'm perfect?" His voice pitches animatedly, making me laugh alongside him.

When things die down, my mouth speaks the truth.

"You know you are."

He nods. "You're right. I am."

Paxton doesn't take compliments well. He's constantly pushing them off with faux conceit. In reality, he's not that guy.

"And you're humble," I deadpan.

"So glad you noticed."

"And a jerk . . ." I bring my hand to my mouth to stifle the giggle threatening to spill out.

"Jeez. Can we just make these damn s'mores already?" He scoffs good-humoredly.

"Thought that might shut you up."

Paxton reaches over and gives me a twig. It's thick enough not to break but small enough to fit the marshmallow.

"Here you go, princess," he says with a cheeky smile. I roll my eyes and stick the marshmallow on the twig.

The fire is like a furnace as I hold the marshmallow over the flames, watching as its surface bubbles and browns slowly. I'm so focused on getting it just right that I barely notice Paxton scooting up next to me.

"Need any help?" he asks, his eyes twinkling with mischief.

I shake my head and keep rotating the marshmallow until it's just how I want it. I pull away from the fire and gently place it on a graham cracker with some chocolate.

"My hands are too small." I giggle as the marshmallow and chocolate ooze from the corners onto my hand. I switch the hand holding it, and when I do, Paxton laughs, too, grabbing the dirty one and lifting it to his mouth to clean off the extra mess.

I shake my head at him and lift the s'more to my mouth to try it.

Both of us take a bite and moan in contentment. It's sweet and gooey with a hint of burnt sugar that lingers on my lips as I savor it.

"I'm so happy it's just us here."

"Agree. I can tolerate you." He takes another bite, groaning. "You're not a pain in the ass like everyone else on this island."

He says it around a mouthful, lips tipped up.

"Hey!" I playfully swat at him.

He swallows, half choking. "Just keeping it real."

"We'll be forced to walk among them soon enough." I inhale deeply, my mood going sour at the thought.

Paxton's hand reaches out, and he lifts my chin so our gazes lock. "What's going on in that pretty little head of yours?"

I think about his question because there's no simple answer. A million things are floating through my mind at this very second.

Is Teagan going to be okay?

Will Theresa keep her mouth shut?

Can we actually wrap up this project?

What will happen to Paxton and me when this reprieve ends?

I tip my chin up, meeting Paxton's eyes. "What are we going to do?"

A crease forms between his eyes. "Meaning?"

"When this bubble pops, and we have to go to work. We have a shit show waiting for us."

We both go silent for a second, each thinking about everything we'll be confronted with. Paxton eventually breaks the silence.

"Well, other than pulling our clients from the production?"

"Yes, other than that, I don't see what more we can do." Paxton nods in agreement.

"You and I both know that isn't a viable option. We all need this."

I nod, knowing he's right. "We can try to talk to Brad and Teagan again. Have a word with Theresa, too."

He groans at the mention of that witch. "Maybe we should all just get drunk." Paxton looks up at the sky. "Yeah . . . I like that plan."

I roll my eyes teasingly. "I'm sure you do, but that's not viable either."

"Buzzkill."

Lifting both hands in a *probably* gesture gets a chuckle from Paxton.

"Truthfully, I think Theresa needs to leave," I admit with a sigh.

"Honestly, I've been wondering why she's even here?" he says, shoving the remainder of his s'more into his mouth.

"I don't understand it either. She has a hold on Teagan that isn't healthy. I don't get it. Teagan is eighteen now. She doesn't need to do what her mom says." My voice rises an octave just thinking about how demanding the woman is of her own daughter.

She seems to care more about money and fame than Teagan, which breaks my heart.

"You feel very passionately about this." I look up to find Paxton staring at me intently.

"Hell, yeah, I do."

He cocks his head and looks at me, but it's like he's seeing something he's never seen before. "Why?" he asks.

I shake my head. I don't want to do this. Not here. Not now.

"It's complicated," I finally say, allowing the fear to dictate my actions.

He nods and says nothing, but his gaze never wavers from mine. He waits for me to continue, but I can only look away. I can't bring myself to look him in the eyes when I broach this subject.

If I talk about my father, I will ruin all the progress we've made. But if I can't talk to him about this, where does that leave us?

I take a deep breath and exhale slowly.

"I know that if I talk about this, you might—"

He cuts me off. "You can talk to me." His hand reaches out and takes mine in his, then he lifts it to his mouth and kisses my knuckle.

It's Paxton's way of reassuring me, of giving me strength.

"My dad is a condescending prick."

At that, Paxton lets out a laugh. His head falls back on his shoulders.

"What?" I cry indignantly.

His head shakes as his chest rumbles with laughter. "That is not what I expected you to say."

"Well, it's the truth; he is. Being the daughter of Thomas Reynolds isn't that different from being the kid of Theresa. Both are controlling, both think they know everything, and both are awful people who only think of themselves. The only difference is, I don't let my father control me."

Paxton continues to look at me, but now it looks like I sprouted a second head.

"Say something," I beg, not liking the quiet after baring my soul.

"You don't have much of a relationship with him, do you?"

"I tried to tell you that, but you were too hell-bent on thinking the worst of me."

He grimaces. "You're nothing at all like I thought." I can feel my cheeks heat at his words. "I'm sorry."

I turn away, my chest filling with emotion.

So much emotion.

I'm overcome by it.

"You didn't know."

He places a hand on my shoulder. "Hey. Look at me," he commands in a soft tone.

I turn back toward him, and a tear falls down my cheek. I swipe it away, embarrassed at how weak I am regarding this topic.

"You thought I was like him, and I get it. It's just . . ."

"Mallory, please. I was wrong. I admit that. Don't cry."

I inhale deeply, pushing down the tears. "I'm over it. I want to move forward." I plaster on a smile that I hope he knows is genuine despite the heavy moment.

He leans forward and places a kiss on my forehead.

"Me, too." He runs his hand down my cheek, rubbing away the moisture. "Say something cathartic."

I lift an eyebrow at his request.

"Go on. Do it," he prompts.

"Fine. You were an ass. Better?"

He bites his bottom lip, trying not to smile. "Much."

Turning toward the beach, I watch the waves crash against the shore. Inhaling, I savor the salty air and tranquility.

I'm determined to enjoy the moment with Paxton beside me.

The warmth of the fire and Paxton's strong grip on my hand give me a unique sense of peace that I haven't felt in a long time.

Soon, the fire starts to die out, and the light fades away. I move to stand, but before I do, warm hands grasp my hand, and he shakes his head. "Not yet."

"And why is that?"

Paxton simply smirks.

Something tells me I'm going to like whatever he has in mind.

Chapter Thirty-Four

Paxton

@**Stargossip:** Low key getting homicidal vibes from Brad. Anyone else?

    @**ZEfronleftBallSac:** Fear of cannibalism is real.

    @**Lexi_H:** Damn, I knew it wasn't just me.

    @**SirKernals_3:** Bro, STFU. You're not funny.

    @**Lexi_H:** @SirKernals_3 It's a fucking joke. Calm your tits.

B EFORE SHE KNOWS WHAT'S HAPPENING, I'M PULLING HER INTO my arms and sealing my mouth over hers, kissing her like a starved man.

It's only been a few hours, but I need her again.

Need to feel her fall apart all around me.

Need to watch her come.

Need to taste her.

Her mouth opens wider, and she lets me in. My tongue sweeps against hers as I devour her.

My right hand fiddles with the string of her shorts, unknotting them but never breaking our connection.

Once they're loose, she lifts without being prompted, and I pull them off her, leaving her in only skimpy cotton panties and a tank.

Pulling back, I look at her with hooded eyes. "This needs to come off." I reach out to pull her shirt over her head before bending down and pulling one of her pert nipples into my mouth.

Sucking until she's gasping for more.

It doesn't take me long to answer her pleas. Unlike before, I don't want to take my time with her. I need her now.

I move to the other breast, and while I lick, I push down my sweats, freeing my rock-hard cock, stroking it up and down.

"Take them off," I say between licks, and I don't need to clarify what I'm talking about. The only thing that separates me from her sweet pussy is her underwear.

"You have to stop for me to take them off." She giggles.

I pull off her breast with a pop and glare at her for stopping me.

"Oh, stop." She laughs. Then removes herself from my lap before she shimmies out of the small scrap of cotton.

"Enough talking. I want in."

She grins up at me, knowing I'm two seconds from losing my mind. Based on the ways her own eyes hood, she is, too.

Lying back, she spreads her legs farther apart, giving me a full, inviting view.

She's fucking divine.

If I wasn't so desperate to be inside her, I'd lick every inch of her body, but I am, so instead, I angle the head of my cock against her.

Slowly, I tease her, moving my dick up and down on her wet slit.

What I would do to fuck her bare.

Leaning over, I reach into my bag and rummage through it until I find the wrapper. I make fast work of sheathing myself.

Any time wasted is a second I'm not inside my girl.

My girl?

Holy fuck . . . nope . . . not going there right now.

Focus, Paxton.

"Paxton," she purrs. "What are you waiting for?"

A grin spreads across my face at her timing. "What do you want, princess?"

"You."

Licking my bottom lip, I ask, "You want me to fuck you?"

"Yes," she moans. "Now."

I answer her plea with the slamming of my hips upward.

Fuck.

She's a fucking queen.

Placing her legs over my shoulders, I slam into her. She's so tight and perfect, and if I could stay here for an eternity, I would.

That's the way I want to go out of this world.

Fucking Mallory.

I retract and thrust back in.

The feeling is sublime.

Like nothing I have ever felt before.

I keep up the pace, basking in the mewling sounds I'm pulling from her.

Sliding my dick out of her and then slamming back in only furthers the noises.

I do this over and over again with the intention of driving her mad.

From my position, I watch as I fuck her, and it's a sight to behold.

The way her eyes roll back, the way her chest heaves. The little pants of breath as she rushes toward release. Reaching my hand between us, I circle her clit with my finger, working her toward orgasm.

Her moans grow more frantic, so I increase the tempo, fucking her relentlessly as I work her over with my hand.

Her pussy clenches around my cock. It's a telltale sign she's about to come.

I pick up my pace, my movements growing frantic and fierce until my balls tighten as her walls spasm around me.

"Fuck." I groan, and she moans at the word. "Come all over my cock." And she does; she explodes around me, squeezing my dick to the point of pain. "Fuck," I repeat as I follow her over the edge before collapsing on top of her.

Yep . . . I could die like this.

Chapter Thirty-Five

Mallory

@Stargossip: The sun is finally shinning. And sources tell me our two favorite agents have been hiding from their clients . . . *together.*

> **@ZFleftBallSac:** No way. Paxton would never.

> **@Lexi_H:** Damn, Paxton woke up and chose boner.

> **@Deathtothesystem:** I thought we got lucky, and they all washed away.

> **@Bitchpleaseme:** @Deathtothesystem You're alive?

> **@Deathtothesystem:** Sadly.

LIKE ALL GOOD THINGS, OUR TIME IN SECLUSION MUST END. THE storm has passed—a thousand years later, so it seems—and last night the power was restored to the island.

Which means back to work today, something I'm not looking forward to.

This bubble with Paxton has allowed me to relax for the first time since I started my company and took on Teagan as a client two years ago.

I've realized that I'm severely overworked.

Completely self-induced. Not that it makes it any better.

I give my all to Teagan, which I don't regret, but it's exhausting.

Now that I'm rested, it's time to get back to my life.

Which brings me to the here and now, leaving this hut and heading to craft services.

"So . . ." Things need to be said, but I don't know how to broach this topic. My cheeks feel warm, but I press on. "What should we do?"

"About?" Paxton asks, eyes focused on his phone. He doesn't even look up at me.

"Umm, us." I want to roll my eyes. What else does he think I'm talking about? *Men.* "We can't let anyone know about us."

"You're right. We can't."

It feels like I've been stabbed in the chest. That he's willing to hide our relationship in the shadows doesn't sit well with me.

Despite knowing Paxton has to agree with me, I can't help but feel hurt that, after the days we spent together, he's not even trying to object.

Not even a little.

Is it too much to ask for him to become one of those crazy, possessive heroes that I read about in books? The type who demands I tell everyone about us. The one who claims to the universe that I'm his and throws me over his shoulder to carry me off into the sunset?

Too much?

Probably, but a girl can dream.

Deep in my soul, I know it shouldn't bother me as much as it does. We don't have a choice, but I want something more. Something concrete, and we haven't discussed anything close to that.

I'm left feeling uncertain, and that sucks.

Will we continue whatever this is after the movie wraps? Is this just an island fling?

None of those things can matter to us right now. We both know that after all the drama this film has endured, it's best that no one finds out. The risk of a leak is too great.

I can already imagine the tweets.

Teagan Steward got the role in Twisted Lily *because her agent is sleeping with the competition . . .*

Yep, this will be staying a secret.

"It will be okay." Paxton squeezes my hand reassuringly.

Despite his words, as I nod, I can't help but feel my stomach bottom out.

I hate this.

It's the way it has to be.

We'll keep our relationship hidden in plain sight till the end of production, and then we can decide what comes next.

With that settled, Paxton and I walk to the door of the hut, and before he opens it, he turns to place a kiss on the top of my head. I melt into the gesture, feeling a modicum of relief. It doesn't have to end . . . yet.

We head toward camp, and his hand falls casually to my hand and then drops just as fast. He can't do that anymore. Not unless he wants us to get caught.

And neither of us wants that.

So instead of holding hands or sneaking affectionate glances, we walk side by side back down the path to craft services in silence.

The air around us swirls with the tension of two people trying their hardest to keep a secret hidden. But no matter how hard we try, I can't help but feel like, soon enough, the secret won't be a secret anymore.

I'm a terrible actress, and I'm not sure I can refrain from spilling my guts.

And that thought terrifies me.

As soon as we make it to craft services, Paxton stops walking.

He's giving me space to head into the clearing alone. I offer a smile before going in search of Teagan.

"Hey." I step up to the table where she's sitting. The first thing I notice when we lock eyes is that she looks tired. Her eyes, usually so bright and full of life, seem dull and strained.

With the break we've had the past few days, that shouldn't be the case. I was tangled up in Paxton, having sex until exhaustion, but I'm still rested. What gives?

"Are you okay?" I ask her, and she smiles sadly before nodding.

"I'm fine," she says and sighs. "It's just been a long couple of days."

She looks down at the table and then back up at me.

"I was nervous about you. I half expected you to demand a different hut so you wouldn't have to be alone."

My heart skips a beat. "I thought you could use the privacy and downtime."

"What about you? If not for Michael, I wouldn't have known if you were okay, clear across the island."

"I was fine." I motion with my head over to where Paxton stands across the grass, talking to Brad. "Paxton checked on me. He even helped me out by grabbing my supplies so I didn't have to."

Teagan's eyes follow my gesture and then looks back at me. "Hmm." Her eyes narrow. "That was nice of him."

I nod, but all I can think about is the suspicion coating her words.

The feeling of my finger tapping has me crossing my arms at my chest to stop my nervous tell.

This isn't going to be easy at all. Teagan is too observant, which could pose a serious problem if she reads me like a book.

My face heats, which is already a mark against me.

"You ready to shoot today?" I ask, breaking the uncomfortable silence and hoping I can distract her from noticing my blush.

"I'm ready to shoot Brad," she mutters under her breath before answering, "I guess so."

She won't meet my eyes, and that concerns me. Something happened, and for the first time, I realize leaving her alone with Theresa might not have been the best move. Anyone would lose their mind being stuck with her for days on end.

"Don't sound too excited." I laugh, trying to break through her solemn mood, but she's not having it.

"Not like I have a choice."

I reach my arm out and place my hand on her shoulder. "You can talk to me if—"

"I'm fine, Mal." Teagan stands from where she's sitting and lifts her head to look at me. "I'm going to go practice for the next scene with Brad. Grab food and catch up. I'll see you later."

With that, she walks away, leaving me alone with my thoughts.

My head spins in a million directions as I make my way to the food table.

What's going on with Teagan, and how can I help her?

No matter how hard I try to sort through the answers, nothing solidifies.

I grab a plate and pile food on it without thought. I'm not even sure what I've grabbed. I'm too distracted.

I'm seated and looking over my breakfast when I feel his presence behind me. I don't need to turn around to know it's him.

My body hums when he's near.

"Want company?" When I hear his husky voice, little goose bumps break out on my arms.

"Think that's a good idea?" I whisper, not wanting anyone to overhear.

"Yeah. I do."

"Have at it." I point at the chair across from me.

When he's on the other side of the table, I realize how awkward it is not being able to be open with him in public. Paxton takes a bite of the food on his plate, looking at me as he does.

"So," I say after licking my fork clean. "Something is wrong with Teagan."

His brow lifts. "Why do you say that?"

"She's acting weird. Cagey."

"How so?" He leans forward in his chair, his elbows resting on the table.

"I can't put it into words, but I can tell something is up." I pause and let out a sigh. "I just wish she would open up to me."

Paxton reaches across the table but then stops. Obviously remembering that we can't do that in public.

"If she wants help, she'll come to you," he says, looking into my eyes with understanding.

Sometimes this job is so thankless. You put your all into it, but if the other party doesn't reciprocate, it all falls apart.

Paxton gets that.

I nod and give him a small smile before turning my attention back to the food on my plate. Thankfully, I grabbed the traditional fare. Bagel, fruit, and cereal. Except I didn't pick up milk or cream cheese.

"Missing something?" he asks, smirking into his coffee cup.

Yet another vital piece is missing.

My head lulls back. "Just my brain."

He chuckles before standing and making his way over to the food table. I watch as he scoops up some items I can't make out from here, and goes about pouring a cup of coffee.

I try not to stare as he returns to our table, but I fail miserably.

"Here ya go," he says, placing the mug of coffee, a carton of milk, a spoon, and a small container of cream cheese he's pulled from his pocket in front of me.

My belly flips. Not only does he know exactly what I need, but he jumped to the task without even being asked. It warms my heart and gives me hope for a future past this island.

"Thank you." I smile.

Considering the amount of thought that went into that, it's such a trivial phrase, but I have to be careful not to gush too much.

We finish our meal in silence, each chancing glances now and then.

It's clear that neither of us knows how to do this. It's too tempting to play footsie with him under the table. Or graze my hand against his—sure-fire ways to raise eyebrows.

All we can do is wait, hope for the best, and pray it doesn't show up in the tabloids.

Chapter Thirty-Six

Paxton

@Stargossip: Word around town is that during the storm, a stick became lodged up Teagan's ass, and somehow, it's still there . . .

> **@Emo_Gurl:** At least she gets some ;)

> **@Musty_rat:** @Emo_Gurl What are you implying?

> **@Lexi_H:** Oop-loving the controversy, spill the tea.

> **@Brad4life:** I feel bad for the branch.

> **@Deathtothesystem:** I hope *Twisted Lily* gets a twisted ball sac.

> **@Lexi_H:** @Deathtothesystem You said it, bitch.

TODAY HAS BEEN PURE TORTURE.

Not only did I have to refrain from touching Mallory, but now I have to deal with Brad and his ramblings about God knows what.

Filming will start shortly, and if I thought the set was dangerous before the storm, it's got nothing on what it's like now. Branches and trees are down everywhere. There are puddles the size of small ponds and cables haphazardly strewn overhead and held on to branches that survived the wind by zip ties.

Let's just hope that holds; otherwise, someone is gonna get fried.

The only good news is that we have power. It was touch and go for a while. While a small crew worked to restore the island, the power cut in and out. I truly thought we would have to stop shooting. But the crew pulled off some miracle, and Stephan concocted the plan to jerry-rig the wires.

The vibrating of my cell phone in my pocket catches me off guard. The last time I checked, the service was still down. I look down at Kevin's name on the screen. I'm sure he's on the verge of quitting with all he's been forced to do in my absence.

Too damn bad. I pay him well, and it's his job to assist.

"What's up?" I answer, putting on my impatient voice. I don't want him keeping me tied up for too long.

"What's up?" he snips. "More like, where have you been?"

I run my hands back through my hair.

"Good to talk to you, too, Kevin. How's the weather where you're at? Good? That's wonderful because I've spent the past few days without power in a monsoon. So, please, continue to jump down my throat about where I've been. Oh, wait . . . I pay *you*." I speak so fast as not to allow him a word in edgewise.

That's the thing about Kevin; sometimes, he forgets that I sign his paycheck and needs a gentle reminder.

"That's a lot to unpack," he says. Papers rustle in the background, and I wonder what he's up to. "So, when are you coming back to the office? Your desk is a disaster."

"Isn't that what I pay you for?" My tone is playful. Despite my annoyance with him at times, he's a good guy.

"And for my witty personality," he replies with gusto.

"Yep. That's it." I chuckle. "I have to extend another week or so. We lost five days of shooting due to the storm."

"What?" He gasps. "Another week? Are you serious?"

"Unfortunately."

He sighs. "Welp, I guess I'll reschedule your appointments."

"You do that. Make sure to make them for three weeks out to buy me time to finish up here and get caught up."

"Will do." There's a long pause before he speaks again. "While I have you, Andrew needs to speak with you."

"Put me through to him."

"No problem. Stay dry," he jests.

The line goes silent as I wait to be transferred. Talking to Andrew is as bad as talking to Brad. The only difference is that I'm Andrew's boss.

"Man, where have you been?" He's annoyed.

Join the club.

"You know where I am. Stuck on an island, shacking up in a hut that barely keeps dry, working with weather that has to be karma from a previous life."

"Yeah, that shit hole is blowing up on Twitter. Last I heard, you guys were roughing it in the middle of a hurricane. The tweets are hysterical. Apparently, you guys are one day away from resorting to cannibalism."

"Hardy har har. There's plenty of fish."

"Should I even ask if that's a double entendre?"

We've just started talking, and I'm already done with this man.

"What's up, Andrew?" I say, trying to get him to the point of this call.

"I wanted to see when you'd be back."

I glance down at my phone, checking the time. "It'll be at least another week."

"What? You can't be away that long."

I count to ten, not wanting to lose my cool. My company has thrived because of my relationship with my team. I won't snap at him because I'm having a day.

"Miss me?" I tease.

"More like I need the help," he barks, and I don't like his tone.

"Can't you do your job without me around? That *is* what I pay you for." I faux yawn. "Do you need me to find someone else to do your job?"

"Nah. I'm good. Have fun in the wilderness. You're not needed."

"Oh, how tides turn. I'll be back as soon as I can. Hold down the fort, and we'll discuss some reward for the extra weight you've all pulled." I hang up the phone before he can say anything else.

I take a moment to observe the chaos on set. Shaking my head, I let out a sigh.

Hopefully, somewhere within that mess is an actual movie being made, but I'm not hopeful.

Someone taps my shoulder. Startled, I turn around to find Natasha looking at me with that annoyingly seductive smile that she always throws my way. I never wanted to sleep with her, but after being with Mallory, I certainly don't.

"Paxton, I need you to come with me," she says, batting her eyelashes a little too relentlessly.

My first reaction is to say no thank you and walk away. I have no intention of doing any more of this woman's job. Every idea implemented to save this production has come from Stefan, Mallory, or me.

But I agreed to play nice and work with the set's publicist. However, I never agreed to ditch the set, and my client, to run off with her. "What can I do for you?"

"We need to talk about the tweets that occurred during the storm."

I haven't even had a chance to get caught up with the tweets. Oddly, it's been the last thing on my mind. "I think that's a good idea. Let's do that later with everyone. It's something all of us should be apprised of."

Her mouth opens and shuts, but I don't give her time to object. I want nothing to do with being alone with this woman. She might be in PR, but she's shown she's anything but professional.

For all I know, she's behind the tweets. I won't give her ammo to roast me with.

I turn around before she can say anything else and quickly walk away.

Before I can stop myself, I'm headed toward Mallory.

I'm a moth to a flame, bound to get singed.

She's standing beside a tree, leaning back with her arms crossed, watching the set with a blank expression. She looks so beautiful at this moment, and I can't help but stop and stare. I'll take this time and enjoy the peace before returning to reality.

Despite knowing I shouldn't, I sneak up on her, grab her hand, and pull her behind the tree. She yelps.

"Shh. It's only me." I turn her around so she's facing me.

Her eyes light up in anticipation, and she opens her mouth to say something, but I stop her, slamming a brutal kiss to her lips.

Fucking heaven.

Chapter Thirty-Seven

Mallory

@Stargossip: Something's up on the set. It seems Paxton and Mallory have both extended their stay. Guess filming isn't smooth sailing, after all.

> **@Betterthanfiction:** Guess it was too good to be true.

> **@Deathtothesystem:** @Betterthanfiction Oh, that's cute. You actually thought this film was being made.

> **@Betterthanfiction:** @Deathtothesystem What's your problem?

> **@Deathtothesystem:** Everything!

PULL AWAY FROM PAXTON, PUTTING MUCH-NEEDED SPACE between us. It's certainly not what I want, but it's imperative we do. We both know why we can't be seen together—Teagan and Brad would be livid if they found out.

It's our job to go to bat for our clients. If Teagan came to me with an issue about Brad that I found to be ridiculous, she would assume I was saying so because of my relationship with his agent, and vice versa.

It's a huge conflict of interest while this movie is in production. Especially considering this film has been riddled with issues.

Doesn't make it easier, though.

"You can't sneak up on me like that," I hiss at him.

"No?" Paxton retorts in an infuriatingly calm voice. His eyes are dancing with a mischievous glint. He's enjoying himself.

At least one of us is.

I'm now riled up and horny, with no means to take care of the problem.

"No." My voice is barely louder than a whisper, but it feels like I'm in a library—and never quiet enough—I'm petrified everyone will hear.

He leans closer, his lips dangerously close to mine again. "What do you want me to do then, princess?"

I step back. I can't be locked in his gravitational pull. I'll never get out if I do. Looking away, I can't bring myself to remind him of what has to be done. That we need to keep our distance.

It feels like a ball of sand forms in my throat, itchy and uncomfortable.

Paxton nods slowly, not needing the words but understanding, regardless.

We stand in silence for a few moments but are pulled out of it by a sound coming from the set.

"Fuck." Paxton groans. "Now what?"

"You go first." I gesture for him to go back to where the commotion is happening.

Once he does, I count to ten and follow him. What I discover is utter chaos. Stefan is yelling at everyone on set, hands waving around, face redder than a ripe tomato. His eyes are bulging out of their sockets, too.

Jeez. What has him going off?

My gaze darts across the space, searching for the reason for his tirade. That's when I find Teagan.

She glances at me, and then her head moves, and if I'm not mistaken, I think she's now looking at Paxton.

It's too hard to tell from where I am, but it's concerning, nonetheless. What is she seeing? Does she suspect?

Picking up my pace, I head over to her.

"What's going on?" I ask when I'm standing beside her.

"Stefan's freaking out." She turns toward me, eyes narrowed. "Where were you?"

I pause, trying to think of how to respond, but then Stefan shouts again.

"Where is the fucking tarp?" he yells.

Tarp? What tarp? Could he be any less specific?

"Where is it?" he bellows, his voice echoing through the entire set. "Can anyone do their job on this goddamn set?"

I have no clue why a tarp is needed or what's so special about it, but it has him in a tizzy, unlike anything I've seen since arriving on the island.

The tension is high, and the clock is ticking, but nothing good will be accomplished if this is the atmosphere he's creating.

Paxton moves toward Stefan. "Calm down," he says in a soothing voice that stops Stefan mid-rant. "You need to take a step back. I promise once you do, you'll find it."

He looks over at Paxton and then nods before turning back and looking at the crew.

"Be ready to shoot in five. Tarp or not." Then Stefan storms toward Michael.

I would have thought the set would be calmer without Theresa here today, but I'm wrong again.

Doesn't matter who's on set. This place is cursed.

I watch as Paxton heads over to Michael and Stefan.

Good.

Paxton can handle this.

Hell, he probably can build a tarp, too. There isn't very much he can't do.

"What has you smiling over there?" I look up to find Teagan assessing me.

Shit.

She's definitely on to something, and that is not good.

"Umm . . . nothing."

Good one, Mal, 'cause you're not being totally obvious.

Her eyebrow lifts, and one side of her lip does, as well. "Really? Because it doesn't look like nothing."

"Is Theresa giving you crap for not having her on set?" I try to divert her attention.

She turns toward them, watching Michael and Stefan talk animatedly.

"Surprisingly, no," she says nonchalantly. "Or at least, not yet. But today's the first day back, so who knows with her."

I sigh. "As your agent, I think, moving forward—"

"I know what you're going to say, and good luck with that. The only reason she's not on my case about kicking her off today is because she claims she has things to catch up on since we finally have power."

It's my turn to lift an eyebrow. What the hell could Theresa be up to?

"But that doesn't mean I'm going to be able to convince her again tomorrow."

"True." I purse my lips. "But we can try to make a case for you if you—"

"If you think that's going to happen, you really don't know Theresa well." She clenches her jaw, and I can tell it's time for me to back off.

Teagan hasn't been the same recently, and right now, like the past few times I've been around her, she is someone else entirely. The sweet, innocent girl I signed is nowhere to be found. In her place is an angry, jaded girl desperate for . . . what? Escape?

She's been like this since the storm, making me wonder if something happened.

Not that she would tell me.

Been there, tried that, and was shot down immediately.

Teagan isn't budging on the information department.

I'm about to change the topic, but Stefan is back and waving her over.

"Time to work," she drawls before heading back to Stefan without another word to me.

I watch as she slinks along, looking forlorn and exhausted. Hopefully, I'm not too late to fix whatever her problem is. She looks on the brink of a meltdown. I've witnessed it before through my father's clients.

I've been around long enough to see the writing on the wall.

I survey the set again and find everything is calm.

"That was fun." Paxton steps up beside me.

I turn to look up at him. "Did you get him sorted out?"

"We found the tarp, if that's what you're asking." He sucks his teeth, eyes turning to slits as he watches the cast.

"Something else wrong?"

He lets out a sigh. "So much, but I don't even know where to start."

"From the beginning?" I raise an eyebrow. He chuckles, but now that I know Paxton better, it sounds hollow and forced.

He looks around before continuing. "Listen, the whole set is on edge. Not only are we behind on shooting, but the storm, well, it did damage to locations we need for key scenes. Stefan is trying to figure out what to do." His voice drops to barely above a whisper. "And the worst part . . . is that it will be leaked."

"How do you know that?" My voice pitches.

He gives me a look that says, *isn't it obvious?*

"Since the storm lifted, the tweets have already started back up. It might be too late for us to control the effects." He shakes his head and takes a deep breath. "I just hope we can get back on track and this whole thing doesn't implode in our laps."

I've been sleeping on the job, and it shows. He's aware of these new tweets, and I haven't even gotten caught up on them. I need to turn my focus from all the dirty things Paxton and I got up to during the storm and back on my work. If I don't find a way to fix this, it could bury Teagan's career . . . and mine.

"Thanks for telling me," I reply sincerely. "I appreciate you not leaving me in the dark."

A few weeks ago, he wouldn't have told me any of this. He would have let me sink.

"I've got to go deal with Brad. I'll see you later."

I nod. His comment is vague, and I spend too much time mulling it over. What's going on with Brad? Is it something to do with Teagan?

Finally, I take a deep breath and say fuck it.

If it is, I'll find out soon enough.

Instead, I find a quiet spot and queue up Twitter, ripping off the Band-Aid and getting caught up. If I don't uncover the leak, this entire movie could be over before it wraps.

Chapter Thirty-Eight

Paxton

@**Stargossip:** Welcome back, cast and crew of *Twisted Lily* . . . I'd say welcome back to Stefan, too, but we all know how that would go over. If pictures tell a story, what would this one say? You're welcome ;) * Picture of half-crazed Stefan attached. *

> @**Cruelgirl810:** I was served meat as a vegan.
>
> @**Bradforlife:** I haven't shit in two weeks.
>
> @**Deathtothesystem:** Why are these people still here?
>
> @**Lastman_standing:** How much is this going to cost me?
>
> @**Sirkernals:** Taxes! I hate taxes.

IT'S BEEN FIVE DAYS SINCE WE'VE BEEN BACK ON SET. FIVE DAYS of pretending Mallory and I barely tolerate each other while spending five days secretly in bed with her every night.

Her thatched roof has been fixed and the water removed. The

place is spotless, more so than mine. Every night as the island sleeps, I sneak into her hut and have my wicked way with her.

Both of us are insatiable.

It's a wonder we can keep our masks on during the day.

To be honest, it gets harder every day. Just watching her talk to another man is taxing on my nerves.

Even right now, as I'm leaning against a tree, supposedly watching whatever shit they are filming, I'm watching Mallory look uncomfortable as Jeffrey rattles on about God knows what.

I will have to ask her about that one of these days.

But the thing with Mal is that neither of us ever talks business when we're alone. It's an unspoken rule.

It's as if we both understand how precarious of a situation we're in. If we let the real world into our bubble, there's a very good chance it will pop.

I watch for a few more moments before turning to walk down the path to get some privacy.

There's a call I have to make, and I can't interrupt filming.

The path is overgrown, dense, and dark. Despite being two o'clock, the sun is only a sliver of light where I am.

The path forks and I take the way that leads back to craft services; at this time of day, it should be empty. It also happens to have the best reception.

Flies buzz around me in swarms, and I swat them away as I move forward. Ever since the rain, the island has been overcome with bugs, which is just one more setback.

Finally, I'm in the familiar clearing, and just like I thought, no one is here.

I take out my phone. The battery is almost empty, but I have enough to make this one call. I key in the number I've been dreading to dial, and as soon as he says hello, I can tell that he knows what this call must be about.

"Let me guess, you're not coming back tomorrow," Kevin answers with a drawl that sounds nothing like his intended accent.

"They still need me here."

"Really?" he pauses. "From what I was reading, other than Stefan, nothing insane has happened."

"It's still touch and go with Teagan and Brad. The moment I leave, all hell will break loose, and I'll have to rush back here." I groan. "It's best I stick it out and ensure this gets wrapped up."

He's quiet for several moments, and I wonder what he's thinking. I don't have to wait long.

"Is this about Mallory Reynolds?"

My head jerks back even though he can't see it. That's the last thing I expected him to say. How the hell would he come to that conclusion?

"What?" I sit down on a nearby chair, needing to collect myself. "Why would you even ask that?"

"That's not a no, Paxton." He laughs.

"Jesus, Kevin. Do you think me incapable of making decisions without my dick getting involved?"

"We both know that appendage leads the show."

I scoff. That's not true at all. Do I like to entertain women? Sure.

At least I did. After having Mallory, that life no longer appeals to me.

"I'm turning over a new leaf," I say, trying for semi-serious.

He's quiet for a moment, and I wonder if the call dropped or if my phone finally died. Then I hear him sigh.

"How far back do you want me to push your meetings? Who do you want everyone speaking to if they need something?"

"Send them to Andrew. Actually, Chris or Beth would probably be a better fit for everyone." That makes him laugh again. "It's just for a few more days. I'll be back soon."

"I'll make sure things don't fall apart around here. But you might need to spring to cater some lunches. These hangry bitches are overworked and starved, and I'm getting the brunt of it."

I laugh. "Done. You've got my card info. Make it happen."

"On it, boss. Good luck with the new leaf."

There's something like a challenge in his voice, but he doesn't say anything, and the line goes dead.

Despite my assurances otherwise, Kevin is right. This is about Mallory.

She needs me here, and I need to be here for her.

I stand, looking at the path ahead of me, and with a deep breath, begin the walk back toward today's location. For the entire trek, all I can think about is what I want to do to her tonight, and I do realize my train of thought isn't where it needs to be.

As soon as I spot Mallory, I can tell she's uneasy. She's no longer talking to Jeffery, who is currently striding away in the direction of Michael. Now, Bill is beside her, and by the way Mallory's body tenses and her eyes dart around, it seems she's looking for an escape route from him. Her shoulders are hunched, and her lips form a thin line. She's obviously done with the conversation, and it makes my blood boil. My fists ball up instinctively as I stalk toward them.

"Mallory," I say in an effort to sound cool and collected, even though fury pulses through my veins. "Can I speak to you?" I do my best to make it sound like I have an issue that needs to be resolved.

We take a step away from Bill, and I ask, "Are you okay?"

"I'm fine," she responds, her voice surprisingly steady. Bill turns to me with a sneer on his face. It's clear he was eavesdropping because he has the balls to say, "This is between Mallory and me. Beat it."

I ignore him, instead focusing my attention on Mallory. She meets my gaze and gives me a slight nod, as if encouraging me to do something.

"Bill." The anger in my voice is unmistakable now, and Bill takes a step back as if sensing how volatile I am.

"What do you want?" he grunts, too close to her for my liking.

"For you to leave Mallory alone."

He cocks his head arrogantly. "Now, why would I do that?"

"Because I'm telling you to." My voice is low and angry but surprisingly calm, considering how furious I am at this guy.

Bill laughs a dismissive sound that sets my teeth on edge. "Just having a little fun. What's gotten into you?" His voice has the sharpness of broken glass. He leans in closer, and I can smell the musk of his cologne mixed with sweat.

I take a step closer, but Bill doesn't back down. Instead, he moves in, ready to throw down. My fists clench at my side, and as I'm about to speak, Mallory steps up beside me and places a hand on my shoulder. "Leave, Bill. Now." Her voice is loud and confident.

She stands tall, her back ramrod straight and her eyes blazing. She may be small in stature, but at this moment, she looks like a giant ready to do battle.

Bill looks back and forth between the two of us, and for a moment, I can see uncertainty in his eyes, but it quickly passes. He grunts and takes a few steps back.

"Fine," he mumbles before turning on his heel and walking away.

Mallory and I stand there in silence for a few moments before she finally speaks.

"Thank you," she says, her voice barely above a whisper.

I nod and give her a small smile. "Are you sure you're okay?" I pause for a moment before continuing. "What the hell was that all about?"

She meets my gaze and nods. "Yeah, I'm fine. He was just . . . being inappropriate. Trying to convince me that we should hook up."

I give her a tight smile. "Come on." I start to walk, and she keeps pace. "I'll talk to Michael later about getting Bill kicked out of here."

"Do you think that's necessary?"

"Yes. He's a predator. If he doesn't get his way with you, he'll move on to Teagan."

"Shit," she whispers, all the fight in her evaporating in front of my eyes. "That can't happen."

We continue to walk, and the moment we're away from prying

eyes, Mallory collapses against me, her shoulders sagging in relief. I wrap my arms around her and hold her close, feeling the hammering of her heart against mine.

"Can we go back to the hut?" she asks. "I'm pretty shook. He was very aggressive."

"Let's go." I take her hand and lead the way, feeling a wave of protectiveness wash over me as we walk away.

I'll make sure that fucking sick asshole is gone and never works in this industry again. Men like him are toxic predators. If he has the guts to pull something like this on a small set, I shudder to consider what he's done to some poor girl, or girls, on other sets. He won't get away with it where Mallory's concerned.

A thought ricochets through my head . . . She's mine. *Fuck.*

Chapter Thirty-Nine

Mallory

@Stargossip: Apparently, losing your cool on the set of *Twisted Lily* isn't just reserved for the cast and crew. Rumor has it that an angry Paxton almost threw down over Mallory Reynolds.

> **@2/14wayy:** He can be my knight in shining armor. ;)

> **@Cloudyqueen69:** I'd gladly let him fight for my honor.

> **@Deathtothesystem:** Am I the only person who sees this as a problem!?

TWO MORE DAYS HAVE GONE BY, AND AS PROMISED, BILL IS OFF the island.

Everyone is back to work, and finally, the film is making progress. Although, I'm afraid to admit that out loud for fear it'll all come crashing down around us.

"Where are you taking me?"

Paxton swings his head around to smile down at me. "Everyone is shooting at the waterfall, so I'm taking you for a little break."

My lips form a thin line, but the corners are tilted up. "A little break?"

His mouth curves up into a grin. "Yep."

"And you don't think our clients will have a problem with that?" I arch my brow, not believing that at all.

"Well . . ."

I wrinkle my nose. "Well, what?"

"They don't really know."

That makes me stop walking, placing my hand on my hip. "What do you mean, they don't know?"

"Stefan decided they were filming an intimacy scene, and since it's a closed set for that . . ." He smirks.

"Wait." I hold my hand up. "They weren't supposed to shoot that until next week."

"I pulled strings."

I lift a brow. "How?"

"I know people." I smack his gut, and he grunts. "It's the perfect day, and with the island's weather being inconsistent, I suggested they get it over with. Stefan agreed."

Taking my hand back in his, he pulls me along to continue to follow him. I'm not sure where we're going, but I let him lead the way. This island is a labyrinth. No matter how long I've been here, these damn overgrown paths feel like I'm lost in a maze.

We make our way to a small dock with a tiny speedboat bobbing against its wood posts. I shake my head. The last time I was on a boat, it didn't go so well for me. This one looks less safe than the other.

"Umm. No." I stop in my tracks, refusing to take another step closer. "Nope. Pass. I don't think so."

"Do you trust me?" he asks, hands perched on his hips. He levels me with a puppy-dog look, and a small part of me begins to thaw to the idea.

"I do . . . but—"

"No buts. You either trust me or you don't." He shrugs.

"You're being evil," I jest.

"Probably, but that isn't going to change, so . . . get your pretty little ass on the boat, princess."

I hesitate for a moment, hands gripping the edge of my shorts. "Do I have to?"

"Well, seeing as, at some point, you have to—I don't know—get back to the set, yeah, you're going to have to."

I playfully stick my tongue out at him. "You suck."

"But you're better at it."

I roll my eyes, and he begins to laugh. "Ass."

"Thought you'd never ask."

A brief shiver ripples through me, but I push it down when I see Paxton extend his hand toward me.

"Come on. I'll help you."

I purse my lips teasingly. "I don't need your damn help."

Moving forward, I step onto the back of the little speedboat. It rocks with the sway of the water beneath us. I grip the side of the boat so hard that my knuckles turn white.

"We aren't moving yet." His mouth quirks with humor.

"It moved." I glower.

"Boats do that," he deadpans, and if looks could kill, the glare I throw at him would make his head explode.

"Mallory, you need to trust me. I'd never let anything hurt you." His voice is softer than usual, and I know without a measure of a doubt that he means it.

He wouldn't. He's a protector.

Little butterflies take flight in my belly and swarm faster when he steps on and sits behind the wheel.

He slowly maneuvers us away from shore, easing into an even pace.

"Relax," he says with a smile, holding out his hand. "You're safe with me."

I take his hand and relax, allowing the wind to blow my hair back, feeling like I'm soaring through the sky.

We speed off in silence for what seems like hours, but what is most likely only a few minutes. The sunlight streaks across the water. I can't help but admire how beautiful it all is. It sparkles on the water's surface like millions of tiny diamonds.

"It's beautiful," I whisper, as if speaking too loudly would break the spell.

He can't hear me over the purr of the motor, but as if he did, he squeezes my hand gently.

Eventually, he slows the boat down. We're far from where we started but close enough to the island to see the shore clearly.

"It's so much bigger than I thought," I say, staring at the large expanse of land.

"Where do you think we get all our supplies?"

"Wait, seriously? Isn't the island empty? Or deserted?"

That makes him laugh. "No. Granted, it's not what you think. It's a skeleton crew, and they don't cross over often. Stefan's rules, but that's where the generators are."

"Wow, Stefan and his insane rules. That man is really bizarre."

"He is." He nods. "But he's also a genius."

"A pain-in-the-ass genius."

His mouth twitches with amusement. "True."

My gaze skates over the vast distance of the ocean and then back to land. The sun beats down on us from above, its rays reflecting off the surface of the ocean and creating a kaleidoscope of blues and greens.

I feel like I'm looking through stained glass out here.

"Now what?" I ask.

"Swim? Sunbathe?"

"Out here?" I gesture around. "How?"

"I'll drop anchor. Then we can spread out up there." Paxton points at the flat front of the boat that is a few steps down and has cushions set up.

"Won't someone see us?"

"Who cares? I said sunbathe . . . dirty girl."

I bite my lower lip, realizing my mind went straight to sex. I turn my focus to laying out and swimming. Sounds relaxing, which I could use after the past few days. "Okay."

That one word is enough to set Paxton into action as he makes work of whatever one needs to do to park this thing, and I pull off my shirt and shorts. I'm not wearing a bathing suit since this was a spur-of-the-moment idea, but my thong and bra are close enough. I'll return to the hut before heading to the set to grab something new.

"You can take that off, too." He steps up behind me, hands making quick work to unsnap my bra while placing kisses on my neck.

"Oh, can I?" I giggle at the feel of his lips on such a sensitive part of my body.

The flimsy material falls to the floor of the boat.

My nipples pebble as the ocean air hits them.

Paxton's hands lower. "You can lose this, too." Then his warm hand lowers my panties down my hips and off my legs.

Once I'm bare in front of him, he places one more kiss on the back of my neck.

Then he turns me around. Our gazes lock, and just as he's about to lean in and kiss me,

a sound of a boat has my heart lurching.

"Fuck. Quick, get down."

Without a second thought, I drop to my knees. "What's happening?"

The buzz of a motor dies down as whatever was approaching veers in the opposite direction.

"Shit. That was close." Paxton chuckles.

"What was close?"

"A boat. But they're far enough away that they couldn't have seen you."

"Are you sure?" My eyes go wide. "Because you told me no one was out here."

"That's not exactly what I said, Mal."

I glance up at him to find an irritating grin staring back at me. "Yeah. You did."

"No, if you remember correctly, you said, and I quote, 'Won't someone see us?' And I said, 'no.'"

"And . . . how is that any different?"

"Because no one saw you, princess. I made sure of it." He shrugs, dismissing my panic.

"By making me get on my knees," I deadpan.

"Well, you *are* hidden," he teases.

I smack his leg. "You're such an ass."

"And that's what you like about me."

Placing my hand on his thighs, I pat his leg for him to look back down at me. "Pax, are they still there?"

"Yeah, but I promise where you're at, they can't see you."

"And I'm supposed to sit here, on my knees, doing what?"

He lifts his brow. "I have a few suggestions."

"Men." I roll my eyes.

"You love it." He's not wrong. I do love his wit, humor, and playfulness. With my hands still on his shorts, I trail my fingers up, all the while still looking up at him. "Princess."

"What?" I respond in my best attempt at a sexy voice. I'm not sure if it's working, but when Paxton's dick twitches in his pants, I think it is.

"What are you doing?"

"You're the one who alluded to it," I say, trying for innocence.

"Do you want me?" I nod at his question. The look he's giving me is enough to make my legs shake. "Take my cock out, princess. Get my cock ready so that I can fuck you."

I can't help the goose bumps that explode all over my body. I'm electrified with lust. It filters through every inch of my body—a heavy feeling pooling in my stomach.

"We can't."

"We can. I would never allow it if someone could see you." His hands rest on my head, his fingers toying with strands of my hair.

"Take my cock out, princess."

My shaky hand pushes his shorts down, freeing his hard length.

I look up at him, but he's looking off into the distance, most likely watching the boat passing by.

All I can do is trust him that they won't see.

And I do.

That's what I realize as I lean forward and wrap my lips around him. I trust Paxton implicitly.

As I take him deeper into my mouth, Paxton threads his fingers tighter through my hair so that he can control my movements. His thrusts intensify as he pushes forward with his hips and begins to fuck my mouth.

His rhythm is brutal and powerful, and I can't get enough, but just as I'm about to reach down between my legs, he pulls his cock out of my mouth and lifts me up off the ground. "Bend over. Because I want to fuck your sweet pussy now."

"But—"

"They're gone." His voice sounds pained, like he's desperate to be inside me. "Bend over, princess. Now."

I love when he's dominating, but I love pushing back even more.

A good submissive, I am not.

"You can't be serious?" My words lack conviction, and he pulls a face that tells me that he knows what I'm up to.

"I never lie about fucking." He smirks, and I do as he says, standing and then leaning my upper body forward.

The windy air whips at my skin, making me shiver with need.

Before I can ask him what he's waiting for, he's sliding in and stealing my breath. I gasp at the feel of him filling me to the hilt.

"Fuck!" he groans as he begins to thrust inside me.

With each drag of his cock through my flesh, I feel myself building toward release, and it doesn't take long for me to fall over the edge. The moment Paxton slips a hand between us, I explode, and not long after that, he's jerking inside me and flooding me with his release.

This moment on the open water is sublime, and I don't want it to end.

Chapter Forty

Paxton

@**Stargossip:** Just spotted Paxton Ramsey taking a sail around the island. So where's the tea, you ask . . . ? He might not be alone. ;)

> @**Fairytalelover:** Please be Teagan. That Ramsey is hot.

> @**Ihatehollywood:** Really? This is what you're calling gossip now?

> @**Twistedtealover:** I have to agree with @Ihatehollywood. Give us Teagan/Brad dirt.

> @**Deathtothesystem:** You all need a life.

NOTHING HAS EVER FELT THIS GOOD.
        Feeling Mallory's warmth surround me is the best feeling in the world.

But then, like a bucket of ice water being dumped on my head, I realize why it feels so damn good.

"Fuck."

Mallory turns over her shoulder, her wide blue eyes searching mine.

"What's wrong?"

My dick is still twitching inside her as I speak. "I didn't use a condom."

She stares at me for a beat, her features blank and unreadable.

What is going through that beautiful brain of hers?

Anger?

Betrayal?

I watch her with an air of caution, silently hoping I haven't fucked everything up.

Much to my surprise, she observes me through lowered lashes, a look of amusement reflecting back at me.

"I trust you, Paxton." Her mouth curves up. "Plus, I'm on the pill. So . . . if that's what you're worried about, there won't be any baby Paxtons running around."

The thought of her having my kid one day has my dick twitching.

At least the thought of trying and the fucking that entails does.

Although, I don't hate the idea of settling down with her and eventually having a family.

What the hell is wrong with you, Pax!

You've known this girl for only a few months, and most of the time, you've spent it hating her. Now you want her to have your kid?

I blame it on the post-orgasmic high and push the thought away.

I pull out of her and then motion to the translucent blue ocean. "Let's wash off."

"That's one way to clean ourselves." She laughs.

Taking her hand in mine, I walk us to the back of the boat.

"On three. One. Two. Three." We jump.

Our bodies hit the water at the same time, my legs kicking out to tread.

The sound of Mallory's laughter rings through the air. It's

infectious, and I can't help but throw my head back and chuckle alongside her.

Now submerged, we both swim around, copping feels under the shield of the water.

Mallory's arms glide as her legs kick out to keep her in place.

She gives me an impish smile and swims away from me. I lunge forward, my hands digging into the water as I propel myself after her.

I'm determined to catch her.

Her laughter turns into a playful scream as she kicks faster, swimming for the surface with all her might.

Finally, I grab on to her slim waist and pull her back into my chest with one arm.

"You think you can get away from me?" I grin.

"Maybe." She giggles, squirming while attempting to stay afloat.

We both float on our backs together, side by side. The sun is warm on our faces, and the water is refreshing to the touch. It's moments like these that make me feel alive.

"We probably shouldn't stay out here too long. We'll attract sharks."

"Sharks?" she screeches, bolting upright. I pull my bottom lip into my mouth to smother my smile. "Are you serious?"

"Maybe . . . maybe not," I say, twirling around in the water.

"Paxton . . ." she warns, and I dive toward her, hearing her shriek before submerging myself.

When I break the water's surface, I'm directly in front of her, pulling her into me with one arm. I place a kiss on her lips. "We need to dry off."

We both climb back into the boat, lying next to each other on the sundeck at the back of the boat, the sun beating down on us.

Mallory turns to look at me, her eyes sparkling with joy. "This is perfect," she murmurs. "Thank you for whisking me off."

I nod in agreement and squeeze her hand. "It really is."

She sighs. "I wish we'd never have to leave."

I'm right there with her. This moment with her is one I'd love to stay cocooned in, but reality awaits us.

"Unfortunately, staying isn't an option."

"How long until you think shooting will be done?"

"Barring no more drama?"

"Yeah, let's assume that." She grows silent for a moment, and I watch as her brows pinch together.

"What is it?" I ask, wondering where her thoughts have drifted to.

"You think it's sabotage or just a comedy of errors?"

"Definitely sabotage," I admit. I've been thinking about it for some time, and there's no way this is all coincidence. Not when you consider the leaks. "I wish I knew who was doing it. Then we could have Stefan kick them off the island and finish this damn movie."

Her nose scrunches at my words, and I realize the way she's hearing them. "I didn't mean it like that, Mal."

"I know."

My eyes widen in challenge. "Do you?"

"Well, no . . . I guess I don't understand what we're doing."

This is the conversation I've been dreading. Relationship talk. It's not that I don't want to go down that path with her. I do. But I also realize it's easy to get caught up on a tropical island away from real life. Back home, we're competitors living different lives.

"Does it have to be labeled?" I ask.

"No." She exhales. "It's probably better that it's not. Especially with all the factors against us."

"Factors?"

I have a feeling she's thinking the same as me, but I'm curious. I don't want to give away that I've thought about factors myself because I don't want her to freeze up on me.

"Well, the haters of this film will have a field day if they find out. Plus, it's also not good for either of our reputations."

"We'd survive."

Why the hell am I arguing this? I have the same damn concerns. It's just not setting well hearing it from her.

"Easy for you to say," she mutters. "You have a successful business. I'm just starting out."

"Well, you can—"

"Don't even say those words, Paxton Ramsey. If, after everything, you still think I'd go, tail tucked between my legs, and ask my father for a handout—"

"Chill out, princess. I wasn't going to say that."

"Oh, yeah? Then what were you going to say?" She sucks in her cheeks. It looks like she's sucked on a sour lemon, and I must refrain from laughing at her.

"I was going to say you can work for me."

Her eyes practically bug out of her head. "Oh, yeah, 'cause that would go over well."

For fuck's sake . . . what are you doing, Paxton?

The idea flew out of my mouth without a single thought. I'm not one to make rash decisions, but when it comes to Mallory, all sense leaves the building. Taking the computers, the desk, even the planted flower half dead on the windowsill with it.

My hand reaches out, and my fingers skim down her arm. "I wouldn't know. It would be a gamble."

"Must be nice not having overbearing parents." She scoffs as I continue to trace small designs into her soft skin.

"It's great. I love my parents. They're the best." I blow out a breath. "What does your father have to do with this? Why does he have any control over where you work?"

"He doesn't. I just mean . . . he has a lot of clout in the industry. Connections with people in high places. I'm afraid he'd come after your business out of spite."

I shrug. He might have connections, but so do I. He can do his worst, and I still will come out all right.

"He can't touch me," I say, sounding arrogant to my own ears but not giving a fuck. I need her to know that I can protect her. Even from him.

"Must be nice."

I halt my movements and meet her snarky gaze. "It actually is. My world is wonderful. You're free to join it."

"I can't with you." She places her free hand over mine, giving me a small squeeze. "Tell me about them."

I pull a face, not knowing what she's asking.

"Your parents?" she prompts.

My confusion melts away, and a huge smile takes its place. "They're great. I love them dearly."

She smashes her lips together, not satisfied with my answer.

"What's there to tell about my family . . . ? I'm one of five kids. Three brothers and on sister. But we're boring compared to what you've probably seen."

"Boring is good."

"It is," I agree. "Mom's a teacher at the high school I attended. Dad works at the marina."

"Cold Spring Harbor, right?"

"Yeah." I'm shocked she remembered that.

"What's it like there?"

I bring up an image of my hometown and smile like an idiot. Home is special to me. Home is where I truly want to be if my job didn't require me to be where the talent is.

"Beautiful. Truly one of the best places on earth. Although bigger and more lively towns surround it, it still feels quaint and untouched by the world. Almost like a secret."

"How did you end up this big-deal talent agent?"

I smirk. "Oh, so you admit I'm a big deal?"

"Shut it. Jeez, I can't take you anywhere. But, really. What's your story? You already know mine." There's no hiding the bite in her voice.

She's soaking up my life because hers has been lacking. She's the daughter of a man whose work is more important to him than she'll ever be. She's purely a pawn in his scheme to dominate Hollywood.

I've heard around town how he talks about Mallory. Like she's a chess piece. A way to ensure his legacy lives on.

I move my hand, placing my fingers on her chin. "I'm sorry, Mal."

She offers a sad smile. "It's fine."

We both go silent because we both know she's lying. It's not all right.

I close my eyes and think back to how this all started. How I first crossed paths with her father. How I was burned and thus waged a war against this woman, who, in a short time, has rocked me to the core.

"The things I love about the town I grew up in, I hated when I was eighteen. I needed to get away, so I went to school in the farthest state I could think of, California. UCLA. I made some friends. Lots of Hollywood kids. Nepo babies, to be exact."

She pulls a face, hating that term because it's what she's been accused of her whole life.

"Most of them wanted to follow in their parents' footsteps. One thing led to another, and with a stocked Rolodex, I tried to work with your dad." I pause, opening my eyes and looking at Mallory, who's watching me intently. "You sure you want to hear this?"

"Yes."

Clearing my throat, I continue. "I was dumb when I pitched myself. I pitched the clients I would bring and the connections I had. I showed all my cards . . . and your father exploited that. He made me believe I had a job there and, well, poached my clients."

Her eyes close, and she breathes in deeply. "He really is the worst." She lifts my hand to her mouth and kisses the palm before placing it over her heart. "I'm sorry, Pax."

I shrug. "It's fine. It all worked out for the best anyway. Had I stayed, I might never have risen to the heights I have. I moved to

New York and built my business as a full creative talent agency. I don't just rep actors. I rep actors, influencers, models, writers."

Her face falls, and I imagine it's because I was forced to move a world away from Hollywood because of her father—a strike against us.

"I moved to New York to get away from my father, too." She tries to make a joke about it, but her voice gives her away. She's heartbroken. A moment of silence follows, and then she looks at me and smiles while she nods as if she is finally seeing something she never saw before. "That's why this is so important to you. You packaged it."

"I did," I say, nodding.

"We'll make sure it gets done—together."

Silence surrounds us, but it's welcome. And as I feel the beat of her heart, my own breathing calms, and soon, we both fall asleep.

I dream of walking around New York City, hand in hand with Mallory.

A dream that's nearly impossible.

Chapter Forty-One

Mallory

@Stargossip: What do you get when the lead actor and leading lady have no chem? Give up . . . *Twisted Lily*. Rumor has it Teagan couldn't fake it if her life or, in this case, her livelihood depended on it.

> **@TeaganLover123:** It's not her fault. Brad is Old AF.

> **@Bradforlife:** She's inexperienced and will never be the actor Brad is.

> **@TeaganLover123:** @Bradforlife Okay, boomer.

> **@Deathtothesystem:** This whole movie is problematic.

> **@SnarkMaven:** @Deathtothesystem You okay? Who hurt you? Your fifty cats?

FEEL LIKE I'M ON FIRE, BUT INSTEAD OF FLAMES, THE SUN HAS burned me to a crisp. Every movement is agony, and my shoulders are screaming in protest as they move up and down.

The salty sea breeze does carry some relief to my inflamed skin, but it's only temporary.

My skin feels like a knife is piercing it.

When we arrive at the movie set, I find Teagan filming her scene on the beach. She's completely engrossed in her work, lost in her own world.

She looks so young and innocent at the moment, but it works. She's truly incredible when given a chance.

With the right guidance, she'll be a star, and this movie will be her stepping stone.

I sit in the shade of a large palm tree and watch from a distance.

Watching Teagan act out her scene is strangely mesmerizing, playing off Brad with so much confidence.

Brad does a great job of pushing Teagan's buttons just enough for her to unleash some powerful emotions.

Watching them interact is special; each movement is perfectly placed and calculated.

It's funny because only a few weeks ago, I never would have thought they could do this. Maybe Stefan's team-building exercises paid off after all.

Teagan knows precisely how to drive her point home, and after a few takes, the director finally calls it, and everyone walks away to take a break. Some head toward craft services, while others plop under the shade of a nearby tree, glancing through their phones.

I should get up. Maybe grab something to eat. I stay put because my skin is too angry with me for the sudden movement, reminding me of my sunburn yet again.

When I wince, Teagan stops walking and turns around, heading back in my direction.

"You good over there?" she asks as she moves closer.

I force a smile. I'm the opposite of good. Every inch of my body hurts, screaming at me for being so stupid that I forgot to put on sunblock, screaming at me even more that I was dumb enough to fall asleep on a boat, in broad daylight, naked in the middle of the ocean, *but I digress.*

"All good here." But despite my words, I wince.

Teagan raises a brow. "Where were you this morning?"

I shuffle from my right foot to my left. "In my hut, why?" I try to keep my voice level as I lie. My hut isn't where I slept last night, but I can't tell her that.

"Well, I went to ask you a question . . ."

I shrug. "Umm, I must have been in the shower."

She narrows her eyes, watching me for a minute, then her gaze darts off to where Paxton stands only a few feet away.

"It's funny. He's all tan, and you're all burnt."

Shaking my head, I play dumb. Playing ignorant is the only option unless I want to tell her the truth, which I don't. "Not following."

"Just noting you both got a lot of sun yesterday."

"Oh, yeah, I just laid out for a bit. But obviously, I didn't bring enough sunscreen."

She looks at Paxton again, and her brow furrows. "Alone?"

"Yep," I answer too quickly. "Why?"

"No reason, although, come to think of it, yesterday we had to shoot a scene in the water, and I saw Paxton on a boat. I could have sworn he wasn't alone . . ."

My heart rams into my breastbone. She was on the boat.

Paxton said she couldn't see me when I was on my knees, but that doesn't mean she didn't see me before or after . . .

Nervous energy cuts through me, and my hand drops to my side where my finger moves to tap my leg, but I stop myself, knowing full well that if I give in to the anxiety, Teagan will see it.

She sees more than she lets on; that much is obvious. Taking slow breaths, I will myself to calm down.

Teagan steps closer to me, her hand reaching out. "What's that?" She's staring at my neck, but she shouldn't be able to see what I'm hiding; it should be covered. Or at least it was.

Shit.

Can she see it?

I thought I did my best to cover it.

While we slept, Paxton's hand was lying on my upper chest and neck.

Now, I'm sporting a tan mark from hell. But it shouldn't be in view. I look down, and that's when I notice the button of my collared shirt is no longer closed.

"It's nothing." I try to laugh it off.

But Teagan doesn't look convinced, the corners of her lips turning down. "That doesn't look like nothing, Mal. Is there something going on?"

I don't know what to say to her. On the one hand, I don't want to lie, but I also don't want this to get out there.

"Nope, nothing," I finally say. "I just fell asleep in the wrong position."

She presses her lips together and nods, then turns away without another word.

I guess she's not convinced and is now pissed that I lied. Not that I can blame her. I'm a terrible liar.

This situation isn't good.

If I were smart, I'd end things now and get my head screwed on right. Do my job and get off this island and back to my life.

That's not what I want.

There's definitely something happening between Paxton and me. Something that I can't quite explain, but when he's around, I feel things. Things I've never felt before.

We're good together, really good.

I'm not ready to admit that to him. Not yet. Not until we figure out how this might work long term.

We lead two entirely different lives, worlds apart from our shared profession.

For now, I can only protect our secret and pray for an outcome where no one gets hurt.

Unlikely.

I search for him in the crowd, and when I find him, my pulse races. This might be a problem. One that signals that when this movie wraps, it's going to hurt leaving him.

I need to push these feelings down for now. That's the only way this will work out while we work on this project together. It's also the only chance I have to keep my heart intact just in case something goes wrong.

For now, what we have has to be enough.

Paxton strides over to me as if he can hear me thinking about him.

"What's that about?" He motions to a pissed-off Teagan, currently striding away from the set.

"Nothing," I say, turning away from him.

He steps closer, his usual grin replaced by a thin lip and a hard jaw. "You sure about that?"

It takes every bit of strength to keep my resolve now. I step back and adjust the collar of my shirt, making sure it's buttoned up this time.

"Yep."

"If that's how you want to play it, but I'll get it out of you, eventually." He winks, and I shake my head at him. I have a feeling he's right. His attention shifts to my sunburn, and his smile fades. "You all right there, princess?"

I let out a frustrated sigh. "Must be nice to be you."

He lifts a brow in question. "I'm a red lobster, and you . . . you look like you stepped off the cover of *Sports Illustrated* with the perfect tan. It's annoying, if you must know."

"Want me to rub aloe on you later?" The look he's giving me should be illegal. It's downright deadly how sexy he is.

This man is trouble.

My gaze darts around to make sure no one heard him, and he shakes his head at me with a chuckle. "I'm not a complete idiot. No one can hear me."

"Debatable, but I'll let this one pass." I smirk at him.

He steps close to me, his face just inches from mine.

"You're not as tough as you think," he whispers and winks before walking away.

I know he's right because my heart is beating faster than ever before, and all I want to do is follow him. To spill my guts and give him my heart on a platter.

Stop.

I can't. Not now, at least.

Instead, I stand still, watching him walk away, my heart aching with each step he takes, wondering if I'll survive the day he walks away for good.

Chapter Forty-Two

Paxton

@Stargossip: I have it on good authority that not only is Mallory Reynolds doing the devil's tango with Paxton Ramsey, but she's got the battle wounds to prove it. That's one hell of a tan line on her neck, or should I say hand mark? Daddy must be so proud.

> **@Coolcat4:** Does she give it up for clients, too? If so, I might have to change careers.
>
> **@Ilovebrad:** As long as she's not banging Brad, I don't care.
>
> **@Meangirl12:** She's fugly. What's he see in her?
>
> **@Coolcat4:** Shut it @Meangirl12, Your jealousy is showing.
>
> **@Deathtothesystem:** The end is near. ;)

"Wake up." I shake Mallory, trying to get her up. I know she's in pain from the sunburn, but stuff is going down right now, and despite her exhaustion, she needs to be awake.

This is bad. Really bad.

"Come on, Mal." I shake her again, to no avail. She's like a rock—rigid and unmovable.

I sit back and sigh. It's like trying to wake a sleeping bear who's been hibernating for a long winter.

Impossible.

"Mallory," I say softly, almost in a whisper. "It's time to get up. We need to talk. You can sleep when you're dead."

Or, in this case, I'm dead, because when I tell her what I need to tell her, she will most likely kill me.

To my surprise, she stirs slightly and murmurs something incoherently. I take a deep breath—it's a start, at least.

"I hurt." She groans.

My eyes rake over her small body, and I can't help but wince. She's seriously toasted.

"I know, princess, but we need to speak. It's bad."

Slowly, she blinks away the sleep. She sits up and looks around, confused for a moment.

"Pax?" She rubs her eyes. "What's wrong?"

"It's out." I blurt out the words with no finesse. Panic is mounting, and I don't have time for anything but ripping off the Band-Aid.

Mallory shakes her head in confusion. "What's out?"

"Us."

Mallory shoots up. "What do you mean *us*? What are you talking about?"

I take a deep breath. "There were some tweets."

Mallory looks at me with disbelief, and then anger slowly creeps in. She pushes the blanket back and moves to stand.

"What tweets, Paxton? What are you talking about?" Her voice shakes with fury.

I can feel the tension building in the air as I start to explain what has happened. "That gossip influencer. They leaked a story about us—that we're . . ."

"We're what?"

"Fucking."

Mallory's eyes grow wide, and she's ready to explode. "That's impossible. Nobody knows, and we haven't been caught. We've been careful, Paxton."

She's on the edge of hysteria. Her hair's a wild mess of tangles from sleeping like the dead, and her bright red skin somehow glows as if she were roasted on a stick in hell.

There might be a need for a priest and an exorcism soon.

I shake my head. "I know, and I'm sorry. But someone knows. Someone saw something and talked. The tweet references the handprint."

Mallory is livid as she paces back and forth in front of me, her hands balled into fists at her sides. She stops and looks at me, her eyes burning with anger. "Who leaked it? Who told them?"

I shrug my shoulders helplessly. "Hasn't that been the mystery of the month?" I rake my hand back through my hair. "I wish I knew. I'd strangle them myself."

Mallory's face contorts in rage, well past what I've seen so far, and then she slams her fists down on the table, making a loud thump.

She screeches a string of curses at the sky, and my eyes fly wide. I've never seen her so incensed. I'm not sure I've ever seen anyone this livid. It's almost as if she . . .

"It was Teagan," she grits out through clenched teeth, breaking into my thoughts.

I'd just been thinking she had an idea of who it was. But Teagan? That is not what I expected. She has to be wrong.

"You need to calm down. You don't know that. It could have been anyone."

"No. Pax, it was her." She strides over to me. "Show me the tweet."

As much as I don't want to give her the phone, I do.

The moment she sees it, her face pales before the blood rushes back in, turning her the shade of a beet. She reminds me of a cartoon character where smoke blows out of their ears.

"It was *her.*" She taps her fingers on the side of her leg.

I grab Mallory's arm, pulling her hand to my mouth and kissing her knuckles. "Calm down, Mal. Let's not jump to conclusions here."

I have to believe she's making this accusation because she's tired, confused, and out of her mind. This is Teagan. *Her* Teagan. The girl she's gone to bat for over and over. Surely, she couldn't have betrayed Mallory so horrifically. It's inconceivable.

"Princess, this is Teagan we're talking about. The girl can hardly look a person in the eye. Do you really think she has it in her?"

Mallory shakes me off, but the anger slowly dissipates from her face.

"You're right," she says after a moment. She takes a deep breath and looks at me, her face solemn. "It's something Theresa would do. Not Teagan."

That gives me pause. Could Teagan have noticed something and slipped up, mentioning it in front of that devil woman?

"We'll figure it out," I tell her.

Her jaw is still clenched, and something tells me there's nothing I can say to convince her of that.

Right now, we're a joke. We're the punchline of every social media influencer.

It sucks.

But what can we do but hold our heads high?

She turns toward me, eyes wild. "We have to deny this. There weren't pictures to prove a damn thing. We can go to Natasha . . . have her help spin this."

"I don't trust Natasha for shit, Mallory. She's more likely to stoke the fire. Our fuckup means fewer eyes on the movie, Brad, and Teagan."

Her eyes close, and a pained look crosses over her delicate face. "You're right. We'll be thrown under the bus and blamed for all that's happened here."

I nod, hating it's come down to this.

One thing is for sure—it's time to face the music.

"Go shower. We need to head out soon. Get ahead of this."

She shakes her head. "I need to think."

I take her by her shoulders and turn her toward the bathroom. "Think in the shower."

Mallory turns around and stares at me, and her eyes look glassy, like she's seconds away from crying. I'm ready to comfort her, but she continues. "Do we have to do this?" Her bottom lip trembles, and I want to physically hurt whoever did this to her.

I don't give a fuck about myself. It's her that I'm concerned about. What will this do to her career? She's just getting started. I already have a reputation as a playboy, so I'll be fine.

"We can't keep running away from the truth, Mallory," I reply softly. "This isn't going away anytime soon."

She turns away. I can tell she's still angry, but she's also sad. Not a good combo. Despite what she claims, I know she still believes it was Teagan.

Either way, we can't do anything about it now. We have to face everyone and deal with the fallout.

This was bound to happen, eventually. I've been acting like a love-sick idiot. It was only a matter of time before someone got suspicious.

Yet, if given the choice, I'd do it again. In a goddamn heartbeat.

The fallout is worth every second I spent with Mallory.

I can only hope that, somehow, we'll end up on the right side of this. That whatever happens doesn't break Mallory completely.

Only time will tell.

Chapter Forty-Three

Mallory

@**Stargossip:** When it rains, it pours, and the news coming from the island is juicy. Sexual harassment allegations. A sabotaged set. An affair between agents. Oh my . . .

> @**Cloudyqueen69:** Pictures, or it didn't happen.

> @**Lastman_standing:** You're sick in the head.

T HE ENTIRE TIME I SHOWER, MY MIND WHIRLS. MY ANGER bounces around from one person to the next, yet it ultimately lands on Paxton.

We both made it clear we had to be careful, and he pushed the envelope at every turn. I repeatedly asked if we were safe out there on the water, and he gave me his word that we were.

Teagan saw him and someone else. We weren't safe. We weren't hidden at all, and he didn't care.

Why? Because it didn't affect him. He's notorious for hooking up with women. His company is established and swimming with clients. Rising stars clamor to work with him. On the other hand, I've been sunk before I could even float.

Once we're both dressed, he follows me out of the hut, but I'm too angry and upset to care.

"Stop, Mal."

I spin around and look him in the eye. "No. This is your fault. I trusted you. Now I need to clean up the mess *you* made."

I can't contain the rage building inside me. I know it's not all his fault, but I can't help but lash out.

"Don't even go there, princess." His voice has an edge that takes me back to the early days when he treated me like shit.

I was a damn fool to think he cared for one minute about anything more than a hookup.

"I'll go wherever I damn well please." I poke my finger in the air before his chest, but he stands firm. "You said we were safe out there on the boat."

"Mal . . ."

"Admit it, Paxton. Don't dance around my question. Not now."

He shakes his head. "It wasn't like that, and you know it. Stop acting like a petulant child for a second, and let's talk."

"Fuck you," I snap, my voice dripping with disdain. I turn back around, stalking toward camp.

I'm going to war, and it appears I'm doing it alone.

"Fine," he says and follows me. "You wanna play it like that? Want to go in guns blazing without a semblance of a plan? Go for it. See how that works out for you."

I march on, the anger swirling inside me like a tornado, emotions raging in my chest like thunder.

Paxton keeps pace beside me, matching my strides with his own.

We make it to the edge of the clearing before I finally stop and turn back toward him. What I find is surprising but a bit too late. His blue eyes are apologetic, but they don't make me feel any better.

"What do you want?" I ask, my voice cold and full of disappointment.

He takes a deep breath and looks up at the sky for a moment before answering. "I'm sorry," he says finally. "I didn't mean for it to happen like this. Things got carried away."

I cross my arms over my chest and let out a humorless laugh. "You think?"

He nods and reaches for my hand, but I pull away before he can touch me. He lets out a deep sigh before speaking again. "Listen, Mal, I know you're mad, but I swear I didn't mean for the press to get wind of us. It was just a mistake." He pauses and then lets out a long breath before continuing. "I wouldn't hurt you. Not on purpose, anyway."

I take a deep breath, some of the anger seeping away. I'm being incredibly harsh and pointing all the blame at Paxton. It's not fair. The person behind the leak deserves my ire.

I need to think straight. I need to get myself in check.

"I can't do this now. I need to have a clear head for Teagan."

He nods and then reaches out to take my hand. This time, I don't pull away. His fingers intertwine with mine, and for a moment, all is right in the world again.

Not right. Complicated.

"Just remember," he says quietly, "everything is going to be okay."

I want to ask how, but I don't.

I bite my lip, fearful of falling apart in front of him.

I'm not about to admit this out loud, but I know it was Teagan. She's been suspicious for some time. Making comments and saying things that give her away. The last conversation we had is what makes it obvious. She saw the handprint and stormed off like a child.

My one client sold me out, and I have no backup clients to keep me afloat.

I look up at him, my heart aching with sadness. "I know," I manage to say.

The truth is, neither one of us knows whether it'll be okay.

He squeezes my hand, then looks me in the eye. No words are spoken. What more is there to say? He'll be okay after this. I won't.

The thing that hurts the most is Teagan. I considered her family.

Guess I should know that family always disappoints.

I nod, unable to speak, and he pulls me into a hug. We stand there for a long moment with his arms around me like a protective shield against the world. I close my eyes, and for a moment, I forget all of my worries and fears and focus on being in the here and now.

His arm reaches out, tilting my chin up, leaning into me. His mouth finds mine, and although we shouldn't, I don't fight it.

So many words are spoken through this kiss.

It has to be okay.

We'll figure something out.

I'm sorry.

Eventually, I pull back, knowing I can't delay the inevitable. I turn and walk away, making it several feet before I turn over my shoulder and take one last look at Pax.

He's standing there, watching me go. His blue eyes look flat and hollow. It breaks my heart to leave him like this, but I need to find her and figure out why she did this, why she betrayed me.

When I get to Teagan's hut, my hurt is replaced by anger. I march up the steps, my heart pounding like a drum.

My hand curls into a fist, and I rap on the door so hard it sounds like the thing might fall in. Good. I hope she knows what's coming to her.

"Teagan!" I yell when she doesn't answer. "Open this damn door."

Silence.

I take a deep breath and pound on the door again.

I consider what to do, but before I can second-guess myself, I turn the knob.

It's unlocked.

The hut is empty, but in the background, I hear the shower running. The room looks similar to mine, a bit messier but the same layout. Beside the bed, I glimpse Teagan's phone on the nightstand.

Without thinking twice, I pick it up.

My breathing accelerates at what I'm about to do. I shouldn't do it because I know it's wrong. But I have to. I need to know, without a doubt. I need to see with my own eyes that a girl I cared for like family broke my trust and, subsequently, my heart.

My hands shake, and this moment feels like an out-of-body experience. I've never found myself in a situation like this. One so terrible, I'm afraid I might not return from whatever I'm about to see.

I close my eyes, take a deep breath, and go for it.

I'm not prepared for what I find. Bile rises in my throat as the full impact of the moment hits me like a ton of bricks.

My chest heaves, and my vision blurs.

Teagan didn't just tip them off about Paxton and me. She tipped them off about *everything*.

The phone falls from my grip as a sob rips through me.

Teagan is @Deathtothesystem, and every single leak that @stargossip posted came from *her*.

Chapter Forty-Four

Mallory

@Stargossip: Tensions are high on set, and no one is safe from the destruction this movie has caused. The only question left to ask is who will make it out unscathed?

    @Iloveme: All bets are off. I think they're all fucked.

    @Betterthanfiction: I'm with @Iloveme. It's not looking good for any of them.

    @Bradforlife: Brad will be fine. Teagan's dunzo.

SOMEHOW MANAGE TO PICK UP THE PHONE AND DISSECT THE evidence pointing at Teagan as the traitor.

I'm staring at the phone as Teagan comes striding in from the bathroom. Her hair is wet, and she's wearing a T-shirt and leggings. She looks so young at the moment. So innocent. It reminds me of when I first met her. Back then, her eyes were full of hope, before she became this jaded stranger.

She stares me down, not saying a word. She's a shell of the woman she once was.

Angry.

Broken.

Done.

As she comes closer, the intensity of the moment is palpable.

"What are you doing here?" she asks, voice full of accusation.

I've known her since she was only sixteen. A beautiful girl I watched grow into the woman before me. She's still gorgeous, but her sneer is new. Ugly.

I shake my head, my eyes filling with unshed tears.

"Why?" I say in a low voice. "Why?" A sob breaks free. I'm trying to pull myself together but losing the battle.

This hurts so damn much.

I straighten my shoulders and steel my voice, determined not to break down anymore. She doesn't deserve my pain. She'll only get my anger. "How could you do it?"

She turns her head away, her face shifting from rage to guilt. The silence lingers for what feels like an eternity before she speaks, her voice thick with emotion. "I had to . . ." She trails off, searching for the words. I shake my head, not allowing that to be her answer.

She owes me more than that.

"You don't understand." Moisture forms in her eyes as her hand lifts.

I cross my arms over my chest, needing the security. "Then explain it to me because I'm having a hard time understanding how you could sabotage this film that we worked so hard to land you."

"That's the thing, Mal. I never wanted it." I can see the truth in her eyes. Her words hang in the air, a strange and heavy weight between us. "This life. This career . . . it isn't *my* choice."

"It was always *your* choice." I spit the words out, growing more frustrated by the minute.

She shakes her head. "I told you I wouldn't do the movie. I tried to get out of it, but you took it upon yourself to fight Paxton.

You got me more money, and my mom . . . she wouldn't let me out after that."

My eyes narrow in on her. Her hands ball into fists, and her shoulders stiffen at the mention of Theresa.

"What do you mean, your mom wouldn't let you out?" I take a step toward her. "What did she do?"

"What didn't she do?" Her voice rises, startling me with its intensity. "She did everything. Most recently, she wanted me to seduce Brad. But if you want me to go back farther . . ." She takes a deep breath. "My mother would withhold my meds as a kid so I wouldn't gain weight. I couldn't let it continue because all I wanted was . . ."

"What?" I need her to let it all out. To open up for the first damn time.

"I wished for it all to end. I-I wished to—" She chokes on a sob.

My world stops—my heart pounds.

I blink, trying to convince myself I didn't just hear what I thought I did. I stare at her in shocked horror. I'm about to speak when she forges on.

"For years, I've struggled with depression and intrusive thoughts. I've tried to stop working . . ." Her head shakes, and she blows air through her nose like a bull ready to charge. "But she won't let me. She hangs everything on my shoulders. The money. The failed career she had." She takes a deep breath, and I don't move. Don't say a word. "She holds it against me that she gave everything up for me. How it's all my fault that she got pregnant and chose to keep me."

I gasp. "She says that?"

Teagan barks out a crazed, humorless laugh. "All. The. Time."

"I . . . I'm so sorry, Teagan."

Her shoulders rise and fall hard. "She's gotten her payback by exploiting me at every turn. I couldn't get away from her. I tried." Her voice wavers, and I hear her choke back a sob. "Oh, God, did I try."

She falls to her knees on the hard ground, and I jump into

action, lowering myself before her. I pull her into my arms and allow her to cry.

Hell, I cry with her.

For her.

Her words echo in my mind. Words that I can relate to all too well. A million emotions course through me, the most prominent being a deep sadness for her. For me.

"I felt trapped, Mal. I couldn't see a way out, and then I thought . . . what if the studio shuts down production? If the movie was stopped, I wouldn't have to do it. I wouldn't have to live this life anymore. My mom couldn't change that. If it were up to the studio— if it was taken out of my hands, she would stop. It would all stop."

I listen to every word, and it allows my anger to cool.

This girl . . . this beautiful, broken girl.

She's a victim like so many other young Hollywood stars. There's always someone out there ready to exploit them. To ride their coattails and rob them dry. To force them to do things they don't want by making them feel it's owed to the predator.

It's so goddamn wrong.

Hatred builds within me for Theresa, and I want to find her. I want to tear her apart.

It wouldn't do any good. People like her are evil. They don't see their own horrible ways.

We sit like this for several minutes, Teagan shaking in my arms. I think about all that she's said. All that she's done.

That's when the hurt resurfaces.

I pull away, staring into her glassy eyes.

"But"—my voice cracks with emotion as I struggle to understand what could have driven her to do what she did to me—"you didn't have to throw me under the bus to make production stop."

She sighs heavily before responding. "I was scared. Scared of what my life would be like if I let this movie be made. If you kept fighting for me."

My head shakes as I try to understand.

"I'm sorry you were scared, Teagan. I truly am, but why—why would you do this to *me*?"

I stand, looking down at her.

Her head tips up, her eyes fierce. "Because I had to make a choice. Destroying your life was standing up for mine," she says firmly. "If I don't choose me, no one will."

"I don't understand that. You could've come to me. Could've confided in *me*. There was no choice to be made where I'm concerned. Did you also sabotage the set?" She nods.

Everything she did to stop production, I get. Taking me down? I'll never understand because it wasn't necessary. She acted without thinking about me.

She takes a shaky breath, tears streaming down her face. It feels like my heart will explode. Her words hang in the air, and my heart breaks.

"I'm sorry, Mal. I'm so sorry for what I did to you, but I thought it was the only way out. I wasn't thinking. I was too tired. Too scared. Too done."

I step forward, wrapping my arms around her and pulling her close. I'm not sure why, after all she's done, but my love for her doesn't end because she made a horrible mistake. She's young and naïve.

What would I have done if I were in her shoes?

Burn the whole place to the ground to get out.

All I can do is hold her in my arms and cry with her, knowing that sometimes we have to make hard choices, and sometimes, those choices have brutal consequences.

I don't know what to say, so I hold her close until the tears stop falling.

Eventually, all the anger and hurt fade away, replaced by a deep understanding of where she's coming from.

We aren't that much different. Both have parents who hurt us. Both of us have felt trapped and at the end of our rope. We've both had to make choices that hurt.

In the end, we just had different ways of getting out.

I take a deep breath and whisper, "It's okay."

With those two words, her body sags into mine. I've offered her my forgiveness and understanding, and that's exactly what she needs right now. All she's wanted is someone to be on her side, and I hope I've proven I always have been.

Teagan looks up at me, her eyes brimming with tears.

"Now what?" she whispers.

We stare at each other in silence, both of us processing this new reality.

"We'll get through this together." I'm not sure how we'll do that, but I'm determined to make things right for her.

"How?" She echoes my thoughts.

I don't have to think about it too long.

"We walk." My voice is strong, letting her know I mean my words. "We'll tell them this movie is done."

Teagan's eyes go wide. "But what about the studio?"

"You let me handle them," I tell her, squeezing her shoulder. "I'll handle your mother, as well."

She sniffles. "Your career, Mal. You'll be ruined."

Moving a step back, I take her hands in mine. "So what?"

"Mal . . ."

"Don't Mal me. This is the only way. You needed me to see what you couldn't tell me. I failed you then. I won't fail you again."

And I won't. I mean that with my whole heart.

Even if it means breaking my own in the process.

I stand in the middle of the set and take a deep breath. My nerves threaten to explode, but I tamp them down and fill myself with strength.

I need to stand up for Teagan.

Teagan's health is the only important thing. When I finally

find Jeffrey and Stefan, I stride over to them, shoulders pulled back, spine straight.

"I'd like to talk to both of you." I hope my firm voice hides my uncertainty. "Alone."

Jeffrey turns to Stefan with a questioning look, to which Stefan merely gives an almost imperceptible nod.

"Sure," Jeffrey says, turning back to me, then swings open the door to the hut behind him, stepping inside. As I'm about to close the door, I hear the voice of the one person I can't deal with right now.

"Mal. What's going on?"

I don't look at him. Not now. Not when I'm only moments from ruining things between us and splintering my heart into a million pieces in the process.

I need to put Teagan's mental health first. It's the right thing to do.

The door has hardly shut behind us when I spit out the words that will put the nail in this film's coffin.

"Teagan needs to pull out of *Twisted Lily*," I say, managing to keep my voice even and firm.

"W-what? Why?" Jeffrey stammers, face growing red.

"The set has become unpredictable and unsafe. It's in my client's best interests to back out of this role."

The room is deathly quiet, save for the ticking of a clock. Jeffrey's face has fallen into an unreadable mask, something he's likely perfected over the years after having to deal with many situations like this.

Stefan's brows furrow slightly, but he doesn't pitch a fit or fight me. His nod makes me wonder if he might understand why I'm pulling her.

"We'll call our lawyers." He's not harsh or threatening. If anything, he seems calm about the decision. He offers a tight smile, his eyes soft and almost . . . understanding. It gives me the feeling that maybe he knows how hard this is for me.

Jeffrey nods in agreement. "You do realize that our lawyers are going to come after her. After you. The amount of money lost because of this is obscene." He looks at Stefan, eyes wild with untamed fury. "She can't be serious," he seethes.

Stefan's hand juts out, signaling for Jeffrey to stop. "We will have to consider this a breach of contract." Again, he's not being harsh. Stefan is only being professional in ensuring I understand the ramifications.

I'm new to this, and he's well aware. I take it as his way of looking out for me, and at this moment, my heart softens toward the eccentric man.

"I understand," I say, offering Stefan a tight, professional smile. I turn toward Jeffrey, not extending the same courtesy.

He's been obnoxious since I arrived. "You can call your lawyers, but my client is still leaving this island today." My eyes don't waver from Jeffrey's. I allow him to receive every bit of my harsh tone and cold stare.

We're at a standstill. There is nothing more I can say or do to make them understand. All that's left is to get Teagan off this island.

"Jeffrey," I say, hand on the knob as I go to leave. "My father won't be returning your call."

His face pales, mouth flapping open like a fish out of water.

He doesn't realize that I have no control over my father. I only said it to have the last word and make him sweat a bit. He deserves it for all the probing.

Stepping out of the hut, I know I should feel like a huge weight has been lifted from my shoulders, but instead, my stomach feels hollow.

So much more needs to happen. Theresa must be dealt with, and I'll have to tell Paxton.

That's the worst of it all.

Even though Teagan can finally be free from this chaos and start to heal, I know it comes at a great cost to Paxton. It's something we won't be able to recover from. This project meant everything to him.

It was the beginning of big things for his agency, and I just squashed it within five minutes.

There's no doubt that this has destroyed something special.

The sun is setting as I walk away from the set, dejected and incredibly lost. My head tilts toward the sky, a mixture of orange and pink.

This is gonna hurt.

I take another deep breath, thinking about what I'll say to him.

A confidentiality clause, as well as not breaking Teagan's trust, has my hands tied. I can't tell him about her issues with her mother or that she deliberately sabotaged this project. In the end, it's going to look like I don't care about him at all.

The air around me is heavy with my thoughts as I return to my hut to pack and prepare for the journey home.

"I thought I told you not to walk around by yourself." I jump at the sound of Paxton's voice.

I stop, closing my eyes and preparing for what's to come. I'm not ready. I thought I'd have time to pack and work through my words.

Turning around to look at him, I offer a small, weak smile. My eyes roam his handsome face, and my hand lifts to rub at the pain in my chest. The time I spent with him is something I'll carry with me always.

"I've never been a very good listener." I shrug.

He takes a step closer. "Are we . . . are we okay?" he asks, searching my face, likely seeing the sadness I feel deep in my bones.

"We . . ." I swallow the lump in my throat, closing my eyes to stave off the tears welling up and threatening to fall.

It's no use. One slips past my lids, dripping down my cheek.

"Mallory," he says, hand lifting my chin. "What's wrong?"

I choke back a sob, shaking my head back and forth, not ready to face him.

"I've got to go."

When I open my eyes, I find his head tilted, a look of confusion written all over his face. "Where are you going?"

"I'm going home," I say so quietly that it comes out as only a whisper.

Another tear falls, and I swipe it away. I need to pull myself together. To be strong. If I'm broken and weak, he'll ask too many questions, and I can't have that. I'll break and tell him things I can't.

"Home?" His voice drops low. "What do you mean, home?"

I straighten my shoulders and look him straight in the eye, playing at being strong. "To New York. It's time for me to leave."

He takes a step back and crosses his arms over his chest. "I don't understand. Did something happen? Is it your father?"

I laugh, but it lacks humor. "This has nothing to do with him. I'm taking Teagan home."

Tears are in my eyes again, and I pray they don't fall. I can't fall apart now. My heart feels heavy. My mouth opens slightly, and I take a deep breath to steady my emotions.

"We're leaving, Paxton. I just spoke with Jeffrey and Stefan—"

His head jerks back as if I've slapped him. "What exactly did you tell them?"

I steel myself for the incoming storm. The time has come for me to stand tall and own my decisions. "That Teagan's out. The movie is done for her."

"Are you fucking kidding me?" He paces. "Were you even planning to tell me? Or were you going to sneak off the island and let me find out that way?"

I step forward and raise my arm to touch him, but then I stop, letting my hand drop. "This isn't a safe environment for her anymore. I have to protect her."

"Safe environment? What the heck does that even mean? Did something else happen?"

"I'm not at liberty to talk about that." Paxton's expression fades from concern to anger.

"I thought you trusted me."

"I *do* trust you, but I signed a—"

His hands lift, and his face pinches. "Save it. I thought things were different. Guess I was wrong." He turns away from me, and now I can't see the hurt in his eyes. "Guess the apple didn't fall far from the tree."

"That's not true, but I have a duty to my client." My voice is barely a whisper now.

He pauses, his back facing me. For a long moment, neither of us says anything. We stand there in silence, my heart pounding in my chest. I watch as his shoulders rise and fall, his head lowered.

Finally, he turns back to me and shakes his head slowly.

"Just go," he says softly. "We both knew this was how it would end." Paxton takes a deep breath, turns, and walks away, leaving me alone and broken.

"Goodbye, Paxton," I whisper into the wind as I watch him walk away.

Taking my heart with him.

Chapter Forty-Five

Paxton

@Stargossip: Welp. That was fun. Now what? What tea do you want?

> **@Bradforlife:** I hear Brad is already on to his next role. Maybe news about that one?
>
> **@Betterthanfiction:** Brad is old news.
>
> **@CruelGirl810:** We can talk politics ;)
>
> **@Cloudyqueen69:** That would be a no, @cruelgirl810.

MY FLING WITH MALLORY WAS ALWAYS DESTINED TO END here on this island. It has officially run its course, yet I can't help the anger that bubbles inside me.

She fucking left and tried to do it without saying goodbye.

That should be enough reason for me to lick my wounds and move on, but no matter how hard I try to convince myself that this is for the best, I'm not ready to let her go.

As I attempt to walk back to my hut and drink away the night, Brad storms my way. His face is red, his eyes blazing like fire.

I try to bypass him, not in the mood to deal with him right now. I need to have a moment of quiet. Time to process what I've just learned and how to deal with the fallout. This standoff was inevitable, but I really hoped it would be later. Like when I was halfway through a bottle of rum.

I probably should have gone straight to him, but to be honest, I don't give a shit about him.

He's going to fire me anyway, so who the hell cares?

"Paxton." His voice booms through the open air as he points an accusing finger at me. "You're done. Your little girlfriend ruined our movie."

The man looks unhinged. I can practically feel the heat of rage radiating from him in waves, like he's ready to erupt.

"Look," I say calmly, trying to defuse his anger. "It's not her fault. Teagan—"

"Stop." He laughs bitterly and shakes his head. "You think I'm stupid?" he says with a sneer. "She ruined it, and since you're fucking her, I'm holding you accountable. So now you're out of a job, too."

"One, despite what you think, I had no clue they were walking. If I did, I would have tried to stop them. Two, I'm hardly out of a job. You're not my only client, and in case you haven't realized it, you're yesterday's news. Newer, hotter talent is knocking down my door. So good riddance and good luck." I turn to leave, done with him. He fired me. I don't have to stand here and listen to another damn thing.

"You and that little bi—"

I spin around, stalking toward him threateningly. "Don't ever talk about Mallory." I step right up to him, looking down at the smarmy asshole.

I'm not afraid of Brad Wright. I don't care who he thinks he is.

I don't care that Mallory left, and I'm fucking pissed at her. I won't let him talk shit about her. Not now. Not ever.

"You're fired."

My eyebrow lifts because I thought we'd just established that. I laugh. "I quit, you fucking joke."

Brad stands there, his expression a mixture of shock and anger.

"You can't speak to me like that," he squeals, sounding pathetic and deranged.

"I'm done with this." Pivoting my back to him, I head toward my rum.

"You think you can walk away like that?" he says, incredulous. "You're done. Finished. Your career is toast."

Brad's angry eyes burn into my back as I walk away, but I don't care because I know he's wrong.

My career isn't over.

I can't help but smirk. I can't believe I've put up with that dick for as long as I have.

I'm finally free of him and all the bullshit he brings.

When the path opens to the two huts, on instinct, I look toward hers. She's probably gone by now, but that thought doesn't stop my feet from carrying me toward hers, up the stairs, and inside.

It's empty.

Of course, it is. She couldn't get off this island fast enough.

The sweet smell of her perfume lingers in the air, the only sign she was ever here.

I can't be in here, surrounded by her scent. My stomach turns, and my breathing grows heavy.

I rush out, gulping in a lung full of air, trying to rid myself of her memory. It hurts too damn bad.

When I've pulled myself together, I rush into mine but find I'm faced with the same problem.

Even though she's not here, she's still everywhere.

Touches of her fragrance remind me of every moment I spent with her.

Of the way she would lie on my bed, blonde hair fanning my pillow.

The white T-shirt she wore mocks me from the chair in the corner. I consider starting a fire and burning it.

Fuck.

Before I can think better of it, I'm crossing the space and swiping the bottle of rum off the counter.

I take a swig, letting the liquid slide down my throat, trying my best to numb everything away.

How much do I need to drink to make her presence in this room disappear?

Something stronger than anger bubbles up inside my body, filling my lungs and making my breathing hard.

How did everything go so wrong? Only a few days ago, it seemed we were on the right path. The film was being made, and Mallory was in my bed.

Now I have neither.

My career might not end because of Brad, but this movie was to be the very thing that took me to the next level.

To the heights of Thomas Reynolds.

Fuck him and fuck her, too.

What was I thinking, getting involved with Mallory? Despite everything, she fucking turned her back on me. She kept me in the dark, and then when push came to shove, she was no better than him. Now both of the Reynolds have taken a stab at ruining my career.

I take a few deep breaths and try to keep my anger at bay.

I can't get off this godforsaken island until tomorrow at the earliest. My only goal is to get so drunk I don't smell her on my pillow.

That's how I'll get through this night. Tomorrow, who knows . . . ?

The only good thing that came out of this is that I no longer have to deal with Brad.

That was a blessing in disguise.

I slam the bottle onto the table so hard that I swear I can feel the floor shake beneath me.

She made a fool out of me. But that's not even the worst part.

No, the worst is that I miss her.

No amount of booze will wipe her from my mind. She is all around me in this godforsaken hut. A ghost tormenting me at every turn.

The memory of her still hangs in the air.

There's only one answer—lift, drink, and repeat.

The liquid flows down my throat, burning like acid as it goes. I don't stop. I'm not sure I could if I wanted to.

Chapter Forty-Six

Mallory

@Stargossip: Finally, more *Twisted Lily* gossip. Things are getting dicey. Lawyers for both sides have been called. Careers ruined. Millions lost. It's about to get juicy!

> **@Ihatehollywood:** Enough already. This is old news.
>
> **@TeaganStewardfanclub:** That studio can stick it.
>
> **@Moviesaremylife:** Moving on . . .

WELL, THE WORLD DIDN'T OFFICIALLY END WHEN I LEFT THE island. It got messy for a while, but luckily, I found a great attorney to take on Teagan's case.

Yep. The studio tried to go after her for breach of contract.

Ironically, the one thing that saved her was the well-documented safety issues on the set. Teagan and her little Twitter stunt saved her ass after all.

By sending the dirt to @Stargossip, Teagan had laid out the whole case.

In the end, the studio was found at fault for trying to make a movie in such poor conditions.

Don't even get me started on the unions. When they got wind of what happened, they were all over it.

Heads rolled, and ultimately, the studio dropped the case against Teagan for breach of contract, trying desperately to sweep the issues under the rug.

On the other hand, I've been hiding in my apartment for the past few weeks.

Trying to find an agency that will hire me.

Unfortunately, it's slim pickings.

Seems that nobody is eager to hire the daughter of Thomas Reynolds.

I can only guess as to why . . . unsavory methods being at the top of the list.

Not that it's the only reason. I'm not surprised since I've been all over the news. Everyone knows how my client, well, former client, walked off set, got on a boat, and just left a movie that would've made her career. Mine, too.

It wasn't just @stargossip that spread the word. The news of what happened on the island, including speculation about my relationship with Paxton, went viral. It became such big news that every media outlet in the world reported on it.

The. World.

This would only happen to me.

The worst part about everything is how it all went down with Paxton. I can't eat or sleep whenever I think about what I did to him. I don't live under a rock. I know my actions took a hit on him and his career. The thing is, I had no other choice, and I couldn't tell him why.

It breaks my heart.

On the island, when everything was fresh, and my anger at Theresa was still filtering in my blood, I couldn't think past helping Teagan.

The abuse she suffered from her mother's actions is unfathomable. But now that I'm away from everything, I can only think about Paxton.

I miss him.

I miss him so much I can barely breathe.

Somehow, in only a few weeks, I went and fell in love.

Doesn't matter, though. He will never trust me again.

The sound of my phone has my jaw locking because I know who's calling.

As if my week isn't bad enough, the ring tone of Melanie Martinez's "The Principal" gives away who it is. . .

My father.

"Dad," I answer, my back muscles tightening as I wait for the lecture I'm about to receive.

I knew this call was coming, but I had hoped I'd have some more time to lick my wounds before I had to speak with him.

It would have hurt less.

No such luck.

Bring on the torture . . .

Lemon juice on a paper cut seems like child's play compared to this.

"Time to come home, Mallory." His voice has my hands clenching at my sides. This is why I don't like to speak to him. There's no, how are you? No concern for my well-being.

Just the need to control me.

"I'm not—"

"No. Enough. I have humored you for the past few years, waiting for you to finally come to your senses, but I can't allow this to continue."

"It's not up to you," I snap, so sick of him constantly acting like I'm a child he can command.

"That's where you're wrong. You've embarrassed yourself and me. You have no other options."

"I'm not going to work for you." I practically scream down the line, and all I get is his laughter in return.

"You're lucky to have me because you couldn't survive otherwise. I opened so many doors for you. You tried and failed."

"You didn't open any doors for me. If anything, your name alone closed doors in my face."

"Stop being dramatic and ungrateful. You've been an embarrassment to my name. You'll come work here, where I can make sure you don't get into any more trouble."

I'm seething. All I see is red as I play his words over and over in my head. He's so much worse than Theresa Steward.

Teagan was strong. She took her life into her own hands, and here I am, a grown-ass woman, allowing this man to pull me down.

No more.

"I'm done. If you can't support me in my choices, I can't even talk to you anymore."

"Don't you dare—"

I don't bother saying goodbye. I just hang up.

Too many other problems are on my plate right now. My rent, for one. It's due, and paying it is going to hurt.

I have a little money put aside, but living in the city is ridiculous.

Without a job, I won't be able to live here for another month. I'll have to break my lease, lose my security deposit, and pray the landlord doesn't give me shit and lets me out of the lease to find a place I can afford.

The only way not to move is to call my father back and beg, and I would rather get a job doing anything else than that.

Which is exactly what I'll do.

I grab my computer, my mind made up.

I'll find a temporary job to buy me time to find more clients. I can do this.

The first thing that pops up on my computer screen is a tabloid article with Paxton's picture staring back at me. Worse yet . . . there's a woman grasping his arm.

My stomach roils, and I know I'm going to be sick.

I don't bother to read the article. It could be his friend for all I care. Seeing his face was hard enough.

I didn't think it was possible, but that one picture manages to break my heart a little more.

Chapter Forty-Seven

Paxton

@**Stargossip:** It seems the studio isn't giving up on *Twisted Lily* after all. No clue when they'll start shooting, but if my sources are correct, they're currently recasting the part of Lily. Any takers?

> @**Teaganfanclub:** We don't care!

> @**Betterthanfiction:** I'll stick with the book. Thank you very much.

> @**Thatsnotmyname:** Brad is washed up. I don't know why they are bothering.

SHIT ISN'T GETTING BETTER.

I thought they said that time heals all wounds, but whoever said that was a fucking idiot.

Because even weeks later, as I walk down a bustling Fifth Avenue, my mind is still consumed with anger and bitterness.

No matter how much time passes, I can't move past what happened on that island.

The funny part is, I don't even give a shit about the movie falling apart or the money I lost when the deal imploded. All I can think about is her betrayal.

She left without a backward glance.

Without a care to what it would do to me.

I survived, of course, but she didn't even give a fuck.

She just plain ole left.

Taking my heart and slamming it on the floor in the process.

Luckily for me, Brad was wrong, and this shit show didn't end my career.

I'm fine.

Still swimming.

In fact, I'm heading to a meeting right now to discuss a different project. One that doesn't involve Brad Wright.

That was the best thing that came of this whole debacle. I never have to see that idiot again.

I'm about a block away from my friend and client, Charles's office, when I stop dead in my tracks.

There, walking toward me, is Teagan Steward.

And as if the betrayal only happened yesterday, the anger builds up inside me as I realize that I have to face her once again.

"Well, well, well. Look who it is," I spit out sarcastically as she approaches me.

Her eyes go wide when she finally sees me, and she stops in front of me, an attempt at a smile on her face. "Paxton, hi." She may be saying hi, but her body language is anything but friendly. Her gaze darts around as if she is trying to find an escape. I don't blame her; she cost me a job and the studio millions.

"I can't believe you have the nerve to smile after what you did." My voice is harsh with anger.

She lifts her hands, almost like she's surrendering. "I'm sorry, Paxton." She inhales deeply. "I didn't have a choice."

"Like hell you didn't," I snap, my tone dripping with disdain. "You could have never signed up for the project in the first place, but no, you just had to screw over everyone else in the process, right?"

Teagan looks down, clearly ashamed. "I didn't mean to hurt anyone, Paxton. I really am sorry."

I can feel the anger beginning to dissipate as I finally take her in.

Her skin is pale, and her eyes are swollen with unshed tears.

Maybe she is sorry. Or maybe she's just a damn good actress. Something tells me it's the first, but either way, I don't want to waste any more of my time on her. "It's fine, Teagan." I turn to walk away. "Just stay out of my way from now on."

"Everyone thinks I picked Mal because of her father, because of her last name . . ." Her words stop my movements, and I cannot help but pivot back to hear what she says. "But I picked her because of her heart. Who else would have given up her career for a client?"

I don't understand the point of this, but the mention of Mallory has my back going ramrod straight and my pulse increasing.

"Well, she does have her daddy to fall back on."

"If you think she would take a thing from him, you don't know her at all," she says, her tone keeping me quiet. "Mallory isn't the average agent."

"That's right. She has a very successful dad in tow."

"That's why my mom agreed. My mom assumed she would eventually leave and go work for her father. But I went to her because she was the only one who asked me if I was okay."

I'm momentarily stunned by what she just said.

"Did you know the first thing she did when we got home was to make sure I was okay? She'd just lost everything—no job, losing her apartment—and still, she made it her number one priority to make sure her *ex-client* was okay . . . that *I* was okay.

"I'm not following."

"You have no idea why we walked, do you?"

"She never told me anything."

A tear falls from Teagan's eyes. She swipes it away and then straightens her back and meets my stare. The lost and sad girl from moments ago is replaced. Her walls are up for what she's about to say. "She got me help. She put my mental health above everything. She gave it all up for me."

"What do you mean?"

"You had to have known what my mother was doing," she fires back, and I shake my head. Sure, I knew her mom was a bitch, but from what I see right now, it was so much more.

"I told Mallory the truth. I told her what my life was really like. That I was at a breaking point and could no longer take it, and she put me first. She lost everything for me. She's struggling—like really hurting. I check in with her, but I know she doesn't tell me how hard it is. She's untouchable. She can't get a job, and it was bad enough where she was living before this. Her new place is . . ." Teagan lifts a finger to brush another tear away. "I know you're mad at her for what she did, and if I know Mallory, she didn't tell you anything, but she saved my life, Paxton. I was *drowning*. My mom—she was slowly killing me. And Mallory—she gave me my life back."

Her words explode inside me. I can feel them as if they are shrapnel ripping apart everything I thought I knew.

Fuck.

What did I do?

And the better question, what did I lose because I was too proud to see the truth?

An hour later, I'm still pacing back and forth in front of Charles's building in a constant loop, but no matter how hard I try, I can't will myself to enter. So, instead, I walk the block more times than I can count, but there is no shaking the conversation with Teagan.

I don't know what to believe or what to think anymore.

On the one hand, I know where she was coming from . . . *now*. But on the other, she didn't even fight.

Sure, she couldn't have told me the full story, but she could have said something.

Anything.

Instead, she placed giant walls around her and closed me out.

Somewhere on the twentieth pass of the building, I walk into the bar next door instead and text Charles, letting him know where I am.

It's dark and dingy here, and the tables and chairs are scratched from years of rough use, but it's getting the job done.

I order something strong from the bartender and then make it a double. Ten minutes later, I can feel the alcohol seeping through my veins like a sponge, soaking up each sip.

I'm almost numb to any feeling but emptiness until I sense someone hovering nearby.

Turning around, I see Charles.

I've been avoiding him since I've gotten back from the island. Sure, Charles is one of my closest friends, but since being back, I've had too much stuff to deal with and have just wanted to be alone.

Until he called for a meeting I couldn't miss.

But apparently, that meeting won't happen because I'm too busy drowning myself in booze.

"Paxton," he says quietly, "you all right, mate?" His voice is soft and measured, but his eyes show concern.

I give him a halfhearted shrug and continue staring into my drink. "Been better," I mutter.

He takes a seat, lifting his hand to order.

A moment later, armed now with a beer, I watch him out of the corner of my eye as he takes his first sip, savoring each drop before swallowing.

"You know," Charles draws out, "you can't keep blaming yourself for the film falling apart. That's not on you."

"It's still happening," I grunt.

"You're not going to be a part of it?"

I shake my head. Since I no longer represent Brad, no one will expect me to return to the island when they finally start filming.

Charles starts talking again, but I don't hear what he's saying. All I can think about is the island and . . . Mallory. I still remember how her eyes lit up when she talked about the movie.

The woman who had my heart and stomped on it without a second glance.

But it wasn't like that, Pax.

I know that now. I know she did it all for her client. Because she's the type of woman who gives up everything for the people she cares about.

I could have been that person to her.

Fuck. Shut up. I take another swig of whiskey, hoping to silence those memories for a few more hours.

Charles pauses for a moment, looking me over before continuing. "One day, you'll be able to look back and realize this was just a part of your journey."

I scoff at his words. "This isn't about a goddamn movie." It's about losing the one person I thought would be—

"What's *really* going on?"

I don't answer. Instead, I lift my drink again and take a giant gulp.

"Is this about the woman?" Charles asks after an awkward silence.

Emotion clogs my throat. I take a deep breath before admitting it for the first time. "Yeah," I grunt, "but the woman has a name . . . . It's Mallory."

Charles nods. "There's more to the story, I assume."

I sit there for a few more minutes, wondering what I should tell him. I'm not sure what to divulge, but with the movie over, there's no reason not to talk to my friend.

"Oh, I understand now," he says before I can tell him anything.

"You understand what?"

"You lost more than just the film. You lost Mallory, too. You love this girl," Charles says, understanding in his voice.

"I can't possibly love this girl," I respond, my voice thick with emotion.

Charles looks at me like he doesn't believe a word I'm saying. "Your disheveled appearance says otherwise."

My gaze snaps away from Charles, and I'm suddenly aware of my appearance. I must look like shit. He's right, though, even if I don't want to admit it.

"Oh, shut up," I mutter before taking another long pull of my drink. "You can't fall in love with someone in a month."

"Sure, you can. Love doesn't make any sense."

My mouth suddenly feels dry as my heart batters my chest.

Is he right?

Fuck.

He's right. I love her. How the hell did this happen?

We sit in silence for a few minutes before I finally speak again. "You're right," I whisper, more to myself than anyone else. "I *do* love her."

Charles pats me on the shoulder and smiles. "It's okay to love someone, Pax. It was bound to happen. Even an arsehole like you deserves to be happy."

"If only loving her was the problem." I bury my head in my hands.

"Then what is the problem?"

I lift my head and look at him. "How to be with her."

"If you can't figure that out, you can't be helped."

"Harsh." I groan.

"Just speaking the truth."

I nod and take another sip of my drink, thinking about what to do. Love has a funny way of making everything seem much more complicated than it already is.

Charles stands, leaving his now-empty glass on the table. "Go get your girl."

Chapter Forty-Eight

Mallory

@Stargossip: Things are happening. Back to the island they go...

    @CoolCat4: We don't care.

    @Meangirl12: Someone put @Stargossip out of her misery.

    @Ilovebrad: I'm excited.

    @CoolCat4: @Ilovebrad Get a life.

THIS ISN'T REAL.

My heart beats faster, like a hummingbird's wings, as I see him standing outside my door.

Obviously, Paxton isn't here. How could he be?

This isn't real.

Maybe I'm still hungover from the pity party I had yesterday.

Lifting my hand, I scrub at my eyes, but when I'm still facing the man who's haunted my dreams for weeks, I realize this isn't a mirage.

Paxton Ramsey really is standing in front of me, and he looks exactly how I remember him from the last time I saw him, just as handsome, but his eyes still look hollow and lost.

I wrap my arms tightly around my chest. "What are you doing here?"

Paxton takes a step forward. "I wanted to talk."

His husky voice still makes my knees go weak. I'm not sure what I expected. It's only been a few weeks. Obviously, his effect on me wouldn't diminish so fast. However, what I didn't anticipate is the fact that it seems to have gotten worse, more potent, and seeing him now, it feels like I'm being torn apart from the inside out.

I hold myself tighter, my finger twitching on my upper arm as I will myself to stay calm. "Why?"

"Please, Mal." His voice drops an octave, and I realize he's as miserable as I am. Maybe even more so. But why?

Narrowing my eyes, I level him with a curious stare. "How did you find me?"

"Teagan." His words make my mouth fall open. Of all the answers, that's the last one I would have expected.

The tapping on my arm picks up, and Paxton must notice it, too, as he lifts his hand, but then he must think better of it because it shortly drops back to his side.

"You spoke to Teagan?" I ask.

"I did . . . and now I want to talk to you."

I nod. "Fine." Not going to lie, I'm still shocked that Paxton is here. I know I should move out of the way and let him in, but I'm having a hard time remembering my name, let alone how to act in this situation.

After what I did, knowing full well what he thought of my father, I never truly thought I would hear from Paxton again. The days and weeks have dragged since the island.

I've been trying to move on, but seeing as my heart is beating so fast that I think it might explode from my chest, I'm doing an awful job.

A part of me wants to smile at him, welcome him into my apartment and my life, but I'm afraid.

I'm not sure why he's here, and I can't afford to let my guard down.

What if he's here to—nope, not going there.

Taking a deep breath in, I look at him, really look at him, and that's when I notice something . . .

For the first time since I've known Paxton, he seems nervous, fidgeting with his hands, shifting his weight from foot to foot.

A spark of hope ignites in my belly.

With all my strength, I take a step back, letting him pass.

As he walks into the apartment, I see what he sees . . . a mess.

I quickly try to tidy up, grabbing a few items off the floor and throwing them into a nearby closet. I turn to face him, unsure of what to say.

Paxton looks around the room, taking in the cluttered mess. "This isn't what I expected."

I feel a twinge of annoyance. "Of course, it isn't. You expected me to have Daddy paying my bills."

"That's not what I mean."

"What do you want to talk about, Paxton?"

He takes a deep breath before speaking. "I know you couldn't tell me."

At first, I don't understand what he's talking about, and he must see my confusion because he lifts a hand, a silent request to let him continue. "After speaking with Teagan, I know it wasn't your story to tell. I should have trusted you wouldn't just walk away without reason. I should never have left it like that."

"Okay."

"I want you to know that I still care about you. I always have."

I feel a pang of emotion at his words, memories of our past flooding back. But I quickly push them aside. "You thought I was like my father—after everything."

"I did, and I'm sorry."

"That's not enough, Paxton. You can't just waltz back into my life and expect everything to be okay."

"I know," he says, his voice softening. "But I had to try. I had to see you again. I needed to tell you . . ." He stops and studies me for a moment as if he's trying to figure out what to say. The anticipation is killing me. It feels like a live grenade has been thrown, and I'm just waiting for it to explode.

"Tell me what?" I implore. Put me out of my misery. Tell me why you're here. The seconds stretch out for what feels like a lifetime, and all the possible things he might say play out in my head.

Finally, he opens his mouth and speaks. "I want you to come work for me."

Okay. Not what I was expecting.

Not at all.

For a second, I feel like I must be hallucinating because there is no way Paxton Ramsey just offered me a job.

My mouth opens and shuts like a fish on its last breath, gasping for air.

"What?" I blurt out before I can think better of it.

"A job, princess. I want to offer you a job."

In my life, I've never been hit with a sledgehammer, but I imagine this is what it must feel like. "Is this some ploy to get back at my dad?"

"Wow. Do you really think that low of me?" I lift my brow at his question. "Well, I guess it would seem fair that you think of me like that, seeing as how I treated you. But no, that's not the reason."

"Then why? Why would you want a washed-up agent on staff? One that, I might remind you, has no clients and zero prospects."

"Nice selling point. Did you add that to your résumé yet?"

"Paxton." That gets his attention. His mouth shuts, and his lips thin. "Why?"

"Because despite everything, despite all you would lose, you still put her first. And that's the kind of agent I want working for me."

He takes a step closer to me, and on a protective instinct, I take a step back. Paxton would never physically hurt me, but my heart can't take much more. Walking away from him was the hardest thing I have ever done, and for the same reason, I'd do it all over again.

"In the month that we were on the island, I watched what you did for Teagan, how you cared for and nurtured her, and I want someone who can do the same. I've had a lot of time to think, and things need to change."

"How so?"

"I don't think enough emphasis is put on our clients' mental well-being and health, and I'd like you to come aboard and oversee that it is."

I shake my head in confusion. "I'm not following."

"Not only do I want you to bring on clients as an agent, but I also want you to go about setting up a division that will foster a good environment for our clients, whether that means bringing on staff to help with drugs, alcohol, and depression, or whatever issues that arise."

My heart hammers wildly in my chest. What Paxton is suggesting is huge. That's what this industry lacks, and I know that if he wants to make it happen, it will change everything. If I'm honest with myself, spearheading a project like this is everything I could ever dream of. I'm about to say yes, but then another thought hits me. Where does that leave us?

If there is no future for us, can I come on board knowing he might have a future with someone else?

My jaw wobbles, but I quickly push back the feeling threatening to explode. Steeling my spine, I erect the walls I have learned to rely on when things get tough.

Paxton stares at me for a second, most likely trying to read me. "Please, Mal. Come work for me."

"Why would you think I'd want that?"

"Because I know you, Mallory," he says, his eyes locking with mine. "You're one of the most compassionate people I've ever met, and that's exactly what my company needs right now."

I shake my head. As much as I want this and as much as this is a dream come true, can I take this job? Before I can stop myself, my damn pride rears its ugly head. "I don't need a handout, Paxton. I can take care of myself."

"It's not a handout," he insists. "I need someone like you to spearhead the program. It's all about ensuring our talent is cared for and has the services they need to be happy. And I think you're perfect for the job. No one would be better than you at this. You've proved it time and time again."

I consider his words, and a flicker of something stirs inside me—a desire to help. But I can't shake the feeling that I need to know where we stand first, and if I find out this is only a job and there is no future for us, can I fortify my walls high enough not to get hurt?

"I don't know, Paxton. I need time to think about it. I'm just—"

"What?"

"I'm not sure. After everything, I'm just not sure if I can work for you," I admit, unshed tears threatening to fall from my eyes.

He doesn't miss them, though. He stares deep into my eyes, and like always, Paxton Ramsey sees me. "What's going on in that head of yours?"

"It's just . . ." My heart hammers in my chest as he steps closer, and now we are only a hair's breadth apart. "I mean, I know it was just a fling between us, but I don't know if I can work with you and see you with—"

"With?"

"Other women," I blurt out, and then bite down on my lower lip to stop it from trembling.

"What are you talking about?"

I drop my gaze, not wanting to look at him. "I saw the picture of you."

He places his finger on my quivering jaw and tips it up until our gazes meet. "Come on, princess. Don't you know?"

"Know what?" I whisper.

"It's only been you."

"I don't—the woman?"

"Is my sister. I'm in love with you. Somewhere on that crazy island, I fell in love with you. I can't let another day pass without you knowing that I love you. That I would do anything for you. That you're everything."

The words hit me like a tidal wave. I want to melt into his arms and never leave, to stay here forever at this moment. Emotions threaten to overwhelm me, and I can't find the words to respond. He stares at me for a moment, his expression tender. "You don't have to say anything. I just wanted you to know how I feel."

He reaches out and takes my hand in his own, squeezing. "I don't expect—" he says softly.

The tears burst from my eyes. "I love you, too."

A smile slowly spreads across his lips, and he pulls me to him, searing his mouth to mine.

Opening my mouth, Paxton slides his tongue into mine, taking full ownership of me.

This is everything I missed. The feeling of his need, his want, his possession.

I feel starved for him.

I'm desperate for him, and as I'm about to pull away and tell him what I want, Paxton lifts me.

I gasp into his mouth, but the sound only fuels him. His kiss grows more primal as he carries me a few steps, placing me back on solid ground and pressing my back against the wall.

Before I know what's happening, my sweats are off, and my thong follows.

His hands roam all over my body, touching every inch as if he's making sure I'm real. That this is really happening.

He deepens the kiss as I feel his erection nudging, and then he slams inside me, taking my breath from my lungs.

It feels so good.

I had forgotten.

It feels like I'm finally complete. The part of my heart I left on the island has been returned.

He picks up his pace.

"What's it going to be, princess?" He thrusts harder and deeper. "Will you come work for me?"

"Yes!" I scream as I fall over the edge, shattering around him.

Catching my breath, I look up at him, my lips parting into a lazy smile. "I can't promise it'll be easy."

"I'd rather have complicated with you than easy any day, princess."

"Me, too."

Epilogue

Mallory
Six months later…

@Stargossip: So you guys are really done with this story?

    @Ihatemovies: Wow, you're finally getting the picture.

    @Betterthanfiction: Books are better than this shit.

    @Lexi_H: Nothing is better than THE END.

IT NEVER ENDS.

There's always one more email to write. Another phone call to return.

But as I sit in my chair, typing away, I realize I wouldn't have it any other way.

Things have been crazy here.

But a good kind of crazy.

The perfect kind.

Ever since I opened the door and saw Paxton standing on the other side, it's been a whirlwind.

Brad's apparently back on set filming Twisted Lily 2.0. His threats were just that, threats.

Teagan's doing great. She no longer talks to her mom and has started college.

And me? Well, now that my father has finally realized I don't need him to succeed, he's reached out and made amends.

We aren't close.

We most likely will never be, but I can't let that hold me back. I have too many good things going on in my life to let the little details bother me anymore.

Paxton wasn't joking when he said he wanted me to work for him.

And here I am, six months later . . . working with him, not *for* him. I made that clear the moment I signed on the contract's dotted line.

Paxton isn't my boss. He's my partner, and we make a powerful team together.

Most people might not be able to live and work with their boyfriend, but that's not us. Having spent so much time together on the island, we know each other inside and out.

It works.

We work.

My thoughts are interrupted when I hear the sound of the door opening.

My fingers halt, and I look up to see Paxton striding in, acting like he owns the place—which he technically does—but that's not why I allow him to barge in. I allow him that luxury because I love the fool.

Once he steps inside, he leans against the wall. "Working hard?" he asks me with a smirk. I roll my eyes and nod.

He laughs at that and then straightens. "Come on," he says, pushing off the wall with a wink. "I promised you dinner."

Shaking my head, I stand from my chair and grab my coat. As

I move to put it on, he crosses the space with his usual swagger. Once beside me, he helps me put it on and then holds out his hand.

"What should we eat?" I ask.

"I know what I want," he responds in his usual sexy and playful manner. My cheeks warm, and I shake my head in disbelief. Being with Paxton will never grow dull—that much is for sure.

"You're impossible. How about that new Italian place downtown?" I suggest, my smile growing wider.

"Perfect," he says, ushering me out the door. "Just what I had in mind."

He starts to lead me to the center of the room, but then he stops abruptly.

"Fuck it," he mutters, and I shake my head in confusion. "I can't wait another minute."

I'm about to ask him what he's talking about when he suddenly drops to one knee.

My heart stops.

"Mallory," he says seriously.

I feel like I'm on the edge of a roller coaster—my heart racing as it drops with the sensation of free-falling.

"What are you doing?" I ask in disbelief although it's obvious what he's about to do.

My pulse races as tears form in my eyes.

"Will you marry me?"

I let out a laugh—I can't help it. "Yes!"

He moves to stand just as I throw my arms around his neck, and then Paxton kisses me. His mouth latches on to mine as if he needs me to breathe. This isn't a sweet kiss. It's a kiss of ownership, and as the room erupts in cheers and clapping, I remember we're standing in the middle of the common space.

My now fiancé, tongue deep in my mouth, couldn't wait a second for us to be alone. He's kissing me like he's fucking me in front of everyone who works here.

If I thought my cheeks were warm before, they are practically on fire now.

Slowly, the kiss and cheers die down, and we pull away from each other.

"I love you," he whispers in my ear as our bodies remain pressed together.

My stomach does somersaults as I realize that we are officially engaged.

The next few moments seem like a blur of hugs, congratulations, and well-wishes.

I can't stop smiling.

My heart overflows with so many emotions that I can't find the right words.

Paxton pulls me toward him, and as he does, the rest of the world fades away. We both know that no matter what happens, our love will never waver or fade. We have each other, and that's all we need.

It feels like the stars aligned and brought us both to that island. Sure, it wasn't easy to get here, but as I look into Paxton's eyes, I know I wouldn't change one minute of the past as long as it leads me to him.

To Paxton.

My forever.

And our forever begins now.

Acknowledgments

I want to thank my entire family. I love you all so much.

Eric, Blake, and Lexi you are my heart.

Thank you to the amazing professionals that helped with Resist:

Becca Hensley Mysoor

Kristie at Between The Wines Consulting.

Melissa Saneholtz

Robin Covington

Kelly Allenby

Jenny Sims

Champagne Formats

Hang Le

Jill Glass

Rebecca Smith

Thank you to Jason Clarke, CJ Bloom, Kim Gilmour and Lyric for bringing Resist to life on audio.

Thank you to my fabulous agent Kimberly Whalen.

Thank you to my AMAZING ARC TEAM! You guys rock!

I want to thank ALL my friends for putting up with me while I wrote this book. Thank you!

To the ladies in the Ava Harrison Support Group, I couldn't have done this without your support!

Please consider joining my Facebook reader group Ava Harrison Support Group

Thank you to all the Booktokers, bookstagramers, and bloggers who helped spread the word. Thanks for your excitement and love of books!

Made in the USA
Middletown, DE
11 June 2023